UP IN THE AIR

WINTER GAMES, BOOK 1

Michaela,
Welcome to the mountain!
xx
Rebecca Sharp

DR. REBECCA SHARP

Copyright©2017 for Dr. Rebecca Sharp

All rights reserved.

ISBN: 9781723833649

This book or parts thereof may not be reproduced in any form, stored in any retrieval system, or transmitted in any form by any means without prior written permission of the publisher, except as provided by the United Stated of America copyright law.

This is a work of fiction. Names, characters, places, and incidents either are the products of the author's imagination or are used fictitiously. Any resemblance to actual persons, living or dead, businesses, companies, events, or locales is entirely coincidental.

Dedication

To all those who've chased their dreams no matter how many times they've fallen.

"Although I do love oceans, desert, and other wild landscapes, it is only the mountains that beckon me with the sort of painful magnetic pull to walk deeper and deeper into their beauty. They keep me continuously wanting to know more, feel more, see more. To become more."

– Victoria Erickson

Your Book Beverage

EFFEN GOOD MARTINI

Ingredients:
Muddled cucumber slices
2 oz. Effen Cucumber vodka
1 oz. freshly-squeezed lime juice
½ oz. agave syrup
5 leaves of fresh mint

Preparation:
Combine ingredients in shaker with ice.
Shake well.
Strain into martini glass.
Garnish with a cucumber wedge.
Enjoy.

CHAPTER
One

Channing

"You can't do that, Channing!" My younger sister yelled after me as I slammed the door to my blue Wrangler. I heard her struggle to get out of the passenger side and try to catch up to me. Yanking my snowboard down off the roof, I trudged along the loose-stone path, letting the board hang behind me as some sort of shield against her disapproving tirade.

I knew what she was going to say, but it was too late. I'd already made my decision.

"Alice, you can save your breath; I'm not changing my mind." My head tilted over my shoulder to inform her. I used her full name as a deterrent, trying to exert my older sister authority over someone who would never listen to me.

"You can't do this. They are going to find out—and that's going to be the least of your problems. When Chance finds out, he's going to kill you," she continued relentlessly as I opened the garage door of our mountain home—a cabin-esque chalet with large windows to take in the view of the mountains no matter which room you were in.

"He's not going to find out," I countered calmly, setting my board up against the wall of the garage, before walking into the house. "Unless you plan on telling him?" With that question, I spun and gave her my very best ice-cold stare.

She had the decency to stop dead in her tracks, eyes widening as she debated how to answer my question—and how to choose between her two siblings.

"No…" The word was soft and reluctant, drawn out just like the thoughts in her head of how to persuade me otherwise. "But, he's going to find out, Chan."

"How? He's not even here and who knows when he'll be back." I spun away from her again, unable to hide the lingering resentment in my tone, heading back through the hall straight for the basement stairs towards my twin brother's room.

Three months ago, Chance had injured himself on the mountain—to the point where the doctors weren't sure that he'd ever be able to ride again. To say that he'd taken it hard would be the understatement of the century; I was his twin and a snowboarder, and I still couldn't begin to imagine how he had felt at the news. From the time we were three, we'd been out on the snow, riding mountains. Before school. After school. *During* school. The mountain called to us and breathed her life into our lungs. After Chance broke his knee, that life support had been ripped from him and as soon as he'd been cleared from the hospital, he'd left Hope Creek; he'd left me.

I clenched my jaw, annoyed at the stinging pain that burned in my chest. *He'd left without a word, a warning, a method of contacting him, or a care for the rest of us who were left devastated. He left without saying good-bye.* After all of that, saying that no one had heard from him since would be superfluous.

He… We… were turning twenty-five this year—adults by every measure. And we had been for a while. Chance and I had been basically living on our own for the past five years. Lynn and Jason Ryder, while loving parents, had always been more hands-off than helicopter. When we turned twenty, they handed us the keys to the house, hugged us goodbye, and began their comfortable retirement in the warm sun of Delray Beach, Florida, leaving us the mountain retreat that had been our family home for the last twenty years.

I didn't blame my parents for moving and leaving us. They'd sacrificed a lot when they realized the talents that Chance and I had.

They'd uprooted their whole lives when we were four to move to the unpredictable climate of Colorado so that we would have unfettered access to some of the best mountains in the country. Our school was used to students in our situation and made accommodations to our studies so that if it was a good day to be on the mountain, we could be there. They'd supported us, sacrificing jobs, friends, and family so that we could pursue our dreams. When it became clear that we were responsible enough to take care of ourselves, they finally did something for themselves. If anything, I admired them for it.

There hadn't been a big debate when they'd announced the move. I saw it in my mother's face that she wanted to ask us to go with them, but knew the question would be pointless; Chance and I would refuse—with every ounce of our beings. We belonged in the cold, on top of a mountain, strapped to a board. Alice, on the other hand, hadn't been as lucky. She was four-and-a-half years younger than us, which meant that she was under eighteen at the time.

Mom and dad hadn't given her a choice.

Ally had been upset at first to leave us—even though she didn't love the snow like we did. Adjusting had been hard for her, but she was only a teen. Change was the norm for that phase of life. It only took a few weeks for her to tan right up. That, combined with a bikini, her bright blonde hair, and the Ryder blue eyes had made her the picture-perfect addition to every beach in the vicinity.

After a few years in the sun and sand, visiting us with our parents during the holidays for a white Christmas, she'd surprisingly asked to move back out here right after graduation. It had come a little out of the blue, but I wouldn't complain about having another girl in the house; it had been Chance and me for so long, I wasn't sure I even knew what makeup or women's clothes looked like anymore. When I asked, Ally told me that it was just because she missed us and wanted a change; she was lying. But, it had been almost five years; how could I expect her to open up easily to someone who wasn't close to her like that anymore?

Ok, maybe not lying, but there was more to the story that my little sister wasn't sharing.

"Fine." Ally huffed behind me. "Chance may or may not find out, but you don't think the judges will? You don't think anyone at the competition is going to realize?"

"How would they?" I opened the door to my twin's room. Everything was exactly where it had been before he left. I hadn't touched anything, assuming he would be back in a day or two. Well, two days turned into a week and a week turned into a month. And, now, we were on month number three, quickly approaching number four, and there was still no word from him.

Well, today, his time was up.

"Oh, I don't know. Maybe because Chance was medevacked off whatever mountain you were on and every indication was that he wouldn't be coming back any time soon." Ally crossed her arms over her chest as I scanned the room. "You don't think it's going to look suspicious that he's magically better enough to compete?"

No, I thought. It had been over the summer so we'd been up in Canada when he'd fallen, which meant that no one around here knew for sure what happened or the final verdict. I walked over to Chance's desk, shuffling through the papers, opening up all the drawers.

"Where the hell would he have left it?" I mumbled to myself, rifling through my brother's personal belongings. Maybe I should have felt like I was intruding, but in my mind, he deserved it for deserting me. *Asshole.*

You know all of those cliché twin-thing questions that always get asked? *Can you read each other's minds? Do you know what the other is thinking? Is there really such a thing as a 'twin-thing'?* Well, my answer to all of them was always 'yes'. We'd always been inseparable, even before we started snowboarding. But once that began, we'd almost become the same person. Our classes in school were the same. We had the same snowboard instructors. We went to the same camps. We bought the same boards.

Yes, *technically*, I should have been riding a women's board, but I'd always been afraid that Chance was going to leave me in the dust. I was always afraid he was going to be better than me and I wasn't going to take any chances at putting myself at a disadvantage—so I always bought the same gear that he did. We helped each other, competed with each other, and encouraged each other—always pushing the other to accomplish the next big trick.

There weren't a lot of females into boarding. *Let me rephrase.* There were a lot of girls into *boarders*, not *boarding*. You know, the kind of girls that curl their hair and do their makeup before heading out on the slopes? The kind that are more worried about a selfie in the snow, rather than *experiencing* the mountain? Yeah, *those*. I'm not talking about *those*. I'm talking about girls that are really into riding—those brave souls are few and far between. Living in Aspen—or the outskirts of it—probably put me into contact with more women snowboarders, but after being around my brother and his friends for so long, even when I met those other female boarders, I just didn't know how to fit in and didn't have the time or desire to figure it out.

Plus, they weren't as good as I was. Not to be conceited, but it was the truth. I'd trained with the boys all my life and they were merciless. Especially Chance and his friends; they weren't dubbed the SnowmassHoles for nothing.

Assholes of Aspen.
Snowmass Assholes.
SnowMassive Assholes.
SnowmassHoles. Of Aspen.

Some things stick with you well after high school has ended.

Anyway, it wasn't just female snowboarders that I stayed away from; it may have been females in general. In trying to be just like Chance, I seemed to have bypassed all those things that other women seem to enjoy and now, it seemed like just too much work for me to learn how to relate.

I caught sight of myself in the mirror that Chance had hanging on the wall opposite his bed—*its particular location serving a purpose that I'd rather not think about.* Gray TOMS sneakers, skinny jeans, a loose cotton Henley tee—I looked younger than I was; I also looked like a boy. The tee was loose and long enough to hide the more womanly curve of my ass and the distinctly lacking swells of my breasts. That combined with my androgynously short blonde hair—buzzed on the sides with only a few inches on the top—always had people doing a double take—wondering if Chance and I were twin brothers. Sure, if you looked hard enough, my eyes were slightly more almond-shaped than his, my lips a little fuller, and—if you caught me on an inhale—you might be able to see the hint of my sad excuse for a chest.

I was the tomboy. I was the girl who hated makeup and dresses. The girl who drank whiskey with the guys and helped them pick up chicks. I was the girl who preferred snowboots to stilettos.

I didn't know how to flirt or be coy or play hard-to-get. I knew how to be one of the guys. And I knew how to snowboard.

Ally, who was glaring at me through the glass, was the complete opposite. She, on the other hand, was a girly-girl, the snowboard-gene skipping her entirely. She'd moved out here a year ago and already she had more female friends than I did. I tended to stick with Chance and the other SnowmassHoles from the mountain—Emmett and Nick. Even though I'd gone out with Ally and her girlfriends a few times, I stuck out like a sore thumb. I'd had to borrow some of her clothes and she insisted putting that makeup shit on my face. My face had been streaked with the stuff the next morning and the guys had given me crap for it—mostly Emmett; it was horrible.

I'd been out with the two of them last night, grabbing drinks after a long day on the slopes. Neither of them had heard from Chance, but we'd gotten to reminiscing about all the good times that we'd had on the mountain. Nick had brought up the makeup incident. He'd said that the only thing good about it was that at least people were able to tell Chance and me apart for once.

And just like catching the front edge of your board, his words had me falling flat on my face, and the potential in his joke knocked the wind right out of me. His thoughtless words had inspired my current problematic plan.

The reality was that when we had our gear on, I can't even count how many times people mistook me for Chance's identical twin *brother*—and that was if we were together; by myself, half the time I was mistaken for him.

Even though I was slightly smaller in stature, the nature of snow gear is that it tends to obscure almost everything about a person—except the eyes, only until the goggles went on. Thankfully, all three of us had inherited our father's bright blue stare. Now, most of the locals at Snowmass knew me because I'd been riding there basically my entire life; they knew that I was Chance's *female* twin. Because when you live in a resort town, if you make it through one off-season, everyone learns your name. And I didn't just make it through an off-season. I was part of a pair that had won countless local and several national snowboarding competitions. Just a local celebrity—no big deal.

But the commission and the judges and the participants in this year's Winter X Games... they weren't locals.

"Yes!" I exclaimed, finding Chance's wallet in his nightstand drawer.

"Are you sure he's not going to come back to do this?" Ally questioned again, chewing on her lower lip.

"He's not. His knee won't be healed in time," I stated matter-of-factly. "But they don't know that."

No, all the X Games commission knew was that they had extended an invitation to Chance Ryder—talented up-and-comer who was named *Snowboarder Magazine's* Rookie-of-the-Year. This would have been his debut at the X Games which were being held next month right in our backyard—at our home base—Snowmass.

Chance had been practicing his quad cork when he fell—currently the most difficult trick a rider could attempt. I'd seen him nail it a dozen times, but it only takes once—and that one mistake—that one edge—was all it took.

One more glance in the mirror told me that the person finalizing Chance's registration needed to look nothing like the person staring back at me right now.

"Ally, I'm doing this," I said to my sister. "So, you might as well swallow the rest of your protests and instead, put your energy into helping me make sure that this happens flawlessly."

She groaned as I walked by her again, taking the stairs two at a time. "What exactly is your plan again?"

"I told you in the car." Walking into the large open kitchen, I headed straight for the refrigerator where Chance's invitation letter was posted—my blood picking up speed as I took it down off of the magnet.

I'd insisted that it go on the fridge—I was so proud of him. He, on the other hand, had wanted to keep it in his room. We'd both taken gold in Slopestyle at the Burton U.S. Open Snowboarding Championships two years ago; last year… well, last year, Chance had taken gold again. I, on the other hand, hadn't placed—a memory that I'd been trying to erase ever since.

In any case, Chance had been the only one invited to the X Games and after his stellar performance, it was no surprise. However, I could see the guilt in his eyes that he'd been chosen and I hadn't and I knew it was because he blamed himself for what happened to me at the Open even though it hadn't been his fault. As much as we competed and gave each other shit, Chance knew that I was just as good a rider as he was.

Snowboarding was still a man's world—there wasn't much he or I could do about it; I certainly wasn't going to punish him for his success.

"I know," Ally retorted. "But, I was in shock and I need to hear it again."

I stared blankly at the words on the paper before turning to roll my eyes at her.

"Well, right now, I have to head over to the mountain to finalize Chance's place in the competition. Today is the last day to register which means that if I don't go down there now, they will give the spot to someone else."

"But, you're going as you?"

I rolled my eyes again. "Yes. I have his license and his invitation.

And I'm his sister. No one is going to question it. They know he was injured. I'll just tell them that he is on the road to recovery but had a physical therapy appointment that he couldn't miss, so I'm accepting the invitation on his behalf. It's just paperwork that needs to be filled out. It will be fine." I repeated the words less for my sister's benefit and more for my own.

"And you aren't concerned at all that they will see just how much the two of you look alike?" Alice raised an eyebrow. "That they might recognize you later? Yeah, I get you wear a helmet and blah, blah, blah, but you aren't identical, Chan, no matter how much you act or dress like one of the guys—you aren't."

She gave me an eye that said most people might be fooled for a second, but anything longer than that made my lady-parts clearly distinguishable.

She was wrong, I told myself. *She was just trying to get me to give up my idea.* I was definitely more compactly built. Ok, so my chest was a solid B-cup in the week surrounding my period, which could be a giveaway, and my hips did have a slight flare to them. However, with the right clothes, I could definitely pass as my brother in the short term.

I bit my cheek. *She had a point, though.*

She had a really, really good point.

A smile broke over my face—the kind that made my sister's eyes turn wary of what I was thinking to remedy her concern.

"You're right, Ally," I agreed. "Which is why I'm going to need to borrow some of your girl clothes right now and you're going to have to put some makeup on my face."

Her eyes went wide. "What?!" She shook her head frantically. Apparently, it was one thing to know about my plan, but it was another thing to be a willing participant.

It was the makeup that had sparked this whole idea. And now it seemed like it had another role to play.

She stood agape. I reached out, grabbed her arm, and pulled her behind me as we went upstairs to where our bedrooms were.

I didn't have time for any disagreement.

The registration office closed at five and considering I finished my lessons early today, picked up Ally at Peace and a Cup of Joe—the coffeehouse where she worked—at three-thirty, stopped to put gas in my Jeep so I could make it back to work later, and then arrived home; I didn't have a whole lot of time left to get back to the resort.

"I can't believe you are doing this," she said as she complied with my request, putting some sort of something on my eyelids. "Stop moving."

"I can't help it. Stupid stuff makes me itchy," I grumbled.

I couldn't believe I was doing this either. Then again, I spent every day of the week taking huge risks with my life in order to pursue what I loved. Posing as my brother in the Winter X Games seemed like a small gamble compared to strapping my two feet to a waxed piece of wood, sliding down a mountain at appreciable speeds, only to fly off of a ledge, soaring into the air, and flipping head-over-heals while spinning. All with the expectation that I would land safely back on my feet.

"Aren't there going to be tons of riders coming to the mountain in the next couple weeks to prepare? Won't they notice how one of the contestants is conspicuously absent on the slopes even though his sister isn't?"

I gnawed on my lip. "Maybe. I'll have to see how they close the slopes. Plus, not everyone practices here before the games. I can just say that Chance is practicing on a private facility—fewer questions that way." Ally just murmured in response, not quite believing my assumption. "Or I could go out there and practice as him. But, that would mean I might have to bring Emmett and Nick into this…" I trailed off, noticing how my sister frowned at their names. "What?"

"Nothing."

Whatever. I didn't have time for her drama right now. "No, I think it's better if I stick to my normal routine—ride in the morning, teach my lessons, and then pull a quick change before I head to the bar. If I see anyone getting suspicious of his absence… well… I'll figure something out." *I hoped.*

I worked at Snowmass teaching snowboarding to every level of rider; that was in the afternoon. That was usually after I'd already spent a few hours on the slopes riding with Emmett and Nick; if the conditions were shit, I'd hang out at Cup of Joe with Ally. And then around six or so, I made my way over to Ice Breakers (Breakers for short)—the upscale bar inside of the resort and bartended there until about midnight. Same routine. Every day. If there was a change in the work schedule and I ended up with more free time, it was spent on the mountain.

The plan is going to work. Just breathe, Channing.

It was a perfectly rational plan. *Aside from the fact that I was impersonating someone in an international sporting competition. Yup, perfectly rational.*

"What, Ally?" I asked again. Even though my eyes were closed while she put the black goopy stuff—alright, *mascara*—on my eyelashes, I could tell she was in deep thought.

"I just don't think any of this is a good idea."

"It's the only idea," I replied firmly, opening my eyes.

"No, not—" She broke off, realizing it was too late, I'd already smudged the stuff on my eyelids. "Not yet."

"This was his dream—our dream," I said quietly, standing and walking over to her closet to pull out a tight lavender sweater. "He might not be here or be able to fulfill it, but he deserves it. If you saw his face the weeks before he fell, you would have known how much this meant to him." *And how much it meant to me to make it up to him.* Swallowing my guilt, I tugged my hoodie and t-shirt off in one motion, grateful that I'd worn my white lace bra this morning—the pink one would have shown through the sweater.

Ok, I'll admit it, there's one area that I did enjoy girly things and that was underwear—the lacier, the frillier, the brighter, the sexier... the better. It was always hidden underneath everything, so no one would ever know. And I was always on the mountain, so let's face it—no one ever did know.

"That invitation is for a Ryder and if Chance isn't going to be here to win it, then I am," I said determinedly. Thankfully, the sweater was over my face to obscure the thickness in my voice.

It should have been Chance. He was always the better rider.

I knew he'd thought he had to win this, not just for himself, but for me. Because of what happened at the Open. But that couldn't be further from the truth. He deserved this title and I was going to get it for him.

"Channing." Her voice stopped me on my way back down the stairs and I spun to face her.

"I know, Ally. I know you think it's a bad idea, but I have to do it which means I have to go," I huffed.

"Have you thought about what would happen?" Her voice followed me.

"I won't get caught—and I don't have the time to think about the consequences if I do; you don't approach a jump worrying about what happens if you fall—you focus on what you have to do to make sure you land." I grabbed my keys off the table in the entryway and opened the door into the garage, heading for my car parked outside.

"No, Chan, I don't mean what if you get caught," she yelled after me as I walked out of the garage and opened my car door. "I meant what would happen if you win!"

CHAPTER
Two

Channing

ALLY'S WORDS REPLAYED OVER AND OVER IN MY HEAD DURING MY ten-minute drive back over to the Snowmass resort.

What would happen if I won?

It was quarter to five and I didn't have much time. I pulled into the Reserved parking lot, knowing that security would recognize my car and let it be for one night. I rarely took advantage of my friendship with Nate, Charlie, and the rest of the security guys since they usually tried to walk me to my car every night—unless the resort was really busy—and fend off any unwanted advances from patrons at the bar (a rare occurrence). I had a feeling that Chance had asked them to look out for me when I started bartending, but now I knew they did it because they genuinely cared about me and not because my brother had asked them to.

Ugh! Why was every freaking spot filled?!

Skiers and snowboarders from all over the world had started to arrive in preparation for the Winter X Games. Not too many yet, but in the next week or so, the mountain would be packed. And lots of special guests meant a fuller VIP parking lot.

Yes! A spot!

I glimpsed a spot near the end of the second row—or what hopefully was a spot since it was partially obscured by the giant Chevy parked next to it. I pressed on the gas and sped up—the minutes were ticking down. Silently praising the Wrangler's turning radius, I swung into the space—and subsequently took out the row of snowboards that had been resting alongside the Range Rover parked on the other side of the open spot, the boards only coming into my view in the last second as I made the turn.

Son of a biscuit! I slammed on my brakes.

Like Miley-fucking-Cyrus, I came in like a wrecking ball.

The sickening smack of the carbon-fiber infused wood against the pavement made my entire body cringe. And the string of expletives that left my mouth I had Emmett to thank for. *Asshole.*

Backing up, I swung my car closer to the other side of the spot, a safe distance from the fallen mass of boards. I threw the Jeep into first and yanked up the e-brake.

"Shit," I swore, climbing down to examine the mess I'd made.

"I'd say it was a strike," a deep voice rumbled from behind me. Accented and unfamiliar, it stirred muscles in my body that I didn't even know existed in ways that I hadn't known were possible.

I spun around, unable to stop my jaw from dropping at the gorgeous man leaning against the side of the SUV with his legs crossed and his eyes on me. My gaze slid uncontrollably up his figure—the dark jeans that fit snugly around muscled legs, a tailored button-down shirt that was stretched almost to the brink of splitting by the broad chest underneath it. His strong jawline, sculpted face, and symmetrical lips were textbook from the only part of my Greek mythology class worth remembering. The molten brown eyes that matched his warm brown hair cut tight on the sides and styled on top completed the Greek-God-meets-rugged-businessman look. And if that wasn't enough, the earthy, masculine scent of him wafted over to me, clinging to every pore as I inhaled deeply.

I didn't smoke, but the SnowmassHoles loved some good weed. *Was this what they meant by a contact high?*

I took in all of him—his stance, his expression, his scent. This man was breathtaking—potent masculinity simmering with complete confidence and pure sex; I clenched my legs together to try to stop the fire that it ignited between them. And to top it all off, he was wearing a freaking blazer.

I was turned on by a man in a blazer. What was the world coming to?

Not that I dated much (read: at all), but I freely admitted to having a type—and that type was your typical snowboarder. Wardrobe: loose jeans, Henley tees, and Vans sneakers– when not in snow gear that is. The problem was that I was too good a friend with most of them to actually look at them any other way. The other problem was that I tried so hard to be 'one of the guys' that none of them could really look at me any other way—especially if they wanted to stay friends with Chance. *Or ever snowboard at Snowmass again.*

But there was no way this guy was a snowboarder. And yet, my body wanted to jump him.

Worst case—he was a skier. Chances were, he was a sponsor, rep, or some sort of agent for one of the riders who'd arrived today. Or—*most likely*—a model for the brands Burton or Ride. Any of those would explain the slew of boards I'd just crashed into.

Son-of-a-biscuit, I was still staring. "Excuse me?" I pretended that I hadn't heard him. The reality was that my brain had completely forgotten what he said because his hotness had seared it from my mind.

"A strike," he repeated as his warm eyes melted over me; the lilt in his voice was definitely Canadian—enough of them came down here to ride for me to recognize it on hearing him speak a second time.

As he looked down my body, every cell underneath his gaze was set ablaze. I sucked in a breath, feeling my nipples harden painfully against the lace of my bra; there was no padding in it which is probably why his smile tightened ever so slightly as his stare lingered barely a split second longer on my breasts.

I'd never felt like this before; I'd always been cold. I lived on the mountain—in the snow; being cold was a fact of life. For the first time, my body felt on fire and to say it was more uncomfortable than being cold was the understatement of the century.

"Well… I… uhh… Yeah, I guess I did strike the boards. I'm so sorry." I was mumbling unattractively to arguably the most attractive man I'd ever seen. Turning quickly, I bent to pick up the boards, examining them to make sure there wasn't any damage. I swallowed a curse as Ally's *tight* sweater made every movement that was normally fluid, awkward and clumsy—and the low neckline was the worst. Yes, it was feminine. No, it was not functional. Not only did I have to worry about the boards falling down, but I had to worry about my breasts falling out.

Not that there was much to see.

"Well, that too." And then he laughed. *God,* he had a sexy laugh. But the smile that it came from… I bent down for the last board because my knees were weak, not because I'd planned on retrieving it right in the middle of his sentence. I bit my lip trying to focus my rapidly disintegrating thoughts as I finished righting the fifth and final board up against the side of the car. "But, I meant it was a strike—as in you knocked all of them down. You know, like in bowling."

I just turned to stare at him. Which, in retrospect, was an even bigger mistake because I looked right into that bright white—*panty-melting*—smile. *Oh, it burned.*

"Oh… Um… Right," I murmured, continuing to stare like a complete fool. It was like I'd never seen a hot guy before.

I had, I swear.

But him…

Let's just say that the terms 'Perfect,' 'Frontside grab,' and 'Lipslide' had been redefined for me. They were no longer names of tricks that I did with a snowboard; they were now the very dirty things I wanted to do with him.

I prayed that Ally's makeup was doing its job to hide the rising blush on my face and that my underwear was holding out against the rush of desire that I couldn't seem to control.

"I don't think any of them are damaged, but if they are I'll be happy to pay to repair them," I said, turning back to my car to grab the papers and Chance's license. "I'm so sorry again, but I have to go—I'm running so late."

His rich, brown eyes just stared into mine as though he were absorbing every last piece of me. For the first time, I was glad that I looked a little bit like a female—the makeup, the sweater—because I wanted his eyes on me. And they were.

Truth—I wanted more than his eyes on me.

Every cell tingled under that gaze. I never cared about dressing pretty, let alone sexy because who was it for? Certainly not any of the people I saw on a regular basis. What was I going to do? Dress up only to put on five layers of outerwear and then cover my face with a neck-warmer, goggles, and a helmet? No, I wasn't one of *those* girls.

I couldn't remember the last time I wanted a guy to look at me the way Mr. Range Rover was looking at me right now. And with a look like that, who the hell would ever need Under Armor ColdGear to keep them warm?

My breath quickened.

Tick tock.

I broke the stare and began to walk by him, heading for the reception area until a large warm hand on my arm stopped me in my tracks.

"Are you going to tell me your name?" My eyes went immediately to his hand resting gently on my arm, the warmth of it seeping through Ally's sweater. But when he asked my name, my gaze returned to his. "So I can at least know who had the pleasure of taking out all my boards."

Duh, of course I needed to give him my name.

"Channing," I replied softly. "Channing Ryder. I'm sorry, I really have to go." I turned and walked away, my arm easily leaving his grasp.

Truthfully, it was a miracle I was walking. For a second, I could have sworn that the number of butterflies in my stomach was enough to let me take flight.

"I'm so sorry," I gasped as I ran up to the desk. It was two minutes after five and I said every prayer that I knew with the hope that they would have a little mercy on me. "I know I'm late and I'm so sorry, but there was an incident in the parking lot and—"

"Ma'am," the woman behind the table interjected. "You're not late. We're here until five-thirty today."

Oh, thank God.

"Oh..." It was all I could say as I caught my breath—and my wits.

This was just what I needed—the lucidity of my brain weakened by my body's distraction with Mr. Range Rover.

"The women's registration is over at that table though." The woman—Pat, her nametag said—instructed me. I swallowed over the lump in my throat and looked down at the documents in my hand.

Focus, Channing.

When I looked up, I tried to imagine myself as Ally—a warm, friendly smile spreading over my face as I acted as girly and un-snowboarder like as possible.

"Oh, thank you *so* much. I'm actually not here to register myself." I paused and threw in a cute laugh. *Or what I hoped was a cute laugh.* "That would surely be a sight for national television." I cleared my throat and ran my hand along the side of my non-existent hair, wishing I had Ally's long locks that I could play with. *Because that's what girls did, right?* "I'm registering my brother, Chance Ryder. I have his paperwork and license here. He's recovering from a minor injury and had to be at a doctor's appointment, so he sent me instead."

I refused to break her gaze even though I wondered if I'd said too much, too quickly.

Pat took the papers from my hand, glancing down at them and then back up at me. Down at them, back at me. She must have done it at least ten times and each time my heart stopped, wondering if my ruse was going to end right then and there.

"I don't know if I would trust her, Patty."

Son of a biscuit.

A shiver ran up my spine as that molasses-smooth voice rolled over my body again. I didn't have a chance to turn around before Mr. Range Rover's broad chest came into my peripheral view. I managed to keep my eyes focused on the woman in front of me though—the woman whose face lit up on seeing this man.

"Mr. Olsen!"

I don't know what else she said because as soon as I heard his name, all those butterflies in my stomach fled back into their cocoons and begged to return into caterpillars. My pulse rocketed and I glanced down to make sure they couldn't see my heart beating out of my chest.

Olsen. Wyatt Olsen. The Canadian, six-time golden, X games winner who also took gold in the Olympics two years ago. He didn't come to compete. He came to win because that's all he ever did.

He was the best which is why he won everything—and made himself a tidy fortune in the process. He was everywhere in the snowboarding world; the best snowboarder that had been seen in years. For all intents and purposes, he was the King of the mountain. Everyone wanted to be his sponsor, everyone wanted him. *What else?* I wracked my brain trying to remember everything that I'd heard about the man. He mostly trained in Canada, so aside from competition season, he practically dropped off the media radar. My brain was on fire and all I truly knew about Wyatt Olsen was that he was good at one thing: winning. Every. Single. Thing.

And that meant that he was Chance's biggest rival in the X Games.

Which really meant that he was mine.

How had I not recognized him? Maybe because the most I saw of him was when he was in snow gear? Or maybe because I was so rushed and flustered over the boards and missing my chance at this hair-brained idea that I'd missed the forest for the trees.

I begrudgingly turned my eyes over to see the woman embrace him. It was no wonder she knew him so well; he'd competed in every X Games for the past ten years or more. And he took gold every time.

Son. Of. A. Freaking. Biscuit.

He was a snowboarder. No wonder I was attracted to him.

If only that realization made me feel better about myself…

"Sorry about that, Miss… Ryder." Pat sighed and looked over at Olsen again. "Normally, the registrant needs to be here in person…" *No, no, no, no.* "However, since Mr. Olsen here is vouching for you, I'll go ahead and mark your brother as registered. If you'll give me a moment, I'll get together his welcome packet, lift pass, and all of the information as far as practice times, trail closings, competition information, etc."

I already had access to all of that since I worked at the resort, but I wasn't going to tell her that—mostly because I didn't want Wyatt-Freaking-Olsen to know.

"Fancy seeing you again so soon, Miss Ryder." He flashed that seductive smile at me again and I would have sworn that my nipples could have cut through ice.

"I thought the desk closed at five and I promised my brother I would handle this so he didn't have to worry," I repeated nervously, unsure of just how much he had overheard. His presence dulled my faux persona. I couldn't focus on being a girly-girl because every part of me was too busy feeling like a woman.

"Ahh. I see." He crossed his arms over that broad chest of his. *Gulp.* "Well, I'm glad you were wrong or I would be out of the competition as well. My flight was delayed this morning, so I was afraid that I wasn't going to make it either. But, it looks like I made it just in the nick of time to come to register and save the day." He nodded over to Pat who was busy collecting all of the necessary papers.

I blushed. "Yes, thank you. I… My brother would be crushed if they'd refused to let me register him. He's been training really hard…" I trailed off before my voice was in danger of breaking.

"Chance Ryder's sister," he mused and I couldn't help but let my eyes return to the warmth of his. "You snowboard, too, if I remember correctly? You won Slopestyle at the Open last year?"

"The year before," I answered quietly. *Last year… Well, I tried not to think about last year.*

He nodded. "Who's better?"

"Excuse me?"

"Who's better—you or Chance?" He clarified. "And don't tell me you don't know. I have a brother. Everything is a competition."

"I wasn't going to. Obviously, I'm the better rider," I replied confidently, yet in jest.

He knew and he smiled. "I'll have to let him know that you said that."

"Oh, don't worry about it. I remind him all the time."

"I can imagine." He laughed. "So, I guess that's good news for me then—that I'll have a chance at beating snowboarding's hottest young gun?"

"Unlikely. I'll make sure to teach him a trick or two to beat you." I couldn't help the laugh that slipped out at the easy banter between us. On the one hand, it was like my conversations with Emmett and Nick, relaxed, funny, refreshing—on the other hand, I wished we were having the conversation naked, which was definitely *not* like the kind of conversations that I had with my friends.

"So, then maybe taking out all of my boards wasn't an accident..." His tone was suddenly very serious and I was immediately on alert.

"Of course it was!" I jumped in, my hand flying up to my chest and grabbing the edge of Ally's sweater, appalled that he would intimate such a thing. "I would never... Unbelievable. I would never do such a thing." I then noticed that I was ridiculously waving my other hand at him, scolding him for the thought.

"Not only that," I continued, crossing my arms over my chest to stop my wayward hands from making any more embarrassing gestures, "but, I didn't even know who you were out there. I didn't recognize you. I thought you were—" I broke off, biting my lip before any more of *those* thoughts slipped out. "It doesn't matter. I didn't know it was you and I'm still very sorry about knocking them down, but really, they are fine." I sucked in a long breath after my emphatic defense, the pause giving me a moment to take in his reaction.

He was laughing. The drop-dead gorgeous man was laughing at me. Again.

I just glared at him, only now realizing that he'd been joking about the whole thing and I—I'd defended myself to my last breath. Literally.

"Alright, dear. Here's the information for your brother and his mountain pass so that he has access to the lifts for practice once we close them off to the public at the beginning of next week."

"Thank you so much." I gave her my most grateful smile before turning back to the man that I desperately wanted to scold.

Except, without him, 'Chance' might have never gotten into the competition.

"Mr. Olsen." I, instead, gave him my most demure, feminine smile.

I had no clue what that was, but I'd seen Ally do it enough times to know that it was a polite parting for someone that you weren't particularly fond of.

"Will I see you out on the mountain? Or around to cheer on your brother?" His voice called after me.

I couldn't help myself. I turned back and replied, "Why? Worried I'll try and sabotage your chances of winning again?"

You're playing with fire, Channing.

"Of course not. I'd just like to see you again." My knees went weak. And then that devastating smile of his reappeared.

I'd ignored it before, but now there was no question that my panties were soaking wet. There was definitely one part of me that was all for his suggestion.

Why did I have to want this man? Of all men? Of all the men in the world, why the one that I was secretly competing against?

"I'll be around, but not to cheer Chance on," I admitted cryptically before spinning and walking out of the hall before he had the opportunity to stop me again.

I had to get to work. Breakers was opening in thirty and I still hadn't eaten anything for dinner.

CHAPTER
Three

Channing

"CHANNING, WHERE THE FUCK HAVE YOU BEEN ALL afternoon?" I heard Emmett's voice ring through Breakers loud and clear and I cringed to myself.

Dick.

Not that I didn't like when my friends came to visit me at work, but this was the most upscale bar at the resort and when they came, well, they tended to say things like that. *And usually do things far worse.* When I'd worked at Big Louie's it hadn't been as big a deal since that place tended to be a local dive—plus everyone there knew the SnowmassHoles *and what to expect.* But here, there were mostly tourists and guests… here, there were limits.

Thankfully, the place wasn't too crowded at the moment. I really liked working at Breakers compared to some of the other bars that I'd tended over the years. It was a relatively new space that used to be a piano bar, but was remodeled just a little over two years ago.

The bar was the main feature in the middle of the room with a column in the center that rose to the ceiling and had expensive liquor bottles decoratively adorning it. The bar itself went in a complete circle around that center column and could maybe seat about twenty people. The menu here was small—mostly made up of meats and cheeses with a few foodie variations on comfort food. Around the bar there were maybe eight tables for people to sit and a few booths along the walls.

All in all, it was a nice spot with good, *overpriced* cocktails where mostly the wealthier resort guests came to drink—which was another reason why I liked working here because it meant good tips and not a lot of drunken messes.

It also meant that I didn't really see any of the people who would be out on the slopes with me during the day. I preferred to keep separate those two parts of my life: the part that I enjoyed and the part that I had to do. Unfortunately, or fortunately, that separation didn't always happen and sometimes my friends did venture up to the land of the fancy to harass me at work; it was more common now that Chance was gone and they weren't at Big Louie's. Before he left, they'd usually all go out and do something at night when I worked—and by something, I mean go out and pick up chicks. Sometimes I'd tag along, but my presence tended to diminish their chances of success and guilt puts a damper on an otherwise enjoyable night out.

I'd been standing at the right side of the bar, just as it wrapped around to the back of the room when I'd heard Emmett. Holding cocktail shaker in my hands, I walked towards the front of the bar to greet him and Nick, shaking the metal container vigorously until my arms started to hurt and my fingers went numb.

Emmett 'King' Jameson and Nick 'Frost' Frost strolled through the bar like they owned the place—their entitlement stemming not from the fact that I worked there but from their title as the SnowmassHoles of Aspen. They were the best local rides—you might call them local heroes if you didn't actually know them. Their SnowmassHole perspective said that everything belonged to them in this town and especially on this mountain.

I could tell you all the stories—all the reasons why they were given this name. All the rules they'd broken on the mountain—riding after dark, stealing keys to the lifts, terrorizing skiers by stealing one ski and forcing them to walk down to the bottom of the mountain to retrieve it. Out of all of them, they were most famous for their Winter Night Games.

For about a year and a half in high school, they'd held weekly nighttime competitions in the park—where riders competed for money, weed, or women. They were held when the mountain was supposed to be closed. Chance organized everything, Frost paid off workers for access to lights and lifts, and Emmett threatened anyone who got in their way. The Games were brutal, most riders trying tricks of their own; injuries were numerous. Ironically, the Games didn't end because they got caught. They ended because Chance and Nick fought over a girl. But that was a long time ago and high school was ending anyway.

The Games no longer existed, but the SnowmassHoles survived.

Chance had become a professional boarder although currently MIA. Emmett, had started his own custom snowboard fabrication business after one year of engineering in college and quickly became famous and wealthy—not that he showed that to anyone. And Nick, who was currently finishing his degree in design and marketing and still seemed content to live at his parent's mansion and off of their support, showed up to class ten percent of the time, and spent the other ninety percent high—either on the mountain or with a woman. Or women.

They were flawed—there was no doubt about it. But they were my crew.

Unlike Mr. Olsen, these two were prime examples of your classic snowboarder; Emmett had red hair—like *bright* red—which is why he hadn't let it grow out since probably the second grade. I didn't know him in the second grade, he was three—*or was it four*—years older than Chance and I. Regardless, from the time I met him, he'd always kept it in a tight buzz—not enough to look completely bald, but close. The effect was this reddish halo that always seemed to be surrounding his head; if only there were little red horns growing from it to complete the look.

And then there was Nick with his dark, short hair pushed disastrously away from his face. Neither of them had the styled cut that Wyatt did. Their off-duty snowboarder attire of loose, dark jeans, a long sleeve tee, and skate sneakers was a distinct contrast to the business casual that Wyatt wore. I honestly couldn't ever remember seeing either of my friends, or my own brother, ever wearing something as put-together.

If I had to think about it—and if I had to admit to it—I would say that both Emmett and Nick were pretty good looking. Ok, if I had to be one-hundred-percent, 'cross my heart hope to die' honest—most girls considered them panty-dropping hot—which is how they got away with being assholes. Emmett was completely toned thanks to hours on the mountain and hours in the gym. That combined with his hard jawline, ginger buzz cut, and jet-black eyes was a heart-stopping combination. Then add on the fact that he was a blatant dick most of the time and well, for most women, that was the icing on the sculpted, Emmett-sized cake—the undeniable asshole attraction. Nick, on the other hand, was just as muscular but quieter, only obnoxious when around Emmett or Chance, and preferred to let the two of them race through the female population of Aspen, staying comfortably in the background. At times you could tell that he had a dark streak that was longer and harder than Emmett's and Chance's combined, but for the most part, he hid it well.

These were all pretty standard traits of ninety-nine percent of the male, snowboarding population. So, if snowboarders were your thing, my best friends—and brother—would be at the top of your 'want to fuck' list.

If you wanted the blonde-hair, blue-eyed, golden-boy look, you went for Chance. If you wanted the dark-eyed, dangerous asshole, Emmett was your top choice. And Nick, well, it didn't matter what you wanted, it only mattered what *he* wanted.

Ok, that wasn't quite true. My perception of them was slightly blinded by the fact that I saw them all as my brothers. The reality was that they were a little more than obnoxious and most days, a lot more than assholes. The SnowmassHoles were kind of like the Three Musketeers, except boards instead of swords, and the only people who needed saving were the ones they set their sights on. As much as I tried to keep them all in line, I was only one person and so ignorance was bliss.

As much as I insisted that snowboarders were my thing, there was a growing part of me that suggested that they might not be—as least not in their classical appearance. Truth be told, I hadn't been around any other kind of guy long enough to consider anything else.

But, technically, Wyatt was a snowboarder… So, there was that.

I shook my head slightly, trying to stop that gorgeous smile from invading my thoughts again.

As Chance's twin, I guess saying that he took the cake on looks was saying *something* about me, too. It was one of the multitude of reasons why I tried to make myself like one of the guys for as long as I could remember—boy hair, boy clothes, boy hobbies, boy *friends*; if today was any indication, the slightest hint of makeup and a piece of women's clothing was drawing far too much attention to all the wrong parts of me. I wanted to be a part of the pack, not a piece of ass. *Not that Chance would have let that happen.*

I watched my friends approach before Emmett made a show of stopping abruptly in his tracks, squinting his dark eyes at me.

"What the hell is on your face?" he asked in mock disgust. "Are you… wearing makeup again? Don't you remember what happened the last time you did that?"

Nick begin to laugh beside him and I rolled my eyes at the two of them. Thankfully, I was used to their attitude.

"Shut up, Shaun White." I said. "It's just for work."

Those black eyes flared at me. He hated when anyone made reference to him and Shaun White—the one famous snowboarder who also happened to have bright red hair. Don't get me wrong—Shaun White was like a god in the Religion of Ride. But Emmett still hated being compared to the guy. He liked to think that he was better—he probably was, but I wasn't going to inflate his ego any more.

"Um, we've visited you at work before, Lil. You never fucking wear makeup to work."

What the hell.

My name was… unique. Also on the masculine side. And it was

a pain to shorten. Ally called me 'Chan,' but that was deemed too lame by the SnowmassHoles back in… seventh grade? Maybe sixth. Basically whenever Emmett had joined our group. I believe his words were: *'There's no way you can ride with us with a name like Chan.'* Therefore, a shortened version of my middle name, Lily, was chosen. It also served a second purpose since I was just a few minutes younger than my dear brother; 'Lil' was their abbreviation for 'little.'

I sent him a glare that said he needed to watch his language and his volume in this place and then quickly made up a lie to justify my answer.

"It's because of the Games. There are a bunch of very wealthy people who are going to be staying here; they want the appearance of their bartenders to reflect the fact that this is their most upscale bar." I poured the drink from the shaker into a chilled martini glass. "They also are going to be stricter on removing anyone who is creating a scene, so don't make me report you," I teased.

"Whatever. Looks like you touched something that you shouldn't have though." Emmett snickered, gesturing towards his right eye. I turned, trying to look into the mirror that was behind the decorative alcohol bottles. "So where were you today? I thought we were riding this morning."

Sure enough, I smeared some of the mascara off underneath my right eye. *This was the problem with wearing makeup when you never wore it—I continued to rub everything as though there was nothing to mess up.*

"I know, I forgot to text you. I had some things that I had to take care of." Translation: when I woke up with this idea on my mind, I needed the morning to figure out how to make it work. I usually sent them a message if I wasn't going to make it so that they weren't waiting for me. "Not to mention, Ally didn't have a morning shift at Cup of Joe, so I had to take her in anyways." I passed the martini to the man sitting in front of me, smiling when he gave me a tip; I tried to ignore the look in his eyes that said he was hoping for some more attention from me.

This must be what happened when you wore make up… and clothes that fit. I'd been getting looks like that all night.

"All right, all right," Emmett said, giving up on his interrogation. "I'm assuming you'll be out tomorrow though, right?"

"It's going to be a fucking disaster with all the competition riders coming in," Nick grumbled. "The next few weeks are going to suck."

Two bar stools opened up around the back so we moved into my territory and they took a seat.

"What beer do you have on tap tonight, Lil?"

I peered over my shoulder trying to see if I could make out what was written on the taps around the corner of the bar. "I think we just got in something from the East Coast. Hold on, let me check."

I walked back around to the front where the row of beer taps was located and sure enough, they'd just installed one for Magic Hat Number 9. I looked up, about to head back down to where my friends were sitting, when I saw a group of guys walk into the bar.

Son of a biscuit. I groaned louder than I should have.

Normally, I didn't notice the comings and goings of anyone in Breakers unless they were coming to sit in front of me and going to ask for a drink. However, when said group contained one Wyatt Olsen, my entire body was immediately on high alert, forcing my attention to the new arrivals. I immediately did a one-eighty and walked back around the bar to Emmett and Nick. I hoped that Wyatt and his friends would stay on the front side of the structure so that I could stay safely hidden in the back; I still hadn't recovered from earlier.

Can't a girl catch a break?

"We have a new Magic Hat on tap," I said to my friends who were still looking through the beer menu.

"Yeah, ok. I'll try that."

Nick echoed, "Make that dos, senorita."

Crap. I hadn't thought this through. A quick glance back towards the door told me that Wyatt's group hadn't made it to the counter yet, but they were definitely headed in that direction.

Thankfully, I wasn't the only bartender tonight. Friday nights there were usually two of us, sometimes even three, one normally working the front of the bar and one working the back and then someone floating.

Tonight, I was working with Andrea who had chosen to cover the front—like she always did. Usually whoever worked the front ended up with a few more clients since people would walk straight in and order, but I wasn't going to argue with her for it. She was a bitch to everyone, but honestly, I didn't mind working with her because she was gorgeous and she liked to flirt with any and all male customers—no exclusions applied—and for me that meant that I was left in relative peace.

Tonight, I prayed that that would still be the case—that Wyatt and his friends would be preoccupied with her.

I ducked my head and quickly scooted around to the front of the bar, grabbing two beer glasses and standing directly behind the tap machine. Out of the corner of my eye I could see Andrea giving me a weird look as I crouched down slightly to better hide behind the handles of the machine. I ignored her—*like I usually did*—filling the glasses as quickly as I could with the Pennsylvania beer. I didn't even look to see where Wyatt was at the risk of being seen. Holding the beers for my friends, I turned and moved back around to the far side of the bar, releasing the breath that I'd been holding when no deep, seductive voice called after me.

"Do you know what trails they are taking from us?" Emmett asked as I sat their beer down in front of them.

"Why would I know what trails they are closing off to the public?" I stared at him, immediately wondering if they knew what I had done. *But how could they?*

"Oh, I don't know, maybe because you fuckin' work here, Lil?" Emmett laughed before he took a huge swig of the pale ale I'd brought them.

Crap.

I cringed. That was a stupid comment my part.

"No. I... uhh... I think we probably get them tomorrow, so I'll let you guys know."

"Have you heard anything?" Emmett asked.

I didn't have to clarify to know that he was talking about Chance. By now I thought they knew that I would tell them if I'd heard from my brother, but maybe with the competition starting soon he'd been hoping for a different answer this time.

I wished I had a different answer to give him.

"No, I haven't."

"Shit. Sorry," he mumbled, realizing that he, too, had said something stupid.

I shrugged and attempted to steer the conversation in a different direction. "So, what did you guys hit this morning? I'm pissed that I didn't get any time out on the slopes today. I can't remember the last time that happened."

"Mostly the park. Trying to get our last runs in before these assholes come in and take over. Although we hit a couple regular runs to get some of the fresh pow still in the glades from last night; it was pretty good." He stopped and began to laugh. "But the highlight of the day was when this dickhead here had the grand idea to try a triple cork off the kicker and ate it so fu--freaking hard." *At least he caught himself the second time.* "You should have seen him lying there—all yard-saled out. Fucking hysterical."

That time he didn't catch himself. Still, I laughed at the story. Thankfully, they were really the only people on this side of the bar, otherwise their Shred—also known as the language of snowboarders—tended to draw eyes. I couldn't count how many times I'd had to translate for Ally what our friends and I were saying. Now, she knew some of the basics; 'kicker' or 'booter' meant jump and 'yard-sale' meant a particularly bad fall, usually involving loose pieces of clothing or gear flying off of you from the impact.

"Oh, shut the fuck up, Emmett." Nick rolled his eyes and downed the rest of his beer.

I laughed at the two of them. They were excellent riders; they'd each won their own slew of competitions and medals and could definitely hold their own in the park. But there were only a few in the country who could successfully pull off a triple, let alone a quad cork; and Chance and I had been two of them.

Although, no one except Chance had seen me accomplish it. He'd helped me learn the trick—spent hours out on the slopes with me practicing before the Open last year. It would have been the first time a woman attempted it. And then, I'd screwed it up and I hadn't attempted it since.

Another obstacle that I would have to overcome if I was going to do this.

"Sounds like you two really need me out there to give you some pointers."

"Holy shit!" Nick exclaimed, hitting Emmett's arm with the back of his hand to get his attention. "Do you see who the fuck is sitting over there?" He quick glanced at me and mumbled, "Sorry."

"No fucking way!"

I rolled my eyes even though neither of them were paying attention to me, assuming they were checking out some chick, as was usually the case. Meanwhile, I decided to accept the fact that their language was not going to be curtailed tonight.

"Channing, seriously; it's fucking Wyatt Olsen," Emmett whispered way too loudly.

Oh God, no.

I'd hoped he would have been gone by now.

Just breathe, Channing. It's not like they're going to call him over here; it's not like they know him.

"I wondered if he was going to be here. I heard rumors that he was retiring after last year," Nick said in awe; the two of them staring like fools.

"Dude's gotta push his fucking luck," Emmett replied.

I'd heard the rumors too; that last year might have been his last, even though he was only thirty or thirty-one. He'd taken gold in the Olympics—what more could you want out of your career? It was the old 'quit while you were ahead' mantra.

For Chance's sake, I'd hoped that it was Olsen's last year. But if he was anything like my brother or myself, it would take a lot more than age to get him off the mountain.

Before I could make any efforts to regain their attention I was forced to turn and leave the conversation for a moment because someone else had taken a seat at the bar and was waiting to be served. He was a younger guy wearing polo shirt and he had that whole prep school vibe going on.

Translation: He was a skier.

"What can I get you?" I watched as his gaze swept over me and I tried to contain the nausea that rolled through me.

What the hell? This is exactly what Andrea was here for—to enjoy the skeevy attentions of all the rich brats who came up here for a drink.

"How about a phone number?"

"How about a drink?" I returned saucily.

"Dirty martini. Extra dirty." And then he winked at me and I desperately wished I could let Emmett spit in his drink before I gave it back to him.

I made quick work of the cocktail, wanting to get away from him as fast as possible—not just because he was a creep, but because God only knew what my two friends were doing at the other end of the bar. As I reached for the olives, I glanced down to them and saw that their gazes were still trained around the corner of the bar—and probably still on Wyatt.

"Do you want to open a tab?" I asked the creep as I put his extra olives into the glass.

He just smiled at me in a way that made my skin crawl. *Whatever.* I was going to assume that that was a yes and be done with him.

I set the glass down, realizing I'd forgotten to put a napkin down first. Mistakenly, I held onto the glass as I reached for a napkin with my other hand. A second later, sweaty fingers closed around mine digging firmly into my skin.

I immediately sent him a hard stare. "Let go of my hand." My demand came through clenched teeth and then, because it was my job, I added, "Please."

"Give me your phone number," he demanded.

I would have just pulled my hand away except that would have caused the drink to spill all over him, which I knew he would then report to the manager and, with my luck, he was probably some rich, important person's kid, and I would end up in big trouble.

I quickly glanced down the bar to see if Emmett or Nick were looking over to see what was taking me so long hoping that maybe they would come to my rescue; they didn't even have the chance.

"I think you should let her hand go."

My heart fluttered at the familiar deep, lilting voice.

Wyatt.

CHAPTER
Four

Channing

I TURNED AND SUCKED IN A BREATH TO SEE WYATT STANDING BEHIND the jerk with his hand on the other man's shoulder applying what looked like pretty significant pressure. The younger guy scowled and looked like he wasn't going to comply in spite of the discomfort he was obviously in. But then Wyatt's one finger pressed slightly into what must have been a pressure point and immediately my hand was free. The jerk yanked his hand back against him.

Wyatt sent me that smile again, saving me and ruining me all in one shot. *I was definitely going to have to get rid of these panties when I got home.*

"I think I'll buy my friend here his drink. I know he has some very important places that he's in a rush to get to." The emphasis in his words made it clear to the preppy creep that he needed to take his drink and go before there was a problem.

Creeper grabbed the glass off of the counter, some of the liquid sloshing up over the side and stormed off around the bar.

I bit my lip, giving my handsome rescuer a small smile. "Thank you," I murmured softly. Recognizing the blush that was rushing to my cheeks, I turned to use the sink behind me to wash the feel of that asshole off of my skin.

"Just glad I could help." He took a seat at the bar and I noticed that he was no longer wearing the jacket; his shirt had the top two buttons undone. *The man must be really letting loose.* "Does that happen a lot?"

"Not usually," I said. "Not up here."

"Good." *Was that a hint of possessiveness I detected?*

I dried my hands and then remembered that I was working and asked, "Can I get you a drink?"

"No, I'm good, thank you. I'm going to be struggling enough tomorrow with the jet lag—I don't need a hangover to complicate it." He laughed, the smooth rumble caressing my skin in a way I wished I could ignore, but more in a way that had me wanting more.

"Sounds like a reasonable plan." I smiled and gave him a glass of water.

"You know, when you said that I might see you around, I didn't expect it to be so soon." He rested his elbows up on the bar, putting his chin on top of his clasped hands. The pose accentuated just how well-tailored his clothes were, straining in all the right places—leaving both too much and not enough to my imagination.

"That makes two of us," I mumbled softly to myself.

A quick glance down the bar told me that, now, of course, Emmett and Nick had their eyes trained on me and the world-renowned snowboarder who wanted my attention—their mouths inconspicuously wide open in shock that I was talking to *the* Wyatt Olsen. I rapidly returned my focus to the man sitting in front of me before he realized my friends' embarrassing expressions.

"Anything good on the menu here?" Wyatt asked.

"Mmm... the mac and cheese, but only because I've never been one for fancy food. Lodge food is the staple of my diet." *Chicken fingers. French fries. Honey mustard. Hot chocolate.* I actually rarely got to eat lodge food anymore since I took the job at Breakers; before that, we'd all met religiously for dinner after my afternoon lessons were over.

He laughed at my response, the sound sending another wave of heat down through my body and out into my lace underwear which were not equipped to handle this type of abuse.

"Any chance we can get some lodge food up here?"

Now it was my turn to laugh. "I don't think so. Maybe for you they would, but you could just go down to the lodge and save yourself the trouble."

"I could." He nodded. *"But you wouldn't be there."*

Smoldering. His eyes were smoldering at me.

Me of all people.

It must've been the makeup. And the sweater.

"Well, that is true…" I agreed softly as I bent down to start unloading clean glasses from the dishwasher had just finished running.

"So, Miss Ryder, do you work anywhere else on the resort or is my time over the next few weeks going to be split evenly between fancy food and the slopes?" He took a sip of the water that I'd given him, his eyes catching mine over the rim.

If it hadn't been before, my blush was clearly evident now—and not the powdered version that Ally had put on me earlier.

"You can call me Channing," I began, wondering just how bad an idea it was to give more information about myself. I pulled my lower lip between my teeth for a moment before my brain magically came up with the perfect response.

"Well, I do teach snowboarding lessons in the afternoon if you feel like you need some instruction or even just a few pointers." I smile sweetly at him as though I hadn't just told arguably one of the best snowboarders in the world that he could use my help.

His stare held mine, his face remained unfazed for a moment before he burst out into laughter. At that point, I couldn't help myself either and I began laughing, too—the kind of laugh that erupts uncontrollably from your stomach and cleanses all tension from your body.

"You are something," he said as his laughter died down. The humor drained from his gaze as it bored into mine, leaving only the foundation of desire that remained. "I think I might have to take you up on that."

"Well, you can make reservations down at the front desk or in the ski shop."

Too late I realized that my furthering of the joke only put me deeper into hot water.

"And can I make reservation for a private lesson there as well?" I sucked in a breath, no longer confident in how to answer. "It doesn't have to be lesson. It could be dinner. Or lunch. Or I'm even willing to accept coffee as a start."

He was asking me out on a date. Wyatt Olsen was asking me out on date. Me –Channing Ryder—the sister of his main competitor (or so he thought). The girl who'd knocked over all of his prized possessions. The girl who just barely looked like one at the moment.

Me.

On. A. Date.

Was that some sort of joke? I thought. *Some sort of ploy to throw my brother off his game?* If it was, Mr. Olsen was going to be in for rude awakening.

"Sorry—I don't think it's a good idea to fraternize with the competition." And I had a feeling that it was an even worse idea to fraternize with *him*.

"Only your brother is my competition, Channing. And you're the one that mentioned fraternizing—I only suggested coffee." Then came *that* smile again and my heart began beating faster than any amount of caffeine could ever accomplish.

Maybe I should agree to coffee. The man did just save me from having to deal with that scumbag.

Come on, Channing, the least you could do is not lie to yourself about why you're going to say yes to coffee.

"Olsen! Let's go, bro!"

Both of our heads turned as the friends he'd come in with must have just finished being entertained by Andrea and were ready to move on with their night.

"I'm being summoned." He sighed, standing up from the bar. "So, coffee?"

I'd hoped this was going to save me from having to decide.

"You can say no, but I'm a slow learner, so there's a good chance

I'll be back here tomorrow night with the same question and the following night and the night after that and, well, I think you get where I'm going with this." His friends yelled to him one more time. "Hold on, Zack!" Holding up a finger, he looked back at me, waiting for my answer.

So, coffee or be harassed at work? Great.

"Fine. Coffee." I agreed begrudgingly, crossing my arms over my chest. My brain was smarting, but my body was already aching to be in a room with him where we weren't separated by a countertop and expectations of appropriate work behavior.

"Where and when tomorrow?"

"I can't tomorrow." *Why? What did I have planned?*

A break—a break from poor decisions like this one and a chance to collect myself.

"Sunday." I offered. "Before my shift here—so, around four. There's a local coffee shop on the base of the main lifts called 'Peace, Love, and a Cup of Joe.'"

He nodded. "What time do you finish tonight?" He asked warily, his eyes narrowing on me.

"Why?" I responded skeptically. *I just agreed to coffee, what more could he want?*

"After what I just saw, I'm not comfortable with you leaving here by yourself. So, I'd like to come back and walk you to your car when you're finished with your shift."

Damn Canadians. Always putting American men to shame.

Most nights I did walk to my car by myself because there was always security around and I never had a problem, but I had a feeling that that answer wasn't going to be good enough for Wyatt. Thankfully, tonight of all nights, my friends were here to keep me company.

"Thank you, Mr. Olsen, but my two friends over there—" I nodded my head in the direction of Emmett and Nick, purposely not looking at them. "—are here for the evening so they'll make sure I get to my car safely." Watching his eyes look behind me, I continued. "I apologize if they're still staring, although I'm sure you noticed it by now."

He looked back at me and, with a soft laugh, said, "I hadn't realized, gorgeous; the only thing I've noticed is you and that sight has held my eyes captive."

Now it was my turn for my mouth to fall open, my heart pounding from his compliment.

Gorgeous. Me. Captivating.

"I'll see you on Sunday, Channing." And with a sexy, successful smile on his face he turned and went back to his waiting friends while I stood there waiting for my limbs to recrystallize from the puddle of mush he turned them into.

One time—it was probably about three or so years ago—I'd fallen attempting a McTwist; it was only the first or second time that I'd attempted the trick and I shouldn't have because the conditions weren't great. I fell *hard* on my ass on the landing, actually, come to find out later, breaking part of my tailbone. But that wasn't the worst part. However I landed pinched a nerve in my back that sent an electrical tingling throughout my lower limbs. It was the strangest thing; I couldn't feel my legs, but they weren't numb. It was the sensation that my body wasn't my own.

And the way that Wyatt had just made me feel, well, it was like that… but on steroids.

I use those few seconds to collect myself as much as I could before I had to turn around to face Emmett and Nick's inquiring gazes—otherwise they would've found me.

"What?" I asked as I walked back over to stand in front of them, their faces speechless for a moment.

"What the fuck do you mean—'what?'!" Emmett exclaimed, throwing up his hands and glancing at Nick. "You were just… you were just having a full-fledged-fucking conversation with Wyatt fucking Olsen. Don't tell us what. Tell us what he said."

"And why he looked like he knew you," Nick added. Sometimes, he was oblivious; other times, he was so perceptive that I swore his slightly-stoned distraction was just for show.

"And why the hell he looked like he wanted to *know* you, if you know what I mean." Emmett's tone hardened and I knew the look that he gave me; it was the one that Chance always did when he saw any guy showing any interest in me. *Over-protective brother on the loose.* Chance wasn't here and it didn't surprise me in the least that Emmett would step into his place—even with all the shit I gave him.

I shrugged, trying to play it cool. "We were having a conversation because he'd helped me get rid of some unwanted attention from some asshole who was sitting at the bar earlier." When Emmett's expression showed his disbelief, I added, "You two were too busy being star-struck by Wyatt and his buddies to notice. Anyway, he was just making sure I was ok."

"He looked like he knew you," Nick insisted.

"I... ahh... I may have run into him earlier today in the parking lot. Well, technically, I ran into his boards in the parking lot."

"What?!" they yelled in unison and I winced, looking around to make sure no one else was on our side of the bar.

"I was running late! And I pulled in too fast and I didn't see his boards propped up against his car until it was too late, so I may have tapped them a little..." They continued to stare at me. "Alright, I freaking knocked them all over onto the pavement. Happy now, assholes?" I huffed.

"Holy fucking shit!" They both burst out laughing and my humiliation for the evening was complete.

"I can't believe you knocked over Wyatt Olsen's boards!"

I grabbed a piece of ice from the ice box and threw it at them. "I know... I know!"

"Holy shit, Lil," Nick said, wiping the tears from his eyes from laughing so hard. "Does he know who you are? That you're Chance's sister?"

"Yeah..."

"Oh man... Good thing Chance isn't competing otherwise he'd probably have a legit complaint that you were trying to take out the competition."

Shit.

I gnawed on my lower lip. I hadn't had time to think about whether or not I should tell the two of them what my plan was. In my mind, their response was either going to be full-on support for the 'gnarly' trick I was about to pull or complete disagreement, in which case they would most definitely strap me to my board and lock me in a closet until the Games were over. When Chance had left, they'd been just as unprepared as I was, but over the past few months his absence had led to an increased protectiveness which is probably why my gut was telling me to hold off.

No, I was going to have to really feel them out and seriously weigh the pros and cons of bringing them into the fold.

I just nodded. "You guys want another one?" In trying to deflect the conversation, alcohol was my best (legal) option.

"Did he ask for your number?" Emmett continued to probe, ignoring the free alcohol that I'd offered.

"No." *At least that I could answer honestly.*

"What was he asked you about? He looked interested."

"Seriously, Emmett!" I groaned, exasperated. "He asked about the food here. He asked what was good. And then he asked if I worked anywhere else on the resort. And then he asked for the name of a good coffee shop. Is there anything else you want to know, Inspector Asshole?"

True. True. True. Mostly true.

Arms over my chest, I glared at him, daring him to question me further. At that point, Nick threw up his hands in resignation. "Well, I'll take another beer if you're offering."

I didn't move, holding Emmett's gaze for another second before he picked up his glass and held it out to me—a gesture signaling that he was satisfied with my answers and ready to move on with the night.

I took three monstrous breaths as I walked around the bar to top up their beers.

CHAPTER
Five

Channing

"**A**LLY!" I YELLED, RUNNING UP THE STAIRS TOWARDS MY SISTER'S room.

If she wasn't ready to leave, I swore I was going to leave without her. It was almost quarter to seven and I told the guys I'd meet them by the lift on the hour, not to mention she had to be to work at seven to open; Ally worked at Peace, Love, and a Cup of Joe—the coffee shop I regrettably told Wyatt I would meet him at tomorrow afternoon.

Unless there was a change in our schedules, she and I rode over to the resort together in the morning; it was the best time to ride—before the afternoon rush. Since I worked late at *Breakers,* Chance was usually the one to bring her home when she finished in the evening. When he left, I think Emmett brought her home a few times before she started getting rides from her friends or coworkers most days.

Had there ever been a time when those two hadn't been at each other's throats?

Some days, if my afternoon lessons ended early or, like yesterday, when I didn't end up having a full schedule, I would bring her home before I had to head back for my night shift.

I banged on the door one, two,—

"I'm ready!" She'd flung the door open wide, standing there in her skinny jeans, Ugg boots, and a different brightly-colored sweater. Her hair was in a loose French braid, small tendrils framing her face that was expertly done with what I was certain was a fair amount of make-up even though it looked very natural. "Sheesh!"

She brushed past me, walking down the stairs.

Somedays, I wished I could be just a *little* bit more feminine like Ally. I wished I could let my short, blonde androgynous haircut grow out to even shoulder length instead of where it was. But long hair—no, even short hair—was a pain to deal with underneath a helmet and against my neck. I couldn't have anything itching or distracting me from my ride.

As for the rest of it all, it wouldn't be difficult to look more feminine; the problem was what happened once I got to that point—evidenced by my interactions with Mr. Olsen. I only knew how to interact with guys as, well, one of the guys. Not to mention the fact that Chance would have had my head if he'd ever seen me flirt with a guy—especially another snowboarder.

To him, all snowboarders were the same as he, Emmett, and Nick; they were all just looking for the next best trick… or so to speak.

I laughed to myself as I turned and followed my sassy sister down the stairs. Who was I kidding?

I had no idea how to flirt with a guy.

"I guess they didn't give you a problem when you went to register?" Ally asked softly as we climbed into the Jeep.

"Not really." She just nodded and turned her head to stare out the window.

Sometimes, she seemed to lose herself in her thoughts—sad thoughts. I didn't know if it had to do with Chance or being so far from our parents or maybe missing all the friends that she'd left behind, but I also didn't know how to ask. Every time I tried to talk to her about her life before she moved back here with us, she closed off and changed the subject.

We'd lived apart for almost five years. She'd grown up with girlfriends; I'd grown up with the boys. I didn't know how to relate to her or get her to open up and I felt like a failure as a sister for it. The only thing that I'd learned that worked to pull her from her melancholy was to distract her, pure and simple.

"I'm putting your sweater in the wash, FYI. I ended up wearing it to work last night, so it definitely needs to be cleaned."

Her fingers strummed against the screen of her phone. "Why? Did someone spill beer on it?! Ugh, that one was one of my favorites, Chan."

"No. Thankfully. Although, Emmett came close by the end of the night." Her head spun towards me, all trace of her previous thoughts gone.

"Emmett was there? Why am I not surprised?" She scoffed and rolled her eyes.

Out of all of our friends, she disliked Emmett the most and it only seemed to worsen with time. I couldn't find a reason for it, besides the obvious, but then again, I'd had over a decade to get used to his abrasive and crude, bordering on careless, personality.

"Yeah. And Nick. I forgot to tell them I couldn't ride yesterday, so they came to check on me. And probably for some free beer."

"Probably," she muttered and I could tell that I was starting to lose her again.

"The next time I ask to borrow your clothes, don't let me. I can't handle the kind of attention that they bring." I laughed a little—*if she only knew.*

"Oh yeah?" Her interest was piqued. "Were you actually recognized as a girl? The horror!" She laughed a little at her own joke and even though it was at my expense, the laugh was worth it.

"Worse," I grumbled.

Now, she turned in her seat to face me. "What does that mean? Did you meet a guy?"

I said nothing, turning into the Snowmass resort. *Was this how it worked with girls? Was this what they meant by 'girl talk?'*

"Oh my God! Chan, did you get asked out?" Astonishment filled her voice as she stared me down, waiting for an answer.

"Why do you say it as though I never get asked out?" *I was slightly offended. I was also trying to avoid answering.*

"Because you never do. Or if you do, you don't go." She continued to stare as I turned the car left, heading towards the Two Creeks lift where the quaint chalet-esque building containing the coffee shop sat conveniently waiting for riders to break from their morning runs for a hot cup of Joe. "Did you?" She put up her hand to stop my answer that hadn't been coming. "No, I already know that you did, so forget that. Is he hot?"

I bit my lip, suppressing the tortured laugh at just how freaking hot Wyatt Olsen was; 'yes' would not have been a sufficient answer to that question.

"You're blushing—so that's a yes." No makeup this morning to hide my reactions. "Who is he? What did you say?"

I stopped my car in front of the coffee shop. "I'm going to be late to meet the guys." I still had to find a place to park in the quickly filling lot and put all my snow gear on. Ally didn't care, buckling down and staying firmly planted in her seat. "Seriously, Al! We're both going to be late."

"So then just tell me what you said and I will happily whistle my way right into work." She flashed a smile at me and knew that she had me.

"Yes, alright. I was asked out and he is hot. He's beyond hot. Like, you could stick his pinky finger in your little frothing pitcher and he could steam the freaking milk for your latte, hot; he was milk-frothing hot." Her smile grew as she began to laugh uncontrollably at my exuberant, ridiculous, yet somehow still lacking, description of just how good-looking Wyatt Olsen was. "Are you happy now?"

She put her hand on the door handle, but continued to laugh while she waited for more.

My hands gripped the steering wheel and I dropped my forehead to rest in the middle of them.

"Yes, I said yes to him. To a date. And I have no idea why and I have no idea what I'm doing." I laughed pathetically at myself before turning to her to plead, "Now can I please get to my friends?"

"Fine, but we are *so* going to talk more about this later!" Her excited squeal sealed her promise as she jumped out of the car.

I threw the jeep in second gear—I had no time for first—and gunned it towards the parking lot of the resort hoping that Emmett and Nick didn't think I'd bailed on them for the second day in a row.

"Well, well, well! Look who decided to show today!" I groaned, wrapping my board behind my back as I trudged through the decent pow over to where Emmett and Nick were tying into their boots. "Didn't recognize you without your makeup on, Lil." Emmett continued to tease.

"Yeah, well, maybe you'll recognize the bottom of my board when I nail the double today in front of your sorry asses."

Step one: Get my double cork down solid.

Step two: Proceed to the triple.

Step three: Don't choke.

"HA!" He clipped in his leading foot and stood, waiting on Nick to finish so we could head to the lift.

"So, lay it on us, Lil. What's the damage for the next month?" Nick locked in his toe strap and we all pushed over to the Coney Glade lift.

They weren't going to like my answer.

"What we thought. Snowmass Park is closed Monday thru Friday for the entire day except to competition riders."

Their string of expletives was lost in the wind as the lift carried us up to the top of the slope.

"What the fuck…"

"What are we going to do?" They literally sounded as though the entire resort was closing, instead of just one trail.

"It's only for a few weeks, guys. Makaha will still be open…"

Makaha was only the intermediate park and would be fine for our afternoon rides. The Snowmass Park, though, contained the Zaugg superpipe; it was groomed much better, had bigger kickers, and overall just stayed in better condition since there were only a few riders expert enough to take it on.

"Makaha blows," Nick grumbled as we prepared to get off the lift. "And it's always swarming with skiers."

We reconvened at the top of the terrain park slope.

"Alright, who's up first?"

"Well, you were talking a pretty big game down there, Lil. I think you should be first on the kicker."

Figures.

I stared down the mostly empty slope, excitement coursing through my veins at the relatively untouched powder that coated the run, the first jump within my sights. I smirked at my crew before pulling my gray neck-warmer up over my mouth. I hooked the clasp of my helmet underneath my chin and pulled my goggles down over my eyes.

Giving them a small salute, I hopped to angle my board to face directly down the hill—my right foot in front. Up until this point, it was the only thing that ever differentiated Chance and me: he rode regular, with his left foot in front, and I rode goofy. After riding for so long, we were both pretty adept at riding switch—or riding with the opposite stance—which would come in handy for this competition. The only time I couldn't change it though, was right before taking a jump—it was too risky to come in with my weaker leg behind. Thankfully, the judges didn't keep track of which way each rider rode—and that meant only those closest to Chance and me would be off-put by that observation.

I sucked in a deep breath and pushed off down the slope.

"Dropping!" I yelled, letting anyone on the other side of the landing know that I was coming.

Pumping my legs up and down, I quickly gained speed. Even just one day off the mountain had sucked some of the life from me and the feel of my body now slicing through the wind, the cold freshness of the air filling my lungs, my board sliding smoothly over the perfectly-pressed snow, immediately rejuvenated me; I felt like I was flying.

And soon, I was.

My body began to bend forward and twist towards the back in the moments just before my board took off from the lip of the jump, launching me effortlessly into the air and into my double cork ten-eighty.

The double cork—and where it gets its name from—is that trick is comprised of a two-fold rotation. First, the more basic element of the maneuver is that you have to spin around at least three times. *Not too hard.* The second part is what makes it incredibly dangerous because you are essentially doing a double backflip *while* continuing to complete those spins.

In the air, twisting and turning, you feel like you are in one of those machines that they use to spin astronauts around; you feel weightless.

In the air, the seconds lingered for just a little longer as my body curved through the air in a practiced arc. I was soaring.

And just when my brain told my body that we were right side up again, my board slid smoothly into the grooves of the landing.

Nailed it.

A huge smile broke onto my face as my right leg swung back to bring me to a stop to wait for the guys. I clapped my hands together in excitement for sticking the landing. The double cork, while incredibly difficult, was something that I was mostly comfortable with now, unless the conditions weren't that great. It was funny to think that back in 2010, when Shaun White had first performed it, they'd almost banned it from the Olympics. Now, if you couldn't do the double, you probably weren't even getting an invitation.

My gaze shot up as Emmett flew over the jump pulling a double backside rodeo—basically back-flipping with what looked like a five-forty rotation. It was smooth and sweet and the reverberating thud underneath my own board confirmed that his landing had been no different.

He turned over towards me and came to a stop while we waited for Nick.

"You land yours?"

"Absolutely." He could hear the smile in my voice.

"Think you can nail the triple?"

My smile dimmed. "I don't know about that—and definitely not today. I haven't gone that hard in a while."

Truthfully, ever since Chance left, we'd all kind of stuck to the maneuvers that didn't push our limits. Maybe it was the fact that one of our own had been injured to the point of no return. But, more than that, I think it was because we'd lost a little bit of our drive with Chance. He'd always been the pusher, always demanding us to go bigger. Emmett might have been 'King' of the Mountain, but even he followed Chance.

Even when we were younger, he'd been like that. If it wasn't for Chance, there was no way I would be as good as I am now; none of us would be.

Anxiety bloomed in my stomach; the only reason I'd landed the triple cork last year was because Chance had been practicing with me every day. I'd been black and blue for two weeks afterward, but he stayed with me and kept making me attempt it over and over again, critiquing each failed attempt and coaching me on how to fix it.

I didn't have that now. I didn't have Chance. How the hell was I going to re-learn this move without him?

Nick flew over the jump, choosing a classic Wildcat (or backflip). He was a little shaky on the landing, but managed to stay upright before sliding over to us.

"You almost tanked!" Emmett laughed.

"Yeah, well, someone left a huge fucking gash in the lip that I'm lucky I was even able to do anything."

"Oh please, don't try to blame this on me, Frost."

"You looked like you nailed the double, Lil." His hand swung out, fisted and waiting for a pound.

"I told you two that I would." My gloved fist bumped his.

"Triple next time?"

"Not today." *What was it with these two?* Nothing for months and now, all of a sudden, they want to see me try and kill myself.

"C'mon. I'm leading and I say we warm up with some McTwists!"

I didn't wait for them to agree, instead taking off down the trail and heading for the half-pipe. One after another, we rode up and down the walls of the giant curve, each performing an Allie-oop McTwist (basically a forward-flipping rotation).

I caught a few more kickers after the pipe before we made it down to the bottom of the run. With the time we took to wait, watch, critique and harass each other, I only had time for one more run before I had to head out, grab a bite to eat, and head over to my lesson.

"You guys have time for one more?" I asked. I assumed that they did since it was Saturday and both of them would be off of school.

"Yeah—I'm good," Nick said.

"Same. Something is off with this board. I need to figure out what the fuck it is before I have to go and make ten of them for the Open. The way I carved yours and Chance's boards was fucking perfect to help with the rotation; I need to go back and adjust this." Emmett bent down and brushed the snow off of his board, examining it as he spoke.

Emmett's snowboard fabrication business was run out of his basement—or so he says; I'd never actually seen it. His waitlist was almost two years out. His boards were expensive as hell. But it was worth the wait and worth the price. His boards could literally make or break your run.

We scanned our passes and jumped back on the lift.

Because of how our high school was set up, it made sense that a lot of us ended up with dreams or jobs that fell into the winter sport's industry, like Emmett and Nick, as well as becoming professional athletes, like Chance and me.

Again, we arrived at the top of the terrain park.

"Alright. Frost, you go." Emmett turned to me and I watched Nick strap in and disappear down the slope in my periphery.

"How can I give you tips if I've never seen you try it? I don't know where you're messing up." I crossed my arms.

"Fuck. Fine." He turned and prepared to drop. "This is going to hurt," he grumbled as he slid off the edge.

I watched him approach the lip, gain speed, and take off.

He hadn't turned soon enough.

I couldn't see past the edge of the jump but I knew that he couldn't have stuck the landing; he wouldn't have completed the flip in time. I bent down to strap my back leg in when a shiver ran up my spine—*only I wasn't cold.*

I looked up to see a group of boarders walking over to the park; the one in the front carrying a board that looked very familiar to me—a board that I'd picked up off of the asphalt yesterday afternoon.

Son-of-a-biscuit.

I quickly locked in my toe-strap, needing to disappear over the jump just like Emmett had done before Wyatt realized that it was me.

I pushed off and flew towards freedom, soaring over the edge, I chose a comfortable 1080, sticking the landing and swerving over towards my crew. Emmett was sitting on the ground, his jacket covered in snow.

Yeah, he'd lost it on the landing.

"I swear, if you made me do that on purpose because of the fucking makeup comments—" Black eyes burned angrily at me.

"Ahh, no." I laughed at the thought though, stopping next to them with my back facing towards the top of the hill. "I think your problem is that you're not prepared enough for the spin right before the take-off; you're not getting enough momentum for the turn, which means you don't have enough time, which means you reach the ground before you're ready to land."

"No shit Sherlock." He smacked the snow next to him. "But it's the board, not me."

The triple was very difficult to master. Last year, before the Open, Chance and I had flown out and rented time at a Pipe and park by Tahoe that was fitted with a foam pit. There we must have fallen a hundred times trying to land the triple. Attempting the triple here would be the first time I would be doing it without a safety net since the incident at the Open.

"You really have to swing your body into it almost when it seems too early. Your body has to start the turn before your feet leave the ground—that's all I can really say." I glanced quickly over my shoulder. Wyatt and the other riders he was with—and what looked like a lone skier—were waiting at the top for us to move on. "Alright, let's keep moving. I don't want to be late."

"Hey, wait a sec." Nick pulled off his goggles and looked up towards the top of the trail. "Is that Olsen?"

Emmett stood to get a better view. "We should stay and watch him. Maybe Miss Makeup over here can introduce us to her new friend."

"Shut up, Emmett. I don't think that's him and I have to go. But, if you two guys want to wait for your man-crush, I'll just catch up with you later." And with that, I swung around them and began to head for the next jump, needing to get as far away from Wyatt Olsen as possible. A few second later, I heard the guys following behind me. *Or at least one of them*

"Damn you flew down that fast!"

Nick hadn't reached the bottom yet, still probably hitting some of the kickers in an attempt to covertly wait and watch Wyatt take some of the jumps.

"I need to grab some lunch and a coffee before my lessons; when you try to teach five year olds how to snowboard, you will understand." I unstrapped from my board, hiding my face for as long as possible.

"You going to Cup of Joe?" Emmett unclipped his helmet.

"Yeah, I need to make sure Ally has a ride home later. I forgot to ask when I dropped her off. Why?" I shook out my hair, hooking my helmet strap around my arm.

"No reason. I was thinking about a coffee, too, so I'll just come with you."

I looked back up the slope—still no sign of Nick.

"Leave him. He wanted to watch Olsen's gang. Let's go." He walked ahead of me towards the caffeine chalet.

CHAPTER
Six

Channing

I wasn't too thrilled about Emmett coming over with me to the café, but I couldn't think of a good reason to tell him not to without it looking suspicious. I just prayed that Ally wouldn't say anything about what I'd been forced to admit to her in the car this morning.

The crisp, invigorating scent of freshly brewed coffee spread right through my chilled body. I immediately saw Ally behind the register, but she hadn't noticed Emmett and me.

"There's Little Miss Sunshine!" Emmett yelled, drawing her—and everyone else's—attention.

I laughed as Ally gave him her best resting-bitch-face.

"Hey sis," she addressed me, then decided to completely ignore the smirking ass standing beside me. "Didn't think I was going to see you again today. What can I get ya?"

"Mocha—my usual. And the chicken pesto panini." They literally made the best mochas in the world. "I know, but I forgot to ask if you had a ride home tonight, since I'm working at Breakers. Plus, I forgot I was teaching five-year-olds today, so I need some sort of stimulant." I loved teaching little kids, but after this morning, they would require more energy than I was able to spare.

"Oh." She bit her lip and looked around. "Actually, Jessa has a prep class for the next couple weeks before her licensing exam, so she can't take me. There's another girl who works here that I could ask—her name is Charlie—but she called off again today; I seriously don't know why they don't fire her, she's always missing work." Ally groaned in frustration. Even though it took some effort to get her here in the morning, once she was here, she was a hard worker and slackers were her biggest peev—after Emmett, that was.

"I'll take Little Miss Sunshine home," Emmett interjected, speaking to me instead of my sister.

Her Ryder-blue eyes iced over glaring at him. "Stop. Calling. Me. That."

He just smiled at her, clearly having no intention of abiding by her request. I didn't know when the whole 'sunshine' thing started—probably right around the time Ally couldn't seem to stand being around him—which had been from day one. I didn't know why it made her upset, I thought it sounded endearing—like something you would call a little sister. But what did I know?

"Sorry, sis," I said, grabbing my coffee and sandwich. "Unfortunately, looks like you're stuck with him for the ten-minute drive home. I think you will survive… hopefully, he will, too," I mumbled underneath my breath. I didn't have time to deal with her protests, so I quickly turned to leave the coffee shop before I was sucked further into their feud. "See you in the morning!" I yelled behind me as I balanced my sandwich on the lid to my coffee and opened the door to leave.

I managed to turn my head back around just to see myself collide with a solid white and blue wall.

The heat, the fresh-spiced scent, and the tingling over my body informed me that this wasn't any wall.

It was a wall of Wyatt.

"We have to stop meeting like this." The sexy, slightly-accented voice released goosebumps down my arms.

Well, that settled that; his voice was still just as intoxicatingly arousing as it had been yesterday.

I'd hoped the intoxication would be similar to a hangover—that after a good night's rest, I would have slept off all the effects.

My underwear was now evidence to the contrary.

I stepped back slightly, refusing to look up until I'd made sure that I hadn't spilled coffee all over his *white* jacket.

I raised my eyes to his smiling ones. "I'm so sorry. I was saying something to my sister and I didn't see you."

"You know, I have to believe that either you are one of the clumsiest people I've ever met *or* you're just looking for ways to bump into me." I scowled. "*But*," he continued, "judging from the moves I saw you pull down the park, it's hard for me to believe that you could ever be clumsy."

"*You should see her in heels!*" Ally yelled from behind the bar. Any guilt I had for making her ride home with Emmett completely evaporated.

That devastating smile broke out on his face, accompanied by a small laugh, while his gaze remained focused on me.

"I was hoping it was the second option anyway," he said a little bit softer so that no one else would hear.

I felt both Ally and Emmett's gaze on me. At least only Wyatt could see my blush and hopefully, he thought it was just because it was cold outside.

"*I'm Channing's sister, Ally! What's your name?*" I groaned. *Why was she continuing to yell?* I swore my cheeks were going to burst into flames. Thankfully, he looked over to her and gave me a moment of respite.

Before the situation could get any more awkward, I stepped to the side, a subtle hint that he should move past me and let the people behind him enter into the coffee shop. And wouldn't you know it, the very next person to walk in behind Wyatt was Nick-fucking-Frost. I scowled at my *friend*.

"Did you bring him here?" I muttered to Nick as Wyatt walked over to order at the counter; his eyes kept returning to me even as he briefly conversed with my sister, making sure that I wasn't going anywhere.

He tried to look at me innocently but I knew better. "What, Lil? He asked if I knew where this place was, so I told him I would show him."

"And did you also tell him that it was me on the park earlier?" My scowl darkened even further.

He gave me that calm smile—the one that said everything was just for his entertainment. "He said he was going to give me some tips" *I should've known.* "You should have seen him nail the triple, even Pride's doesn't look that smooth."

My gaze dropped to the floor at the mention of my brother—and at the mention of the feat that I had yet to accomplish.

"I hear that you've been practicing your triple cork." Wyatt's voice returned to our conversation and I wished I could shoot laser beams from my eyes at a certain SnowmassHole.

Oh, God. Hopefully he didn't mention anything about Chance.

"Did you?" I sent him a too sweet smile at which point, Nick excused himself with a fake sheepish look to go order some coffee. *He'd better hope that Wyatt held up his word to give him some pointers, because the only thing he was going to learn from me was how to get his ass kicked.*

"That's pretty impressive. I don't think a female has done that in competition yet." The admiration in his eyes was genuine.

"Well, the only competition that I'm in is with my brother—and if he can do it, then I know I can, too."

Wyatt laughed as he took a sip of his coffee and the way he licked his lips afterward, well, I quickly gulped down some of my own drink in order to swallow my groan.

"A healthy sibling rivalry, I see." He nodded to someone who walked in behind me. "Thankfully, my brother, Zack," he paused and nodded to the third guy walking into the place behind Nick, "ended up on the wrong side of the fence—he ended up being a skier—so, we can still be civil to each other."

So that's who the lone skier had been.

I followed his glance to see another equally (not really that equally) handsome man approaching the counter; he hadn't paid a single bit of attention to us, but he was, however, completely focused on Ally behind the bar. I also noticed that Emmett's protective growl was now trained on Ally instead of me; I chalked it up to the big brother instinct of his.

"Alright, well I gotta run. I have a lesson starting in a few minutes—so, unless you want to come heel/toe it with about ten five-year-olds…" I waved 'bye' to my sister and my two friends—none of whom were paying any attention to me. *Great.*

"I'll walk you over there." It wasn't a question and before I could protest, he reached around and opened the door for me, waiting for me to walk through.

"You don't have to," I muttered as I tore into the wrapping that was covering my panini.

"I want to."

How could I argue with that? Especially when I wanted him to, too.

"You're an excellent rider and your friends really admire you." Our boots crunched in the powder as we walked toward the lesson area.

"You've barely seen me ride; you can't know how good I am." *I was pretty excellent. When I didn't choke, that is.*

"When you take your first step onto the snow, you know exactly what the riding conditions are going to be like—whether the snow is too moist and there's going to be drag on your board or if the powder is perfect and it will be smooth sailing. It's the same when I look at a rider—when I look at you. I only need those first tracks to know." He sighed and I knew he was staring at me, but I refused to look over; his compliments were too unnerving.

"You should really stop complimenting me," I blurted out, unprepared for the verbalization of my thoughts.

"Would you rather I kiss you instead?" His smooth-as-molasses voice mingled with the tantalizing lilt of his accent snuck up on me and ripped the breath right out of my lungs.

So shocked as I was by his question I tripped over my own boots.

Stumbling, I began to slip in the snow that had turned to slush from all of the foot traffic.

Wyatt grabbed my arms and hauled me against his chest to stop my embarrassingly sudden lack of coordination and imminent fall.

The oxygen in my lungs and my brain was gone, replaced only with *him*—hard, hot, and everything male.

"Still can't decide if you are clumsy or if you just like running into me," he whispered softly, his breath brushing against my cheek as I lost myself in his eyes. "I think I'd rather kiss you now, Channing."

My mouth parted.

Just like earlier, standing on top of the slope, I eyed the kicker that was in front of me—only this one had a name: Wyatt Olsen. Only this one, I had a feeling, was going to send me faster and higher into the air than any jump I'd ever taken. The same adrenaline pumped through my veins; not fear, not uncertainty, but pure, potent need to take the risk of crashing and burning because the reward would have me soaring.

My hands curled into his jacket and instead of responding with words that were sure to be an awkward, incoherent mess, I pushed up on my toes and flew towards the jump, my body tensing and preparing for flight as I planted my lips firmly on his.

I'd shocked him with my brazen response, but only for that split second. Then, his lips slanted over mine and I was weightless and airborne in his arms. His tongue pressed against my lips—lips that opened willingly for him.

Damn, he tasted like strong, masculine coffee—a brew that, I can assure you, is much more addicting than any caffeine that Cup of Joe had been selling.

"I'm not clumsy," I muttered, our breaths mingling in the millimeters of space between our lips.

I dropped back onto my feet, releasing him and stepping back. "I'll see you around," I stammered awkwardly, turning and walking towards the little group of munchkins and their tiny, tiny snowboards.

"Tomorrow, Channing. I'll see you tomorrow." I turned, my eyes unlocking the promise in his as I nodded.

Crap. Tomorrow. All of this I would be reliving again tomorrow.

God, I couldn't remember the last time I kissed a guy; hell, I couldn't even remember the last time I *wanted* to kiss a guy. I'd been too focused, too determined over the past few years trying to keep pace with my brother. Chance had been getting much better, much faster than I had and, well, we'd always been in this together and I didn't want to get left behind. So, I'd thrown everything I had into training because I wanted—no, I needed to win.

Ally had asked what would happen if I won?

I was beginning to fear that the real question now was: *would winning taste as good as Wyatt?*

"Finally!" Ally's footsteps came racing around the corner from the living room into the front hallway of our house.

I froze in my tracks, tossing my keys in the basket on entryway table. "What? What's going on?" I tugged off my beanie, watching in a fog as Ally approached me. "Are you ok?"

I was completely drained from the day—first, with the ride I had this morning. Then Wyatt... and more Wyatt. Then the adorable but exhaustingly rambunctious kids in my lesson, and finally, my shift at Breakers.

I thanked the Mountain gods that they had two other bartenders on staff tonight in addition to me; even though I made less, I probably would've been asleep on the bar by now without the extra reinforcements.

All I could think on my drive was how much I just wanted to get home, take a hot shower, crawl into bed, fall asleep, and dream of Wyatt.

And then get up and do it all again tomorrow.

"What! Of course, I'm okay. I've been twiddling my thumbs,

waiting for you to get home so that you can tell me about one Wyatt Olsen." She crossed her arms over her chest and smirked at me.

"Ugh," I groaned, dropping my head back; I was too tired to talk about the man. "It's past midnight, Ally. I have to go to bed. Some of us have to work tomorrow," I grumbled and walked around her, heading for the stairs.

"Don't care," she said sweetly as she followed me into the bathroom, deciding to continue with her interrogation as I stripped down for my shower. "So, I don't really think I need to ask this, but is Wyatt the guy that you have a date with? Because holy hotness—you were totally right about him being able to steam milk. Heck, I'd let him froth my milk—"

"Ally!" I yanked back the shower curtain and glared at her for her dirty thoughts.

Only I was allowed to have dirty thoughts about Wyatt Olsen. And that thought right there was a big problem.

"Well, maybe if you would just tell me what I want to know, I wouldn't be forced to talk so much."

"Yes." I succumbed to her demands as I shampooed my hair. "I have a date with him tomorrow. At the coffee shop. If you say anything to Emmett or Nick though, I will pour beer on all of your sweaters."

"Why would I say anything to either of them? Especially Emmett. Which, by the way, I'm still really mad that you asked him to bring me home. You know what happened after you and Prince Charming left? Your Mr. Milk-frother's even more delicious younger brother decided to hang out and chat with me for a little bit after the lunch rush slowed down."

Mr. Milk-frother. I was never going to live that down.

I murmured to acknowledge that I was still listening to her while I massaged conditioner into my scalp.

"He even offered to take me home when I was done. But, because you asked Emmett, I wasn't allowed to go home with sexy, Zack Olsen. Oh, no—according to King Emmett, I was only allowed to be escorted home by him."

I hoped that the noise from the shower hid my laugh at my sister's overly dramatic tale of her disagreement with Emmett.

"Sorry, Ally. I'll let Emmett know—"

"No! Don't say anything to him. I refused to speak to him the entire way home and I refuse to waste any more time on him right now."

I turned off the water, reaching out for my towel, and pulled the shower curtain open.

"So." *Uh oh. I didn't like the look on her face.* "Have you kissed him?"

Son of a biscuit. Was the fact written on my forehead or something?

"YOU DID!" And then she started jumping up and down and I swore to myself that I was going to make her get a second job because she had way too much energy for almost twelve-thirty at night. "HOW WAS IT?!"

I groaned. "If you stop yelling and jumping, I'll tell you that it was really, *really* good."

Even though she bit her lip, it did nothing to stop the squeal that escaped.

"It was really… incredible." I winced at how lame my details of the event were. However, I just didn't know of any word adequate enough to describe everything that he made me feel.

"This is so exciting!" She clapped her hands, following me down to the other end of the hall and into my room. "And you're going to see him again tomorrow. Jeez, from what I've witnessed of your love life, chances are you're going to be married by the end of the week!"

"Rude." I dug into my drawer of brightly colored underwear, pulling out a royal purple thong with a little bow detail on the front. "And I don't know if I'm going to see him after tomorrow—I don't know if I should see him after tomorrow."

"What do you mean? Why not?" Her face fell.

"Because he's in the competition, Ally. Not only that—he's the one who will win unless I beat him; he was Chance's biggest competition." I shook my head, sitting on the side of my bed. "If he finds out… if he realizes… that it's me underneath that helmet, it will ruin everything.

I can't let him get close enough to realize."

"But…" She came and sat down next to me. "You really like him; it's written all over your face—and, I'm sorry, but even my makeup skills can't hide it."

"I don't know what I'm going to do. I'm too tired to think or decide anything right now. I'll see what happens tomorrow."

I climbed underneath the covers, hoping that would signal to her that I was going to bed and she should too. But she made no move to leave.

"Channing, I moved only a few months ago, but I have not seen you go on one date with a guy. I haven't even heard you mention a guy besides our brother and his friends. I understand that they're your friends, too, and I understand that you and I have different personalities, different interests, but you can't sit there and tell me it's only because of snowboarding that you haven't had time to even have a crush on someone. I know better than to believe that excuse because I've seen Chance and Emmett and Nick go out for the express purpose to meet girls, whether it's just to hang out at the bar or hook up with them; they've made time to still live their lives. Why haven't you?"

I stared at her, the emptiness inside of me echoed with the truth of her words.

"You don't have to answer me, but you should at least answer that question for yourself. I've seen you excited about a lot of things—from winning the Open to landing a 'kicker,' to seeing Chance get his invite to the X games, but I've never seen you like this. You compared the man to a freaking milk-frother for crying out loud." She sighed and stood and then looked down on me as a mischievous smile grew on her face. "All I'm saying is that I think you could use a good frothing."

"Oh dear Lord," I turned and groaned into my pillow as Ally walked out of my room, chuckling to herself as she closed the door behind her.

Freaking milk-frother.

But right now, I didn't care. A smile crept onto my face as I closed my eyes and easily drifted off into my sweet, frothy dreams.

CHAPTER
Seven

Wyatt

"**W**HAT DO YOU MEAN YOU HAVE TO GO?" ZACK THREW UP HIS hands. "We were just killing it, bro."

"*Bro*, I told you, I'm meeting Channing for coffee." I pulled off my helmet and began to unstrap from my bindings.

"Yeah… Not your usual type there, big brother." He stabbed his poles into the snow next to him and crossed his arms over his chest, looking at me and expecting me to justify myself.

It was true; not on purpose, but I normally had a thing for curvy, feminine brunettes who were *not* riders—no pun intended.

Channing Ryder was the complete opposite of that.

When I'd heard the crash of my boards the other day, I walked around Zack's rental car, prepared to lay into whoever damaged my shit, until I saw her—her hand pulling at her short, boy-cut blond hair before she frantically jumped down from her Jeep and began to pick up the mess she'd made of my most valuable possessions. My body's reaction had taken me completely by surprise; instantly hard, instantly aroused, and instantly uncomfortable in the clothes that I was wearing.

She wasn't curvy in the slightest. Everything about her was tight and compact—the thought making my cock throb against my jeans. And she was just bordering on feminine. Even though her makeup was done and she was wearing a preppy, feminine sweater, it clearly wasn't her norm with the way she pulled at the tight fabric, annoyed as it restricted her movements and the way that she inadvertently rubbed one of her eyes, not realizing that it slightly smeared whatever was on it.

I had to stop and stare for a minute; I had no other choice, since words eluded me.

But when I finally said something and she spun to look at me, well, I'd broken body parts that had a far less devastating effect.

The first thing I couldn't help but be drawn to was her brilliant blue eyes. They were the most incredible sapphire I'd ever seen—like the sky on a clear day from a mountaintop ten-thousand feet above sea level—the kind of brilliance that also takes your breath away.

Her sweater clung tightly to her lithe, petite form, the slight swells of her small breasts peeking out from its edge. As my gaze dropped over them, I could see the faint outline of her nipples hardening underneath my stare, the knowledge making my balls tighten painfully. *Hell,* in different clothes, without makeup, she probably could have passed for a boy and yet, my hands twitched with the need to feel her flesh; my body begging to be inside of her as I imaged her body wrapped around me.

I'd crossed my legs, thankful that she seemed intently focused on righting my boards, so that she couldn't see that I was a breath away from tossing them all back on the ground, pressing her up against my brother's car, and kissing her pink, full lips.

No, she wasn't my usual type—*and I'd never wanted anyone more.*

That alone should have told me that I should have been better prepared for my next realization. From the second she touched my boards, I knew immediately that she was a snowboarder. She picked up my gear like she'd done it one-hundred-thousand times before…

And then I walked inside to registration to learn that, of course, the one woman who'd literally crashed into my life, inflamed my body, and stolen my breath was the twin sister of my biggest competition.

And a respectable boarder in her own right.

I had to wonder why she then seemed uncomfortable in her own skin; part of me hoped that it was because of me—because she was just as attracted to me. The other part of me whispered that there was more to it.

If I hadn't seen her handle my boards, or realized who she was, I wouldn't have pegged her for a snowboarder right away. There was a certain appearance that riders tended to go for, even women, and the makeup and girly sweaters wasn't it; just like the button-down shirts and sport coats weren't typical for men.

Knowing both parts, it made more sense why she seemed so uncomfortable. My suspicions were confirmed later at that bar—*Ice Breakers*—when I saw her again. The makeup that she was wearing was slightly more smudged from forgetting that she was wearing something that she usually wasn't. The sweater that she had on had the sleeves rolled up and when she'd talked to me, her arms remained crossed over her chest as though she was trying to hide her attractiveness.

All that to say that Zack was right, she wasn't usually the type that caught my eye. But not only had she caught it, it seemed like she blinded me to everyone else. After we left Breakers that night, Zack and his friends had wanted to go to a local dive bar down the road—Bar Louie's, or something like that—to pick up girls. I begged off, saying that the jet lag had me beat. The truth was I couldn't get Channing off my mind—and I had no desire to even try.

She was the intoxicating combination of fire and ice. Awkwardness and sass. Tomboy and total woman. She had a confidence in who she was and what she was doing, but more than that she had a contentedness with the unknown—a quality that eluded me.

I turned back to my brother, wondering what his point was. "Yeah, so?"

He put his hands up to suggest that he meant no offense. "Just saying. Although that sister of hers, now she is a ray of sunshine." He winked at me.

I gave him a look that said he'd better watch himself.

Bending down, I picked up my board and said, "I'll catch you later at the house."

"Yeah." He put his goggles back on, pulled his poles from out of the snow, and gave me a salute as he skated over towards the lift.

Checking my board, I headed for the locker room in the lodge to get out of my snow gear, wondering just what it was about Channing that had me so enthralled.

Normally, snowboard chicks didn't do it for me, mostly because a majority of them were only doing it to be 'in' with the guys. But after seeing her on the park yesterday—and watching her nail a 1080—I knew that snowboarding was a part of her, just like it was a part of me and that realization had only caused my admiration to grow.

I'd looked her up as I lay in bed last night, trying not to think about the erection I couldn't shake. I read about her and her brother—the Wonder Twins, the snowboard reports liked to call them; they were both incredibly talented, winning multiple national competitions and podiuming in Slopestyle at the Open. It brought back memories of the days when I'd competed in those events—now, I practiced and saved my strength for the X Games and the Winter Olympics.

Another sign that my life on the mountain was coming to an end.

My entire life had been about winning, about dominating this sport, and I'd made it to the top. Now, the problem was, I didn't know how to get back down. All I'd ever done was win and succeed at this and everything that it involved—from the sponsorships, to the modeling gigs, to the ads and TV stints here and there. I was the best and now, everyone expected me to just take off my crown and quietly pass it on, probably to Chance Ryder, no less.

And then I'd read about Channing's run at the Open last year. Damn woman had attempted a triple cork—hardly accomplished by men, never by a woman—in her Slopestyle run. And she'd bailed the landing. Even just looking at the photos of her lying there in the snow, my body had vibrated with the need to go to her, gather her in my arms, and tell her that she was incredible for attempting the impossible and that she'd nail it next time.

Something told me that she wasn't the type who would ever say that she needed comforting, even when she did.

Back in the safe disguise of normal clothes, I walked over to the café. Checking my watch, I realized that I was a few minutes early, but that was ok. I didn't want her to have to wait—or have the time to change her mind.

I didn't give a shit who her brother was or that he was my competition; he could have been Shaun-fucking-White for all I cared—*I wanted to win and I wanted to win her.*

Channing, on the other hand, I was sure felt like she was betraying her brother by flirting with his rival. At this point in my life, the X Games was exactly that—a game, but for someone like Ryder, it was the jumping point for what could be a very successful career. I didn't know Chance personally, but I would hate to think he'd blame his sister if he lost.

I pushed the door open into the coffee shop, half-expecting to run into my date in the process, but she wasn't there yet. In fact, the place was pretty dead. I took a scan of the room with its coffee bar and display case in the center, small table on either side, and then couches and cushioned chairs along the edges by the windows. There was only one other couple in the place and they were on the other side of the coffee bar.

Walking up to the counter, I found myself continuously glancing back over towards the door, waiting for Channing to walk through it. I was greeted by a younger kid working the counter who was either really tired or really stoned. I guess Channing's sister—*Ally*—wasn't working today.

She'd probably done that on purpose.

I walked over to the register and ordered two mochas, seeing as how that was what she'd had in her hands yesterday, I figured it was a safe bet. I also figured that if I waited for her to get here before ordering, she would refuse my attempt to buy her coffee and I didn't want to waste my time with her arguing over who was going to pay.

Sorry, sweetheart, it might have just been coffee until those sweet lips of yours touched mine; now it was a date and the only person who was paying for anything would be me.

I carried the mugs of sweetly strong liquid over to a small table near the corner of the room that had two large armchairs on either side. Setting them down, I took a seat in the one that faced the door.

Damn, my body was hardening by the minute as I waited for her to get here.

The bell at the door dinged as it opened and in walked my blonde-haired, blue-eyed kicker.

Channing

Before I could turn around for the fourth time, I threw open the door to Cup of Joe and walked inside, immediately regretting my decision.

I was toeing the line, letting whatever attraction there was between Wyatt and me grow. If I wasn't careful, I was going to catch an edge and wipe-out before I even knew what hit me.

I didn't have to scan the room to know he was already here. The familiar goosebumps sprinkled like snow over my skin, but instead of cooling me, my temperature began to rise. I turned my head to see him relaxing in one of the chairs in the corner. The place was mostly empty since it was almost dinner time; the majority of visitors would be just coming off the slopes and changing for the evening ahead.

I gnawed on the corner of my lip as I walked over to him, watching as his eyes darkened with desire.

I subjected myself to the excited harassment of my sister this morning when I asked her if she could do my makeup again and loan me another top; I insisted that it was for work, but she obviously didn't believe my terrible attempt at lying. So, instead of my usual Gap black boyfriend jeans and t-shirt for work, I was presented with some dark, designer jeans that were just a hair too long. And then she gave me a gray, long-sleeve top that had a V-neck cut. I'd held it up and determined that it was going to be far too small, but sure enough, it fit. And by fit, I would use the expression 'fit like a glove' except that no glove I'd ever worn had molded to every curve of my body like this.

I sucked in a breath as he stood when I made it to the table.

"Channing." I squeezed my thighs together at the onslaught of the accent, followed by the swift descent of his head to kiss my cheek.

"Hi." My voice was completely breathless. "Wyatt."

Smooth.

He motioned to the other chair and as I sat down, I noticed there were two drinks on the table.

"You ordered me a drink?" Was I asking or stating? I didn't even know.

"A mocha." He smiled and I was then forced to cross my legs. "I saw that's what you ordered yesterday."

"Oh." I picked up the cup, letting the heat pleasantly warm my hands. "I could have gotten it." I began to blow some of the steam coming off the top of the liquid, looking up at him over the rim of the mug.

His expression darkened. "Not when you're on a date with me, you won't."

I froze mid-blow. "This isn't a date."

"I beg to differ." He had the nerve to smile and take a sip of his own drink.

"You said it was just coffee." I took a sip.

"And then you kissed me." And then I practically choked. "Which turned *this* into a date."

It was totally uncalled for for him to bring that up.

"You—" I broke off, knowing I didn't have any rebuttal against the truth; I had kissed him. And the way he put his lips up to the side of his cup was making me want to do it all over again.

He smiled triumphantly before continuing, "So, your sister works here?" The change in the conversation was a relief to my thoughts that were quickly losing themselves in the memory of his mouth for the umpteenth time today.

"Yeah." I nodded. "She was living in Florida with my parents, but moved back out here a few months ago."

"Ahh… She seemed like someone who enjoys sand over snow."

That was definitely the truth. "She does—just like my parents. Only Chance and I seem to have gotten the frozen gene." Even though he laughed, I cringed for mentioning my brother.

"So, I've met some of your friends, I've met your sister from a distance, but I've yet to meet your brother." My insides turned to ice. "I'm guessing I'll see him out on the slopes tomorrow."

No. No. No. No.

Even though he said it as a general musing, which made complete sense since he seemed to have met everyone else in my life except for my twin brother, my mind was still racing.

"I… ahh… probably not," I mumbled, trying to inject calm confidence into my voice. "Chance still has to go to physical therapy in the mornings, so he's probably going to be practicing offsite until the competition."

I could've sworn that I saw his eyes narrow ever so slightly at my answer but then he shrugged casually and replied, "I'd heard that Ryder was injured, but I'd thought it was something much more serious. Glad to hear he's on the mend."

"I'm sure." I couldn't keep the sarcasm from my voice, but I hoped Wyatt didn't notice.

"Seriously. I want to compete against him." His gaze caught mine before he let loose a devilish grin. "I want to win against him."

I scoffed at his assumption. Wyatt wouldn't be winning. And he certainly wouldn't be winning against Chance.

"I don't think you're that lucky," I mused calmly, taking a long sip of my delicious mocha.

"Well, I'm here with you, aren't I? On a date, no less." The man's confidence killed me. Most snowboarders were cocky assholes, but Wyatt… he was confidence bathed in class; he took what he wanted in a way that had you wishing you could give him more.

I took another sip of my drink to avoid responding.

"Are you jealous?" The bluntness of this questions startled me. "Sorry, I didn't mean..." His foot-in-mouth moment made me smile; *at least I wasn't the only one.* "So, even though he skis, my brother Zack and I used to get in huge fights years ago when we both boarded and started competing. I didn't know if it was a sibling thing or maybe just a guy thing. We're good now, but we were bad; it was bad." He shook his head at the memory.

I laughed, rubbing my thumb along the outside of the coffee mug that was now almost empty due to my nervousness. "I think it's must be a guy thing. Or maybe it was because we never could compete in the same contests. I don't know; we always worked together, always pushed and helped each other. I think I wanted to make him better because it made me better—and vice versa, I'm assuming."

"Or maybe it was the twin thing?" The question was asked half in jest, but I knew from experience that he wanted to know if such a thing existed.

"It is real," I admitted and he raised his eyebrows. "At least for us. Maybe because we have the same passion—I don't know. I don't know about the whole telepathy part—" *Because I certainly wished I knew what my twin was thinking right now, disappearing into the world with no word to those who cared about him most.* "—but, I feel more for Chance than I do with my sister. I love her to death—most days—but whatever Chance feels, I feel it, too."

"Amazing." And he meant it.

"I don't know about that. When he fell and we... weren't sure whether he'd ride again or not, I think my heart stopped with his."

Strangely enough, his eyes dropped from mine at the mention of not riding again. I knew the R-word had been thrown around after the Winter Olympics last year, but wasn't he excited for the next stage of his career?

And then, just as quickly, his eyes were back on me and he smiled. "Well, I'd still like to meet him at some point—preferably before the competition; I've heard pretty incredible things about his skills."

"He's very talented," I agreed softly; there was no question about that.

"So are you." My eyes darted up to his. "Going for triple cork at the Open. Very bold of you, Miss Ryder."

I stirred the spoon in my coffee cup absentmindedly, rather preferring not to talk about that incident.

"Bold or stupid?" I laughed to myself and muttered ironically, "Kind of like kissing you." *Perhaps I shouldn't have said that last bit out loud.*

He raised an eyebrow at me and then smiled. "Definitely bold. Without a doubt."

"Well, I still haven't decided."

"I'd be happy to give it another go if it would help you make up your mind."

I sucked in a breath so fast that I started to choke, quickly coughing to hide the fact that my body was screaming '*yes*'. Very emphatically, I might add.

Instead, I send him a look that said, 'Really?' and he laughed.

"Hey, a guy's gotta try." He shrugged, finishing the last of his coffee. "The coffee here is *really* good."

I nodded in agreement.

"I know you have your brother, but if he's practicing somewhere else, I'd be more than happy to help you with your triple."

I flushed, my eyes dropping down. "I… umm… thanks." *Ok, enough was enough with putting me in the spotlight. It was time for this suited snowboarder-in-disguise to take some of the heat.*

"So, what are you doing here, Mr. Olsen?" I asked with my very best investigative, reporter voice.

"Trying to stop myself from leaning over and kissing the most beautifully intriguing woman I've ever met," he replied so nonchalantly that I almost spit out the last sip of my mocha that I'd drained from the cup. "How about you?"

I wiped my mouth with a napkin, trying to compose myself.

"That's not what I meant."

"Doesn't mean it's not the truth, sweetheart."

I shivered at his endearment.

Gorgeous. Beautiful. Intriguing. Talented. Sweetheart.

I think that was more compliments than I'd gotten total in the first twenty-five years of my life. The only endearments—if you could call them that—that I got, besides the occasional 'sis' from Ally, were… well… a variety of inappropriate terms that Chance, Emmett, Nick and I shared amongst ourselves.

Who was this woman he was talking about? I struggled to believe that it was me.

I didn't know how to respond, so I didn't. Instead, I pressed for the answers that he was avoiding.

"What are you doing here? Rumor had it that you were retiring after last year." I sat back in the armchair, crossing my arms over my chest only to release them when I saw how much cleavage this shirt was capable of revealing.

"Can't always believe everything that you hear."

"Are you thinking about it?" I was now really curious. His entire demeanor had changed, his confidence somewhat diminished, replaced with a general air of uncertainty.

"Yeah, of course." He ran his hand through his sculpted hair. "I don't know that I have a choice."

"What do you mean?"

"It's time for me to pass the torch—or so they say. I'm on top right now and my sponsors want me to quit while I'm ahead. Too much young, new blood out there, willing to try things that I'm not sure my body would easily recover from anymore."

"Why? You're not that old," I retorted, struggling to believe what I was hearing.

"Oh, thanks," he returned sarcastically with a laugh.

"I mean… that's not… you know what I meant." I blushed again and began to gnaw on my lower lip.

"Don't do that," he said gruffly. I watched his hard body tense underneath his fitted clothes.

"What?" I froze. Did he mean don't ask about him? Don't ask about his retirement?

He bent forward, resting his elbows on his knees as his hands came up and cupped over his mouth for a second before they dropped and he responded, "Bite your lip like that." Immediately, my mouth parted in a small 'oh.' "You have no idea how badly it makes me want to kiss you again."

My pulse skyrocketed as my gaze was lost in his. We just sat there for I don't even know how long, both afraid of what would happen if either of us moved. What was brewing between us was the tremors before an avalanche and another inch toward one another would precipitate the fall.

"I should head over to Breakers and get ready for my shift." My soft voice ending the impasse between us as I pulled back from the ledge, back to safety in the space.

His mouth thinned and he nodded. Standing, he picked up both of our cups, letting me lead the way over towards the counter and the door. I walked slowly, waiting until I heard the sound of the porcelain cups rattling before I pushed the door open into the cold, flurrying weather.

I knew I should have grabbed my ski jacket instead of this flimsy 'fashionable' blazer that Ally insisted on.

The wind swirled the snowflakes around me. Even though the sun was setting, the white-gray clouds completely blocked out the sky with the snow that would continue to fall. *Looked like tomorrow was going to be a good day to ride.*

"Channing." I shivered, turning towards my name, my hands clutching the stupid blazer closed over my chest; I never had to worry about this with a sweatshirt.

"You can't walk to Breakers in that." He swore and took off his jacket. "Here, wear this." I opened my mouth to protest until he said, "Please." I ducked my head in stunned acquiescence as his arms reached around me to put his jacket around my shoulders; no one had ever done this for me. Hell, my friends would have taken this opportunity to give me crap about dressing like a girl again. *Cocky assholes.* But Wyatt...

Wyatt could be cocky—demanding coffee, insisting on a date, hinting at a kiss—but then he did something like this and my entire body melted in spite of the cold. My shivering stilled as my desire spread from the center of me out over my body. I didn't need his jacket; I just needed him.

"That should help keep you a little warmer," he murmured with lips that I knew could do an even better job as he pulled the coat tight across my front. I couldn't help myself from breathing deeply as his hands moved over my chest, my body aching for even the barest hint of his touch. In his presence, I felt alive. I shouldn't want him. I shouldn't want this. He was the competition. *Or was I just a coward?* I looked up into his sinfully handsome face, letting the warmth of his tone and gesture seep into me—into all the empty holes in my life that I'd tried to hide from.

Just this once, Channing. Let yourself feel for just this once.

And then, in a move that I would add to the list of bold and brainless ideas, I responded breathlessly, "Kissing keeps you warm."

His eyes widened. Again, the unexpected coming from me. His expression said, 'do you mean that?' I boldly stared back at him, daring him to find out.

And then, his lips crushed mine.

Wyatt wasn't kidding when he said that he'd been trying to control himself in there. This was nothing like the kiss we'd shared yesterday. This kiss demanded. It took risks; it explored the unknown. It hurdled us towards something that couldn't be controlled. I may not have kissed a lot of guys, but I was a fast learner. His tongue demanded entrance, mine took control.

Soon enough, my arms were wrapped around his neck. His jacket would have been on the ground, in the snow, if his arms hadn't been locked like a vise around my back, holding my body flush against his heat.

Well, there went another pair of underwear.

Now, instead of shivering in the cold, I felt relief every time a gust of wind blew against us; my body felt like it was on fire. Heat poured out of me in waves as my body begged to be burned. I wanted to be closer to him, without the layers. His right hand slipped down to grab my ass; I was now thankful for the designer jeans that let him mold his hand over my flesh. He yanked my hips against his and I felt the hardness of his erection pressing into my stomach. Those butterflies that I'd felt before? The poor things were now incinerated by the wildfire inside of me.

He held me close, but still my hips ground against his, needing more of whatever it was that he was giving me—needing more of him.

I wanted to be with him; and suddenly, I didn't care what it did to my chances of winning gold in Slopestyle. I'd never felt like *this* before and I wanted to explore whatever *this* was, no matter the cost.

The thought sent me flying back. I caught his jacket before it fell, wrapping it around me as we stared at each other trying to catch our breaths.

"Holy shit, Channing," he said hoarsely.

"I have to go."

His hand grabbed onto my arm—onto his own jacket—to stop me. "I need to see you again."

"I don't think that's a good idea," I whispered thickly. "I'm sorry. This was a mistake."

And then before the heat that still throbbed between my thighs overwhelmed my caution and had me throwing myself back into his arms, I released his jacket from my grasp—freeing myself from his—and took off down the path towards the main lodge.

This was the first time I'd ever shown up to work thinking that I was the only one in the bar tonight who actually needed a drink.

CHAPTER *Eight*

Channing

SON OF A BISCUIT.

My hands fells to my sides in the soft powder that puffed up above me. I'd been right; the snow that fell last night left a blanket of soft, fresh pow on the mountain today, just waiting to be explored. I pulled my goggles up onto my helmet, letting the snowflakes drift onto my face. The snow clung in heavy plumes to the branches of the trees, making them appear like giant Q-tips rising up from the ground. Everywhere I looked was white; everywhere I looked was a clean, fresh start—untouched and untainted.

I felt the cold snow and earth under my back as I deeply inhaled the crisp air. It wasn't the ocean—the mountain didn't actually move underneath me—and yet, it still felt alive, breathing its strength into me.

That feeling never got old.

Its unchanging solidarity was a firm base underneath my body, giving me a rock to cling to when everything else in my life felt like it was up in the air. It was here when I landed, it was here when I fell, it was the foundation that lifted me up to reach for the stars. It had no expectations; it had no judgment. It didn't wonder why I was so good or not good enough. It didn't look at me wondering where my brother had gone or why he left. It didn't pass over the surface of me, ignoring the woman underneath.

Most look at the mountain as something to best—a challenge to defeat; most had it all wrong.

I didn't come here to conquer the mountain; I came to the mountain to conquer myself. I came to break through my fears, my boundaries, and everything that held me back.

But today, I seemed to be conquering nothing. Not my frustration on the fourteen-week mark of Chance leaving—but who was counting? Not my fear of the triple cork. And certainly not my complete confusion over everything that I felt for Wyatt.

I heard the faint echo of Emmett's voice as he signaled his drop onto the jump. We'd been out since seven this morning—determined to get first tracks in the park. I warmed myself up slowly today, gradually increasing the difficulty of the jumps that I pulled. About an hour ago, partially at the instigation of Emmett and Nick, and partially because I knew I was going to have to attempt it at some point if I was going to win gold in slope style, I went for the triple cork.

I was calm, I was confident, and the conditions were great. And just like last year at the Open, I choked on the take off—not getting enough speed or initial rotation to complete the move. It hurt, but I got up and pretended like it hadn't.

Frustrated, I tried again. And again.

And now, I lay in the snow at the bottom of the landing wallowing in my failure and the soreness pulsating throughout my body.

"I think you were closer that time." Emmett pulled up next to me, plopping down on the ground.

I knew deep down, it wasn't just technique that was holding me back; there was a fear inside me that reared its ugly head just as my board was about to leave the safety of the ground.

"I don't know what I'm doing wrong," I grumbled. "Everything feels perfect going into it, but somehow I still end up here."

"Well, I'm sure Frost can empathize with you there."

"Hey, fuck you! I heard that." Nick came toward us, swinging his board to an abrupt stop and showering Emmett and me with snow.

"Ugh." I pushed myself up to sit, ignoring the pain in the right side of my hip from landing on it three times now. *Definitely going to be a bruise there.*

And on my tailbone. But, it was hump day, so what did I expect?

"You could always ask your buddy Wyatt to help you, you know," Emmett interjected sarcastically and I shot him a cold stare.

For the past two days, he'd thrown in his snarky comments about Wyatt every so often and this was no different. I'd told him to drop it, but like that was really going to work.

I didn't know what his deal was, but he disliked Wyatt and even more than that, he really disliked his brother, Zack. But I wasn't about to defend the man that I hadn't seen in two days; I was trying to forget all about that sexy piece of snowboarder. That was what was most frustrating about Emmett's comments—not their sarcasm, but because they reminded me.

And I didn't need any help remembering.

I'd given in to my body—my feelings—telling Wyatt to kiss me again and for a second, I'd allowed myself to relish in the fact that I was doing something for myself—not for my friends or my brother or my sport. And then, when the thought burned through me, even hotter than my desire for him, that I was willing to risk everything else to figure out what the pull was between us, I knew I was making a mistake.

This. The Games. Winning.

It was everything that I'd worked towards. Even though I hadn't been the one to technically be invited, I *knew* that I belonged there just as much as Chance did and I needed to prove that.

Wanting Wyatt was a wager that could cause me to lose everything I wanted.

It was also a wager that could end up giving me everything I need.

That nagging thought I usually managed to suppress until just before I passed out from exhaustion into a world of dreams where I was free to do with Wyatt exactly what I craved.

Outside the coffeehouse, when I left him standing out in the snow, hadn't been the last time I'd seen him that day. I managed to lose myself in my shift at Breakers, again grateful for Andrea's stony silence and the steady flow of patrons while we worked. However, just as I finished wiping down the bar at the end of the night, Wyatt strolled into Breakers, that molten gaze of his locking onto me. I don't know how he got in because we were closed, but he did. I stared dumbly at him wondering if I was imagining his presence.

"I'm walking you to your car," he said firmly. It wasn't a question and his tone told me that it was pointless to get into a debate with him over it because Wyatt always won. "I know you said you couldn't see me anymore and I will gladly respect your wishes, but this—your safety—is nonnegotiable."

Again, he effortlessly strolled along the line between cocky and class. A gentleman with a demanding edge.

I started to open my mouth, my natural instinct to at least make the attempt to refute his assertions, but I was just too tired. And if I was honest, I wasn't ready to let him go cold-turkey—not that night at least. So, instead, I clamped my lips shut again and just nodded, finishing up the last few things that I had to do around the bar before walking out and leaving Andrea to lock up.

We walked out to the car in silence. He stayed a respectable distance away, all the while I'd wished he'd walked closer; his proximity would warm me.

"Can I ask why?" His deep voice echoed through the practically empty parking lot as we came up to the side of my jeep.

I turned to look at him; he looked as tortured as I felt. "Because." I felt like I had to at least try to give him something. I couldn't tell him it was because I was going to be competing against him. I couldn't tell him that it was because being with him would mean lying to him and I couldn't have my first… whatever this was… be constructed around a lie. Plus, could I even have the drive to win when it meant that someone I cared about would lose?

I couldn't tell him any of that. So, I tried to give him as close to the truth as possible. "First, you're my brother's competition." *Not technically a lie.*

"Bullshit." He took a step towards me which had me stepping back, putting my back up against the side of my Jeep. "I don't care about who your brother is and he shouldn't care who I am. The Games are just that; but *this* could be so much more." His hand came up to my cheek, his thumb brushing over my lower lip as it parted, allowing me to suck in a breath at his touch. Wyatt grinned at me. "Unless you are trying to sabotage me, but in that case, this would only help him. And if you aren't, then he should be happy to know how easily distracted I've been from everything except you."

I bit my lip, quickly releasing it when I heard him growl underneath his breath.

My mouth was dry, but I forced a swallow anyway. "Right now, I'm focused. I'm working towards something—towards winning the Open in February. I want to be the best and if I'm going to get there, I need to give my skills every ounce of my attention because the odds are against me—a female landing a triple cork. February in Vail is not that far away and I know that if I put everything that I have into practice, I will win." I sighed. "Right now, I can focus; I can make winning my priority." *Be careful, Channing.* "Now, kiss me."

Wyatt stared at me in confusion. "Don't make me ask you again," I demanded hoarsely, prepared to relish in the feel of his mouth and body one last time.

He didn't.

Closing the distance between us, his lips dropped onto mine, one arm snaking around my waist and pushing me back against the side of my car, his body coming up flush against mine. I'd asked, but he took—and it was like all the hours we'd spent apart had never existed and we were right back where we'd left off. But this time, because we both knew it wasn't going to last, there was an urgency that consumed us both; there was a need to devour the other and take every last drop of the intoxicating passion between us. We kissed for several minutes until the pressure twisting inside of me drew painfully tight, begging to be unknotted and unfurled into an orgasm. I didn't want it to end—I *needed* it not to end—which is why every cell of my body raged against me as I just barely pulled back from his kiss, our breaths mingling in the cold air surrounding us.

My eyes flitted up to his gaze. I could see he wondered why I'd asked him to kiss me after telling him that I couldn't see him anymore.

"Before you kissed me, I was focused on my goals—focused on the dreams that I've had since I was a child. But, right now," I whispered, my words caressing his lips. "I don't know who I am or what I want. I don't care about my job or the mountain or landing a triple or winning gold. I don't care about anything except kissing you again and again and again because when I'm with you, everything that I've ever wanted and worked towards is up in the air and the only thing grounding me is you."

His arms tightened around me. "And that's a bad thing, Channing?"

God, I loved the sound of my name on his lips. I squeezed my legs together as the pressure squeezed just a little bit tighter, begging for release

"For me, right now, it is." I pressed my mouth to his one more time before I pushed myself away, cracking open the door to my jeep and sliding inside. "Thank you for walking me to my car. I'll make sure that security takes me from now on." I didn't look at him again as I threw the Jeep into first and pulled away—I couldn't. I could barely focus on the road as pointless tears formed in my eyes.

Wanting Wyatt was a dangerous game—one that I just couldn't afford to play right now.

So why did it feel like in leaving him to focus on winning, the only thing I'd done was lose?

"Earth. To. Channing." A snowball hit the back of my helmet and I spun to look at Emmett. "Where did you go, Lil? I was fucking kidding about asking Olsen for help—no need to go all ghost on me there."

"I know," I blurted out, brushing the snow off of me. "Just trying to figure out what the hell I'm doing wrong."

And trying to ignore the part of me that insisted that Emmett had a good point—even if it had been said in jest.

"Yeah… sure." He pushed himself up to stand. "We good?"

I nodded. "Yeah, you go this time," I insisted; I was done with the stupid, elusive triple cork today. "I gotta head out after this one anyway."

It was almost eleven thirty now, which meant that I could finish this run before I had to grab lunch and head over to my lessons for the afternoon.

A group of three boarders blew past us, avoiding all of the jumps. "Fucking hate Makaha. Damn posers." Nick stood up grumbling.

That was the problem with the intermediate park, riders who weren't skilled enough to do any of the jumps—*but wanted to be*—would blow down the trail, stop and stare at the kickers, and then just keep going; it threw off the whole flow.

With the Snowmass park and pipe closing this past Monday, Makaha had been crowded all week—making it even more difficult for me to really focus on my triple cork; instead, I was too busy worrying about who was watching—or who was in my way.

"Dropping!" Emmett yelled out over the slope, letting anyone who was on the other side of the landing know that they better move their ass unless they wanted to get hit.

I pulled my neck-warmer up over my mouth as I chewed on the corner of my lip. Wyatt was one of the few people who knew how to do this and do it well—he would probably be the only other one attempting it in the Slopestyle competition. Was it right to ask him to help his competition?

He didn't know that… and he had offered.

I pushed myself up off my very sore ass, swearing that I was going to take a nice long bubble bath at the end of the week for my efforts.

I cupped my gloved hands around my mouth. "Drop!"

This time when I flew down, I stuck a ten-eighty; I'd had enough torture for one day. We reconvened at the bottom of the slope, my gaze straying over towards the lift for Snowmass like it had done every time we'd finished the run—trying to catch a glimpse of Wyatt.

"You heading out?" Emmett pulled off his helmet, immediately reaching for a beanie in his jacket pocket and putting it on.

"Yeah, I have two lessons this afternoon," I said as I unstrapped from my board.

Nick pulled off his helmet, running his hands through his dark, matted hair. "I think I'm going to go too; I have a project that was due on Monday that I still haven't finished."

Emmett snickered. Nick was a procrastinator—too busy with women and weed to focus on school especially because it was only because of his parents that he was going. He liked to push the boundaries—or just believe that they didn't exist for him. He enjoyed getting himself in too deep seemingly for the sole pleasure of getting himself back out again.

Emmett, on the other hand, was always organized, on-time, and by the books—typical for an engineer. And typical for a control freak. They always took turns taking jabs at one another. Usually, it was Chance who'd stepped in between them both to settle things. Chance was a phenomenal people person when he wanted to be and he was the great mediator between all of us.

I picked up my board and waved as I walked towards Cup of Joe.

If there was one other person who'd had a shot of pushing Wyatt from my mind, it was my brother. This was the longest I'd ever gone without talking to him… or seeing him. I know that he didn't leave to hurt me—but it had. And now that I was back on the slopes practicing the triple again, the hurt in my heart was even worse. Every time I fell, I heard his voice in my head, telling me to get back up, that we would try it again.

The worst part was that these memories made me angry at him—for leaving, for not contacting anyone, and for not being here when I needed him. I knew it was selfish, but we'd always been there for each other and instead of letting me be there for him through his recovery, he'd decided to do it on his own. And I was angry at him for putting me in a position where I had a rational reason—an arguably necessary reason—to want to spend more time with Wyatt.

I walked into the coffee shop feeling more frustrated and defeated than when I'd finished my last run.

"You ok, Channing?" Ally's voice greeted me immediately as I walked in the door.

I gave her a soft smile and nodded. "Can I just get my usual?" I set my helmet and gloves on one of the tables. "Maybe with some extra whipped cream on the mocha."

She raised an eyebrow, knowing that meant something hadn't gone well; extra whipped cream was only reserved for emergency pick-me-up situations.

I sat down while she took the order of a few people who'd walked in behind me before she came over to bring me my coffee and sandwich.

"What's up?" She plopped down in the other chair. Even with an apron on, coffee grounds stuck in random places, and her hair loosely contained, my sister looked beautiful. I ran my fingers through my boy-short hair, trying to pull all the strands to one side so that they weren't sticking up all over the place—a pretty pointless effort. Part of me wished I could look like Ally did all of the time; a different part reminded me that Wyatt made me feel like I *did* look like that all of the time.

"Nothing." I sighed. "Just bailed a lot this morning. And yesterday. And Monday. My head's been all over the place."

"What were you trying to do?"

"The trick that Chance helped me learn for the Open last year. I need to nail it if I'm going to win." I bit into my sandwich.

I didn't have to say it for her to understand what my problem was—that I needed Chance's help and he wasn't here.

"But, I'm just not getting it anymore and we're stuck on the crappy park with a thousand other riders, so I'm struggling to focus."

"I wish I could help you," she offered sweetly.

"I know, sunshine."

Ally huffed. "*Please,* not you too. I hate when Emmett calls me that." I chuckled and the fact that I was laughing seemed to mitigate some of her annoyance.

"I thought the place you usually snowboard was going to be even more closed off to regulars so that you could have more privacy to practice?"

"Yeah, it's closed off to regulars—that's the problem. Only competitors are allowed in."

Her blank stare was like a smack to the back of my head and I realized what she was about to say just as the words left her mouth. "But, Channing, you are a competitor." Her hushed whisper was a giant lightbulb in my brain.

"Oh my God. What the hell was I thinking?" I shook my head. "You are a genius, baby sis, and I would kiss you right now if it wouldn't cause me unimaginable pain to move at the moment."

I had Chance's pass which meant that I had access to Snowmass; unfortunately, Nick and Emmett wouldn't be able to get in and I'm sure they'd hold my board hostage until I told them how I'd managed to gain access, but the point was that I *did* have access. And I was going to need it. Already the thoughts of how I could find time to ride over there were running through my mind.

She laughed. "Do you have a ride home tonight?"

"Yeah," she murmured and her face flushed bright red.

"Ally?"

"I have a ride!"

My eyes narrowed. "Who?"

"Zack." An innocent and excited smile crept onto her face. *Of course, she had to be seeing Wyatt's brother.*

If I thought my momentary wish for her effortless beauty was bad, the sharp stab of jealousy I felt now was a hundred times worse. Jealousy over the fact that she could so easily go after what she wanted, whereas both of my wants were conflicting.

"There you are, Princess."

Speak of the devil.

Zack approached my table and bent down to kiss my sister on her cheek, causing her to blush even more. *Woah, seriously? Was it really at that point already?*

Says the one who was up against her car, tongue-deep with his brother the other night.

I had no justifiable cause to question…

"Hey, Channing." He finally noticed me.

"Hey," I replied quietly, wondering just how much he knew about what happened between his brother and me.

"Hey, Little Miss Sunshine, I see your apron, but what I don't see is why you aren't over here taking my drink order." Emmett's voice wove into our conversation. *He was such an ass.* I hadn't even seen him walk in, but he was now standing against the counter, his arms crossed over his chest. Even though I assumed he'd said the words in poor jest, his tone had an edge to it and there was a dark scowl on his face as he looked between my sister and Zack.

I didn't blame him, I was feeling a little protective of her, too.

Ally frowned and rolled her eyes, murmuring 'Excuse me' before she abruptly stood and walked back over behind the counter to take his order.

Zack's eyes followed her before they narrowed back on me. *Well, he knew something, that was for sure.*

"How are you doing this morning?" he asked genially.

I waited for the other shoe to drop.

"Alright. Took a few nasty spills this morning so I'm trying to recover before I have to go teach a lesson." I cut myself off before I started to really ramble. "How's your brother?"

Oh, what the hell, Channing?!

I winced at his look of surprise, hiding my unfortunate awkwardness behind my coffee mug as I took a nice, long sip of my mocha, licking off my whipped-cream mustache.

"He's alright." *Oh, good. Short and sweet answer—time to move to a different topic.* "He'd be better if you hadn't decided not to see him anymore."

Crap.

"I… I have a lot going on right now. I'm sure he does too with the Games coming up. He said himself that I was a distraction."

He laughed, drawing Ally's curious attention away from Emmett who was almost completely blocking her view of us.

"He needs a distraction, trust me." Zack rubbed his forehead as he continued, "Damn idiot is looking at these games as though they are the end of his life. It's a *game;* dude needs to chill and stop putting so much pressure on himself." He started, realizing who he was talking to and what he was saying. "Sorry. Forget I said all of that."

Ally practically skipped back over to us, effectively ending any further conversation about Wyatt which was a good thing on so many levels, not the least of which was that I hadn't really told Ally that I'd called it quits on whatever was happening between him and me.

"Guess what we're doing later today?" Ally giggled, glancing up at Zack. Her voice was a little loud considering that we were all sitting right there—loud enough that even Emmett heard her as he stood waiting for his coffee, his attention jerking to her. I wasn't sure I really wanted to hear the answer to her question, but it looked like I wasn't going to have that option—and neither was anyone else in the place. "Zack is going to teach me how to ski!" She let out a squeal and clapped her hands in excitement.

Oh, that wasn't too bad. I mean… skiing was… but I guess it was a forgivable sin.

Emmett let out a bark of laughter and all of our eyes turned towards him.

"You hate the snow, Sunshine." He snickered. "Do you even own snow clothes?"

Her mouth fell open and she turned to me; to her credit, she didn't respond to his taunts. "Channing, tell your *friend* to mind his own business."

I put my hands up. "I mean, you did kind of announce it to everyone, Al, but I'm not getting in the middle of this. You two are old enough to handle it."

My sister huffed, turning back to Emmett who was still quietly laughing to himself. "For your information, I don't hate the cold or the snow. I don't even hate snowboarding. I just hate you."

Oh, boy. Fighting words.

"I'm really excited to learn how to ski." She refocused with a sweet smile on Zack and completely turned her back to Emmett who stood there vibrating with anger from her words.

"Well then. On that note, I think I should head over to my lessons," I murmured, recognizing that I'd quickly become the third wheel at my own table. Ally and Zack barely broke their gaze from one another to say goodbye to me as I stood to leave.

Raising my eyebrows at Emmett, I paused by him on my way out.

"You're just going to let her hang out with that douchebag?" he bit out.

"She's an adult, Emmett, and I'm not her parent. She can do what she wants. Plus, it's only skiing." I sighed. "Maybe if you stopped baiting her, she'd be a little nicer to you."

"Chance would never be ok with this," he practically sneered.

Guilt washed over me and before I said something that I would regret, I turned and left. Another situation that Chance would have handled with ease—or at least definitively, but I, on the other hand, only seemed to have made things worse.

For the first time in a month, I pulled out my phone on my way over to the lesson area and dialed Chance's number. It went immediately to voicemail; I didn't expect anything different. *'Hey, this is Chance, leave a message and I'll drop you a line as soon as I get it! Have a gnarly day!'*

My eyes welled with tears even as I chuckled at his ridiculous recording.

"Hey, Chance. It's me. Where the hell are you? Don't you think it's time to stop running?" My voice broke, clogged with emotion. I hung up the phone. It was stupid—and I'd probably left him a thousand messages like that over the past three months, but sometimes, I just couldn't stop myself; I needed him.

Wiping the tears that had frozen onto my face, I dug deep for a smile that tried to elude me, the corner of my lips finally rising as I saw my group of little riders waiting for me.

"Hey, Channing," Tammy, one of the other instructors, greeted me.

"Hey," I said, dropping off my board in our breakroom. "Didn't think I'd see you today."

Tammy was the 'head' instructor—if there was such a thing. She coordinated all of the schedules and classes and she was whom I reported to on the days she was there. She also worked part-time for the Open Hearts daycare center. She was a skier, but I tried not to hold it against her. She also happened to be one of Ally's closest friends since she moved back—they'd been friends before Ally moved and I was glad to see how they picked right back up where they left off when she came back. Between her and Jessa Madison—ironically, Chance's high school ex-girlfriend—Ally had found a group of friends that filled in all the girly gaps that our relationship lacked.

"Yeah, I know. I just couldn't stay away," she said wryly, but I knew she meant it. She loved her job. "You've got a full class this afternoon."

"Yeah and it looks like mostly girls!" I was always excited when my classes were dominated by girls, for mostly obvious reasons—the biggest being that snowboarding was still a male-dominated sport and this gave me hope that in the coming years, that would change.

"Actually, Tammy, I'm glad you're here," I began. "I wanted to talk to you about the upcoming weeks. I know we have the whole powder clause, but I noticed that some days the lessons are kind of light, so I was thinking about blocking myself off a few afternoons to spend more time out on the slopes…"

On the resort and even in the town of Aspen, a lot of the local businesses had what was called a 'Powder Day Clause' which meant that if it snowed the night before and the powder in the morning was perfect, work got rescheduled; the day was meant for the mountain.

"For time on the slopes or time with a certain snowboarder?" She winked at me and I swallowed my groan.

Ally and her freaking big mouth.

"I don't think so…" I tried to let her down gently. "Unlike my sister, I'm trying to steer clear of any and all Olsens." I said the last as I opened the door back outside to the safety of my lesson, filled with little humans who didn't care about Wyatt or winning, love or losing.

CHAPTER
Nine

Channing

I towel-dried my hair, listening to Ally run frantically back and forth down the hall between her bedroom and the bathroom. Weeks ago, Ally had asked that we do a girl's pizza-and-movie night tonight. Feeling guilty for not spending a lot of time with her since Chance had left, I agreed; I'd requested off of work and everything—which was a pretty big deal given that it was a Saturday night and all. So, why was she rushing around like a maniac?

Because she was ditching me for Zack.

I came home from my lessons this afternoon prepared and ready for some sister-sister time, which I knew would include a discussion about what happened with Wyatt; I still hadn't found the time to tell her. Although, in my defense, it wasn't completely my fault. She and Zack had been together literally every second of her free time this past week. So, even when I was around to talk, she wasn't. And when she was, I wasn't.

And even though I was slightly annoyed that I'd taken off of work only to have her bail on me, I couldn't whole-heartedly complain since I'd just finished taking the most amazing bath.

I picked up my phone and called our local Papa Don's pizza, ordering my usual *with* mushrooms. Looked like I was going to have a Netflix and chill night with myself. I was still debating whether I was going to finish *The Crown*, the latest Netflix series that I'd started or go straight for the classic chick-flick, *The Notebook,* and lose myself in the kind of love story that I'd never admit to anyone that I wanted.

The doorbell rang and I immediately heard Ally's voice yell to me, "Channing! It's Zack! Can you please get that!!" It wasn't a question.

I pulled on my yoga pants over my lime-green lace boy-shorts and my 'Evolution of Snowboarding' t-shirt and skipped down the stairs, haphazardly running my hand through my short, wet locks.

The one good thing about super-short hair—dry time was almost non-existent.

I saw some movement through the glass of our front door, for a second wondering if I heard voices coming from the other side, but I didn't think twice about it before pulling the door open.

I should have thought twice.

"Hi, Zack…" I wasn't looking at him though, my eyes were trained on the dangerously familiar, delicious chocolate eyes and the even sweeter mouth that came along with them. "*Wyatt.*"

I stared, frozen. The question '*what is he doing here?*' crossed my mind for only a split second before the answer came readily to my mind and out of Zack's lips.

"Ally told me to bring him—said she was abandoning you and this would make up for it." He smiled and I knew it had been a conspiracy between them. I now regretted every moment during the week that I'd spent grateful to have avoided the whole Wyatt-conversation with my sister. "Can we come in?"

Deep breaths. No reason to be rude. Yet.

"Of course, sorry. My sister seems to have forgotten to mention that little detail to me earlier." I stepped back, pulling the door wide and letting the two of them walk inside.

If it was any consolation, Wyatt seemed marginally uncomfortable as well, although not enough to overshadow the flare of desire in his eyes at seeing me—or the response that it provoked in my body.

If I thought that a week was enough to dim what I felt for him, well, I was very, *very* wrong. Just as I shut the door, Ally made her appearance, wrapping her arms around Zack's neck and kissing him in front of Wyatt and me.

My face flushed as I looked to the ground—it was the only safe spot; I didn't want to look at my sister making out with a guy. I also didn't want to look at the guy that certain aching parts of me wished I was making out with.

Wyatt cleared his throat and it made me want to kiss him for a whole different reason—it ended the PDA that was going on for far too long in front of us.

"Sorry," Ally said, but the smile on her face told me it was more like a 'sorry-not-sorry' situation.

"Alright, Princess, we should get going." Zack wrapped his arm around her waist and pulled her towards the door and a few seconds later, they were gone and I almost wished we were back at the part where they were still making out because then at least I wasn't left alone with the object of my desire.

I turned to him, but before I could even open my mouth, he said, "I'm sorry. Zack made it seem like you knew. I can go, I'll just have to call a cab." My brows furrowed. "I rode over with Zack…"

My lips formed a silent 'oh.'

I swallowed over the lump in my throat as my heart began to beat louder and louder in my ears.

What should I do? Tell him to stay? Smile and wait for him to leave?

I *wanted* him to stay. I *needed* him to go.

Maybe just one night.

No, Channing, you can't do that. You've been over this. Maybe if he was anyone else, but he's not.

He pulled out his phone and my mouth betrayed me.

"Just stay." I put up a hand to stop him as the soft words escaped my mouth. "Just stay for a little."

He stared at me, silently asking if I was sure about that. I dropped my head in a half-nod, crossing my arms in front of me.

"I'll stay for as long as you'll let me, gorgeous."

When he talked like that, I wanted to let him stay forever.

"I don't know if you are hungry or not, but I ordered pizza. Hope you like mushrooms." I turned and began to walk towards the kitchen.

The front door of the house opened into a huge, two-story foyer, light from the large window above the door streaming through to illuminate the space. There was a formal dining room to the left and my dad's old office to the right. Both of those doors were shut because Chance and I rarely used those rooms.

The Brazilian hardwood floor of the hall led back, past the staircase to the second floor, to the large kitchen on one side and the living room on the other with a small morning room space in between. The entire back wall of the house was covered with windows providing a nice view of the woods behind it in the summer; in the winter, once the leaves were gone, we could actually see the lights from Snowmass in the distance. The second floor didn't extend all the way back, which meant the ceiling was vaulted, making the space feel even larger than it was.

The kitchen was Cherrywood and granite, with modern appliances, and a gas stove; my mom loved to cook.

"Lucky me, I love mushrooms." I heard him say as he followed me. When I stopped in the kitchen, next to the island in the center of the room, he spoke again. "This is a great house."

His presence completely changed the space. Wearing fitted jeans and a crewneck sweater, he looked like he belonged at the table talking business with my dad over a Scotch, rather than on the slopes risking his *very* pretty neck.

"Thanks. My parents bought it when we were little… when Chance and I began riding. They enrolled us in Pine Wood Academy which is a few miles down the road; it's a school geared toward kids who have a desire or talent for winter sports. That's where we met Emmett and Nick." *Way to ramble.* "Anyway. The house. They left it to us when they retired to Florida."

"And they didn't think you'd just have one giant house party when they left?" he joked, pulling out one of the counter stools and taking a seat.

"I've tried to keep those to a minimum. Usually—thankfully—Nick hosted that type of thing at his parents' mansion since they were never home. The only party I want to be a part of is the fresh pow-party on the mountain. I can't speak for my brother and friends now." I smiled ruefully. "But, I'm sure you know what I mean."

He laughed. "I'll be honest, I was interested in both kinds of parties at one point in my life. Not anymore…"

"I'm hoping Chance and the rest of the SnowmassHoles get to that point soon. I try to keep them out of trouble, but I wouldn't say that I'm usually successful with it."

"SnowmassHoles?"

"Their nickname in high school. Kind of stuck with them after all of the shit that they pulled."

He chuckled. "I can imagine."

"Ally, though, I try to look out for but most days it's actually the reverse. She originally moved with our parents, but then a few months ago, she moved back out here with us."

"Why do you sound surprised?" *He heard that?*

"I guess because she's never been much for the cold or the mountain." I shrugged. "Maybe she missed us, but I sometimes get the feeling that she moved back here to hide." A loud sigh escaped me. "But, having grown up with the guys, I'm not that great at getting that sort of information from her."

He rubbed his hand over his mouth and my lips tingled, wishing they could take its place. "People have to open up to you in their own way, in their own time. Especially family. I can see how much she respects and loves you, so I don't think you are the obstacle that she's trying to overcome."

I looked at him for a moment, taking in his words and relishing how they seemed to soothe the guilt that had been gnawing at me for some time now.

"Can I get you something to drink?" I changed gears, pulling open the fridge even though I knew that there weren't a whole lot of options. "We've got water, green tea, umm…" *I really was not prepared for guests.* "There are two bottles of Lagunitas beer that Emmett left here the other week and I think Chance has some whiskey around here somewhere."

Cringe. Don't keep mentioning Chance.

"I'll just take water, thanks," he said with that sexy, half-smile of his. "So, pizza and a movie?"

I let out my breath when he didn't question where my brother was, probably assuming he was out with the guys. "I'm a classy girl, what can I say?" I pulled out two glasses, filling them with water. "You're welcome to stay… for the movie…" I offered quietly.

He was already here so I might as well go big or go home.

Before he had a chance to respond, the doorbell rang; the pizza was here. I didn't even make it around the island before Wyatt was down the hall and answering the door, paying for the large pie that I'd ordered.

He turned around holding the box of pizza. "I told you, gorgeous, you're not allowed to pay for anything when you're with me; that's not how I work."

I threw my hands up in defeat and walked back into the kitchen to pull out plates.

"So, what else do you do, Channing?" he asked, setting the box down on the counter. "You bartend, you teach snowboarding lessons, you ride."

"Well, I don't have time for much else after all of that to be honest." I laughed, sliding a piece of pizza onto my plate. "How about you?"

"If that wasn't the million-dollar question…" he replied, picking up a slice and biting off the steaming end. "I snowboard. I'm not sure that I really have any other talents."

"Is that why you're still riding this year?" His eyes darted up from the pizza to mine, watching as I took a bite, surprised that I'd asked so bluntly.

"Yes and no." He sighed, taking a seat again at the counter. "I didn't feel ready to retire. I also have no idea what I'm going to do with myself once I do."

"Sounds exciting."

He let out a bark of laughter. "Or terrifying."

"Well, isn't that what we live for every day?" I asked distractedly, trying to keep the hot cheese from melting off the side of my pizza. "You know, when we fly down the side of a mountain, most times into the air to do some arguably life-threatening maneuver? Exciting, yet terrifying. That's why it's so addicting."

"True." He nodded in agreement. "Maybe that's why I can't seem to stay away from you." He grinned devilishly at me.

Unprepared for his remark, I coughed, choking on the bite of pizza that I'd taken. He had the nerve to smile even bigger, knowing exactly how his words were affecting me.

"Snowboarding is just all I've known for a very long time and all of a sudden, it seems like it's coming to an end. I wish I'd taken the time to have more of a life—to have other interests to now fall back on."

"I know what you mean," I said and he raised an eyebrow at me. "But the mountain is a part of you. It breathes life into you. It's like a limb—you can't cut it off just because competing isn't an option anymore. And, not for nothing, you don't dress like a snowboarder, so you could always fall back on modeling."

"What's that supposed to mean?" he asked, grabbing another slice.

"You know… the nice pants, button-down shirt, nice jacket… not your typical vans, jeans, and a t-shirt…" I shrugged. "I'm just saying that you always look very nice."

He laughed. "Thank you, I think? I don't know that I ever dressed that casually, but especially not now. I'm almost thirty-one. I should at least start looking like an adult even if I don't behave like one." He winked at me and I had to set the remainder of the crust of my pizza down. "All this coming from the one who wears clothes and makeup… for what I'm still trying to figure out."

"What's wrong with wearing makeup?" I asked defensively.

"Nothing. It's just clear that it's not the norm for you, so I'm wondering why you started." His gaze bored into mine.

"Maybe I just wanted to look a little more like a girl sometimes." I shrugged nonchalantly.

"Sweetheart, trust me, there's no mistaking you for anything but." As if to emphasize his point, he shifted in his seat, adjusting himself. I quickly turned my gaze down to my plate. I was in sweats and a tee—with damp hair, no less—and this man was somehow still attracted to me.

What was wrong with him?

"If you want my opinion, it's entirely unnecessary; you are even more gorgeous right now without it." His heated gaze raked over me. *Crap.* A night in with Ally meant I hadn't needed to ask for her make-up assistance. A night in with Wyatt was a whole different situation—one that she'd left me inadequately prepared for. I ducked my head trying to hide the blush that crept onto my cheeks. "Plus, I'd rather no one else be tempted to look at you the way I am right now," he growled with a possessiveness that made me ache to be claimed.

"So, what are your options?" I tried to redirect our conversation.

"The usual. Continued work with sponsors, coaching… I don't really want to work with professionals though. They get enough help."

"Well, based on what I know about you and how quickly you rose in the snowboarding world, there isn't a doubt in my mind that whatever you decide to do and set your mind to—you will succeed." He stared agape at my unquestioning faith in his abilities. "I mean, you're Wyatt Olsen; all you do is win." I tried to tone down the seriousness with a little jest, one that did manage to have him cracking a smile.

"You do have a point." He brushed his thumb over his lip, sending a quiver through me.

"Plus, you're only thirty. You literally could do whatever you wanted." I rested my elbows on the counter while I continued with my train of thought. "I mean, my parents moved out here when Chance and I were five, so they would have been like thirty-seven or so. They used to work in New York City for big financial firms and then, when they moved here, they both did something completely different. I guess they could have found similar jobs, although probably not at companies as large as the ones they'd worked for, but they didn't. My mom went back to school to become a nurse and my dad began teaching at the University of Colorado. Both were totally outside of what they'd done before." I paused, chewing on my lip for a second, noticing how intently he was staring at me. "Even now, well, my dad's working on his golf game, but my mom decided to become a yoga instructor. So, I really wouldn't be worried if I were you."

"I'm not worried, just wondering, I guess. Up until now, everything had a plan and a point. Now, it's all up in the air."

"Mmm," I murmured, wishing I knew something else to say. "What do your parents do?"

"They're both doctors in Montreal. My mom is originally from Brooklyn—part of a large Italian family. My dad was doing his residency at Columbia when they met and I guess, the rest is history."

"Oh." *Still. Life is never that simple.*

"What?" He laughed.

"Well, I think I see why you're stressing. Doctors... Type-A personalities... they always have a plan." He nodded, tapping his fingers on the counter. "Still, I'm sure that they struggled with where their careers were going at some point or another; you probably just don't know about it."

Even though I sounded confident, he didn't look convinced and I couldn't blame him; they were his parents after all, he would probably know.

"You could teach. I mean, it doesn't have to be the little ones like I do. You're a gold medalist; you could instruct or coach other professionals, offer classes and stuff." He was staring again. "I'm sorry, do you not like to teach? I shouldn't have assumed."

"Honestly, I don't know. I've never done it." He stood and picked up both of our plates, taking them over to the sink, and beginning to wash them.

"Sorry," I apologized again. "I didn't mean to just barge into your personal shit."

He turned the sink off and grabbed a towel to dry the dishes. "Don't apologize, Channing." He laughed softly and shook his head. "Somehow, in the last few minutes, you have managed to make me feel calmer about the inevitable, upcoming changes in my life, than I've ever managed to feel." *Oh, shit.* "For the first time, the thought of leaving the sport competitively doesn't fill me with dread and uncertainty."

My stomach clenched. I could hear how heartfelt his words were. I could hear that my attempts to put him at ease had helped and my insides warmed at the knowledge; *I'd helped Wyatt Olsen*—famous snowboarder who always seemed like he had his shit together. Except, in that moment, he wasn't famous; he was just a man, faced with a big life change, asking for help. For an instant, my thoughts drifted to my brother who had been in a similar, yet different, scenario—both of them being forced to leave the sport that they loved.

Maybe that's why I couldn't resist trying to break through to Wyatt—because Chance had never given me the opportunity. Maybe that's why I risked the intimacy that this conversation brought—because if I couldn't help Chance, at least I could help *him*. And then there was the part of me that pounded in my chest, demanding I admit that I'd helped him because I wanted to—because I wanted to be closer to him.

I stood there, arms over my chest, one foot rubbing down along the length of my calf, all while chewing on the inside of my lip.

I'd thought about this off and on—mostly on—for the last few days ever since Emmett had said it. I knew that there were so many problems—so many potential ways that this could end badly. But the thought in my mind that drowned them all out was this: *I needed Wyatt if I wanted to win.*

More potent than the thought was the feeling in my heart and, well, everywhere else in my body: *I needed Wyatt.*

I would be lying if I said that the words that came out of my mouth next were entirely motivated by my need to take the gold in Slopestyle, by my need to do this for myself and my brother, to make him proud—*and to prove that I could*. The truth was that I wanted to spend more time with this kind, protective, albeit demanding, and milk-frothing-hot gentleman. And *this* was the only legitimate reason my brain would accept for my being able to do that.

Because even though I would be spending time with him, it was going to be all business.

I swear.

"So, teach me."

He set the last plate down on the counter and turned to stare at me; I'd surprised him again, but at least I'd refrained from begging him, in some way, to kiss me. He waited and his silence made me anxious, second-guessing my brazen request.

"I mean, you don't have to." I laughed nervously. "What am I saying? You have to focus on your practice—just like Chance—I didn't mean—" I rambled, throwing the mention of my brother in there just to clarify why I hadn't asked him in the first place.

"No." He shook his head. "I want to. When?"

"Monday."

"Where?"

My head ducked down—it should have been a clear indicator of the lie I was going to tell. "I can meet you at Snowmass park in the morning. Chance isn't using his pass, so, I mean, as long as you don't tell…"

He chuckled. "Your secret is safe with me." *He had no idea that he was the last person my secret could be safe with.* "Are you sure, Channing?"

I nodded. "Yes. I mean, you're just going to help me nail my triple… not anything else." My awkwardness was becoming even more apparent; *of course not anything else, Channing, why would you even say that?*

Wyatt smiled at me. "Just the trick." I nodded to confirm as he took a few steps towards me, closing the space between us. He stopped just in front of me and I felt my breath becoming shallower as my body became more alive. "Nothing else?" I didn't know if it was a question or a statement—and I think that was the whole point. His head dropped closer to mine as he said it, that incredible mouth of his within my reach.

A delicious shiver trickled down my spine, inciting that familiar pressure that began to roll deep inside of me. *How did this happen every time I was around this man?* I wanted his help, but I couldn't want him. My body hadn't seemed to have received the memo, though.

What have I done?

"Nothing else," I answered breathlessly.

Now his eyes were on my lips and I licked them out of habit, seeing his body tense ever so slightly as desire raced through him.

"So, no kissing?" He clarified as his hand came up, a large index finger tracing down along my cheek to brush along the fullness of my lip.

I breathed against his hand, feeling my nipples harden against my shirt, my heart slamming against my chest. "Definitely not."

"And definitely," he broke off as his finger trailed down the side of my neck, soft like snow as it grazed over my pulse that was rapidly firing underneath my skin, "no touching?"

Again with the ambiguous questions and statements. My breathing was ragged as his finger moved lower, reaching the neckline of my shirt while his intoxicating gaze remained locked with mine; my blue eyes hazy with the storm that brewed inside of me. That lone finger crossed the boundary of the fabric of my tee and I stopped breathing altogether. My thighs were clenched so tightly together, trying to ease the throbbing between them.

"Yes," I whispered shakily. Immediately his finger stopped, just at the top swell of my breast. I bit down hard on the inside of my cheek to stop myself from immediately retracting my word. I sucked in a breath, my chest rising higher than normal begging for his touch to continue on to my breasts.

He leaned in close to my ear. "Are you sure about that, Channing?" His finger dropped an inch lower, teasing me with its proximity to my nipple—the aching peak painfully hard against the lace bralette that I had on.

No. Not by a long shot. "Yes." *Liar.*

He didn't say have to say it for me to see in his gaze that he knew I was lying. But, he didn't push any further and I was glad, because I would have given in.

Maybe a few days was enough to make me stronger.

His hand dropped back to his side and he walked towards the living room where the TV was on, Netflix waiting for me to make my choice.

"So, what's on the schedule for tonight?" He turned and asked.

"I already planned on watching 'The Notebook' so…" I trailed off, grinning at him with a small shrug as I followed him into the room.

He laughed, taking a seat on the couch. "Your house, your rules, Miss Ryder. I have no car, so I am at your cinematic mercy."

"You just have all the luck don't you, Mr. Olsen?" I teased. "The truth is I have a borderline unhealthy addiction to the sappiest chick-flicks ever produced. However, if you mention this in public or to my friends I will have to go after your boards again."

Chick-flicks were a weakness—just like lacy lingerie, but I was only going to admit one of those to him—for right now at least.

I sat down a respectable distance from him, scrolling through the titles until I found the Nicholas Sparks film. Dimming the lights, we settled into the couch, letting the movie distract the both of us from attraction that lay patiently waiting in the air.

I made it to the part where my exhaustion won its first battle. Tipping over—in the opposite direction of what I really wanted—I lay my head on the pillow at the end of the couch, bending my knees and scooting my legs and feet onto the sofa, carefully avoiding any contact with Wyatt.

"Rough rides this week?" I heard him ask softly.

I turned and looked up at him. "Yeah, pretty brutal. As evidenced by the fact that I'm asking for your help. Why?" The movie continued to play in the background while I waited for his answer.

"Give me your foot." I stared blankly at him. "I'm going to rub your feet. Unless you're weird about that." Ryan Gosling's voice hid the soft groan that escaped from my lips.

That sounded incredible.

"No, I don't," I murmured, sliding my legs out. Wyatt grabbed my ankles and pulled my feet onto his lap, adjusting himself underneath their weight. I immediately refocused my gaze on the TV, grateful that the dimmed lights meant he couldn't see me blushing. I could feel his erection underneath my left foot as he picked up the right one and began to rub.

It felt so good.

And I felt so guilty. I bit my lip to conceal my moans as he rubbed the aching soles of my feet; it felt incredible—even better than my bubble bath. I felt guilty knowing that while I was relaxed and enjoying every second of his touch, my proximity was only making his predicament worse. Even just from the brush of my foot, I could feel how hard he was, constrained in his jeans.

No, Channing. Just watch the damn movie.

I refocused on the screen, letting the pleasure of his touch radiate through me, trying to ignore the discomfort it was causing him and the guilt it was causing me. A few minutes later, exhaustion finally won the war. It was a good thing I'd seen the movie before, because the next thing I knew, I woke up alone on the couch with a blanket over me; the TV and the lights were off and Wyatt was gone. Holding the afghan tight around me, I pushed myself up, seeing a note on the coffee table.

My eyes squinted in the dark.

'*Monday morning. 6AM. Cup of Joe. Sweet dreams, gorgeous.*'

CHAPTER Ten

Wyatt

"Hey, mom," I answered my cell.

"Wyatt! Honey!" Mary Olsen's voice exclaimed over the phone. "Oh, I'm so glad you called. How's practice going? Your dad and I can't wait to see you!" I smiled at her enthusiasm. Even after just about thirty years in the medical profession, my mother's energy and love of life hadn't been diminished by the demands of her job. Dr. Mary Olsen was the chief oncologist at the Royal Victoria Hospital in Montreal. Maybe it was because she encountered death on a daily basis that made her appreciation of life seem more vibrant than most.

"Good, mom. Good." I took a sip from my water bottle, eyeing up the sandwich in front of me. Zack ditched me for lunch again to take Ally out, so after our morning ride, I was in the lodge eating alone; figured it was a good time to check in with my mom. "I told you that you and dad didn't have to take off to come out here again." My parents insisted on coming to every one of my competitions as though I were still in high school, instead of twice that age. Both for support and probably to be safe in the knowledge that if something did happen to me, there were two doctors in the immediate vicinity that would be able to help.

"Don't even start with me Wyatt James Olsen; you know we wouldn't miss it." She harrumphed on the other end of the phone and

I heard some shuffling and groaning.

"Are you trying to take in all the groceries in one trip again?" I laughed. My dad hated when she did that.

"Don't you dare tell your father." I laughed harder. My parents had been happily married for thirty-nine years. They were one of those couples that everything just seemed to work out for—the kind you secretly want to hate because of how perfect their life together had been, but can't because they are just so genuinely nice that it's impossible. "You know I hate leaving them in the car. Plus, I have a Bunko game tonight with the girls, so I can't just leave them sitting. I can't."

"Alright, alright. But you owe me," I teased. My eyes glanced out the window of the lodge into the distance where the ski and snowboard lessons were being given, searching for *her*.

I hadn't been lying when I told Channing on Saturday night that I couldn't stop thinking about her. Her slightly awkward, unfiltered thoughts, the way she insisted on one thing, only to turn around and kiss me in the exact opposite fashion. She was everything that drew me to the mountain—the beauty, the surprises, the adaptability, the constancy, the challenge. Channing stood there, challenging me to find out more about her, daring me to work my way closer to her, and drawing me deeper into her magic.

After my last serious relationship—that ended amicably—with Emelia, I'd *sworn* on everything that was holy that I would *never* watch that godforsaken chick-flick, The Notebook, again. But, as soon as Channing had mentioned it, my first reaction was 'perfect'. Not because I wanted to see the damn thing again or even that I wanted to see it with her; no, I wanted to see her—the woman who was always with the guys, always one of the guys, the woman who didn't seem to have any interest in trying to be attractive (not that she needed to try), and the woman who was more focused on riding than relationships—I wanted to watch her; I wanted to watch her face and know why she picked a movie that was so fucking focused on only a relationship—focused on a couple that couldn't or shouldn't want each other. I wanted to see it in her face that that was what she wanted.

Because if she did, I knew I'd fucking move the whole goddamn mountain to make her want it with me.

I hadn't given a shit that my cock throbbed against the hard denim of my jeans, begging for her. *Well, I did give a shit, but I ignored it.*

It was my own fault anyway—I shouldn't have gone down the *'no touching,' 'no kissing'* road, but I couldn't stop myself; I'd been playing with fire, putting myself that close to her inferno. I could see in those seductive, sapphire eyes of hers that she wanted me—that she wanted more—but I wasn't about to coerce it from her. I wanted her to say it; I needed her to tell me it was ok to take—*and fuck, did I want to take...* But more than that, I wanted to be the winner in her war against herself.

I wanted to win her want.

I wanted to take that tight body of hers up onto the countertop, get rid of her t-shirt that was far too big and, more surprisingly, far too sexy. My finger had moved lower onto her shirt, torturing myself, along with her. I wanted to take her small, pert breasts—breasts that I would have normally considered lacking—and cover them with my hands; the thought of them being encased in my grasp, completely possessed by my touch, did things to my mind and my dick that were beyond comprehension.

And then those legs. I bit my cheek at the memory. Even though her t-shirt had hidden all the benefits of the yoga pants that she'd had on, I knew her legs were strong from riding. *And I wanted them locked around my shoulders as my mouth devoured her sweetness.*

I shifted in my seat, glancing down to confirm that my snowpants and jacket were doing an acceptable job of hiding my raging hard-on. *Fuck, Wyatt. Pull yourself together.*

I was on the phone with my mother for fuck's sake.

I cleared my throat, hoping it would clear my mind. "Did you always know you wanted to be a doctor?"

"What? Oh, I don't know about always." She laughed and I could hear her opening the refrigerator door. "I knew I wanted to help people; the doctor part came later. Why do you ask?"

"Just wondering. Trying to figure out exactly what I want to do after this year."

"Oh, sweetheart," she cooed like every mother would, "you know I didn't get my license until after your brother was born, right?"

"What?" I set my sandwich down, my mouth full of the turkey, avocado, and tomato lunch special. *What was she talking about? She'd always been a doctor.* "You've always worked in the hospital."

"Yes, but not as a doctor." She laughed again, surprised that I had no idea what she was talking about. "I mean, you were almost six when I became a doctor, so I doubt you would remember much before that, but I was a nurse up until I had you. So, yes, I still worked in the hospital, but it wasn't until after you were born and I was home taking care of you that I decided I wanted to become a doctor."

I listened in complete shock. Not that my parents would intentionally keep anything from Zack or me, but somehow this had never come up in conversation before. She'd always tell us stories of when she worked at the hospital when she was pregnant with Zack, but I'd always just assumed it was as a doctor.

"Yes, I was in my residency when I had your brother. I can't believe you didn't know this."

I shook my head. *I couldn't either.*

"Maybe I did and I forgot; I don't know."

"Either way, I was a little older than you when I made the change. You're young, Wyatt. I don't care what your sponsors and everyone else are telling you; you have a whole life ahead of you to conquer more challenges. This was just the warm-up."

I smiled to myself at her over-confident and calming words. I knew she and my dad would always be in my corner and I loved them for it. Her revelation had my mind reeling slightly.

"Well, I wouldn't say that it was particularly warm…" I laughed and she did, too.

"Very funny."

"Speak of the devil, your other son is heading my way now, so I've got to run. Love you, mom." She returned my sentiment just before I hung up.

"Who was that?" Zack eyed me suspiciously.

"Mom." I chuckled, standing to put my gear back on.

"Did you tell her that her favorite son said hello?" He smirked.

"Well, yeah, I was the one who called her, so I did say hello," I shot back. This banter was the norm for us—always poking and prodding each other. It was a game off the slopes, but on the slopes, it had turned into a disaster—literally a full out brawl on the side of the mountain that resulted in our snowboards sliding down the rest of the trail without us. Needless to say, after that incident, Zack had signed up for ski lessons at the next opportunity.

My little brother smiled at me with a look that said he'd get me back for that one later. "Did you know she was a nurse before she had you?"

He looked confused for a second. "Yeah. You didn't?" *What the hell.* I didn't answer, pretending to be focused on my task. "You seriously need to stop stressing about this. You're going to win Slopestyle and Big Air and then you'll have all the time and money to take a breather and figure out what the hell you want to do with your life."

"Do you think I'd be a good teacher?" I blurted out, unable to stop the thought that Channing had planted in my mind from sprouting.

Zack laughed in surprise. "What? What do you mean? Like teach snowboarding?"

"Yeah."

He stared at me, processing the thought. "Seriously?" The word was part laugh, like I was making a goddamn joke. *Fuck.* I grabbed my stuff and walked around him, heading for the stairs out of the building.

Stupid idea, Wyatt. You're good at one thing and you're not going to be able to do it anymore. Get over yourself.

"Hey, hold up there, bro!" Zack jogged up behind me, clapping his hand over my shoulder to halt my determined strides towards the board check. "Seriously, hold up. I didn't mean you wouldn't be. I just wasn't expecting that at all and I needed a minute to think about it."

I turned my head and raised an eyebrow at him, handing the kid behind the gate the keyring for my snowboard. "You know I can be slow at times… all that head trauma you inflicted on me as a child." *Now I knew he was really trying to make up for his dick response.*

Grabbing my board and passing a buck to the teenager. I moved towards the lift, not waiting for Zack while he retrieved his skis.

"Alright! I'm being serious, Wyatt!" A snowball hit the back of my head and I spun to face him, dropping my board into the powder at my feet. "C'mon. Gimme a sec."

"Ok, answer," I replied curtly, zipping up my jacket and putting one foot on top of my board.

He took a deep breath, knowing he had one more shot. "First, I don't know a whole lot. I do know that you taught me how to drive stick because mom was too afraid and dad was too impatient. I know that you helped me study for my exams so that I could go get my Masters. I think you tried to teach me how to snowboard before I left the darkside and came into the light, but I don't really remember that far back." I laughed and shook my head at the brief humor interjected into his answer. "I think you'd actually be a great teacher, but not because of any of those reasons."

I raised an eyebrow. "What the hell do you mean?"

He laughed at the memory he was about to recall. "The other day, I agreed to teach Ally to ski. Now, granted, I was a little preoccupied with more than just the skiing part, but I will willingly admit that I am a fucking horrible teacher. I could not, for the life of me, find the right things to say to get Ally to move the way that she needed to. I mean, she looked like a disaster on the bunny slope—like if she wasn't gorgeous and it wasn't completely my fault, I probably would have left her there." I glared at him. "*Kidding!* Calm down. But you get my point. After, I don't know, twenty minutes—*maybe*—all of my patience was gone. Don't worry," he put up a hand, "she felt the exact same way. Thank God, Tammy took pity on us and came over to give her some tips which immediately improved the entire afternoon."

"My point is, is that experiencing how difficult it is to actually try to teach someone something and knowing how many things that you've taught me in my life—especially since I was probably not the best student—I really think you'd be a fucking great instructor. I mean, you sure as shit have the skills for it."

He stopped there, stepping into his skis as I stood speechless for a second. *How did he remember all that?* Maybe I had fallen one too many times on my head—first, not knowing or remembering that my mom had been a nurse for years before becoming a doctor and now forgetting all the times that I'd taught, not just my brother, but friends, classmates, and girlfriends different things over the years.

"So, do you really want to teach? Or are you just looking for another excuse to get close to Channing? Because I already helped you out there once, buddy; not my fault you didn't seal the deal."

And my obnoxious little brother was back.

I yanked one of his poles from his hand and tossed it behind him. "What the hell, dick!" I just laughed as he skated over to retrieve it, waiting until he'd turned around before I spoke.

"Yes and while this does happen to be my other excuse, it's also not the reason I asked," I answered cryptically.

"What are you talking about?" Zack pressed as we got on the lift, headed for the park. They hadn't even started checking passes yet, so we'd decided to risk his presence on the restricted trail.

"Yes, I'm considering teaching or opening some sort of coaching school once this year is over. I also agreed to teach Channing the trick she's been trying to nail."

"You sure that trick isn't you?" I smacked his arm. "*Kidding!*" He pretended to nurse his wound. "So, what you're saying is that this was all Channing's idea?"

Shit.

"Maybe," I grumbled, wishing the damn chairlift had a turbo button. *Ok, it had been her thought.* Not that it hadn't crossed my mind in the past, but never for more than a second. But when she mentioned about her school… As soon as the notion had crossed her lips, it had given me pause. *Or maybe it was because it had crossed her lips…*

Hearing her tell me that I had potential for something other than winning, other than competing—that my skills wouldn't go to waste and I could help people—*teach people;* it changed everything.

"Interesting…" He trailed off. If he was expecting me to say more, he wasn't going to get it. "So what does she want you to teach her?"

We pulled up to the top of Snowmass park. There were a good number of riders on the park already. Today would probably be the last day I could sneak Zack onto the trail with me; not a big deal, he had friends—and now, apparently Ally—to keep him entertained.

"Triple Cork," I replied as I bent down to strap in. Even though he skied, Zack knew exactly what I was talking about—some trick names were universally known throughout both sports.

Zack laughed and I should have known where this was going. "Yeah, I bet you want to triple cork her." I shot up and whipped a snowball at him, which he easily dodged, beginning to head down the slope as he yelled behind him, "That's the one where you flip her over…" *Dick.* I tried to stop the laugh that was coming at his ridiculous insinuations. "And then spin her…" His voice echoed up the slope.

"Fuck you, Zack!" I yelled down after him. I slowed my board knowing that if I tried to catch him I was going to miss the entire run. I chuckled again. *That was my brother, fucking dick.*

I couldn't say that he was completely wrong though. I'd basically been in a perpetual state of arousal since last night. *No,* since the moment I'd met her.

Angling my board towards the next kicker, I aimed for the takeoff, flying off the edge into the trick Zack had just mocked.

Weightless. Carefree. Alive. Up in the air. *Just like everything was between Channing and me.*

Now, all I needed to do was convince her to want to fly, rather than to be afraid of the fall.

Channing

Tomorrow.

My stomach was even tighter about the prospect that it had been the night before the Open.

I tossed and turned onto my back for about the fifth time, my body trying to get comfortable in my own bed; it wasn't the bed that was the problem. I pulled the note he'd left me off my nightstand, reading over it again. I'd replayed what had happened between us over in my mind probably a thousand times already today—from the conversation, to the point where I almost gave into wanting him. The torture of having him standing in front of me, feeling that we both wanted the same thing, and knowing that he was waiting for me to make it ok… it was like I'd been trapped on the lift, above the slope I so desperately wanted to be on, but couldn't get there.

I groaned, thinking about how foolish I'd been to think that trying to take gold in the Men's Slopestyle competition was going to be the hardest thing about the X Games. *No, the hardest thing wasn't going to be winning when I currently couldn't; the hardest thing was wanting Wyatt when I shouldn't.*

Maybe it was his attraction to me that kept drawing me in—the unfathomableness of it all; that I could meet him with my damp hair in disarray, wearing a t-shirt and yoga pants, and the man looked at me like he wanted to rip everything from my body, strap me to my board, and have his way with me.

Clearly, my mind had also replayed what *hadn't* happened between us—but what *could* have.

After trying to keep the conversation on Ally's date with Zack last night, I still couldn't escape her interrogating questions about what happened with Wyatt. Especially since they'd come home to me passed out on the couch, Wyatt—who'd covered me with a blanket by that point—still gently rubbing my feet as movie credits were just finishing. She'd said that Zack had started to have a good laugh until she threatened to make him do the same thing.

"Did he complain when you put that on?" Before I even got out an answer she continued, "I can't believe you picked The Notebook! I knew I should have warned you about him coming. You could have totally scared him away, Chan."

If only it could have been that easy... Except this was Wyatt 'Always Wins' Olsen and right now, he wanted to win me.

Then, I had to hear her drone on about how incredible and sweet Wyatt was. She swore to me that Wyatt had no idea that I had had no idea that he was coming; it had been completely her and Zack's plot. I *still* couldn't even get in a word to scold her about that before she was on to how happy she was for me. Her final thought on the subject was to insist that I not do something stupid, like try to break it off with him for my "own dumb reasons".

Apparently, I was only allowed one stupid idea at a time and currently that position was filled with my impersonation of Chance.

"You didn't tell him, did you?" Her head had spun to me so fast I thought her neck was going to snap.

I shook my head frantically. "No! Of course not. Are you kidding? I can't tell him that I'm his competition..." I blurted out. "Especially not after I ask for his help."

"Wait. What?" She crossed her arms, her eyes narrowing on me. "Do you mean you asked him for help with the competition?" I just swallowed, trying to think of the best way to answer the question. "Do you mean that you asked the guy that you like to teach you, unknowingly, how to beat himself?"

"Maybe," I mumbled underneath my breath; the way she put it did make it sound kinda-sorta-really bad.

Shit.

A million reasons had flown through my head, a million excuses to give—"I needed help and he was the one who offered" or "He might be interested in teaching riders after this year, so I thought I would give him a chance to practice" or "I really wanted to see him again but I couldn't admit that to myself, so instead, I asked him to help me thinking that *it would be a legitimate cover-up for my embarrassingly incapacitating desire to be close to him no matter the cost to him or me."*

Ok, not the last one because the last one was the truth and the truth was only getting in the way of my target: winning. Even though I'd inadvertently admitted that I would be seeing him again, I still ended up cowering away from revealing to her that there could be nothing between Wyatt and me—and that I'd told him just as much. *Maybe if I had told her that, she wouldn't have looked so disappointed in me as I ran out of the house.*

Although, as I lay in bed tossing and turning for the better part of an hour, my mind tried to figure out a way for that not to be the case. I had to ask myself, what was going to be the worse distraction—continuing to deny the desire between us or diving in with the hopes that it would release its hold on me?

Maybe if I just fucked him and got it over with, I could move on with what was really important to me. Riding. Winning.

Back and forth. *Heel to toe.* I carved through the options in my head. *Why couldn't everything be as simple as the mountain?*

Tomorrow, I had to see him. Tomorrow, I was going to be alone with him again. My only saving grace was that we would both be covered with layers of clothing on the side of a mountain instead of comfortably clad in the seclusion of my kitchen with the suggestive undertones of a chick-flick to incite poor decisions.

Tomorrow my two biggest desires became one. The man and the mountain.

As I drifted off to sleep, I wondered who would come out on top?

CHAPTER
Eleven

Channing

My teeth chattered together as I jogged towards Cup of Joe with my board. I was two minutes late, but it was *So. Freaking. Early.* I swore that there was more than an hour's difference between six and seven AM because I felt like a zombie. I prayed that the instant coffee I'd chugged on the drive over would kick in soon.

Of course, Wyatt was already there waiting for me, his pristine white jacket and black pants blending in with his surroundings. His held his board on one side of him, leaning casually against it as I approached. My stomach tightened familiarly. *Maybe he should consider modeling.*

"Sorry," I mumbled when I got close enough. His eyes took me in—over-sized gear, no makeup, and my skin flushed from the cold and, well, *him*.

"Couldn't wake up this morning?" He teased.

"Something like that." I set my board down and zipped my jacket up higher. "Although this cold is doing a pretty good job." He chuckled as we both bent down to strap in.

"I can help with that if you want." His gaze caught mine and I knew we were both remembering my ridiculous suggestion of kissing to keep warm. *No kissing, Channing.* I was about to reiterate my ground rules when he reached in his pocket and held out his hand to me. "Hand warmers. If you want them."

Oh.

I smiled slightly and took them. I didn't really need them at the moment; I just wanted the excuse to touch him. We pushed over to the Village Express lift in silence, my eyes looking around to see that we were legitimately the only people here aside from the two guys working the lift. The Express could seat six, so I made sure to sit a reasonable distance from him on the bench. Although, if I had sat closer, I might have been a little warmer—the cold air biting into my skin as we flew up the side of the mountain.

"How were your lessons yesterday?" He asked, watching me through his goggles; I couldn't see them but I'd felt his eyes since we'd sat down.

I'd been staring out towards where the lift would drop us off, still acutely aware of every slight movement of his body. When he spoke, I forced myself to keep my focus off of him even as I answered. "Good. Busy. There are always a lot of people who come in for the Games, so the lessons get filled up quickly."

"I thought about what you said." *Oh boy. I'd said a lot of things.*

"I'm afraid to ask—but which thing in particular are you talking about?" *Hopefully, not about the kissing—or no kissing. Or touching. Or coffee. Or dates.*

"Not that. Don't worry, Channing, I'll respect your wishes." I swallowed over the lump in my throat, partially relieved and partially disappointed by his words. "I meant about teaching."

"Oh. That." I'd almost forgotten about that.

"Yes. That." He laughed. "I'd really never considered it before—I'm not sure why, but now I can't seem to let the thought go. But if I'm seriously contemplating it, I want your honest opinion when we're done with this if you think I'm any good at it."

"You want my opinion?"

"Of course." His tone suggested how ridiculous he thought my question was. "I mean, I appreciate that Zack and my mom both think that I would be good at it, but they are family; they don't count."

"You told your brother and your mom?" I squeaked out, praying that he didn't tell them that it was my idea.

"Is that a problem?" I could hear the confusion in his voice.

"No. Of course not. I mean… I'm just wondering… did you tell them it was my idea?"

"Well, it was your idea…" *True.* "Zack says 'thanks', by the way. I think I've annoyed the living shit out of him trying to decide what is next for me." I sat there in silence. "Is that not ok?"

Why was I making a big deal out of this?

Because Wyatt was making a big deal out of me, I answered myself.

"No. Of course, it's ok," I answered quickly. *Lie.* I didn't want to be thanked for a future that I couldn't be a part of.

The end of the lift approached, so we swung the safety bar back above us and glided easily off the chair.

"Ready?" He turned and asked as he strapped himself into his board while I sat down quickly to do the same. I nodded. Wyatt immediately turned and moved down the Sunnyside trail towards where the entrance to the terrain park broke off. I pushed myself back up and began to follow.

Even though I quickly gained speed, I was still several feet behind him.

"What—Where are you going!" My head jerked to the entrance of Snowmass as it flew past me on the left. He'd blown right by past the trail. There was no question in my mind that I needed to continue to follow him… wherever he was taking me. Finally, he began to carve and slow down to the point where I could yell to him. "Did you fall asleep there, Olsen? The park is back that way."

"I thought you wanted me to teach you?" Came his cryptic response, as he veered to the right and stopped in front of the Big Burn lift.

"I do…" I muttered, quickly unstrapping as he was already moving to catch the next chair. This one only sat four, which meant that when it captured my seat, I was much closer to Wyatt than before; *and my body immediately reacted to the difference.* "But last I checked, the triple cork required a kicker and all of those are in the parks... and we just passed the entrances to all of the parks."

His arm came up to rest along the back of the lift, partially around my shoulder. "Channing, do you trust me?" Our heads were close, encased in helmets, and covered with goggles, but none of that mattered to my traitorous body and the desire that rolled through it.

"Yes," I replied quietly. *I just didn't trust myself.*

"Good." He smiled. "Because we aren't going on the park today."

"What?!" I exclaimed, shaking my head. *No, no, no; this wasn't right. I needed to be on the park.* "I need to learn the triple, Wyatt. I don't have time to waste doing... whatever it is--" I broke off when his left hand turned my helmet to face him, his helmet clanking against the front of mine. I froze even though I knew there was no way it was physically possible for him to kiss me right now with all of our gear in the way.

"Channing, calm down." He stared at me—into me—and I swallowed the rest of my protests. His hand held me there.

"Tell me what happened."

"What do you mean?" I whispered.

"At the Open." *Oh.* My body shuddered at the memory I kept trying to suppress. Our breaths mingled in the few inches that separated us, the warmth clearly visible in the cold air surrounding us. *I wasn't cold though.* Losing myself in his eyes, I began the story that had yet to be spoken from my mouth.

"Chance and I were both invited to the Open. There was no question that he was going to win it—I mean, *you* weren't there—he was—*is*—so good. I told him I wanted to learn the triple and I remember him turning and looking at me—deadly serious—and nodding as though he expected nothing less from me." I laughed sadly, not because it was funny, but because the memory of my brother stung. "We rented time at a park that came with an airbag base to practice, and for two weeks he trained me—taught me how to do it. And I did." I felt Wyatt's surprise even though he stayed silent; he didn't know that I'd actually landed the trick before. "I did it; I've done it. I remember he was so proud. And then the competition started—men first; Chance took gold." I swallowed hard, remembering my brother standing and smiling on top of the podium.

"What happened?" Wyatt pressed quietly, bringing me back from the memory.

"Nothing," I said, blinking rapidly to disguise my tears. "I choked, that's all." *All he needed to know.*

He would have pushed further, but the lift was ending and we had to get off. Slipping onto the snow in silence, we both came to a stop at the top of the surrounding trails.

"Can you tell me what we are doing up here?" I asked, the resignation in my voice clear.

"We are up here to forget about the pressure," he said simply. I just stared at him like he had two heads. "You're stressed about nailing this triple and there's no way that you're going to land it if you are stressed. If you've landed it before, it's obviously not your skills that are holding you back; it's your mindset—and having you attempt the trick over and over and over again when your mindset is the problem is going to get us nowhere."

Interesting. I bent down to strap my back foot in. "So, then what are we doing?"

"We're going to ride the mountain." His answer punctuated with that devastating smile. "We're going to explore the Powerline glades and just enjoy the powder."

"I don't know—" A snowball hit me in the chest. "Hey!" Without a second though, I bent over, balling snow inbetween my mittens to return the shot. When I stood, he was right in front of me; my breath caught at his closeness.

His hands reached for my hips and my skin burned underneath all the layers I was wearing. He pulled my body against his, the snowball disintegrating in my grasp as my hands came to steady me on his chest.

Again, I knew that there was no way he could kiss me, and yet the realization only made my body ache for it more. Instinctually, my legs tried to close to ease the pressure between my thighs, but my feet were strapped in, preventing me from alleviating the torture.

Even though my arms slightly separated our chests, from the waist down I was flush against him, legs spread, with his hips directly between them. Through the snowpants and jackets, I could feel his arousal, pressing hard against my core.

"What are we doing?" I demanded breathlessly even as my gloves gripped into his jacket, my hips uncontrollably arching against his.

I saw his jaw clench with the restraint it was taking not to break his promise to me. "This morning," he rasped, "we're going to forget about the competition, forget about the pressure. This morning, we're going to just have a little fun." I sucked in a breath. "Think you can do that, Channing?" He whispered hoarsely, his mouth trapped inches away from mine because of our helmets.

I never dreamt that this was how a helmet would save my life.

I moaned in response, not trusting my words or my body that pressed itself against him. He growled, his eyes darkening with desire. And then he was gone.

He gained speed, flying into the fresh powder and disappearing into the trees. It took me a few seconds to find my wits and catch my breath. It had been weeks since I'd been down any of the other trails on the mountain—and even then, Emmett, Nick, and I usually just did one trail as a warm-up and then stuck to the park. I tried to remember the last time I'd spent an entire day just exploring the mountain. *I couldn't.*

The first time, I took the glades slowly, familiarizing myself with the trail and the conditions. Trees and powder everywhere, we carved the first tracks in the virgin snow, and met down at the lift. I could only look at him confusion that my body felt—torn between needing to focus on the competition and wanting to throw caution to the wind and enjoy the day. "Again," was all he said. The second pass I moved with more speed, slicing a new path down the mountain; that time, when I arrived at the bottom, there was a hint of a smile on my face, my worries becoming buried with each run. The third time, I pulled up to the lift and I couldn't have wiped the happiness off my face if I tried; that time, I turned to him and insisted, "Again." *Not that he had any other plans.*

We made it back to the top of the slope and I eyed up the trail; this time, I was going to let loose. Wyatt started down first and I let myself indulge in the sight of the smooth agility with which he moved; he was an artist and his board, the brush, painting a masterpiece on the side of the mountain. Turning my board in his direction, I gained speed, breathing in the cold air, letting it bring my body to life. I carved down amid trees, flying past their snow-capped branches, feeling the powder spraying up against the exposed skin between my goggles and my neck-warmer. My smile became uncontrollable.

This was the beautiful contradiction of the mountain: it could be both elevating, yet grounding. *And right now, I needed grounding.* I loved being up in the air, where anything was possible. But this—the chance to shut everything out, the competition, my brother, my fears, my desire, *this* was the rush of living in the moment. And my heart pounded its vehement approval against my chest.

I managed to see Wyatt stopped amid a cluster of trees off to the side of the glade just before I would have flown past him. He was facing up the mountain waiting for me. And without thinking or caring, I swung a wide heel turn to come up behind him and shower him with snow; I cut into my heel-edge so hard to stop that, combined with the laughter that was now bubbling out of my smile, I fell right onto my ass and I didn't even care.

He held his arms out, looking down at his snow-sprayed front, and then over at me, cracking up in the snow. I couldn't stop it—the laughter spilled out of me like an avalanche, tears streaming down and then freezing on my face.

Wyatt pulled down his face mask, partially mouthing the word '*What?*' before he broke into a huge grin.

For the first time, in a long time, I didn't have any weight on my shoulders. *And it felt incredible.*

"You think that's funny, do you?" He asked rhetorically. "I see how it is." He bent down, balling up snow in his hands.

I knew it was coming, but I couldn't stop laughing long enough to do anything except bring my mitts up over my face to shield it from the snow that scattered as his snowball hit my stomach. Not only could I not stop laughing, it made me laugh harder.

I didn't know if something was wrong with me, but everything felt right.

"It looks like you're having a little bit of fun." He grinned in success. I finally began to calm just enough to breathe, pushing myself up to sit, and grabbing snow from between my legs. "You sure you want to do that?" He raised an eyebrow, daring my next move.

Yes.

I whipped the snowball at him, aiming for his chest, but landing a little bit low... My laughter immediately stopped as he groaned, his hand dropping the snowball he'd made in retaliation and coming to hold his cock. My hand jumped up, covering my mouth, as I waited on edge for his response.

His left hand reached up to pull his goggles off of his head, tossing them into the snow beside him. "You're going to pay for that one, sweetheart," he groaned, pulling off his gloves and dropping them on top of his goggles.

"Wyatt—" I broke off, raising my hand as a stop as he unclasped his helmet, pulling it off his head to join his gear that was buried in the powder. "I'm sorry--" My hands planted on the ground as I tried to push myself back as he stepped towards me, desire glinting dangerously in his eyes that I could now clearly see. I quickly found that I only had a few inches behind me before I was backed up against a tree. "I didn't mean—" I bit my lip, swallowing as he crouched in front of me. I heard the zipping noise of my bindings release before I comprehended that he'd just unstrapped my feet from my board. And by the time I realized that, he was kneeling between my legs, his face in front of mine.

I watched in slow motion as he pulled my goggles from my face.

"I can't tell if you are just clumsy." *Click.* My helmet strap released. "Or if you just like putting yourself in these situations with me."

I gulped, trying to find my bearings. "Wyatt… we agreed…" My voice was desire coated in desperation.

"I know," he replied, his knuckles tilting my chin up as his thumb brushed over my lower lip—a lip that parted duplicitously, begging for his touch. "But I have a question for you."

His hand slid underneath the side of my helmet, pulling it up off my head. I held my breath as his face came closer to mine, slipping to the side at the last moment; his lips just barely grazed along my cheek until they reached my ear.

There he paused, my eyelids dropping shut as the serenity and silence of the mountain was broken only by the pounding of my heart that I was sure was echoing all the way down the slope.

And then his lips began to move, his words the barest caress into me. "If a tree falls in the woods and no one is around to hear it, does it make a sound?"

My heart stopped. *If he kissed me in the woods and no one but us would know, was it still breaking my rules?*

My eyes flew open and I turned my face slightly towards his just as he did the same. If there was any space between our lips, there was a good chance it was too small to be measured. Like where the sky meets the earth, my blue gaze met his.

The moment froze between us like the eerie stillness before an avalanche. And then my lips moved, uttering the word that made the weight of our desire exceed the strength of our dissents.

"*No.*" Barely audible, it shattered our sculpted, structured restraint. And then the landslide began.

His mouth took mine. Just like the mountain, Wyatt's tongue carved into every crevice of my mouth, before dueling with my own. I moaned against him. The waves of pleasure that I'd just been riding down the slope ignited under his kiss. *Here*, there was no one but us. There was no competition, no impersonating, no nosy siblings—*nothing but us.*

My arms wrapped around his neck, my hips grinding up into his. Through all of the clothes, I could feel his hardness pressing against my core, a cure for the friction that was building inside of me.

Even though I was surrounded by cold and snow, I was on fire. *"I'm burning,"* I murmured against his mouth. A second later I felt his hand reach between us, unzipping my jacket. He pulled me tighter against him and I awkwardly tried to wrap my legs around his waist—a little difficult because of the bulkiness of my snowboard boots. I got them far enough though that it put the ridge of his arousal right where I needed him.

I clutched around his neck, clinging to our kiss—the only place where skin touched skin—as I rocked my sex up against him, groaning as pleasure rocketed through me. One of his hands laid claim to my waist, locking it in place as his body began to move against mine. His other hand slid up to cup my breast—my small flesh easily engulfed by his palm. In spite of my bra, cold-gear, and woolen t-shirt, he found my nipple immediately and I knew the layers had done nothing to conceal my body's reaction to him.

He pinched the swollen flesh through my clothes and I gasped into his mouth.

"What are you doing to me?" He groaned, his mouth sliding and nipping all along my jawline as he began to press his erection against my core.

"The same thing you are doing to me," I moaned and he pinched my nipple again, sending fireworks straight down to my center. *"Again."*

Wyatt bit down on my earlobe as his fingers squeezed the hard bud of my nipple again; my hips slammed up into his. *How was he doing this to my body—ripping it apart with the barest of touches?*

Our bodies were glued to one another, yet not touching—*another contradiction created on the mountain.*

It was the most exquisite torture—and it was the reason why I felt my orgasm beginning to roll through me. I wanted nothing more than to feel every inch of his bare body against mine—inside of mine, but instead we were trapped by the layers between us. It was why even the slightest touch created a tidal wave inside of my body, knowing that what I truly wanted was still denied to me.

Like the ivy, my legs clung to his hips as he began to grind his swollen cock furiously against the very center of my desire.

"*Wyatt...*" His name breathlessly escaped my lips. The friction inside of me was building and I couldn't stop it even if I wanted to. "I'm going to come..." I gasped, not caring how idiotic I sounded—like a damn high-schooler—getting off from dry-humping a guy. Maybe it was because I hadn't had an orgasm in so long or maybe it was because I wanted this man with a desire that I'd never experienced before.

"*Christ, Channing.*" His mouth tore into mine again. My chest arched into him, experiencing the first tease of my release as he rolled his erection relentlessly against my aching sex. I was drenched and the waterproof pants that were meant to keep the water from seeping in, were now preventing my wetness from soaking out. "*Take it,*" he demanded against my lips as his fingers tweaked my nipple hard one last time. My orgasm erupted inside of me like a volcano—starting at the bottom, its molten burn working its way up my body until every cell felt like it had been charred; I couldn't see any of it, but I knew my skin was coated in goosebumps, all of my hair standing on end. My legs tightening like a vise around his waist as my hips undulated against him, the intensity of my climax momentarily blinding me.

I felt his lips leave mine even though I could still feel the ragged rhythm of his breath on my skin. I remained pleasurably paralyzed against him as I slowly began to come down from the high, my brain and thoughts trying to regain their footing.

"What are you doing?" I finally managed to whisper, knowing that I had been the only one of us to find release. My legs slid down off of his hips as his stormy gaze met mine.

"Torturing myself." He gave me a small smile before he pushed himself up and off of me; standing, I could see what I'd felt a moment before: *just* how unfulfilled his body was. Immediately, the cocoon of heat that had comfortably covered me was gone. I still couldn't find the strength to move as I watched speechlessly while he picked up his helmet, goggles, and mitts from the snow, putting his gear back on.

"We should get going. I want to make sure you have enough time for lunch before your lessons."

I just nodded, swallowing over the lump in my throat. The subtle reminder of the real world that awaited us at the foot of the mountain jarred me into action. I zipped my jacket back up, grabbing my helmet as I stood.

"Channing," he rasped my name and I looked up at him. "I'm sorry—" he broke off, smacking his glove against the side of his leg. He waited a second even though we both knew I wasn't going to respond before he angled his board and began to move down the mountain.

I moved back onto the trail from the security of the glade, weaving my way around the many skiers and snowboarders who were now out on the mountain. I didn't see Wyatt again until I reached the bottom where he was waiting for me.

My stomach clenched at the painful mixture of guilt and frustration on his face.

"Tomorrow. Same time." I didn't even have the chance to nod before he added, "I promise this won't happen again." My gaze fell. I should have asked for that promise from him, but I wasn't going to. And yet, I still got it even though I didn't want it.

"See you then," I managed to say calmly, hoping that my face showed the expectation of holding him to his word instead of the disappointment that I actually felt. He unstrapped and walked towards the lodge, probably to grab some food as well, but leaving me my own haven at Cup of Joe.

I stood there for a second longer, trying to absorb everything that I was feeling. The knowledge that this wouldn't happen again stood in front of me like a mountain—only it was a mountain that my body craved to conquer.

CHAPTER
Twelve

Wyatt

For the first time in my life, I hadn't stuck to the plan. Watching Channing as she slept on the couch the other night, I had realized something—she may have plans, but she was driven to a fault; she was determined and focused to the point where she didn't know how to let loose. Which is why she couldn't even make it through a movie—a chick-flick, no less—without passing out from exhaustion. Watching her lie there sound asleep and completely at ease had me wondering when was the last time she did something for fun.

I'd then gleaned from Zack, who'd questioned Ally, that Channing hardly ever went out, and not just because she worked almost every night at the bar. When she did go out, it was for a drink with her guy friends and she was never out long.

Channing Ryder may think that she had it all figured out, but what she didn't know was how to have fun. *Yes,* snowboarding was love and life—I get that, *trust me,* I really did, but there was more of life to enjoy.

And when I learned that she'd landed this trick before, but no longer could, I realized what was going on. Maybe not entirely since I could hear in her answers that they weren't the whole truth, and while I'd already made up my mind that I would find out that truth at some point, it wasn't my focus right now. Right now, I realized that what was holding her back was the pressure that she was putting on herself—*for whatever that reason was.* She was letting that pressure slowly crush her, suffocating her skill right out of her. Channing needed to relax; she needed to just have some fun.

I knew there was no way I was going to be able to convince her to do that *off* of the mountain, so I'd compromised: we'd stay on the mountain, but out of the park where all of her self-imposed standards lay waiting for her to fall all over them.

As soon as I had the idea, I knew it was the right one. I felt it in my heart—which was another realization for me, but one I wasn't going to explore at the moment.

I'd expected her hesitancy, her questions, and the fact that it would take her time to warm up to the idea. *Hell,* I'd even expected my desire—planned on the price I'd have to pay to be around her, hoping the cold would at least numb my senses a little. What I hadn't expected was the mountain.

Maybe because it was so early, maybe because it had just snowed, maybe because we'd been the only ones up here—there were a lot of maybes to account for the magic.

Yeah, she'd nailed me right in the dick—that was already throbbing—and I one-hundred-percent had planned on retaliating with a similarly-sized snowball. But when I looked at her sitting there in the snow, her face flushed from her laughter and the cold, her chest rising and falling rapidly, her legs spread and strapped to her board, I couldn't stop myself from finding my way between them.

I knew that I'd asked before taking her pleasure, but I also knew it was a question that she wasn't going to refuse; I saw her surrender in her eyes the second my helmet hit the snow. And for that, I felt like the biggest ass.

For the first time in my life, I resented winning.

I'd promised her no touching, no kissing. And when I made that promise, I knew that I wasn't just swearing it to protect her from my desire, but to help protect her from her own. I could see the way it ate at her to want me—her brother's competition—which is why I'd settled with myself to maintain a respectable distance until the Games were over when my career on the mountain was done; then she would no longer have cause to feel that sense of betrayal.

And Day One, I'd gone and broken it. I resented myself for winning her desire, which is why I'd called it quits for the day. Not to mention my dick had been so painfully hard that it would have been impossible to train in that condition.

Even though I'd like to think it was a moment of weakness, I seemed to be having lots of those moments around her. So, I put on my game face and for the rest of the week I went to the other end of the spectrum. My plan didn't change—we stayed away from the park the entire week. But I kept our conversation—and more importantly, our contact—limited and focused on the mountain. I wasn't going to let her—or myself—down this time; she deserved more than my weakness.

Channing

Five days.

It had been five freaking days since I'd been on the park, since I'd taken a jump or tried to get any sort of air. Annoyingly, that wasn't the tally that I'd been keeping in my mind. No, my mind counted the days that had passed since Monday, since Wyatt gave me my orgasm in the glades.

Four days.

Only four felt like *four-ever*.

I relived those moments every day, but mostly every night, still struggling to believe that he pulled an orgasm from me without even touching me. After which I dreamt about what would happen if he were.

When we'd parted ways that morning, I felt in my bones that I wasn't going to have to worry about Wyatt trying anything like that again. I saw the look on his face—the one that said he was punishing himself for breaking his word far more than I would have.

I was the one who'd said it was ok, after all...

I hadn't known exactly what to expect on Tuesday when I'd arrived at the mountain, but what I got was professional-snowboarder-Wyatt. He wasn't rude or curt, but I could tell that he was being very careful with everything that he said, everything that we talked about, and especially making sure to keep his physical distance.

We'd stayed away from the park, but that didn't mean he hadn't given me pointers on my stance. We talked a lot about the triple—about what I thought I was doing wrong, what my problems were when I'd originally learned it; we talked through the entire thing.

And now it was Saturday and we were sitting at the top of Snowmass park. He'd surprised me after our second run by making his way here instead of back onto the lift.

"Are we actually hitting the park today?" I needed to clarify.

"Yes, ma'am." He smiled—it still made my knees weak. "Time to work your way back into the air." *Finally.*

I felt the rush of adrenaline roll through me. "So, am I going for it?"

"We're going for fun." I sagged a little at his response, taking it as a 'no'. I felt relaxed after a week away; looking down the slope, I didn't feel the weight that the pressured anticipation of needing to nail this trick had put on me before. It had been a long time since I'd looked at this slope as something just for fun instead of something that I needed to be better at—something that defined me.

"Alright, let's start with the double."

"But I can do that one." For some reason, I insisted on protesting.

"Right." He nodded up at me from where he sat. "But you don't practice until you get it right, you practice until you can't get it wrong; and I've seen you get this one wrong." I huffed, but I couldn't argue with him about that. I didn't land the double every time, not that that was what he was implying, but my double wasn't as solid as it should be. "I'll be at the landing." He pushed up and off down the trail, casually carving alongside the first kicker before coming to a stop.

I shook my arms at my side, suddenly nervous about doing something that I knew I had a decent chance of landing. Adjusting my goggles, I angled my board and took off towards the lip.

Spin. Flip. Land.

As soon as my board planted firmly on the snow beneath me, I smiled at my success and turned over to where Wyatt was waiting. I pulled to a stop, planting my hands on my hips. "Well?" I asked confidently.

"You start the flip too late." *What?* My spirits sank. It was one thing to be critiqued when I fell or when it was clear that I'd messed something up, but I was always easily annoyed when I felt like I had something and was told that it was still wrong. It was that annoyance that had gotten me into trouble the last time.

"I landed it," I retorted.

"I never said you didn't," he answered, standing back up onto his board. "And it's fine for the double, but when you try to turn that into a triple, that's where you are going to run into problems; if you start the flip too late here, that means you won't have enough time for three rotations when we move on."

"Ok…" I crossed my arms, waiting for him to tell me what I was supposed to do about it.

"As soon as you come off the lip, your hand needs to be grabbing the edge of your board. I think you are waiting a second or two into the jump before doing that and it's putting your entire timeline behind," he continued. "For the triple, you need one rotation on the way up, one at the top, and one on your way down. You're waiting until you're too far up before starting." He nodded to the next jump. "Again."

I waited until he was next to it before starting to gain momentum, remembering what he had told me.

"Better, but not quite," was the feedback I received after another successful landing. "Again."

I huffed, my frustration rising, as he rode off, waiting for my third attempt.

This went on for another forty-five minutes and another complete pass and a half down the park. I pulled up to him, just like I'd done the past twenty-some times, only this time my patience was worn thin.

"You know you put a signature on your tricks?" He asked, amused as I slid to a stop beside him.

I made a face. "What are you talking about?"

"A signature. A tick." He laughed. "Every time your left hand lets go of your edge and you land, that hand immediately brushes the side of your pants, like it got dirt on it from touching the bottom of your board."

What? I just stared at him. I'd never noticed. A fact that made me more annoyed. Here I was, like a trick monkey, doing the same thing over and over and over again, feeling like I wasn't making any difference in anything important.

"It's not a problem, obviously," he reassured me when I didn't respond. "Just wondered if you knew. It's cute." His gaze immediately broke from mine as he uttered the words, realizing that for the first time in four days, he'd come within the vicinity of the line he was determined not to cross. Clearing his throat, he looked down at the last jump. "You're almost there. Do it again."

He'd gone to turn and ride down to the next jump when I determined, "No." I was tired of doing the same thing. I was tired of him critiquing a jump that I'd never asked for help with. I was frustrated that I'd wasted a whole week of *not* attempting the triple when the Games were only two short weeks away. "I'm done with the double, Wyatt. I've nailed it every damn time. Whatever is wrong with it, isn't important anymore. It's almost been a week of this crap. I'm going for the triple."

"Channing," he growled, his expression, one of knowing concern, was familiar to me, but I ignored it. "I can't stop you; you are a free woman. But you asked for my help, you asked me to teach you, and

I'm telling you that you aren't ready."

"I don't believe you," I returned defiantly, tears brimming in my eyes, his words an echo from my past. And before he could say anything else, I swung my board around him and headed for the last jump, determined to prove myself right—*determined to win.*

Sometimes angry frustration is a great motivator. Other times, it blinds you to the facts of reality. And those facts were that Wyatt knew what he was doing and I should have listened to him.

I gained speed, not because I needed it to fly, but because I needed it to flee. Wyatt's words had reminded me of what happened between Chance and me the night before I competed in the Open last year and I so desperately needed to run from the memory.

Everything felt perfect—the drop, the grip, the take-off, the spin, the rotat—.

They always said that 'pride comes before the fall.'

This time, the *'thump'* that connected on the landing wasn't the hard wood of my board, but my hard,stubborn head.

Fuck. Fuck. Fuck. I groaned loudly, feeling pain radiate from my head down throughout my body. The tears that welled in my eyes though, those were not only from my embarrassment, but my disappointment in myself for not listening to someone who was looking out for my best interests. *Again.*

I peeled my eyes open to see Wyatt running towards me. He'd unstrapped and I couldn't even see where his board was. *Stupid man abandoned it on the slope to get to me; I was fine.*

"What the fuck were you thinking, Channing?" He roared at me and my eyes widened in shock. I'd been expecting concern, not anger. *I was the one who had tanked, after all.* He knelt in front of me, carefully but efficiently pulling my googles off of my face, unstrapping my helmet and lifting it from my head. "I *fucking* told you, you weren't ready." He took my face in his hands, tilting it slightly from one side to the other, swearing underneath his breath. "Did you black out? Do you feel lightheaded at all?"

I tried to shake my head 'no,' but he held it steady, forcing me to rasp the word out over the lump in my throat and through my dry lips. I wasn't lightheaded; if anything my head felt heavy as it pounded from the impact.

"*Christ*, you landed right fucking on your head." *No shit, Sherlock.* His hands moved into my hair, rubbing around my scalp to feel for any bumps, I assumed. Tears began to slip down my cheeks.

"I'm fine. I had my helmet on."

"Thank fucking God." His gaze returned to mine, noticing the trails of water on my face. "What's wrong? What hurts? Tell me what hurts."

My pride.

It wasn't that I'd wanted to show off, but after this entire week of doing what Wyatt suggested, we'd arrived at the park earlier and I'd felt so at-ease, completely confident that I could do this; until I couldn't. It was just like what happened before the Open and then he'd said just what Chance had—and I ignored him just like I'd ignored my brother. And now, his part-angry, part-tortured, part-caring question sent me over the emotional precipice that I'd been straddling.

"Nothing," I said forcefully, turning my face in his hands, trying to get them off of me. "I'm fine. I'll be fine." I twisted out of his grasp.

"Channing..." His hands moved to my shoulders, but trying to calm me right now was like trying to talk down a hurricane.

"No!" Now, I was yelling, my frustration derailed by the tears I couldn't stop. I pushed him away and pushed myself up, almost falling again as my head protested the sudden movement.

"Channing!" He reached for me, his tone sharp with anger. "Don't fucking move like that. Jesus Christ, you just landed on your head. You need to sit."

I shook my head even though it made the pain worse, hardly hearing him. "No... I can't... I have to go..."

"Absolutely fucking not. You need to stay here so I can go get someone to make sure you're ok."

"No!" I yelled again, barely able to see him through my tears. I turned my board and began to move; I felt Wyatt reach for me but my jacket slipped from his grasp.

"Channing! *Fuck!*" His curse echoed down the mountain. I needed to get out of here. I didn't know why he was so upset, we were almost at the bottom anyway. My legs wobbled a few times as my balance faltered, but I kept going knowing that it wouldn't be long before Wyatt was back on his board and coming after me.

Sure enough, I just made it to the bottom, stopping off to the side where there weren't too many people congregated and unstrapped my bindings when he flew up in front of me.

Yanking his feet from his board, I stared into his eyes that burned with vehemence. "*Are you fucking kidding me right now?*" He was yelling and I stood there frozen, my brain hurting too much to move. "*What the fuck is wrong with you! You could have a concussion and you're fucking riding down the mountain like it's no big deal!*"

"I'm fine, Wyatt!" I yelled back, his body swimming every so often in my gaze. "I'll be fine, I just need to sit. I just need to be. Alone." My vision blurred again and not from my tears. I groaned, bringing my hand to my head.

"*Bullshit, you are not fine.*" He kicked his board out of the way, his hands gripped my shoulders and tried to pull me against him. I pulled away again, but this time, I stumbled as a wave of dizziness overcame me. *Maybe I wasn't exactly fine...*

All I knew was that I'd just relived a memory that I'd been trying to forget—and not only had I relived it, but I'd succumbed to it in front of Wyatt. I didn't know if it was the head injury or the fear of disappointing him that made me feel nauseous, but I knew I needed to get away.

I tried to push past him, completely forgetting all about my board lying in the snow. I was about a curse and a half away when my vision started to go black and I was grateful for the vise-like grip that clamped down on my shoulder before I was hoisted into his arms. I wanted to protest, but even though the quick movement had probably saved me from falling on my face, it also jarred my already traumatized brain.

I groaned and tried to push against him with no avail.

"Please, Channing," his voice was suddenly soft like velvet against my head and I could have sworn that I felt his lips brush against my scalp, "please let me take care of you."

No, I thought. *Not him. He couldn't. I couldn't let him get that close.* My senses began to calm down to the point where I could press harder against his chest, staring up at him through watery eyes. "No. Please, no." I started to shake my head, feeling the sobs I wanted to let loose building in my throat. "No, Wyatt! No," I insisted louder, knowing I was probably drawing stares from the people we were walking past.

"Hey! What the hell are you doing, Olsen?" *Thank God.* Emmett's voice resounded from somewhere off to the side.

"Emmett!" I yelled and then he was in front of Wyatt, blocking his path. I reached for my friend, catching Wyatt's pained expression along the way.

"What the hell is going on?" Emmett demanded again.

"Damn woman fell on her head and then proceeded to continue riding down the mountain before anyone could check her." Emmett stared at me and I silently pleaded with him to help me. "After which, she almost collapsed over there, hence why I'm carrying her to the damn first aid station."

"I'm perfectly fine, King," I tried to say confidently. "I fell; it happens all the time. He's being overbearing."

"What the hell is the matter with you!" I could feel the fire in his tone as it washed over me. "*Christ,* and I thought when you'd decided to go for the triple that you were being an idiot, but this, right now, puts that whole stunt to shame."

Now, I was crying and I refused to do it in front of *him*. I writhed in his arms, forcing him to set me down where I immediately wrapped my arms around Emmett—not that we particularly hugged a lot or that I needed a hug, but my head *wasn't* right and I was afraid if I stood on my own I would end up proving Wyatt right.

I hazarded a glance over to him and my heart ached with the hurt and concern that I'd etched into the strong lines of his face. I wanted…

well, it didn't matter what I wanted; I couldn't have what I wanted.

"Take her to get her head checked," Wyatt demanded, his eyes boring into Emmett. There was a dark undercurrent in his tone that suggested doing anything to the contrary would be ill-advised.

I closed my eyes as another wave of nausea and dizziness spread through me and when I opened them again, Wyatt was gone.

"What the hell have you done, Lil," Emmett grumbled as he turned, keeping one arm firmly around my shoulder, guiding me towards the first aid station. Whatever beef he had with Wyatt and his brother was momentarily forgotten as he was determined to obey Wyatt's demand.

This time I didn't protest. I did feel like something was wrong with my head.

More concerning to me though was how I felt like there was something wrong with my heart.

CHAPTER
Thirteen

Channing

"A**RE YOU SURE I CAN'T GET YOU ANYTHING ELSE?**" Ally asked for probably the fiftieth time.

"No!" I insisted with a sigh. "Go get ready." I was lying on the couch, preparing for movie night number two, wondering when the last time was that I'd had two nights off.

Emmett had taken me to have the doctor on staff check my head. Dr. Lam had said that, at worst, it was a minor concussion, but that I should take it easy through the weekend, which translated into: no teaching, no bartending, and *definitely* no riding. Yesterday, I'd had no problem agreeing to it; I had felt like shit and Ally had insisted on babying me—which provoked an argument between her and Emmett over whether or not I could take care of myself. I was actually in the room, but it seemed that neither of them wanted my opinion.

Today, though, was a different story. My head felt a thousand times better—unless I stood or turned it too quickly—but Ally still insisted on playing nursemaid. I said a silent prayer to the gods when she'd told me that she had a date scheduled with Zack, but that she could cancel if I needed her.

I vigorously assured her that I didn't.

Bless her heart, but I was counting down the minutes until Zack showed up to take her away; she was like a helicopter parent. Meanwhile, I dreaded the prospect of being alone with my thoughts which would only be occupied with one thing—Wyatt.

Guilt gnawed at me, making me far more uneasy than the head injury for how I'd treated him. I didn't know what I'd been thinking in the moment, but now when I looked back, all I could see was his face as he came up to me. He'd been white as a sheet, afraid that I'd really hurt myself and even though that fear had turned to anger, I'd thrown his feelings back in his face. The one that killed me though was his face when I reached for Emmett. I shuddered at the memory.

I needed to talk to him, to apologize. But first, I needed to get through the weekend without doing any more damage to myself. And then I would figure out a way to make amends to the man whose only crime was caring about me—a man who probably had no interest in speaking to me ever again.

The clicking of Ally's footsteps flew down the stairs and she jogged awkwardly in her thigh-high boots around the couch, coming up behind me to plant a kiss on my head. "Zack's here. I gotta go! I'll be home later. *Call me if you need me.*"

"Yeah, yeah. Go." I shooed her away, hearing the tapping of her heels slowly disappear as the front door opened and shut. I looked at the TV, wondering what I was going to watch tonight. About to reach for the remote, I heard the front door open and close again.

She probably forgot something; that was so Ally.

It took me a few seconds to realize that the footsteps weren't being made by someone wearing heels and when my gaze flew towards the hallway, my heart jumped into my throat.

Wyatt.

And roses.

And take-out.

In my periphery, the soup that Ally insisted on making me—*because a head injury must be the same as a cold*—no longer looked as appetizing as the sight in front of me.

"Hey." The rumble of his voice warmed my body, feeling like I'd been deprived of heat since I'd last seen him. Tonight, he looked tortured—as much if not more than on Friday.

I pushed myself to sit up straighter against the side of the couch, licking my lips. "Hey," I answered quietly.

He looked down at the flowers and back at me. "I'm just going to give these guys some more water," he murmured as he walked over to the kitchen sink to fill a vase with water. While his focus was momentarily elsewhere, my hands quickly rose to run through and smooth my hair that I hadn't given two seconds of thought to for days.

"I'll just set them here if that's ok?" My hands dropped, hoping I looked marginally decent as I nodded; he set the vase of flowers on the countertop.

I didn't respond, too distracted by the gorgeous man who had clearly come to grovel even though I couldn't fathom for what. His dark, fitted jeans followed his muscled legs effortlessly over to the middle of the kitchen. He was wearing a crew neck sweater underneath a blazer and looked like he was about to take his girlfriend out on a nice date, instead of bringing food and flowers to the crazy, careless tomboy who had not only treated him poorly, but looked like a complete disaster in my semi-tight sweatpants, t-shirt, and sweatshirt.

My stomach clenched with desire as he walked towards me, still holding the bag of take-out boxes. The intensity on his face broke me.

"Wyatt—"

"No, wait," he interrupted, setting the bag next to the bowl of soup that I knew was going to be left untouched. "I'm not staying, but I needed to apologize to you."

"No, you—"

"Please, Channing," he rasped. "Just hear me out for one minute and then I'll go."

What if I didn't want him to—apologize, leave, any of it...

He sighed and ran his hand through his hair, messing its sculpted appearance. I bent my legs in front of me, a subtle indication that he could sit on the couch if he wanted. He glanced down at my movement, but instead he crouched down on the floor next to me.

"I need to apologize for my behavior the other day. I shouldn't have yelled at you like that, but I saw you fall—I saw your head hit the ground and *Christ*, it was like the life got knocked out of me. And then you didn't get up right away—" His mouth clenched shut and I saw his jaw muscles flexing as he tried to contain his emotion. When his eyes met mine again, I saw the turbulence in their depths. "And then you insisted on finishing the run." He shook his head. "Don't get me wrong, I still think you are insane for doing all of that, but I shouldn't have treated you like I did." His eyes dropped to my hand, his own fingers locking tightly as though he wanted to grab mine, but refrained from crossing that line. "I was so fucking scared." The last was barely a whisper into the space between us.

I blinked a few times wondering if this was reality or if the bump on my head was causing me to hallucinate the gorgeous gentleman kneeling in front of me taking fault for something he didn't deserve to.

"Ok, I'll leave you to your night," he murmured when I didn't respond. My eyes jumped up and my hand reached out and grabbed his, stopping him in his tracks.

"No. Wait. I… I can't let you apologize." I started to shake my head but stopped remembering that that was a no-no. "You didn't do anything wrong; it was my fault." I choked, my chest tightening as those same suffocating memories began to reappear. "What did you bring?" I looked over to the bag of food that smelled amazing. I wasn't trying to abruptly change the topic but my brain was running from the past.

He blinked and then realized what I meant. "Chinese. From Master Wong's. Ally said it was your favorite." His head ducked as he cleared his throat.

"You asked Ally?" I don't know why that surprised me; he always managed to do the most thoughtful thing possible.

"I used Zack's phone to call her yesterday. I… I wanted to come to apologize then but she said you were sleeping already. So, I told her I would stop by tonight." His eyes dropped to our hands that were still intertwined, neither of us moving to break the contact. "I wanted to bring you some food and she said this was your favorite. I figured by today you would be contemplating doing something stupid like not abiding by the doctor's instructions so this is my attempt to bribe you into staying put."

I frowned at him even though he was completely right about how I was feeling.

"Well, thank you," I murmured. "Ally made me soup. I don't know what she thinks is wrong with me…" We both laughed and my hand squeezed his a little tighter.

Wyatt cleared his throat. "I should go."

I ignored his statement because I couldn't bring myself to say just how much I needed him to stay. "Do you want some of the… what did you get?" I turned, finally pulling my hand from his to open the bag and beginning to pull out the cartons.

Pork lo mein. Sesame chicken. Egg rolls. Fried rice. Sweet and sour chicken. Pepper steak.

"I see what's going on here." Wyatt raised an eyebrow at me. "You're trying to feed me into a food coma so that I *can't* move for the next two days."

"Whatever it takes." He laughed.

My stomach growled. Looking at Ally's soup, I would have sworn that I was *not* hungry. But with the Chinese food sitting there… it was a whole different story.

Wyatt stood up and my eyes followed him intently, fearing that he was leaving. But he was just going to grab some forks from the kitchen. He handed me one, my whole body aware of the second that our fingers brushed.

I picked up the carton of sesame chicken, digging in to one of my favorite dishes. "Chinese is my favorite—after lodge food." I smirked at him, taking another big bite.

"Well, I thought about bringing you some fancy food from Breakers, but I figured you might enjoy this more." He teased back.

"Just a little." I smiled and reached for the lo mein. "Were you out today?" And then as if to justify my question, I said, "I watched it snow last night."

"I wasn't." He didn't elaborate, instead his eyes narrowed on me. "Did you not sleep?"

I shrugged my shoulders. My head had been throbbing last night, but I refused to take the pain medication that the doctor had prescribed; plus, I kept replaying what I'd said to him so I'd hardly slept.

"Not really."

"How are you feeling?" His voice was hoarse with concern.

"Alright. Much better today." I went back to the sesame chicken—it was the best thing on the menu. "I was thinking about going back out tomorrow…" I admitted with a sheepish grin, causing him to glare at me until he realized that I was joking.

I watched him open up the fried rice. He had to be uncomfortable sitting on the floor, but I didn't say anything. There was a silent acknowledgment between us that he was staying for the moment, even though I knew he would continue to insist that he should leave.

"Everything is just very sore," I continued, trying to break the silence. "Between the head and neck and then my hip was already hurting from last week… I'm falling apart." It was a white lie; my injuries didn't bother me that much.

I was falling apart for him.

"What did the doctor say?" He asked.

"Didn't you ask Ally?" I found it hard to believe that he'd waited a day and a half to find out.

"I want to hear it from you." Again, my heart skipped a beat.

"Nothing major. At most a minor concussion. I'll be back out on the slopes with you in no time, Olsen, don't worry."

"I wasn't," he replied. "At least not for the reasons you think." Desire immediately rolled through me. I didn't know if he was referring to our retreat into the glades, but that's all I could think about.

"I can't believe I fell," I said quietly, bringing us back to that afternoon. "I mean, I can believe it. That wasn't the right thing to say. I guess I can't believe I tried it." My admission was a necessary blow to my pride if for no other reason than to make sure I didn't try it again.

"You were riding the high. And I'm sure I was annoying as shit telling you that your double still wasn't right."

"You were telling me the truth." I set the carton of chicken down, feeling completely, disgustingly full. "It was my problem that I didn't want to listen. I seem to have this problem not infrequently." I began to hint towards the reason for my reaction that was bubbling underneath the surface, begging to be told. "Sometimes, I get an idea in my head that I *know* I need to and can accomplish even when it's not the truth or it's not the best thing to do." *And Wyatt didn't—and couldn't—know the full extent of everything that I was saying.*

"Goals… determination… it's nothing to be ashamed of, Channing." He handed me my glass of water and I took a sip.

"I know. But there's a limit to when those things are a good idea."

"You'll be able to do it." His emotionally-charged gaze locked with mine. "I know I said you weren't ready, but I didn't mean forever, Channing. You are an incredible rider. There's no doubt in my mind that you'll be able to nail this in the next few weeks. I want you to know that I have complete faith in you."

And that was the difference between him and Chance: Chance had never admitted to his faith in me that night, maybe assuming I knew that it was there—which I'm sure it was—but I'd needed to hear it.

"Chance said the same thing," I said quietly, staring down at my hands as they played with the strings of my sweatpants. I felt Wyatt pause while collecting the empty cartons of food to look up at me. "When he was teaching me the triple. He was practicing it over and over again because it was what he was going to do—what he did—in his Slopestyle pass; it was what won him the Gold."

I watched as Wyatt's large hand covered mine, stilling the anxious fidgeting of my fingers. "What happened, sweetheart?"

I wondered if he could feel the rise in my pulse from just his slightest touch.

I didn't care that he was touching me; I didn't care that he called me sweetheart. And I didn't care about the stupid competition right now.

I couldn't look at him, afraid that the tears would really begin to fall then, but I continued softly. "The day before the Open started, I landed it; it was only Chance who was there, who saw. But I landed it." I laughed a little to myself. "I was so freaking excited—I remember tackling him in the snow, laughing and crying at the same time. And he was excited too. He'd been nailing it all week, so practicing it hadn't been that much of an achievement for him, but to help me land it… He was so excited."

I pulled one of my hands out from underneath his, using the sleeve of my sweatshirt pulled up over my hand to wipe the tears from my cheeks. Remembering that night was emotional, but remembering my brother was even more so. Especially now, after Wyatt, after falling, after everything… I wished he were here so badly.

"That night, I told him I was going to do it in my heat the following day; I wanted to take gold the same way he was going to. He looked at me just like you did earlier and he said the same exact thing." My voice cracked with sorrow. "He told me that I wasn't ready."

"*Shit.*" I heard him say underneath his breath and then, before I could raise my arm again, his hand was on my cheek wiping away one tear after another with his thumb.

Before I really lost it, I blurted out the rest of the story. "I freaked out. He'd been so happy for me and then to tell me that I shouldn't do it… We'd fought before, but not like this. He thought I was being reckless. I thought he was being unsupportive; I even accused him of being jealous that I would steal his thunder—to be the first woman to land a triple." The laugh that tumbled from my lips was pained. "We didn't speak the rest of the night. Or the following morning. Obviously, I chose to do what I wanted and I bombed the landing." I inhaled shakily. "I probably didn't have the skill to land it again at that point, just like I didn't today. But that's not why I fucked it up. I remember getting up to the lip of the jump, like I was watching myself riding in slow-motion, and all I could think was that he wasn't there—he wasn't watching—because he didn't believe in me. And it broke me."

I'd never told anyone the story, letting them assume whatever they wanted about the incident; on the outside, it wasn't a big deal in the long run; on the inside, it had shattered something inside of me.

Hearing myself recount that night, that day, broke me and I couldn't stop the sobs from spilling. I'd held them all in since my fall; I didn't cry at the doctor's, I didn't cry when Emmett brought me home, I didn't cry when I vaguely told Ally what happened, and I didn't even cry at all today wondering how I was going to apologize to this gorgeous, kind, and caring man.

"*Fuck*, sweetheart." I couldn't really see through my tears, but I knew that his face was in front of me even before his forehead rested on mine. "*I'm so fucking sorry.*"

"No," I gulped, "not your fault... just can't take feeling like someone I care about doesn't believe in me."

I heard him swear again as his lips crushed mine.

Maybe it was the bump on my head. Maybe it was the fact that I was mandated by the doctor *not* to focus on the parts of my life that had, well, dominated it forever. And without those clouding my mind, the only other part of my life seemed to be *him*. I didn't want it to dominate me... *I wanted to drown in it—in him.*

Moaning, I leaned into the kiss. His hands angled my face, leading me deeper into the depths from which I knew I wouldn't return. He tasted like a drug—a rich, addicting spice that spread through every cell in my body. Nothing hurt anymore—not from the fall, not from the memories; there was nothing but him. Even though the kiss was for comfort, it wasn't soft or gentle—and I didn't want it to be. Our tongues fought each other, each spar building the burning pressure between my thighs. And I needed more. I needed to be consumed.

"I'm sorry," he groaned as he tore his lips from mine. I gulped in air, reaching up to grab his hands and keep them on my face. "I'm sorry, Channing. I shouldn't have done that. I promised you... *Fuck.*" He didn't pull his hands away by his head turned to the side slightly and I knew that I was losing him. "I don't... I just can't let you think that I don't believe in you, gorgeous." A pained laugh escaped him. His thumb brushed over my lower lip that was swollen from our kiss. "I just can't do it. You know what I think of you? Most days, I think I believe in you more than I believe in myself. Hell, lately I feel like I only believe in myself because of you." His eyes returned to mine, fire searing straight to my core as his words shot right to my heart. "You are so fucking fearless, so determined—you are so unlike anyone I've ever met. You know exactly what you want and you will do whatever it takes to make it happen. You work two jobs and still manage to be one of the best female boarders I've ever seen. And you make sure to find time to help your friends, your sister… and me."

Was I breathing? I couldn't even tell anymore.

"And it doesn't faze you because it's like you know exactly what is going to happen; you know it because you know you're going to make it happen." Finally, his gaze captured mine, overflowing with admiration, desire, and something more. "I don't just believe in you… I am in *awe* of you."

My heart was beating out of my chest as my mouth parted, my response coming from a place deep down inside of me that had been fighting for a voice ever since I'd met him. "I don't know what's going to happen, Wyatt," I whispered. "Right now, I have no fucking clue." My fingers tightened their grip on his hands, making sure he wasn't going to let go. "I don't know what's going to happen when I tell you that I want you to stay, that I want you to forget about your stupid promise and stay with me tonight. But I don't care."

I saw his jaw clench and I knew he was battling with himself over what he should do, probably wondering just *how* hard I'd hit my head after all.

"All I know is that when you are here, everything feels right, and when you aren't, there's a hole inside of me that hurts. Please," I whispered. "I don't know what's going to happen tomorrow; all I know is that I don't want to hurt tonight."

Even though he was still kneeling on the floor, he closed the slight distance that separated our faces, and I felt the warm caress of his breath against my lips and into my mouth as he rasped, "I would do anything to take your hurt away, gorgeous." His lips brushed mine. "You never have to ask me for that."

And then his mouth covered mine, only this time it was no longer with the drug-like craze, but with the tenderness that told me his only goal was to make me forget every ounce of pain tonight.

CHAPTER
Fourteen

Channing

H E KISSED ME LIKE I WAS THE MOUNTAIN AND HE WAS DETERMINED to explore every slope, every corner, every glade to its fullest. For minutes he did nothing *but* kiss me, steadily building the ache down in my core to frustrating heights. At some point, with his hands still cupping my face, he moved my head to lean it gently on the side-arm of the couch; his mouth staying locked with mine.

"So damn sweet, Channing," he groaned into my mouth before claiming it again.

My hands had moved to thread into his hair. *Knowing that I was the one to mess it up made me even hotter.*

"*I want more,*" I said against him, sucking his tongue into my mouth. I moved one of my hands onto his chest, running it down over the hard planes of his stomach, reaching for the front of his pants. I shuddered, feeling his hard length jump underneath my touch and hearing how he exhaled an expletive at the sensation.

But, his hand took my wrist and moved it back up to his chest. "Tonight… just let me make you feel whole."

I bit into my lip in anticipation and then his hands were on my waist, underneath my sweatshirt and tee. Goosebumps spread from where his fingers claimed my bare skin. With his eyes locked on mine, he pulled both pieces up over my stomach… my chest… and then, I bent forward so they could come off of my body completely.

His jaw muscle was practically vibrating as he looked down at me, my small breasts covered in a comfy, albeit lace bralette, my nipples hardening underneath his gaze. I watched him watching my chest rise and fall, the burning desire in his eyes making my core melt even more.

They didn't look like much, honestly, but in his eyes, it looked like they were everything.

His hand started on my stomach. I couldn't move—I couldn't breathe—I needed his touch. Hearing my thoughts, it slid up and covered my right breast. I gasped and Wyatt's head dropped onto my stomach with a groan.

"I've dreamt of this since the glades," he said against my stomach kissing and sucking on the skin. He groaned as his fingers found my nipple, my body arching into his touch as he tweaked the sensitive skin. I moaned his name, feeling wetness seep between my thighs. "So damn perfect."

His eyes met mine even though it was a fight to keep my lids open, my body overwhelmed with and needing the pleasure that I'd tasted earlier in the week and was now finally getting more of. His right hand slid up to my other breast and I watched as the possessiveness with which he kneaded me exponentially increased his desire. His hands engulfed my small, pert tits but instead of feeling embarrassed, his response to that fact made me feel inexplicably powerful.

His left hand continued to toy with my nipple while his right reached for the edge of the lace, pausing for a split second to give me the opportunity to stop him. Instead, my wanton self moaned, "Please."

It only took the slightest tug of his fingers to bare my breast to him, my nipple pink and begging, jutting up from milky-white skin.

He didn't pause this time; I don't think he could stop himself as his mouth slid up my stomach and captured the aching peak in his mouth. My hands returned to his hair, holding him tight against me as his mouth and hands teased the parts of me that seemed to have a direct line straight to my sex; my thighs pressed against each other as the ache became too much to bear.

"*Wyatt,*" I moaned again, not knowing how to say what I wanted. Yet, he heard what I needed.

He tugged on my nipple with his teeth and I felt the first hint of my impending climax. My stomach quivered as his hand moved over it, his fingers breaching the waistband of my sweats. I inhaled sharply as I felt the first brush of him against my folds.

"You're drenched," he groaned painfully, biting my nipple again before he came for my mouth.

My hips had a mind of their own as I felt one finger enter me. "So fucking wet, Channing..." Then two fingers, stretching me. I tongue dove into his mouth, trying to pull more from him as I felt the waves of pleasure rolling and begging to crash over me. "I'll take your hurt away." He shuddered against me and then pushed a third finger inside of my sex. I gasped. I was small and he was stretching me to the point where I was about to come from the pressure. "You're like an ocean, gorgeous," he rasped, "and I'm so fucking thirsty."

A second later he was gone from me, my eyes darting open just as he grabbed the edge of my sweats and tugged them down over my hips, baring my core to him. He yanked off his jacket and tossed it onto the other end of the couch. I could see the hard, distinct outline of his erection through his pants. He just stared at me lying bare before him, like he was branding me with his gaze.

My legs bent, spreading slightly as I tried to reign in the cells of my body that were determined to explode—a subtle invitation to where I needed him. I felt the couch dip underneath his weight as he knelt between my knees. I wasn't breathing—*I knew I wasn't*—but *I wasn't sure I needed to.*

His hands, tanner than my skin, ran slowly up my thighs, my sex clenching in anticipation. His head bent, the soft fabric of his navy sweater brushing on the insides of my legs, forcing them wider to accommodate the breadth of his shoulders.

"Has anyone ever done this to you?" He growled, his fingers slipping lightly—*too lightly*—over my folds.

I was barely coherent, barely able to process his words. *Done what? Kissed me? Ate me? Or made me lose all rational sense for the sake of passion?* All I knew was that my brain might actually explode if I didn't feel his mouth on me soon.

"*Channing,*" he growled louder, biting into the skin of my inner thigh just enough for me to register the brief pain, "*has anyone ever tasted you?*"

Now, I heard the question and immediately gasped, "No. No one."

I thought I felt the cool breath from his curse, but then my world evaporated as his mouth covered me. His tongue licked along the length of my slit and my eyes widened in shock and pleasure.

"So fucking sweet," he rasped into my sensitive skin just before his lips closed to suck on my clit. I whimpered, holding his head with both my hands as I raised my hips closer to his lips, desperate to get more of this feeling that promised to destroy me. "All fucking mine."

I panted his name, feeling my body tightening rapidly towards my release. My eyes were squeezed tight as I pushed myself against his face, shamelessly begging for more. Then his fingers joined the torment of his mouth, brushing along my entrance as he continued to drink from my core.

I bit my tongue until it bled, acknowledging that Wyatt's mouth devouring me was the best thing to ever happen to my body since snowboarding.

"Say it," he raised his head, staring at me with heady eyes, his lips glistening with my juices.

"All…" I breathed out. "Y-yours." His tongue replaced his fingers, thrusting inside of me in a way that felt more penetrating than actual sex. I shoved his head deeper between my thighs feeling my climax beginning. Oh my God.

Oh my God.

My orgasm ripped through every achingly tense muscle in my body. I didn't know it could feel like this. So powerful. So intense. Like whiplash, it flung me into the depths of exquisite pleasure over and over again, rolling through me in waves.

Oh. My. God.

I finally blinked my eyes open to reality and the incredibly arousing sight of Wyatt's head still between my legs, gently lapping at my core, bringing me back down to Earth slowly. *Shit.* My hands looked like they were about to pull out his gorgeous hair the way I was still clutching to his head. I quickly released them, the sudden movement causing his eyes to rise to mine.

Even though my body burned for him—burned for more—that look made heat flood into my cheeks for a whole different reason. He kissed me gently before pushing himself up and pulling my underwear and sweats back over my hips; my panties sat uncomfortably bunched against my tender skin and I would have rather just taken them off but I wasn't going to.

"What now?" I asked quietly.

He smiled slightly at me, "Now, you get some rest because as soon as your doctor's orders are up, I'm getting that sweet ass of yours back out on the slopes and nailing that triple, solidifying your place as the most impressive—and sexiest—woman I've ever met."

Son of a biscuit, I felt like I was about to cry again, his ridiculously simple words touching my heart. I didn't trust myself to respond, so I just nodded trying to blink back the now-happy tears.

I saw him wince as he bent to retrieve my shirt, his pants digging into his arousal painfully. *I couldn't let him leave like that—although what he'd just done to me was going to be a tough act to follow.*

"Wyatt…"

"Sit up," he said gruffly, and I complied, raising my arms above my head so he could slip my sweatshirt back on. As soon as it was over me, I dropped my hand to cup his arousal. "*Fuck,*" he swore and stepped back.

My brows furrowed with hurt and confusion. *Why didn't he want my touch?*

He pinched the bridge of his nose as he knelt in front of me, taking my hands in his.

"I want to make you feel good," I blurted out dumbly, wishing I'd said something just a tad bit sexier, but I just wasn't that kind of girl.

His hand cupped my face, and his eyes stared intently at my lips, as though he were picturing them somewhere else on his body. "I know, sweetheart, and I do." My lips parted. "I'm more than good with what just happened here. I'm more than good knowing that not only did you give me the privilege to take away your pain, but that you trusted me with a part of you that no one else has had before." I couldn't look away from his eyes and the depth of emotion in them that was swallowing me whole. "Relieving *this--*" He glanced down at his cock that looked like it was about to poke a hole through his pants, "—would be nothing compared to the pleasure you've already given me."

His head leaned in and he claimed my lips softly one more time. I could taste myself on him, the pleasure that he'd freed inside of me; it began the ache in my core all over again.

"I've won a lot of things, Channing—the Open, the X Games, the Olympics—but none of them tasted as sweet as you." *Swoon.*

I groaned as he pulled his head back to stand. *I didn't want him to go.* "I'm going to go fill the bathtub for you and then I'm going to go," his eyes darkened, "before I break every gentlemanly attempt that I'm making right now."

Break them and take me, I wanted to say but he was gone before I had the chance.

I sat frozen for a second before taking the opportunity to adjust my clothes, fixing my underwear that were wet and uncomfortably bunched up against me and righting my shirt and bra. I grabbed my cup of water, gulping down several mouthfuls in an attempt to moisten my throat that felt as dry as the desert. I looked around for my phone, finding it wedged between the cushions of the couch. I saw there was a text from Ally.

ALLY
On our way back. Karaoke crowd was unacceptable.

I smiled to myself. *Poor Zack.* Ally had an unhealthy obsession with karaoke and it was her first suggestion whenever she was given the chance. I looked at the time. Her text had come through ten minutes ago, right when my phone was the last thing I would have noticed.

Good thing Wyatt had turned me down... otherwise that would have been a very uncomfortable situation for Zack and Ally to—

"Helloooo!" Ally's sing-song voice rang out through the hall. *What timing...*

I heard two sets of footsteps approaching me so Zack must have come inside with her. "Glad to see you haven't moved!" She was smiling and completely serious.

"Of course not. I knew what I'd have to put up with from you... all of you... if I did." I rolled my eyes.

"How you doing there champ?" Zack asked. "I hope you enjoyed your sister's soup." He winked at Ally and looped his arm around her waist. I watched her return his smile, only hers didn't quite spread all the way across her face.

"I... I went with the Chinese food. Sorry, Al." I shrugged sheepishly, knowing she'd see the empty cartons in the garbage anyway.

Zack's head looked over his shoulder and then back at me. "Hey, where is that big brother of mine?"

I felt my face reddening by the second even though my answer was completely harmless. It was going to take at least an hour to be able to think of the man without seeing his face between my legs and his mouth devouring me.

"Yeah, Chan, where is Mr. Milk-Frother?"

Zack's eyes shot to my sister as he began to laugh; I didn't care about him. But, of course, that exact moment was when my Mr. Milk-Frother strolled back into the kitchen just in time to hear Ally's comment.

"Mr. Milk-Frother?" Zack had the audacity to repeat.

At least my face had a legitimate reason for being beet-red right now, I thought as I groaned and tried to sink deeper into the couch, refusing to look at any of them.

"Zack…" Wyatt's raspy voice drawled through the space, a subtle suggestion that he should let it go.

"You're definitely going to have to explain that one to me later, babe," he whispered not-so-quietly to my sister.

"Alright, we should get going." I heard Wyatt walking towards me. He picked up his jacket off the couch, throwing it on, his eyes locked with mine. I could hear Zack and Ally 'saying' their goodbyes, but Wyatt and I could only stare at each other. "I'll see you Monday."

This time it definitely wasn't a question. "Thank you," I answered softly. I saw him glance quickly to his brother and my sister who were still too preoccupied to notice us, before he took two steps towards me, his head bending to my ear.

"No, gorgeous, thank you." I shivered. And then his mouth claimed mine hard and fast because he needed to and because neither of us were the blatant PDA kind of people; especially when whatever was between us was as undefinable, yet as unstoppable as a snowstorm.

A second later he was gone, pulling his brother out with him, leaving my sister grinning just until the door shut when seriousness rained down on her features.

"I'm injured," I began preemptively. "My brain is too traumatized to answer questions right now." Clever, entertaining, but not enough to stop a sister on a mission. I stood as she rounded the couch—my eyes darting not-so-inconspicuously over me to make sure there was no evidence of Wyatt's touch.

"What happened?" She crossed her arms, looking from me, to the couch, to the untouched bowl of soup.

"I said nothing." I smiled sweetly at her before turning towards the kitchen, anticipating my bath. "Thanks for the soup, sis," I tossed over my shoulder, attempting anything to keep control of the conversation during my escape, "but Wyatt brought me food. So, unless you want it, you should probably throw it."

"I'm fine. But don't worry, *sis*," she returned, her tone oozed sweetness, far more than mine—*practice makes perfect*, "there's plenty more soup in the fridge. Did you think I just made one bowl?" I swallowed my groan. "You can have some tomorrow for lunch!"

Son of a biscuit. Damn soup... and damn sister.

"You want to know how I know that you're lying, that it's not just nothing?" Her laughter floated behind me as I tried to escape to the stairs and I knew I was in trouble. "Because your freaking sweatpants are on backwards—and I have a feeling they aren't the only things!"

My head jerked down, pulling out my waistband. Sure enough, my sweats, which in my defense looked the same in the front and the back, were on backwards. *No wonder my freaking underwear felt so uncomfortable.* I groaned out loud, taking the stairs two at a time. I breathed a sigh of relief when I didn't hear her footsteps behind me.

I thought—*hoped*—she'd given up as I turned on the water, only to be mostly naked when she came barging into the bathroom. My hand flew to my chest to stop my heart from jumping out of my chest.

"Are you trying to give me a stroke?" I stepped into the steaming, lavender-scented bathwater.

"Are you trying to avoid my question?" She pushed herself up to sit on the sink counter, smiling at me and waiting for me to cave. "Don't bother answering that—I know you are. But, I'm not going to leave you alone—and lucky for you, I'm the one who is taking care of your brain-damaged tush for the near future. So, unless you want soup for *every* meal, I suggest you start talking."

I closed my eyes; she drove a hard bargain.

"I apologized to him for making him out to be the bad guy on the mountain the other day." She wasn't impressed. And I wasn't going to tell her the whole story so that she would be; Emmett had said enough when he'd dropped me off before they began fighting. "He apologized for yelling at me. We talked a little and then ate some dinner."

"I really do have a *lot* of soup left." Ally flipped her hand over, pretending to examine her nails in boredom.

I groaned and half sunk underneath the water, wishing I could disappear underneath its surface. "What do you want, Al?"

"The truth about what's going on between the two of you. I mean, we come home one night to see you two relaxing on the couch. You don't say anything about it. Then, I have to hear from someone else that you're blowing off Emmett and Nick to spend time with Wyatt even though you two sure don't act like a couple around anyone."

"I haven't had a chance to really talk to you—you're always with Zack!"

She huffed and rolled her eyes. "Don't you start with me too." Her eyes narrowed on me. "Did you tell him to say that? Did you tell him to say something to me?"

My face scrunched at her. "What? Tell who to say what?"

"Your asshole friend, Emmett. He said basically the same thing to me tonight. Is there a problem that I'm hanging out with Zack?"

"When did you see Emmett?"

"Oh my God. At the karaoke bar, which is why we left. I told you that the crowd was unacceptable; I couldn't stand being in that jerk's presence one more minute." I closed my eyes, listening as her anger got the better of her curiosity. "He literally must have done five shots in the first five minutes of being there, only to come over and give me attitude about how the Olsen's show up and we lose our 'pretty little heads.'" I peeked one eye open; Ally was really getting worked up about this. "Then going on about how I was spending too much time with Zack and that I was too young—*can you believe that!* I'm almost twenty!"

I bit my lip so that I wouldn't chuckle at her distress. I didn't know why she let Emmett get to her; then again, I didn't know why he insisted on trying to get to her. I'd have to talk to him.

Ally threw her hands up. "No. I digress. And, if you couldn't tell, I'm not in the mood. What is going on with you and Wyatt?"

"Nothing." I sighed. "I don't know. Honestly. I don't know. There's obviously *something* going on between us, but I keep fighting it."

Until tonight.

"Why?"

I stared down at my toes peeking up above the water. "Because," I admitted softly, "I don't want to hurt him any more than I have to." My confession wasn't just to her.

"What are you talking about?" She slid down off the counter.

"I asked him to help me learn the trick that will help me beat him in the Slopestyle competition."

"Wait, what?"

"I asked him to help me. That's why I've been ditching Emmett and Nick in the mornings. I asked Wyatt to teach me the triple because I told him I wanted to attempt it in the Open. Only, I'm really going to attempt it in two weeks in our Slopestyle run. I basically asked him to teach me how to win against himself, only he doesn't know that. And if he figures it out, I don't want that betrayal to be magnified by any feelings that we may or may not have for each other."

Silence.

I hazarded a glance at her; she still looked angry.

"Well, I think it's safe to say that those feelings are there—the roses alone should have been a clue. But I think you need to make a choice to either explore them or keep him out of your life for good, because letting *this* linger for the sake of a stupid trick, is cruel. If you don't want him, then break it off. If you do want him, then you better figure out just how much because there are some things in life more important than winning, Channing." My mouth dropped open and then shut again, begrudgingly admitting that my *baby* sister had a very good point.

It wasn't just a 'stupid trick,' but she was right nonetheless.

"Alright," she sighed, apparently giving up on our conversation, "I'm going to bed. I'll see you in the morning."

Her hand stopped on the doorknob as I said, "Ally…" She looked over at me as I reached down to open up the drain. "Thank you," I paused, "for the soup, I mean."

That earned me a small smile from her as she left me to dry off in peace.

I *did* want Wyatt. And tonight, I wasn't afraid to admit to that, even if it was just to myself. Maybe it was the trauma to my head from falling; more likely it was the trauma to my unused heart from falling for *him*.

I had this nagging feeling that at some point, as stupid as it sounded, I was going to have to make a choice between Wyatt and my brother. But not giving in to my feelings for Wyatt would have been like never attempting the triple again—it would have been letting the fear of the unknown limit me from reaching for the stars; *and I wasn't that kind of girl.*

Look out, Wyatt Olsen—I don't know what it is or what I do to make you want me, but you better strap on your helmet, because it's looking mighty cold on Monday and I'm going to need you to keep me very, very warm.

CHAPTER
Fifteen

Channing

"Channing!" I groaned as Ally banged on my door. "It's almost eleven!"

My eyes flew open, the realization that I had nothing to do today—no boarding, no lessons, no work—only coming after the point where adrenaline had already flooded my body and I sat up in bed thinking that I was late.

"What's up?" I croaked, wiping my eyes open wider.

"How are you feeling? How's your head? Any headache? Dizziness? You know we need to call Dr. Lam if you notice any new symptoms."

I pinched the bridge of my nose. "Only from your helicoptering." I flashed a quick smile at her frown. "No headache. No dizziness. Just a severe case of laziness."

"Well, I don't know the last time you had a day off, so I think it's just what the doctor ordered." She flipped her hair over her shoulder, instinctively causing me to run my fingers through my own. "Anyway, Zack wanted to come and take me to lunch and I didn't know how you were feeling and I didn't want to leave you. But, since you're doing fine, I'm going to let him know he can come get me."

"Ok, sure. Yeah, I'll be fine." I turned and walked back into my dimly lit room away from the light in the hall.

My room was nothing special and sparsely decorated. There were a few frames of mountain photos on my wall that I had taken over the years at wherever Chance and my competitions had taken us—Vermont, Canada, Wyoming—and then two photos on my dresser: one of Chance and me at the Open last year and one of our whole family at Christmas. The only other decorations were medals and trophies of the competitions that I'd won—reminding me what I'd always been working towards. Everything else though was white—the walls, my dresser and nightstand, my bed and bedspread. I like to think it was because I loved snow and not because I was just *that* basic.

Picking up my phone and pulling it off the charger, the screen lit to show several messages. *Tammy, Nick, and Emmett.*

I opened up Tammy's first, knowing that I'd left her high and dry for an instructor for lessons this weekend.

TAMMY
Hey, just want to see how you're feeling! Don't worry about your lessons! I asked Jax to cover them and he was more than happy to. Just focus on getting better and I'll see you soon!

I quickly tapped back out a reply, grateful to have her as a friend and coworker, thanking her for everything. I didn't even remember talking to her that day which meant that either Emmett or Wyatt had let her know what had happened and why I wouldn't be making it to my lessons; since Emmett was with me at the doctor's, that only left Wyatt who'd made sure that everything was taken care of. *I wasn't surprised by his thoughtfulness even in the face of my thoughtlessness.*

NICK
Hope you're feeling better!

Typical, canned response from Frost, but that was a lot for him. Last, I opened up the text from Emmett.

EMMETT
I'll be by later.

Typical Emmett. Caring, yet controlling to a fault. I wasn't sure what 'later' meant since I received the text at eight this morning, but it's not like I had big plans today anyway. *Unless Wyatt was coming by.*

I bit into my lip wondering if he was going to come over with his brother. *What was I going to say?* My stomach clenched. *'Thanks for the take-out and for eating me out'?*

I groaned. *Nice, Channing. Real nice.*

Maybe this is why I didn't get involved with guys because I had no idea how to deal. I mean, the man had just had his tongue inside of me—did that make us a thing? Did that make us official? Because, even though I wanted him, I wasn't sure I wanted that right now; I still couldn't let myself drop out of the Games. I just couldn't let my brother down like that.

I waited until I heard my sister's door shut before heading into the bathroom to brush my teeth and wash my face. I may not have a serious head injury, but I sure looked like I did—my eyes were groggy, my hair was sticking out in all directions because I'd climbed into bed with it wet last night.

My head jerked up as the doorbell rang. *Zack. Maybe Wyatt.*

I wanted to see him, but I didn't want to see him like this. Hearing Ally heading for the door, I quickly ran my hand underneath the faucet, trying to subdue my short locks, trying to press down the strays before I walked out into the hall.

I was only to the top of the stairs when I heard Ally yell, "Channing, the asshole—I mean, Emmett is here to see you."

My pace immediately slowed as I reached the bottom of the steps, just as my sister stormed around the corner. For a second, it looked like she was on the brink of crying, but my neck burned as it tried to follow her and see for sure; the muscles cramped from my fall and forced my head back straight again to see Emmett standing in front of me.

"Lil." Emmett's voice rasped. His face looked angry and tortured and I wondered what had just happened between him and Ally. *I forgot that I wanted to talk to her about that.* "How you doing?"

"I'm alright." I smiled and tilted my head, signaling that he should follow me into the kitchen.

"Nick says 'hey.' He's behind on some shit, but he said he'd see you Monday."

"Yeah, he texted me." I reached into the fridge, pulling out a pre-made yogurt shake. "You didn't talk to Tammy about my lessons, did you?"

"Fuck. No. I probably should have though. Did they not have anyone to cover?"

I slightly shook my head, twisting off the cap. "No, no. It's fine. They are fine. I was just wondering…" *So, it had been Wyatt.*

His jaw muscle flexed as he rubbed his hand over his red halo of hair. "What were you doing with Olsen?"

His tone immediately had me on the defensive. "What do you mean?"

"I mean, what the hell was he doing carrying you down from the mountain?" His hand came up to stop my smart-ass response that he was carrying me because I'd just fallen on my head. "Not what I meant. Why were you with him? I thought you were picking up extra lessons and that's why you weren't riding with us in the morning."

I felt my cheeks beginning to flush. I may have alluded to that. I was afraid to admit that I'd taken his sarcastic suggestion to heart; I was afraid of the questions it might bring.

"I asked him to teach me the triple." I made sure to keep my gaze locked with his, showing confidence in spite of my concern.

"Jesus…" He swore. "Why? Chance already taught you; you don't fucking need him." His black eyes glistened like dark diamonds at me.

"Over a year ago he taught me. And I haven't done it since. Obviously, I'm still doing something wrong because I can't nail it and I need someone to coach me who can tell me exactly what I need to change. And, in case you haven't noticed, Chance isn't here—for *any* of us anymore; he's gone.

"Channing…" His voice was a warning that I sounded like I was about to say something that I didn't mean—*only I did mean it.*

"I don't know when he's coming back and I'm not going to bank on it anymore. He. Is. Gone. And I don't care about the fact that he can't snowboard anymore—at least competitively—the mountain wasn't the only goddamn thing here that he cared about." I sucked in a ragged breath, feeling angry tears clogging my throat. "Or maybe it was. And that's what I need to accept because I need to move forward. I need to learn the triple. And I need to learn that I can't rely on my brother like I thought… like I did."

Emmett was surprised by my outburst and honestly, I'd shocked myself with my vehemence. I felt it bubbling up inside of me ever since he left, but I kept pushing it down because I should feel bad for him; I should feel empathetic and sympathetic and every other pitiable emotion for him. So, I buried the anger even though I knew it couldn't stay buried forever—pieces of it kept breaking up and floating to the surface.

"You know that's complete bullshit, right?" He asked casually.

"Why are you defending him? He left you, too. He stranded all you SnowmassHoles."

Emmett lightly pounded his fist on the countertop. "Because I'm a grown man, Lil—and you're a grown woman. Yes, Pride is my friend and yes, I'm fucking concerned for him, but you act like you are nothing without him." He let out a harsh laugh. "You always have. I get it—you're siblings, you're twins—but you're out there always trying to best him, to be him, instead of just being yourself." His words paralyzed me. "You aren't angry because he fucking left; you're angry because you've fucking followed his path for your entire life and now, without him, you think you don't know where to go." *This was hurting; this was really hurting.* "How about instead of resenting your brother for trying to deal with his own shit, you look in the mirror and deal with the real problem."

I wiped a frustrated tear from my eye, hating to cry in front him. I needed to change the conversation away from Chance—and away from the thoughts that struck too close to home.

I had lived in Chance's shadow—or at least shared the spotlight with him—for so long. *Maybe I was angry because without him, I was starting to realize that I didn't know who I was.*

I didn't want to talk about my sibling anymore—at least not that one. Now, I was angry at Emmett for throwing all his perceptions on me with no warning and I wasn't going to let this end without making him feel just as uncomfortable about truths that he was equally wanting to ignore.

"Yeah?" I wiped away one last tear before smirking angrily at him. "How about you take some of your own advice? Are you still refusing to see your mom?" I knew that was a trigger and he was ready to fire at me. "Or how you deal with the real problem between you and Ally? I saw how upset she looked just now; she's always upset whenever she mentions you or has to see you or ride with you." I leveled a hard stare on him; *it was my turn to ask the probing questions.* "Why is that? What's going on? What happened between you two?"

His mouth thinned and I wondered if he was going to answer me. I watched as he walked behind me to open the fridge and grab a water bottle; he and Nick always made themselves at home here—our unofficial other siblings.

"She's a hormonal teenager. What else do you expect?" He ignored my first question which was no surprise. He never discussed Miriam.

Interesting answer. "She's turning twenty in like a month, Emmett. Not a teenager for much longer." I took another sip of my drink, trying to listen to him but more trying to calm my nerves.

"I don't know what you want me to say, Lil." *Why was he angry at me? He was the one upsetting my sister.* He sighed. "Look, Chance isn't here and I'm just trying to look out for the both of you and I don't think she should be seeing Zack. He's too old for her and he's a douche."

Zack was only my age—maybe a year older than me, which would make him a year or so younger than Emmett; I didn't think that was a big age gap. And I didn't think that he was a douche.

"She's just having fun," I murmured. "She can take care of herself and I think Zack is a nice guy. I mean, they did get pretty intense pretty quickly, but it's fine."

"Yeah," he scoffed.

"What was that for?" Now, I was getting pissed.

"She's a kid; she doesn't know what the hell she wants or what she's doing. The whole reason she's here is because she's running away from something and whatever it is, she running straight into the arms of stupidity." His words came as a surprise to me, immediately starting to turn the wheels in my head, seeing my sister in a whole new light and wondering just what I'd been missing. Before I could recover from those thoughts, he spat, "Plus, I didn't realize that fucking his brother automatically made him a nice guy."

My eyes shot to his, my face immediately flushing with embarrassment at his words even as my body radiated with anger. "What the hell is your problem?" He had the decency to look surprised by my outburst. "First off, I'm not *fucking* his brother." *Not yet, at least.* I swallowed a groan. "Second off, I can't believe you just fucking said that to me, dick." I whipped the lid of my yogurt drink at him. "If Chance were here, he'd tell you that you've gone too fucking far. You're like a brother to me and I know you care about both Ally and me—and I'm grateful for everything that you did for me on Friday, you know that I am. But, as your friend, I'm going to look out for you here and tell you to sort out whatever is up your ass and causing you to be more of a jerk than usual because it's becoming a problem."

I didn't know what the hell happened between him and Ally, but I was tired of having to deal with the repercussions from both sides, especially when my own life was walking on a tightrope between winning and wrecking. "Figure it out and then handle it with my sister. But, I don't see Zack leaving the picture any time soon, so you better figure that shit into your plans."

He glared at me for a minute, then slowly drank down the remainder of the water bottle. I felt my mouth parting, tempted to say more just to break the silence, but I didn't know what else to say. A cold smirk spread over his face and I cringed, really thinking about what I'd said. *He was an ass, but he was a caring ass; maybe I should have been a little more patient.*

"Alright then. Guess I'll see you two around then," he replied callously as he crushed the water bottle between his hands. Ally chose that moment to come back downstairs, her gaze on Emmett cold and unfazed. "Enjoy your Olsen obsession." He'd been talking to me, but I wasn't sure that he was anymore. Ally just ignored him, walking into the living room to sit on the couch.

I watched Emmett's jaw flex before he stalked towards the front door—apparently fed up with both Ryder sisters. I followed a few steps behind, suddenly afraid of leaving things the way they were between us.

I'd already lost one brother. I didn't want to lose another.

He swung the door open and before I could say a word we saw Zack standing on the other side, about to knock.

"Hey, man," Zack greeted him with a smile.

Emmett just scoffed in disgust and I heard him mumble "cradle-robber" underneath his breath as he walked out. Even Ally's excited footsteps as she flew past me didn't entice him to turn around; he was done with us.

For right now. I knew at some point, the mountain would bring us back to good terms—it always did.

"What's his problem?" Zack asked; I was unsure if he was talking to Ally or me, but I just stayed silent hoping that she would answer.

"He's an ass," came her annoyed response. "I'm ready."

With a sigh, I turned and tried to mitigate the situation that Ally was instigating with her response. "He's just very protective of us both and concerned about me after the fall and everything…" *Too vague. Too quietly indistinct. But it was the best I had.*

Zack just stared at me for a second—a second for me to realize that Wyatt wasn't with him. My spirits immediately sank until he shoved a bag in my direction.

"Here. The glorified messenger was told to give you this care package from my *dear* brother." My heart gave an extra thump as I took it from him.

"Thanks," I murmured.

"What did you get?" Ally asked, trying to look inside.

"I thought you were leaving." I didn't want to share; she had her man. I was going to enjoy whatever Wyatt had sent alone, with his memory.

She rolled her eyes. "Fine. I'll just see it later."

"C'mon, doll." Zack wrapped his arm around her waist and led her through the door.

"Call me if you need me, Chan!" Ally yelled over her shoulder, but I was already shutting the door; *I was fine.*

I began to look through the bag as I walked into the kitchen; whatever was inside smelled delicious. He'd definitely sent food. *Thank God.*

Each item inside was accompanied by a sticky note on top. The first was the delicious smelling one.

'*So you don't have to eat soup again.*' I smiled, popping open the lid to see Pad Thai inside.

'*So you don't have to decide what to do. (Although I can't stop you from falling asleep.)*' I laughed, pulling the note off to see 'A Walk to Remember' underneath—one of my favorites; after this morning, I could use a good cry.

The last thing was the smallest. I lifted it out to read, '*Dessert. Spoiler: it doesn't taste as delicious as you.*'

Son of a biscuit.

My heart flipped and I crossed my legs as the memory of him between them hit me like a wrecking ball. I leaned against the countertop, laughing ridiculously at myself. It was only later than I actually took the note off to see that it was chocolate.

Emmett was right; I'd been trying to *be* my brother for so long, to want what Chance wanted, that I was afraid to want anything for myself. Until now.

I wanted Wyatt; he was the first thing that I wanted for myself and I'd be damned if I was too afraid to take him.

CHAPTER
Sixteen

Wyatt

I'D FORCED MYSELF TO STAY AWAY SUNDAY, SETTLING FOR SENDING her some Thai food, a DVD copy of *A Walk to Remember*, and some dark chocolate. Thai food because I wasn't going to send Chinese again, more Nicholas Sparks because she'd fallen asleep during the last one and I liked reminding her of her guilty pleasure, and dark chocolate because… well, what woman doesn't like chocolate? Plus, it was just like her: decadent, delicious, with a subtle hint of fucking ecstasy that kept you coming back for more.

I'd spent the day on the slopes, knowing that the snow was the only thing that would be able to keep me from her—*but just barely.*

There was nothing that could keep my thoughts from her though—*her and the sweetness between her thighs.*

I groaned, my cock stirring at the thought, hoping she was just as tortured by my note as I had been. She'd tasted so damn fresh, melting on my tongue like snow—and I'd been the one to make the first tracks over her, claiming her as mine.

Yeah, when her head was concussed and she probably wasn't in her right mind. But the look on her face, the way her body ignited under my touch, the way she'd begged for me to make her feel good; I couldn't turn her down. I'd come to realize that there wasn't anything that I could turn her down for. And while I couldn't regret it, I also wasn't going to let it happen again until I knew for sure how she felt.

And I swore that I wouldn't sleep with her until the Games were over; I wouldn't allow any chance for the possibility of doubt to enter her mind that maybe I was just using her to get to her brother to win the competition.

I knew he mustn't be happy about whatever was between Channing and me—or between Ally and Zack for that matter—because I hadn't seen him at all. He'd probably opted to go out with Emmett and Nick whenever he heard an Olsen was coming over. I wanted to talk to him; I wanted to tell him just how serious my intentions toward his sister were becoming and that this competition could go fuck itself for all I cared. I only cared about her.

But he didn't know me and just knowing how protective I felt about her after only a few weeks, I wouldn't believe me either.

It had only been a day, but I was so anxious for her to get here already.

I zipped up my jacket, looking up to see Channing approach. Forget a little black dress and heels; I'd taken this woman in her snow pants and boots any day.

"Hey." Her blue eyes pierced right through me.

"Hey."

A gust of wind blew through the silence between us. It wasn't an awkward silence though; it was the kind of stillness that preceded the kind of moment where I threw my board down, hauled her into my arms, and took her right here at the base of the mountain. Or where I forced those desires to remain at bay and we pretended that tearing each other apart wasn't what we both wanted most.

"How are you feeling?" I picked up my board and we began to walk toward the lift, opting for option number two.

"Fine, but I felt fine yesterday too; I could have been out here."

"Well, your brain and I thank you for deciding against it," I teased as we strapped in.

"It was mostly because of Ally's wrath that I didn't attempt it." She laughed. "Although, I will admit that the chocolate and the movie coaxed me into being comfortably sedentary."

"Not the Thai food?"

"No. That saved my stomach from having to endure three meals consisting of Ally's attempt at chicken noodle soup—which I'm pretty sure came from a box yet she still somehow managed to mess it up." I laughed, looking over at the grin lighting up her face as we rode up the lift. "Was the movie a subtle hint that I should keep my chick-flick watching to solitary evenings?"

I shook my head, laughing a little harder. "Not in the slightest. However, I would like it if you could at least stay awake for it when I'm there, although you're pretty adorable when you sleep."

I knew that I wanted to try to cool things off between us until the Games were over because, given another opportunity, I wasn't sure that I'd be able to control myself or my desire for her again; but I couldn't stop myself from complimenting her every chance that I got.

"So, what's on the agenda for today, Master Yoda?" She asked as soon as we came to a stop off the lift. I didn't object to the change in subject.

"The park." She raised her eyebrows, but she didn't say anything, pulling her goggles over her head before strapping in. I watched as she went ahead of me, ducking as she tossed a snowball half-heartedly back over her shoulder at me.

"Start with the double," I said as I came to a stop beside her at the top of the run. "And take it easy." I cautioned her, wondering if it was the right thing to do—putting her back up in the air her first day back; she wouldn't accept anything less.

"Yeah, yeah," she sighed and we both dropped onto the trail.

"Last run?" I questioned, even though I knew it was. We'd stayed in the park all morning and, not only had she not fallen, but she'd managed to nail the double to perfection. I'd even suggested to take a break and do some other tricks as a breather, but she wouldn't hear it; I'd never seen someone so determined before. She'd put her mind to doing this and as I watched her do the same jump over and over again, I knew that there was nothing that would be able to stand in her way.

Keeping her in the park—in the open—had also forced me to keep my hands to myself since the trail was completely devoid of trees and much wider than some of the other runs, making any type of seclusion impossible.

But now, we were on the lift and she was staring off as though something was on her mind.

She nodded; her nonverbal response making me wonder even more.

"You're pretty quiet over there, Miss Ryder," I mused. "I'll admit that I'm a little afraid of what you might be plotting in that pretty head of yours."

She laughed, murmuring, "Nothing."

"Let me guess. You're trying to think of the best way to convince me to let you try the triple today—your first day back after nearly breaking your neck attempting that very trick." I wouldn't put it past her and I wasn't sure that I could say she wasn't ready—not after how she did today. Although, it had been a long morning, probably not the best time to try.

She looked about to respond, but waited until we were off the lift.

"No, that's not what I was thinking, Mr. Olsen." A bit of cheekiness returned to her voice. "Actually, I was going to ask if we could do the glades."

Now, I was shocked. I would have thought that with all the time we spent on the mountain last week and then with her missing the whole weekend, she wouldn't want to shred anything but the park until she nailed her triple; again, she surprised me.

"Fine with me." I clipped in.

"Hope you can keep up!" I looked up at her words to see her already sailing down the mountain. *Oh, so that's how this was going to go?*

I gained speed; I was going to catch her.

And then I was never going to let her go.

Channing

My heart had been in my throat all morning and I couldn't seem to get it to go back into my chest. Even when Zack had shown up and given me the care package from Wyatt, I still felt disappointed that he hadn't come himself. I wanted to see him again, especially after *everything*...

God, I was acting like a teenager, replaying the events of the night over again in my mind, but they were so much better than the movie he'd sent—which I still watched, but mostly because he'd sent it. I was turning into one of those girls that I'd always sneered at: the ones who put on makeup to go to the mountain hoping to pick up a snowboarder of their own. Granted, I didn't have the makeup on today—*I wasn't that far gone.*

I showed up at our normal meeting spot wondering just how awkward I was going to make this.

The answer was very awkward; I was going to make this very awkward.

The second I saw him I felt a rush of moisture between my legs and my nipples hardened and instead of being grateful for the layers to hide it, I wished he could see just how much I wanted him; a day apart had only made it worse.

Now, we had time for one run and it was like nothing had happened between us. He wasn't cold or rude, but he also didn't act like he'd had his tongue all over my privates forty-eight hours ago. *And that was unacceptable.*

I smiled to myself; good thing I was determined to remedy it. "Hope you can keep up!" I taunted him, flying towards the privacy of the glades. *This mountain was about to get a whole lot hotter.*

I made sure he was close enough behind me to see as I veered off the loosely designated trail into the trees. The ride was a little bumpy since it hadn't snowed in a few days; apparently they were calling for a decent snowsquall at the end of the week. *Yes, I'd resorted to watching the weather channel after the movie had ended.*

I swung my board to a stop in a small clearing, quickly unstrapped and dug the side into the snow so it didn't slide away. And then, I waited.

"Channing!" I heard a few seconds before I saw him carving through the trees. I was going to yell back, but I could tell the second he spotted me. "What are you doing?" He skated to a stop.

Now or never.

I jogged in front of him, standing close enough to prevent him from being able to bend down and unstrap.

"Channing..." He rasped, standing stock-still as I reached up, pulling his goggles up off of his face so that I could look in his eyes. His expression shifted and I knew that he wasn't mistaking where my actions were leading.

I bit my lip, lowering my gaze for a moment. The temperature in our own little glade was rising quickly with the tension between us. My hands found his chest and the sharp intake of his breath through the layers. "What are you doing, gorgeous?"

I began to pull the zipper of his jacket down. "Warming us."

Wyatt groaned. "Channing, I don't think this is a good idea." *But he didn't stop me.*

My breathing was heavy as my pulse skyrocketed. "Why not?" I dared him for an answer.

"Because--" he growled as my hands rested on his chest, "you are still recovering..." I hoped he stopped because he knew what a load of BS that was.

"And I wasn't the other night?"

"The other night I should have been stronger. I shouldn't have taken advantage." My hands skated lower onto his stomach. "You... said you didn't want this."

"*I lied.*" I looked up at him. "*I want you.*"

My hand dropped down onto the front of his pants, the thrill of success and anticipation as my fingers found his hard length throbbing for my touch.

"*Fuck*," he rasped and in it I heard the end of his dissent.

His mouth dropped to mine and my tongue immediately sought his. We devoured each other, needing more than what our clothes and present circumstances could accommodate. *But that didn't mean I didn't have a plan.*

My hand teased him through his snowpants before finding their fastening. I made quick work of the zipper, eagerly reaching underneath the waistband of his briefs to feel his hardness.

"You have no idea how much I want you," he whispered against my mouth. Lightning struck throughout my body, leaving a tingling mess of desire in its wake. I tugged his briefs and pants down slightly, pulling his erection out slightly so that my hand had freedom to move. His hiss at the cold air on his cock was quickly transformed into a groan as I began to pump my fist down his hard, hot length. "Pretty fucking cold out here, gorgeous," he laughed painfully.

I smiled and grabbed his lower lip between my teeth, sucking it hard into my mouth before letting it go. "Have you learned nothing from me, Mr. Olsen?" He groaned as I fisted him harder, his hands coming to rest on my waist to steady himself as he tried to balance on the edge of his board so he didn't slide into me.

I stopped my hand, waiting for his eyes to shoot open to look at me.

"Kissing keeps you warm." I felt my inner muscles clench just from the look of confusion-shock-anticipation on his face. *Was it possible to orgasm just from pleasuring someone else?*

I dropped to my knees right in front of his board, locking my lips around his tip.

"Oh, fuck…" His hand speared into my hair as I took my time sucking him all the way into my mouth, knowing that the harsh transition from cold to hot must be exquisite. Once inside, I swallowed, letting my throat muscles caress his head, feeling it pulse and release a small taste of his desire against my tongue.

He groaned my name, holding my head tight against him as my tongue licked and teased up his length as I took his cock in and out of my mouth. My own body was on edge knowing what I was doing to him, feeling his legs shake as his feet remained locked in his bindings, forced to keep his muscles flexed to stay balanced on the edge of his board even though they wanted to give way. His hips began to move, pushing himself against the back of my throat harder and faster.

"I'm going to come, gorgeous," he rasped, but I could feel the tremors in his erection before he even got the words out. In response, I slipped my hand down to cup him and he exploded. His shout echoed into the silence of the mountain as I felt his desire coat the inside of my mouth. He pumped into me, riding out his orgasm, and I swallowed every last drop, wanting to savor the delicious proof of how much he wanted me.

Slowly sliding his erection out of my mouth, I quickly pulled his clothes up to shield him from the cold. Hazarding a glance up at him, I was met with the potent desire that clouded his eyes as he looked at me.

"*You...*" He began hoarsely. I shot him my best confidently sexy smile before purposely licking my lips as I stood back up in front of him. "That was the fucking hottest thing I have ever done." His words were like a caress on my self-conscious and sensitized soul. I bit my lip again and he immediately raised a hand, his thumb pulling the flesh from between my teeth, silently assessing the soft skin that had just ripped him apart.

"We should go," I murmured with a small smile. There weren't too many riders that would venture this far off of the trail, but I didn't want to take any more chances.

I turned and took one step before his arm snaked around my waist, pulling me back hard against his body. I lost my balance and I was surprised that he was able to remain standing—still being strapped to his board, his muscles overly exerted from what I'd just done.

"What makes you think," his voice caressed my ear, "that I'm just going to let you walk off without my turn?"

Cold air rushed into my lungs as I sucked in a breath, feeling the palm that had been splayed against my stomach, drop to find its way underneath my jacket to the waistband of my pants.

"Wyatt..." I moaned, feeling the clasp of my pants release from around my hips, "what if someone comes?"

"Gorgeous, you were just on your knees with my dick inside your mouth." He laughed harshly. "I don't care who finds us; I'm not letting you down this mountain until you've had some part of me inside of you."

My head tipped back against his shoulder as his hand dove underneath the edge of my lace underwear and into my folds.

"You are so wet for me," he growled as he bit into my neck. "Soaked, gorgeous. You are soaked. *God,* I want to taste you again—taste your honey."

Somewhere inside of me his words registered as his fingers teased my clit. My hips pressed against his hand begging as I felt one finger enter me and it was just like the other night—his touch lighting matches, inciting me to explode. I moaned louder as another finger entered me. Before I had a chance to accommodate it, he pushed in a third, causing me to gasp his name.

My knees weakened and I wondered who was this woman—standing on the side of a mountain, fully clothed, back pressed against one of the sexiest snowboarders in the world with his hand down her pants? If I thought secretly sucking him off on the mountain was sexy, I could only imagine the picture we painted right now—at first glance, probably innocuous. On further inspection, the cold and the layers were not enough to stop him from finding and taking my sex.

"Mine," he said harshly against my ear, making sure I heard him through the fog of my desire.

"Am I?" The question coming from the part of me that ground against his hand, begging for more of everything—everything with him.

"From the second. My lips. Tasted yours." Each phrase was

punctuated with his fingers plunging inside of me, sliding easily through my slickness to fill me. "Say it." *A fourth finger. How was this possible?* My body shuttered on the verge of fragmenting into a million pieces—unique and fragile like snowflakes; I was going to die from the pleasure—the fullness—I was sure of it. I was stretched and soaking and begging to be splintered.

I panted, feeling my impending climax roll through me, liquefying every muscle in my body. "Yours," I barely managed to get out. Then it was only two fingers delving completely inside of me, bending at the end to rub against that sweet spot. And if that wasn't enough, his thumb pressed over my clit mercilessly.

It was an earthquake and a tsunami. Multiple orgasms ravaging me from inside and out. I let the earth shatter around me and the waves of pleasure drown me with only Wyatt as my rock to hold me steady. My body came apart in a way I hadn't known was possible—a way I hoped Wyatt's touch knew how to put me back together.

"I lied." Ever so distantly I heard his words drift into me. "*That was the hottest thing I have ever seen.*" It was hard to find the strength even for just a small laugh as my muscles continued to clench around him. Slowly, he pulled his fingers from me but I refused to move. I wanted to stay locked against him.

"*Now*, we should go." I peered up at him, his smile weakening my body again.

Reluctantly, I forced my legs to work, buttoning my snowpants as I stumbled through back over to my board. I sat down to strap back in—there was no way I could do it standing right now, my limbs were jello. I heard him groan and what I saw when I looked over devastated me: Wyatt, watching me while he sucked the remains of my desire off of his fingers.

"Something to hold me over." He grinned seductively, pulling his goggles back over his devious eyes and starting back down the mountain.

As soon as he was just out of sight, I tipped back into the cushion of the snow, one of those ridiculously happy, sated, irrevocably enthralled smiles bursting onto my face—the kind of smile that Allie (the one in the movie, *not* the one related to me) had during the whole "you're a bird—I'm a bird" scene in 'The Notebook'. Only we weren't birds; we weren't animals. We were a force of nature—a snowsquall; a tempest of wind and snow obliterating everything else around us.

CHAPTER
Seventeen

Channing

"LIL!" NICK'S ARM CAME AROUND MY SHOULDER AS I TURNED, looking for who called my name. "You look totally fucking fine." Letting me go, his eyes did a quick, platonic, once-over as I set the glass down on the bar. "Emmett! She is totally fine you fucking dick!"

Emmett was approaching us, previously distracted by some blonde by the doorway. My ice-blue stare wasn't completely thawed after everything that he'd said and it looked like the anger hadn't completely disappeared from the black pits of his. We were both stubborn; it was now a waiting game to see which one of us caved first and forgave the other.

"You should have known better than to believe me." His voice calm and unconcerned. He took a seat next to Nick at the bar. Breakers was pretty dead, even for a Tuesday.

"Yeah, well, maybe if it hadn't been a head injury, I would have called your bluff. I didn't think you would lie about her head being bandaged up." Rolling my eyes, I turned to laugh to myself and pulled out two glasses to pour them some beer. "I meant to stop by yesterday, Lil, but I was finishing up a project late last night."

"Yeah? A project? Is that what you are calling them these days?" Emmett laughed, clarifying our friend's half-assed attempt to conceal that he'd either been too high or otherwise occupied to leave his house.

"Fuck you." Nick washed down his grumble with the IPA that I'd served them both.

"Was he lying when he said that Olsen was helping you learn the triple?"

I flicked my eyes to Emmett who just stared blankly at me, suggesting that I was the one who'd gotten into this and I better own up to it.

"Uh… yeah, he is."

"Shouldn't he be worrying about practicing for the X Games?" *Yes, he should.*

I shrugged, pulling out more glasses from the dishwasher and inspecting them for any water spots. "Well, it's only in the morning before my lessons."

Although, how he found the energy to do anything afterwards was beyond me. This morning played out similarly to yesterday—except for the interlude in the glades. Today, we'd stuck to the park the entire time—in full view of all the other competition riders who were growing more numerous by the day. I nailed every jump and he'd told me we'd be spending time on the triple by the end of the week; I should have been ecstatic. Instead, all I could think about was how I wanted to spend time with him…alone.

"Still… the Open isn't for another couple of months; you have plenty of time to learn. The Games are in like two weeks…" I bit my tongue; *why wasn't he dropping this?* "Although, I guess he'll be leaving after the Games so you wouldn't have him to help you then…"

The glass shattered on the tile floor, slipping easily out of my hands that were paralyzed by Nick's words.

"*Shit.*" I swore, grabbing a towel and bending down to clean up the broken mess that looked a whole lot like my heart. I hadn't even thought about *after*. Wyatt wasn't from here—he wasn't even from the US—what did I think was going to happen?

"You all good there, *Channing*?" Emmett's use of my full name suggested he knew exactly why the accident had occurred. Which is why I ground out, "Fine" and kept my eyes on my task.

Meanwhile, Nick continued on, superficially oblivious to deadlines and heartbreak. "He *does* win everything, I probably wouldn't be concerned about it either." I stood, dumping the shards of glass from the towel into the trashcan. "Do you think he would have time to teach me some things again? Maybe just like an hour or so. He knows his shit—and I would know it, too, if I hadn't been so stoned."

Wyatt would be happy to know that. Sort of.

"I… ahh… I don't know. I'm sure if you ask he would." I saw Emmett smirk out of the corner of my eye. Sometimes, I could see why Ally got so aggravated by him. *I really could.*

"Maybe I will." Nick smiled but his focus had already moved to the blondes that Emmett had been talking to when they walked in.

Emmett jumped into the conversation then, nodding up to the TV screen that was currently showing the weather, "You think this storm is going to be as big as they think?" Nick and I both turned to look at the weather map showing projected snowfall.

There was an impending snowstorm coming the end of this week or beginning of next; a blizzard was brewing and the talking heads were still debating when we would get hit and how hard. We mountain kids, on the other hand, wondered if it was going to deliver on the incredible powder that they were suggesting.

"I hope; I hope we get a powder day. They've been few and far between this year." Their voices faded into the background, droning on about the potential snow dump and what they were going to do. A few nods and murmurs escaped me so there would be no concern that I'd gone catatonic, but I was hardly paying any attention. The benign topics were good to pull Nick's eerily penetrating questions off of Wyatt and the Games and whatever else he might think to ask about me and the famous boarder; they were not so good at keeping my thoughts away from the one thing I hadn't considered: *Wyatt leaving.*

I'd thought of everything but that. I'd finally decided to go after what I wanted—what was between us—and I felt like I'd been blissfully floating up in the air and now, when I was about to land, the ground had been ripped out from underneath me.

"What do you think, Lil?" Nick's persistent voice focused me. From their expressions, it wasn't the first time this question had been posed to me. *And for the life of me, I couldn't remember what he was referring to.*

"Sorry... brain damage..." Was my mumbled excuse.

"Next week. I'm done with my semester and I said we should go out and celebrate." I blinked twice. "You can even invite your sister and Olsen and whomever." Emmett's hand tightened perceptively around his glass at the mention of Ally and an Olsen.

"Oh, yeah. Sure. Sounds good." My chin bobbed mindlessly. Part of me wanted to invite him. The other part whispered, '*No point of inviting him, of letting him further into your life if he's only going to leave it.*'

"Speak of the devil." Emmett downed the rest of his beer letting my confused stare follow his over to where Wyatt had just walked into the bar. My heart jumped painfully. *When was the last time he'd come to visit me at Breakers?*

I turned away from them and grabbed a glass, filling it with water to hide my consternation.

"Olsen!" Nick exclaimed ruefully. "How did you know we were talking about you!"

Great.

"All good things, I hope." I faced them, squeezing my thighs together. I was like freaking Pavlov's dog—as soon as I heard his voice, my body salivated for him. When I met his gaze, he winked at me and it was all I could do to set the glass in front of him and not dissolve into a pool of jelly.

I looked down at my watch—it was almost time for me to go. They'd put me on light duty all this week after my fall, which meant that I was done around eleven, leaving the other bartender to close. Wyatt had come by last night and walked me to my car—I shouldn't have been surprised to see him tonight.

"I'm done for the night, guys." Emmett appeared to be ready to go since the moment Wyatt had arrived. Nick's expression barely flickered—he was called Frost for a reason and not only because it was his last name.

"Hey, Olsen. I was just talking to Lil here," Wyatt's eyes jumped to me at the nickname and I could hear the question in his mind—'Lil' sounded nothing like Channing, so where did it come from? "and I was wondering—I know you're busy with practice and –" He stopped to glance at me with a knowing smirk. *Great. Frost had known the whole time.* "—everything, but I was wondering if you might have time to help me with a few things in the park."

"Yeah, man. Sure."

"We could meet you on Makaha tomorrow if you want," I offered, suddenly fearful of spending more time alone with Wyatt, getting too attached, and having him break my heart when he leaves. Out of the corner of my eye, I saw Wyatt's eyebrow rise, surprised that I'd sacrifice some of our time together, but he smoothly went along with it.

"Yeah, man. I'd be happy to, but tomorrow isn't going to be good." He cleared his throat, glancing over at me. "I wanted to talk to you about our practice for tomorrow and Thursday because I have some meetings that came up in the mornings, so I'm not going to be able to make it to the mountain until after you start work."

Oh. What meetings? Where?

Instead, I replied nonchalantly, twisting the towel I was holding in my hands, "Oh, that's fine. I'll just ride with you guys tomorrow--"

"That's what we're here for—SnowmassHoles—back-ups for when your hook-ups fail you." Emmett interjected acerbically. Before I could go off on him, he stood and strolled back over to the door where the blonde and her friends were lingering again.

"Sorry," I murmured.

"Yeah, whenever works for you," Nick refocused the conversation, not giving two-shits about Emmett's rudeness. "I'd be so fuckin' appreciative. Even what you showed me the other day, man, *so* helpful. You can ask --" He was about to say Emmett. "Really good stuff."

"Glad to hear it. I should be clear Friday morning. Unless you want to meet up one afternoon this week?"

"No, let's do Friday," I said cheerily. Nick was too undetectably perceptive even when he appeared oblivious. I couldn't trust him not to say anything about Chance when I wasn't there or realize what I was doing.

"Works for me." Nick stood. "Alright, Olsen, Lil, I'll see you guys later." And with a mock salute he joined Emmett.

"Lil?" Wyatt turned to me.

"Meetings?" I raised an eyebrow in return.

He chuckled. "Alright, alright. Why don't you clean up and I'll walk you to your car?"

I nodded and quickly finished the few tasks left for me to do, leaving Stevie—the other bartender—to close.

"It's my nickname," I began, "because 'Chan' was too lame. So, they shortened my middle name, Lily, to 'Lil'." I heard his 'ahh' of understanding. "Plus, they are like my brothers, so I think it also worked out to be short for 'little' as in 'little sister'."

"Channing Lily Ryder." His hand snaked down my arm and intertwined his fingers with mine. *Don't let go*, the thought burning to escape my mouth.

"That's me." My voice was quiet.

"Perfect."

Yes, you are, I wanted to say. Instead, opting to create a safe space between us. "So, what are these meetings for?"

"Mmm… I don't want to say—yet."

"What the hell!" I smacked his arm. "I told you--"

"I'll tell you!" He laughed. "But I just need a few days." His face became more serious and my mind began to turn down a dark road. "I had an idea about what I want to do after the Games—when I'm done competing, but I needed to talk to a few people back home first. I want to make sure of a few things before I can tell you."

Fear gripped me. *Back home.* In Canada.

"Hey," he stopped and pulled me back to him, "you ok?"

My eyes blinked rapidly, trying to stop my tears from falling. "Yeah, just tired." I smiled weakly, turning towards my Jeep that was only a few feet away.

"You sure?" His thumb rubbed along the back of my hand. "Maybe you should take it easy tomorrow morning instead of heading back out on the mountain. You don't want to do too much too fast."

My car lights flashed as the doors unlocked, signaling me to respond to him.

"Yeah. Maybe." I pulled my hand from his. "I'll see how I feel." My hand was on the doorknob when large, warm hands on my waist spun me to face him. One hand cupped my cheek.

"You can tell me." His eyes pierced right through me and I felt the undeniable truth of his words weaving their way into my soul. "Whatever it is, Channing, you can tell me." His thumb brushed over my lip. "I may not have been in your life for very long right now, but I promise you that I intend to be. I may not know you as well as your family or friends, but I promise you that I intend to work towards remedying that every single day. I may be the last person you think that you can trust right now, but I promise you that I would *never* do *anything* to hurt you."

Was it possible for a heart to swell so large that it stops? Because I swore that mine had.

I couldn't stop the tear that forged a path of heartache down my cheek. "Don't cry," he rasped.

"I can't help it. N-No one has ever said something so sweet to me before." I huffed, feeling a few more tears follow suit—*since when was I so emotional?* "How are you this wonderful?" I couldn't stop myself from asking with a pained laugh. "Don't answer that; I-I don't want to know. All I know is that I'm searching for a shooting star tonight, wishing that I could believe everything that you've promised." I couldn't help myself from trying to bring down my expectations, afraid of the fall from the height they were quickly dragging me to.

He chuckled, leaning into me. "Gorgeous, I have more sweet truths for you than the sky has stars and I swear to you, you don't have to make a wish on mine for them to be true."

His lips came for mine and I gave them willingly. The kiss was soft and tender, a mirror to his words. His tongue showed me their truth, coaxing from me not only trust in him, but trust in my feelings for him. By the time he pulled back, I knew that if he felt for me a fraction of what my thudding heart felt for him, there was no way he was leaving when the Games were over.

"You should get going," he breathed against my lips.

"But I want more kisses." *Not ashamed.*

He laughed slightly, dropping one more quick kiss on me. "If you stay, you're going to get a whole lot more than kisses." His response punctuated with a roll of his hips against mine—lightly, but enough for me to feel how hard he was.

"You say that like it's a bad thing." My hand on his chest began to drift lower before his fingers around my wrist stopped it.

He pulled my palm up to his face, kissing the center, stepping forward to push me up against the side of my car, his entire body molding to mine. "Channing, make no mistake, I want every inch of you to be mine—and it will be. But not when you're tired, not when you're recovering, and definitely not when how I feel about you is an uncertainty in your mind." He held my gaze prisoner. "You want to give me your body, and fuck, do I want it, gorgeous, but that's not all I want. And I'm not the kind of man who settles for second-best." And then the sexy, confident, snowboarder had the nerve to wink at me while I was melting into a puddle at his feet and say, "I'm Wyatt Olsen, sweetheart; you know I always win it all."

"And what if you lose this time?"

"I won't let that happen." He kissed me hard and then pushed himself away with a groan. "I'll see you Friday, Channing."

My legs were shaking, making my stick shifting awkward and jerky as I drove home. Every word he'd said echoed in the silence of the ride but not loud enough to drown out the fear that was rapidly rising again: *what if he left?*

What if I gave him my body and it wasn't enough?

What if I gave him my heart and he took it with him when he left?

CHAPTER
Eighteen

Channing

Friday morning lessons had been pushed back to Saturday—and I'd had to find out through Ally. I was almost tempted to not show up, but my traitorous heart wasn't having any of it.

'*Zack wanted me to tell you that Wyatt can't make it this morning, but he'll be there tomorrow.*'

A million questions burned angrily through my mind, only fueling the embers of doubt that had been flickering persistently over the past few days. After she'd told me, I clicked on my phone to see a text from an unknown number.

WYATT
Morning, gorgeous. I hate to do this, but I have to cancel our lessons this morning. Have to be on a phone call with some big-wigs back home. Time difference makes their lunchtime our morning. I'm going to make it up to you big time. Several times, in fact. 😉 <3

My anger had retreated knowing that he hadn't used our siblings as messengers. I chewed on my lip, still wondering who those 'big-wigs' were and why they wanted to talk to him. *Did it have to do with the news that he couldn't tell me?*

The suspense was killing me. That, and the desire. '*Several times.*'

Goosebumps ran up my spine.

I pulled out my phone again, checking for any more messages from him. Nick and I were waiting where we usually met up, only this time was the first time I had gotten there before him.

"He'll be here, Lil, calm down." *Easy for him to say.* Nick was plopped down in the snow doing something that I probably disapproved of on his phone.

"Yeah, well that's what he said about yesterday and then cancelled." I glared down at him and retorted. Of course, as soon as I looked back up, I saw my sexy, secretive snowboarder walking towards us. Damn man was always making me eat my words.

"Sorry I'm late." His smile begged me to forgive him; I'd learned a while ago that I couldn't resist his smile.

"No problem, Olsen. We just got here. Right, Lil?" Nick replied coolly, his eyes flicking between the two of us.

"Yeah, just fifteen minutes ago." I shrugged. I knew my annoyance and frustration wouldn't last long against Wyatt and his always-right words, so I took what I could get.

"Alright, well let's get going."

We strapped in and headed for the lift. Nick plied Wyatt with questions the entire ride up—none of which inquired as to what had made him bail on us yesterday. I wasn't able to get a word in by the time we slid off the lift, heading for Makaha.

"What should I start with?" Nick asked.

"You want to warm up one and then we'll go from there?" Wyatt suggested.

"Dropping!" And then Nick was gone, leaving Wyatt and me alone at the top of the slope—still too early for any other riders to be out.

As soon as Nick disappeared over the first kicker, Wyatt unstrapped from his board and hauled me into his arms. I hadn't fastened my helmet yet which made it all the easier for him to pull it from my head as his lips crushed mine.

Three days. It had been three days since our conversation in the parking lot and I'd tried to tell myself, tried to pretend like those three days had passed as normally as any other day during the B.W. (Before Wyatt) period. But they hadn't.

Like candy, I dissolved underneath his tongue. His kiss quickly broke me down, wearing through the hard, frustrated exterior that I'd tried to keep up.

"So damn sweet, Channing," he whispered against me. "*Fuck*, I missed you, gorgeous." And then his mouth tore into mine again before I could respond. Even though I was tethered to my board, my arms wrapped around his neck, pulling me as close to him as possible.

His hands slid from my waist around to grab my ass, rocking my hips against his thick ridge. Desire grew between my legs where I'd been aching for him for days. I groaned into his mouth, debating whether it was too sappily wanton to ask him if we could just practice this all morning.

"Sorry," he breathed heavily into the space between us, our ragged breaths made obvious in the brutally cold air around us. "There were so many things I wanted to say, but I need that… I needed you first."

I'd always been enthralled by those plasma globes in the mall; the ones with the electrical rays that looked like mini lightning bolts shooting out from the center to the outside of the globe, convening underneath your fingertip if you touched it. That's what I felt like with Wyatt—a damn plasma globe—an electrical storm brewing in my core and shooting out to every cell in my body, my desire converging on his fingers—his touch—on my skin.

"It's ok," I mumbled.

"I know you're mad that I couldn't be here yesterday," he asserted. *I was*, but I wasn't ready to admit it, so I just shrugged without really giving an answer. His fingers tipped my chin up to look at him, the truth easily distinguishable in my eyes. "I'm sorry I had to cancel, gorgeous." His lips gently touched mine. "I'm sorry and I'm going to make it up to you tomorrow."

Ironically, I was less interested in how he was going to make it up to me and more interested in what had caused him to have to make it up in the first place.

"Who were you meeting with?" I watched his expression shudder.

"I had a call with some investors back in Montreal," he explained, but I needed more.

"Why?"

He smiled. "I can't tell you yet; it's a surprise." My frown deepened and I turned my face from his. I didn't like surprises; surprises were just secrets in disguise. I didn't like being kept in the dark where my fears could take hold of me; fears that told me that one day I was going to wake up and Wyatt was going to be gone with no note, no explanation, and no way for me to recover. *Just like Chance had.* "Hey, hey, hey." His hand on the side of my face turned me back. "What's wrong?"

"Nothing," I grumbled. "I just don't like not knowing."

He sighed. "I don't think that's it, but I can't force you to tell me the truth." Just like I couldn't force him to tell me his secret. "I've been thinking a lot about what I'm going to do after the Games," he continued, "and I thought of an idea—inspired by you—but I don't know if it's going to work out yet. All indications are yes, but I need another week or so to know for sure if I can get the funding."

Now I was listening intently. "For what? What are you doing to do?"

He smiled. "That's the part I want to surprise you with." My spirits sagged again. "If you'll let me." My eyes shot to his, hearing his words.

Wyatt was giving me the choice. He saw that it was bothering me and instead of trying to convince me or insisting on his way, he was giving *me* the choice whether he told me or not. Why did he have to be such a gentleman? Why did he have to be so perfect?

In that moment, I could have said no. I could have put an end to my misery and found out whether he was planning on leaving one way or another. I could have picked me and my fears—instead I chose him. I saw his excitement, but more importantly, I saw in his gaze the unwavering belief that whatever he had up his sleeve, he truly believed would make me happy. And I wasn't going to be the asshole to spoil it.

So, I decided to trust him. "Yes," I sighed. "But I won't promise that I'm going to be entirely happy about it until you finally tell me." Even my subsequent pout came out playful instead of serious.

"I would expect nothing less." He kissed me again. "But it will be worth the wait."

I grumbled an incoherent response, taking my helmet and putting it back on.

"Alright, how about you show me what you've been working on the past few days without me." He winked at me and smacked my ass before walking back over to his board.

God, I prayed trusting him wasn't a mistake because seeing him this morning had driven home the realization that the past three days had been miserable without him.

The first run went smoothly as a warm up for both Nick and me. Out of the four of us—Nick, Emmett, Chance, and me—Nick was the least interested in pursuing a professional career out of the sport. He rode for fun—or maybe because he liked cheating death. He rode to get away from his family and whatever shit happened when he wasn't throwing drugged and drunken parties at their house. There was a reason they called him Frost—because what was on the surface was only a remnant of the coldness that existed in the dark.

Then came King—or Emmett—who competed but was always more interested in designing and modifying the boards to give other riders an advantage. And finally Chance and I who competed to win— to make a name for ourselves in the world of winter sports. The difference between all of us made our friendship easier since we weren't each intent on having the competitive advantage. That was why I was surprised when Nick wanted to learn more from Wyatt—I doubted that he would have even asked Chance to teach him some of these things.

Then again, everyone seemed to be acting differently around Wyatt—Nick's concerning interest, and Emmett's growing distance, frustration, and protective stance had become distant, frustrated, and protective; and then there was Wyatt's effect on me.

Is it possible to know that you are acting differently and yet, at the same time, more like yourself?

"Lil," Nick's voice gained my attention as we sat on the lift, "are you working tomorrow night? My classes Monday morning were already cancelled."

The big snowstorm was officially slated to hit late tomorrow night and into Monday morning.

"Nope," I replied. "Jim told us yesterday that Breakers was going to be closed tomorrow and Monday; they say we're going to get pretty heavy powder." Jim was the manager of Breakers and he'd begrudgingly informed us that the resort was closing the bar in preparation for the storm; if it were up to Jim, he would have had us sleeping on bar tables so that we could stay open.

"Should make conditions great for the Games…" Nick surmised, looking to me and Wyatt for a response. *There was no way he could know… was there?*

"Definitely." The bar on the lift went up, ending the conversation.

The next few hours flew by. Without Wyatt's full attention, I stuck to jumps and maneuvers that I hadn't done recently, knowing that the triple cork wasn't the only thing I could do in my Slopestyle run—there had to be other elements included. Wyatt asked if I wanted to attempt the triple again, but I shook my head. Not today. I wanted him all to myself and I wasn't keen on spending the rest of the morning falling in front of one of my best friends.

Even just in one morning, I could see how much Nick had progressed with Wyatt's help; I hoped that it was further proof to him of how good an instructor that he was—patient, kind, able to explain things in a variety of ways, and supportive.

I, on the other hand, was only impatient with myself which led to frustration—as evidenced by my head injury. Chance had no patience for himself or for anyone—giving up quickly and easily. I put up with it because he was my brother and I didn't let it get to me. Chance was good at a lot of things—teaching was not one of them.

"Alright, that's it for me this morning," I said, unstrapping from my board. "I'm going to grab a coffee and head to my lessons."

Wyatt looked over his shoulder. "You good, Nick? Or you want to go again?"

Nick raised his eyebrows, surprised that Wyatt would be willing to continue to work with him without me there.

"I mean, if you have time for one more run and then I should probably go to class." He grinned and I knew immediately that he'd missed at least one class to be on the mountain this morning; they'd probably tried to move up classes from Monday if the school was going to be closed.

"Yeah, sure. I'm just going to walk Channing over to Cup of Joe; if you want to head back up, I'll meet you there in a few." Nick's smile widened as he turned and made his way back to the chairlift.

"You don't have to walk with me," I said quietly, taking my gloves off and unzipping my jacket.

I felt his arms snake around my waist as he came up flush behind my back. "You know why that's not true," he whispered into my ear. My stomach quivered as I felt his hand on my bare skin.

The next instant his hard warmth was gone, standing a step in front of me, holding out his hand. I gulped, realizing what he wanted. With a mind of its own, my hand raised to his, letting him intertwine our fingers together as we began to walk towards the coffeehouse.

I bit down on my lip, watching the eyebrows raise of some of the boarders we passed as they recognized him, if not me. Every time I glanced down at our hands, my mouth tried to smile, my teeth keeping the expression firmly under control.

This. The holding hands, the kissing, the riding, the watching movies while he rubbed my feet and I fell asleep, the teaching, the touching—*everything*. I wanted it all with *him*.

He was there again after my shift at Breakers to walk me to my car, asking how the rest of my day had gone. I was a little nervous about him and Nick spending another run alone, hoping that Nick wouldn't mention Chance; he must not have since Wyatt acted as usual.

"You were great with Nick this morning," I couldn't stop myself from complimenting him. "I've helped him in the past, but I don't think I've ever see so much improvement in one morning as when you work with him." *And when he's not completely stoned.*

"Thanks, gorgeous." He tugged on my hand that he'd insisted on holding again, pulling me against his side so that he could drop a kiss on my head. "It's probably because I'm not as good-looking an instructor—harder to get distracted."

I burst out laughing. I *highly* doubted that was the case, but I loved him for saying it.

No. Wait. What?

I didn't love Wyatt; I didn't. I just… really, really liked him. That's all.

"I think you're just trying to butter me up." I eyed him slyly.

"I might be." He squeezed my hand and I felt my heart tighten in response.

"And why would that be? I already said that you didn't have to tell me your surprise." My steps slowed, seeing my Jeep in the parking lot. I just wanted to stay a little longer with him.

"Did I hear you say that you have off tomorrow night?"

I looked up at him, but his gaze was off in the distance—it felt like purposely avoiding mine. "Yes… because of the snow that they are calling for. Why?"

"Does that mean I might be able to request your company for the evening, instead of having to settle for the fifteen minutes between Breakers and your car?" Now, his eyes met mine, brimming with desire.

A thrill of anticipation went through me. I didn't know what he had in mind, but I knew that this was going to be his way of making it up to me. The thought made me hot all over.

"You might be able to," I said coyly, eagerly awaiting his response.

Instead, I was met with silence as we closed the distance to my car. His hand slipped from mine, hooking around my waist and turning me against his chest. I felt the breath rush out of me as my lips parted.

"At the risk of being shut down on this question for the second time," he rasped, staring into my eyes, "can I take you on a date tomorrow night, Miss Ryder?"

I smiled. "I think you can, Mr. Olsen."

I melted into the kiss that followed. He may only get fifteen minutes for the walk, but he could have claimed the kiss for equally as long. By the time his lips broke from mine, I was panting, my arms around his neck holding me steady so I didn't collapse at his feet.

"Come home with me." The words were out before I could stop them, let alone think about what I was saying.

Wyatt looked just as surprised as I by the statement before need vanquished the emotion. Then I was flat up against the side of my car, his mouth clinging to my neck as he thrust his thigh up between my legs, pinning me to the vehicle. I moaned as it pressed against my sex, my hips involuntarily beginning to rub against the hard muscle of his leg, trying to ease my ache.

"Not tonight, gorgeous," he murmured against my neck.

I whimpered, both from his refusal and from the need that was torturing me. I gasped as his hands slid from my waist to cup both of my breasts, his thumbs immediately finding my hard nipples.

"What are you doing?" My question a breathless mess.

"Saying good night," he replied tightly as his fingers teased the aching peaks. My head fell back against the back window of the Jeep's soft-top as my legs ground my core against his thigh.

What was he doing to me?

"S-someone could see." *I didn't care.*

"No one is here, Channing." He bit my earlobe and pulled it into his mouth. "Now, ride me."

This was so stupid, so blatant, so sexual... *so hot.*

He sucked hard on my neck and I felt my sex clench with the

beginnings of the orgasm that it had been craving for days. I pushed myself harder and faster against his leg, not caring if the whole damn mountain was standing in the parking lot watching me climax against it.

"That's it, gorgeous," he growled as his hands switched to firmly kneading the small mounds of my breasts. I shoved them harder against his grasp as he spoke. I felt my folds slipping against my underwear that were completely soaked through, the friction of the lace against my clit driving me crazy. "*Take it.*"

I exploded against him, my orgasm pulling from every cell in my body and shattering them into pieces. My hands death-gripped his shoulders as I rode the waves of pleasure against his body. When I finally returned—dazed—into reality, I heard his heavy breathing against the side of my neck.

"So damn hot, gorgeous." His head rose to gently kiss my parted lips. "I will never fucking tire of making you come."

I moaned softly as his hands returned to my hips to steady me as he lowered his leg and consequently my feet to the ground.

I let my hands slide down from his neck, but he grabbed my wrists before they got lower than his chest. "I'll pick you up at your place tomorrow at six-thirty." He kissed each palm before stepping back from me.

"W-what about you?" I mumbled; there was no clarification required. I didn't need to see the hard ridge outlined in his pants to know that he was just as aroused as I had been, but I did see it and it looked incredibly uncomfortable. I also saw a dark spot on his left pantleg where I'd rubbed against him; *guess it wasn't just my underwear that I'd soaked through.* I jerked my gaze back up before he noticed, suddenly embarrassed by my desire.

"I have to go take care of a few things here for tomorrow—for our date," he replied cryptically with a mischievous wink. "Plus, you're still hesitant to trust me—and hesitant to tell me why. So, I'm going to keep giving you everything you need until you realize that I'd never do anything to hurt you."

I grabbed the door handle as my knees gave way—and *not* as an effect of my earth-shattering release.

"More sweet truths, Mr. Olsen?" I said huskily, bringing back our conversation from the other night.

He smiled. "I can keep going if you want. Or maybe you'd like me to switch it up to dirty truths?" Both of my eyebrows raised. "I have plenty of those too. Like how the fact that you were so drenched just now that your sweetness soaked through my pants." I watched as his fingers rubbed over the spot I'd noticed a minute ago. "Makes me crazy with the need to taste you, gorgeous."

I felt my face go beet red. "I... umm... I think you can stick to the sweet ones." My eyes fell to the ground even though my heart raced at his arousing words.

I heard him chuckle. "Goodnight, Channing."

"Goodnight, Wyatt."

CHAPTER
Nineteen

Channing

"Where are we going?" It was the third time I'd asked since opening the front door and letting him and Zack inside. Tonight, the roles were reversed; Zack and Ally were having a night in and Wyatt was taking me... somewhere. All I knew was that I was supposed to dress comfortably.

"Can't tell you."

"Have I been there before?" I eagerly watched the familiar scenery pass as we pulled out of my driveway; the flurries had already begun to fall even though the heaviest part of the storm wouldn't hit until tomorrow.

He laughed. "Yes. Well... yes and no."

"What does that mean?" I exclaimed. "If you don't want to tell me, you at least have to be explicit in your answers." I huffed. "When was the last time I was there?"

That one he didn't answer.

"Are you sure that I don't need to be wearing something nicer?" I glanced down at my yoga pants and the fitted tee that I'd borrowed from Ally. "I could have asked Ally for something nicer."

"You look beautiful." He flashed me a devastating smile.

I sighed, turning in the passenger seat to look out the window; the drive mirroring the route I took to the mountain every morning. I jumped slightly when Wyatt's hand reached for mine, holding my fingers tightly. My gaze narrowed as he made another turn.

"Are we going to the mountain?" I spun and asked him.

He looked over at me and smiled again.

"But everything is closed."

"Not everything."

Instead of turning in our normal lot, he pulled in the first entrance that led to the left-most side of the mountain where the Two Rivers Café was located. My curiosity was killing me, but I knew he wouldn't answer even if I asked.

He parked in the main lot and I followed him out of the car. The trunk swung open and I saw snowboots, a large cooler, and another good-sized bag that was zipped shut. I raised my eyebrows at him, but still he said nothing.

Pulling out the cooler and bag, he set them on the ground before retrieving a pair of boots. "You'll need to put these on."

I recognized them as Ally's. *Little jerk was in on this.*

He grabbed the second pair while I shoved my feet into my sister's shoes. When he was finished, he took my sneakers from my hand, set them in the trunk, and closed it. "Let's go."

"Snowboots but no snowboard?" I wondered.

"Not tonight."

"So this is why you said yes and no…" I mused. "I can't remember the last time I made it over to this side of the mountain."

"It's a good spot." I partially took his word for it because everything was dark –closed because of the storm. I followed him quietly, waiting for the next clue as to what was going on while we walked through the cluster of buildings at the base.

The Two Rivers chairlift was lit up. *Weird.* Then I realized that we were walking towards it.

"Wait… where… how…" I trailed off as Wyatt turned and smiled, holding up a set of keys as he unlocked the door to the lift operator's box and turned it on. I watched the chairs begin to move slowly up the mountain.

"Keep moving, missy," he teased as he walked right by me, waiting for the next chair to come around. I quickly hopped over next to him, not wanting to get stuck on the lift by myself. In the dark.

We sat down and Wyatt set the cooler and bag on the seat between us.

"How did you manage this?"

"I know people." He laughed. "I *am* Wyatt Olsen."

Even my eye roll couldn't dampen my smile. "I've never been here at night. I've never been on the mountain after dark." Most mountains, except those on the East Coast, closed right around four or so. I'd only been on a few that had night skiing, but this was different; the mountain wasn't lit with trail lights. It was completely dark except for the hazy glow cast on it by the moon and the stars.

"Beautiful, isn't it?"

My head spun, taking in the panorama around me as the chair took us higher; I could now see the lights of the town behind us in the distance. I looked back to him and realized that he'd been staring at me the entire time.

My mouth parted. "Incredible," I whispered and it was so silent that I might as well have screamed the word.

We jogged down the slight slope when the lift reached the top and I laughed. "I don't think I've ever gotten off the chair without being strapped to a board before."

"First time for everything." Hoisting the bag over his shoulder he began to walk.

"Those everythings seem to happen a lot with you," I murmured, following his footsteps in the snow.

"That's what I was going for gorgeous." He smiled at me over his shoulder.

"Where are we going?" The light from the lift was dimming as we walked farther away.

"Right here." He stopped and I came up behind him. Ahead of us was one of the small warming huts that was open during the day for skiers and boarders to stop in and heat up before heading down the slope.

"There?!" He walked up to the door and opened it. *Guess there was no need to lock it when there was no lift running to bring you here. Except for tonight.*

I shivered and walked quickly inside behind him. Even though by the time we got to the top the flurries had stopped, it had still dropped to a bitterly low temperature. Inside the hut it was much warmer, having been heated during the day and slightly insulated. The inside was pretty sparse. A wide, wooden bench on one side of the room and a small window opposing that had a shelf underneath holding a first-aid kit, a few boxes of granola bars, and water bottles.

Wyatt set the bags down and walked over to the temperature control panel on the wall, turning it on. The soft hum of the heat bulbs sang above us—placed in between the two ceiling lights.

Wyatt turned to face me, the most heart-throbbing smile spreading onto his face. Before I could even ask, he answered me, "I packed us a picnic."

"A picnic?" I should have seen it coming but I was completely surprised.

"A picnic on the peak." He grinned.

I continued to stare, flabbergasted as the man who could have afforded to take me anywhere in town and save himself the effort, instead took me to the one place that felt like home—a home that we were making together.

He opened the bag and out came blankets—lots of them. He shook one out and laid it in the floor. I bent down to straighten the corner that was next to me.

"Why did you do this?" I couldn't help but ask.

"What do you mean?" He pulled out two smaller, draw-stringed bags that opened to reveal pillows for us to sit on.

"All of this. I mean, you said date and I figured you were going to take me to some fancy restaurant."

"Is that what you want?" He stopped and looked up at me.

I wasn't going to lie. "No."

"I didn't want to be surrounded by people. I wanted to talk to you and I wanted you to feel comfortable." He stood. "And I knew the only place you would be truly comfortable was here—on the mountain."

"Thank you," I whispered. *How did he know me better than myself?*

"Don't thank me yet. You haven't tried my food." He laughed as he opened the cooler and began to unload a feast that inconceivably seemed to fit inside.

"Wait, you made all of this?" Bread and cheese, salad, meatballs, pasta, chicken parmesan, and cannolis.

"I'm not very skilled with ethnic food, but Italian I can do." He looked up at me. "Sit, gorgeous. Stay awhile."

As soon as I bent down, I was assaulted with the delicious scents that burst into the air as he opened each of the containers—like the best Italian restaurant times a thousand. Grabbing one of the pillows, I plopped down onto it and crossed my legs.

"So, that's what you went to do last night—get the keys for the lift?" He nodded. "How did you manage that?"

"I can't give away all my secrets," he teased. "One last thing…" Reaching back into the bag, he pulled out another thinner sheet that unrolled to reveal a wine bottle and two plastic glasses. He held one up to me, silently asking if I would like some, so I nodded.

Watching him pour the wine, I took in the magical scene before me—the spread of food cradled amidst a sea of blankets, everything softly lit by the warm red of the heat lamps. In that moment, with the silent and stunning comfort of the mountain underneath and around us, I admitted to myself that I was falling rapidly in love with Wyatt Olsen.

"Thank you." The red wine fell right in the middle of dry and sweet—not that I had a preference either way.

He handed me a paper plate. "Dig in." I didn't have to be told twice; I wasn't the kind of girl that held back when it came to food—especially food that smelled as delicious as this. "I know it's not quite the fancy food you're used to from Breakers…"

I laughed. "Thank God…"

"So," he began, biting into the piece of Italian bread that he'd smothered with the cranberry goat cheese, "I have a question."

I paused and looked at him, silently encouraging him to continue as I dug into the salad on my plate.

"On a scale of one to ten, how much would you say that your brother hates me?"

I gulped down the massive bite of partially chewed lettuce, ironically so that I didn't choke on it. "What do you mean?" I squeaked out—immediately wondering if he'd heard something, if Nick had said something...

"I haven't seen him since I got here, Channing. And I don't mean on the mountain to train—I get wanting to practice in a private space after an injury." *Well, that was good at least.* "So I don't think I'm assuming too much to say that he hasn't been around because he's upset about what is going on between us—and probably between Zack and Ally, too, but I'm his biggest competition."

I took another bite of the meatball and pasta to give me a second to think of how to answer. My stomach rolled, revolting against the prospect of lying to him about Chance.

"He doesn't hate you." *Not yet, at least.* "He hasn't said anything specifically to me about well... yeah... When he got injured, I think it kind of forced a change in his perspective and I think that right now, he is just trying to focus on himself and getting back to where he needs to be," I replied, partially pleased with myself at how truthful my answer was even though Wyatt didn't understand it fully. "So, I don't think it has much—or anything—to do with you as much has it has to do with himself." I took another bite, waiting for his response.

I watched him absorb my words, the only sound between us was the gusts of wind blowing outside.

"Ask me something." I just stared at his demand. I'd been expecting him to say something else about Chance, but relief bloomed when I realized he was letting me change the subject.

"About what?"

"Me," he answered. "Anything about me."

I thought for a moment. "When was the last time that you lost?"

He burst out laughing. "Man, you like to hit where it hurts." I grinned at him. The man won everything though. I wanted to know. "Let me think. The last time I can remember—and don't hold me to this—was my sophomore year in high school. I honestly couldn't tell you which competition it was; Zack might remember. But everyone thought I was going to win and I didn't."

"What happened?" I was really intrigued; I wanted to hear that he wasn't a superhuman snowboarder.

"I fell pulling a seven-twenty."

"Seriously?" That was a pretty easy trick—especially for how good he'd been at the time. He nodded, but something made me ask. "What aren't you telling me?"

"What do you mean?" He took another bite of his chicken.

"I know that look and tone because I gave it to you a few weeks ago when I told you about what happened at the Open last year. What's the rest of the story?" I demanded, scooping a chicken breast onto my plate.

He chuckled. "Alright, Miss Ryder. I did it on purpose." I raised my eyebrows, my mouth full of food. "It was Zack's birthday that weekend and at the time, we were both competing in snowboarding. He hadn't wanted to do this competition, but I'd baited him into it. The night before, my mom made some comment inadvertently about how we were going to celebrate 'when I won'. Zack got pissed because it should have been a discussion about his birthday celebration, not a celebration of my win. He was so mad he wouldn't speak to me the rest of the night or the following morning."

"So, you bailed so that your win wouldn't overshadow his birthday?" I finished for him.

Wyatt nodded. "We were just kids, but seeing his face that night—even though it had been a mistake and my mom apologized—I realized that there are some things more important than winning; there are some things worth losing for."

Son of a biscuit, I felt like I was about to cry. I knew what he meant—I saw it the day that Chance was invited to the X Games and

I wasn't. He wanted to refuse out of concern for me; the difference is that I knew and I hadn't let him.

I looked up to see him watching me intently. "I want to show you something." He stood, quickly clearing the plates and containers from in front of us. "Come here." He extended a hand to me, pulling me to stand.

"What?" I watched him start to put his boots back on.

"Shoes on, Ryder. Let's go." I loosely laced Ally's shoes around my ankles, standing back up as Wyatt draped one of the blankets around my shoulders. "Brace yourself, gorgeous." He opened the door and the bitter cold assaulted me.

"W-why a-are we going b-back outside?" My teeth chattered as I followed him out the doorway and into the darkness of the night; the flurrying that we'd walked through at the base of the mountain had made its way to the top, the flakes gently falling around us, glimmering from the faint light of the hut like tiny sequins or sparkles shimmering in the night sky.

Without all of my snow-gear, the cold was a different story. It was the kind of cold that another fifteen minutes outside and my nostrils would be so frozen and numb that sucking in a breath would collapse them against the inside of my nose.

Wyatt walked maybe ten steps away from the warming hut before stopping. When I came up beside him, he wrapped his arms and blanket around my shoulders, holding my back against his hard and deliciously hot chest, creating a warm cocoon around me.

"Look up," he whispered in my ear.

Tipping my head back against his shoulder, I gasped at the sight above us. Thousands of stars twinkled in the black sky above. Even though my house was a respectable distance from the center of town, the stars never looked like this. On the top of the mountain, it felt like the whole world disappeared beneath us, leaving just the two of us, the snow, and the stars.

"This is incredible," I murmured, my words not even doing the scene justice; I no longer felt the cold, I was so wrapped up in this experience—so wrapped up in Wyatt.

"You are incredible." He nibbled on my earlobe, the static of desire shocking right down to my core. His words faded into the wind as we just stood there, his arms holding me tightly, as we were enveloped in the magic of the mountain.

"I think I might be falling for you." My whisper wafted into the night.

His arms around me tightened and I knew that he'd heard. I turned in his embrace, looking up to meet his gaze. "I'll catch you, gorgeous," one hand slid up to brush my chin, "because I've already fallen."

The moment was frozen, our emotional confession holding us hostage with its weight. Ever so slowly his head dipped down, my breath releasing when his lips claimed mine. His first kiss was soft and tender and I felt like my entire life was up in the air. When he kissed me a second time, I wasn't sure that I ever wanted to come back down. The gentle urgency was replaced with a demanding desire that took just as much as it gave.

Tearing his lips from mine, both of us gasping for air, he uttered, "Let's go inside. I want dessert."

I shivered—*not* because of the frigid temperature or more rapidly falling snow. His hands moved to my ass and lifted; quickly realizing that he intended to carry me, I wound my arms around his neck and locked my legs around his waist. Each of the ten steps back to the hut was torture as his every footfall shoved his erection against my core.

He didn't set me down—not to open the door nor once inside. Kicking the door shut, he pulled my boots off one at a time before moving to remove his own. I clung to his neck for dear life, chuckling as he managed to accomplish the task not only without injury but with relative ease. Slowly, he knelt, bringing us to the ground.

I lost myself in his next kiss, barely registering the feel of the pillow underneath my head or the blanket underneath my back. I kept my legs locked around him and he answered my desire, grinding himself against my core as his tongue thrust into my mouth.

One of his hands stayed on my cheek while the other moved to my chest, inching its way up underneath my shirt.

"Take it off," I begged. His hoarse breath rushed against my neck as he growled his assent, gripping the edge of my tee and dragging it over my head. I had no idea that this was what he was planning, but I was glad that I'd chosen my black and bright blue lace bra, the underwire making what little shape I had much more attractive.

Then his mouth was on mine again, his fingers cupping me through the lace, his thumb using the fabric to tease over my nipple that I desperately wished was in his mouth.

"Can I taste you, gorgeous?" He rasped into my mouth.

I moaned, "I need you to." I didn't have to say anything else. My legs dropped to the side as he hooked his fingers underneath the edge of my yoga pants and tugged them down, rocking back on his heels so that he could pull them completely off.

"*Fuck*, Channing." His eyes smoldered down at me, realizing that my panties matched my bra. He stared at my body like he wanted to eat me alive and underneath that kind of gaze alone, I felt like I was on the edge of an orgasm. "Did you do this on purpose?"

"I always wear matching." I watched how every muscle in his body looked like it was tight enough to burst.

"*Jesus Christ.*" The thrill of power shot through me, hearing his words. I relished that *I*—the tomboy, the girl that passed for her brother, the girl with no girly clothes or habits—could make him weak.

"Is matching underwear your weakness?" I teased breathlessly, trying to ignore the ache in my body that needed him to touch me.

His eyes jumped to mine and my breath caught at the intensity of desire inside of them. "No, gorgeous. *You are.*"

I lost my breath, my hips jerking up as the tremors of release begged to be set free.

His hands spread my thighs, his right hand sliding up my inner leg straight to my core. He didn't pause or tease, instead his two fingers slipped right underneath the edge of my panties and straight inside of me, curling against that magical spot that only he could find.

"Who knew," he groaned with a hint of a laugh, "that I could be on a mountain and be able to dip my fingers in an ocean at the same time." I could only press myself against his hand, needing more. "You're so wet for me."

Then his fingers were gone to rip my underwear off of me, baring my glistening folds to his gaze. His hands dove underneath my ass, holding my hips up as his mouth descended on me. I almost came at the first touch of his tongue over my clit and then again when his groan vibrated against me.

"*Please, Wyatt*," I whispered. I was too close. My body felt like it was about to rip itself apart if I didn't find my release.

He heard my need and he gave it to me. His tongue and teeth devoured me, alternately thrusting inside my core and then flicking over my sex. The way he ate—he was just as hungry as I was.

My desire snowballed into an avalanche that thoroughly wrecked me. I loved hearing his name scream from my lips knowing that there was no one but us to hear it. My hands that had somehow made it onto his head, my fingers in his hair, now dropped to my sides as my whole body turned to jello.

Under heavy eyelids, I watched his head lift, his eyes meeting mine, his lips wet from my desire. I wanted him to kiss me. I wanted *more*. And for a second, I thought he was moving up my body, but instead he pushed himself back on his heels.

"What's wrong?" I rasped, leaving my legs spread, enjoying the possessiveness in his gaze.

"We should get going." His voice was painfully hoarse and I was completely confused.

"I don't want to go," I said softly, pushing myself up to sit, my legs forced to one side of me. "I want to stay… with you… tonight."

He ran his hand through his hair, swearing underneath his breath. "We can't… we shouldn't…"

I didn't know what he was talking about; I didn't understand why he continued to feed my desire and ignore his own. It hurt and my chest began to burn with the pain. My gaze broke from his darting to the window so I could collect myself before any tears fell. And that's when I realized that we didn't have a choice.

"We can't leave, Wyatt," I whispered, my eyes remaining locked on the window—a window that was completely white on the other side. "It's a snowsquall out there."

CHAPTER
Twenty

Channing

His head jerked to the window and I saw reality register on his face. The storm wasn't supposed to start until much later in the night, but in the mountains, nothing was that predictable. And, instead of a blizzard, this one had gone from flurries to a full-on whiteout in the last thirty minutes. There was no way we could leave the hut now; I doubted that we would even be able to find our way to the lift, let alone whether or not it was safe to ride on one during this kind of storm. In a snowsquall, visibility was measured in inches, temperatures in the negative, and wind in the extreme. We were safe in the warming hut, there wasn't any question about that, but there was also no question that we couldn't leave until it calmed down.

His hand rubbed his forehead. "*Shit,*" he groaned.

"I don't understand," I continued. "Don't you want to…?"

His eyes flew open and he knelt in front of me, grasping my face in his hands. "Channing, you have no idea how badly I want to fuck you right now; I can't even say it nicely because that's how deranged my desire is making me. But I won't…" He exhaled harshly. "I don't want there to be any doubt."

"About what?" My brows furrowed.

"I don't want you or your brother to think that I'm using you—that I slept with you—just to throw him off during the games. *You are not a game to me.*" His breathing was ragged.

I gulped. Now, I understood. Now how Wyatt had been acting made sense—why he'd been torturing himself this way. "H-he wouldn't think that," I said softly.

"Would you?"

I shook my head. "Of course not." The horror of the thought was expressed in my tone.

"Because this is one of those moments, Channing, where I'd pull out of the Games if you did," he rasped harshly, his thumbs rubbing back and forth on my cheeks. "This is one of those moments where there is something more important to me than winning."

"What is it?" I breathed out, letting my heart stop as I waited for his answer.

"You," he murmured. "*Love.*"

My heart started again with a vengeance. "If it's more important than winning, it should be more important than my brother. If this isn't a game, then don't let them come between us." And then, with every ounce of need and love I had and could no longer deny for this man, I said, "Be with me, Wyatt. I need you to love me tonight."

I saw his wall crumbling brick by brick. "I don't... I don't even have any protection with me."

"I'm on the pill," I whispered. *And I had been for as long as I could remember so that I was regular and so that my cramps didn't screw up my riding.*

His forehead dropped to mine and he groaned like I'd just ripped his heart from his chest. "Do you trust me?"

"Yes." *Unquestioningly. Unwaveringly. Unbelievably.*

Wyatt

I wanted this to be good—to be magical—like the rest of the night had been, but I knew I was too far gone to be able to make that happen. *I needed her too fucking badly.*

Like the storm outside, my desire for her burned white and blinded me to everything else. I felt my muscles twitching as I snaked one arm around her back, my hand cupping her perfectly rounded ass to lower us both back onto the disheveled bed of blankets.

I seized her lips on our descent, her arms linking around my neck, just like her legs did when we landed on the floor. I plunged my tongue into the hot warmth of her mouth, roughly mimicking the motion with my hips, slamming my erection into her core.

"*Wyatt.*" She moaned my name, her hips grinding up against my arousal deliberately. The need for her escalated excruciatingly, my cock throbbing against my pants. I knew then and there that if she rode up against me like she rode my thigh the other night, all of this would be over far too soon.

My mouth broke from hers, gasping in air as I tried to control my body. I looked down at her rapidly rising and falling chest. Her rosy-pink nipples erect underneath the sheer lace of her bra, begging to be sucked. I moved the hand that was underneath her, sliding it up to unclasp her flimsy excuse for a bra before I yanked the damn thing down off of her shoulders, the lace rubbing roughly against her white skin.

Freed from their cage, her small breasts captured my gaze—the thought of kneading them with my big hands making my heavy erection tingle. I engulfed one small swell with my hand, groaning at the jolt of possessiveness that shot through me. They were small, but they were the perfect size to make me hunger for more of *her*.

Channing slid her hips against me again, her wet sex rubbing against the denim of my jeans. I pressed my hips down, pinning her against the floor so she couldn't torture me anymore. Her shudder of pleasure was almost my undoing as I rolled the plump skin of her nipple between my fingers.

"*Christ,* Channing," I rasped, "you're making me lose it."

"At least," she answered breathlessly, arching her chest into my hand, "this will be one loss that you will enjoy."

I groaned, bending my head to take the begging peak of her nipple into my mouth, first grasping it between my teeth before sucking on it ravenously. I feasted on it for a few minutes before turning my attention to her other breast, my hand taking the place of my mouth on the first. She melted against me, moaning my name over and over again. I knew how sensitive her nipples were—I knew that a few more bites and licks would send her over the edge of another orgasm. But I was greedy. I wanted—*I needed*—to be inside her for this one.

My cock was agonizingly hard—to the point where I couldn't distinguish whether each slight movement elicited pleasure or pain.

"You're mine," I rasped against the goosebumps surrounding her nipple. I slid my tongue down the slope of her breast, briefly licking her sternum before planting a kiss on the soft skin.

I kissed my way down her stomach, reveling in the way her body quaked underneath the slightest touch.

"Breathe, Channing," I instructed her, feeling her chest move raggedly underneath my hand.

"I can't," she answered breathlessly. "Not when your touch takes my breath away."

Inhaling deeply, I licked the crevice between her thigh and her sex. I inhaled her desire before letting my tongue run up the length of her folds. Her hips seized as I pulled back, standing up to remove my clothes. Ripping my shirt up over my head, I looked down at her perfectly fit and flushed body, her nipples, her sex, and the marks left by my mouth the only things blushing pink against the creamy white of her skin—each of those glistening from my touch and her desire.

As I unzipped my jeans I felt just how wet she'd made the fabric over my fly. I sucked in a breath as the release of pressure around my cock almost sent me over the edge. I carefully pulled the denim and my briefs down over my arousal, feeling her heady gaze on me. I tossed my clothes onto the floor, now standing just as naked as she, my body ready to pounce.

I watched her subtle invitation—the way she bit her lower lip, her chest rising on an inhale and her legs parting ever so slightly. And then my gorgeous nymph murmured huskily, "You're mine."

I lost it. Dropping to my knees, I pressed the length of my body against her. Our moans in sync as the heat of her sex touched the hardness of mine. My teeth found her neck as I raised my hips, the head of my cock trailing down to her entrance.

I hadn't planned for this. I should have been more prepared. I should have taken more time preparing her. I should have made sure—again—that she was ok with this. I should have been in better control. But I wasn't. I'd lost everything to her.

And as I sheathed myself inside of her hot and impossibly tight core, I admitted that she was right—this was one loss that was far too incredible and far too enjoyable to regret. I heard her gasp at my sudden entrance into her body and I begged mine to hold for just a second so that I could make sure she was ok. Maybe I did… maybe I didn't… All I knew was that I felt her hips rock against mine—begging for more—as my name left her lips; whatever shred of control I had disintegrated.

I thrust into her once, twice, three times. She was small and so damned tight, but her throaty groans each time I entered her forbade me from stopping. Just like I'd imagined, her legs were incredibly strong from a lifetime of snowboarding. They tightened almost painfully around my waist, encouraging me as I slammed into her. I thrust harder and faster, feeling every cell in my body tingling.

"*More,*" she gasped. I loved her rhythmic moans that followed—and the way they made my swollen cock ready to explode. I felt her and subsequently lost every other sensation; her grip on my erection tightened as her orgasm began and it sent me over the edge. My hips jerked uncontrollably, my thrusts unrestrained as my body finally found the release it had been desperate for.

We came together like the storm—suddenly and with a fury that obliterated anything in its path.

I collapsed on top of her, our breathing ragged for minutes on end. With a groan, I slid out of her, grabbing some napkins from one of the bags and handing some to her before quickly wiping myself. A quick glance at the window told me it was still snowing furiously outside—a sharp contrast to the warm, heady musk that pervaded the small hut.

"You ok?" I, surprisingly, struggled with the question, afraid that I had hurt her, gone too fast, too rough, too *everything* for her. I turned on my side, pulling one of the blankets up over both of us. "Sorry. I lost control there."

When she turned toward me, the sated sigh combined with the smile on her face told me that my fears were unfounded. "All I have to say is… that is the best kind of losing," she murmured with a small grin, "the kind where we both win."

I laughed at her silly joke. "Seriously, Channing," my hand cupped her face, "I didn't hurt you, did I?"

"Honestly, my entire body is numb with pleasure so I couldn't tell you. But, even if you did, I'd be the first in line to sign up and have you hurt me again."

I bent and kissed her forehead, loving how she immediately snuggled closer to me. I may not know exactly what was going to happen once the X Games were over, once I retired from competing, but I did know that waking up with her in my arms everyday was non-negotiable. And I sent up a silent prayer that all my planning this past week would fall into place.

"When was the last time you had sex?" I knew my mouth had been her first, but she hadn't been a virgin. She had, however, been tight as all hell which made me believe that she hadn't been with someone in a while. A violent stab of possessiveness ran through me; I didn't care who it was, there would be no one else after me.

"A *long* time ago," she mumbled and I could hear her drifting off to sleep. "Was only two times." Her hand came to rest up against my chest and one foot slid between my legs. "Some boarder who moved East for college. Wasn't anything like this… why I never did it again."

I stayed silent, not wanting to disturb her any more. She surprised me by whispering against my chest, "How about you?"

My fingers lazily rubbed over her back. "A few months." Her response was just a sigh. "But it was never like this…" I continued softly. She breathed heavily against my chest and I knew she'd fallen asleep.

Still I answered the question that I imagined she would have followed with. "Because I've never been in love with anyone before."

․․․

The light glimmering over my face from the small window of the hut woke me. Channing was still fast asleep against my chest, her soft breathing caressing my skin. I felt around the blankets next to me for my cell; it was almost six-thirty. We needed to get going. I hadn't planned on us staying the whole night, but we'd both drifted off into a deep sleep to the sound of the wind and snow.

I trailed my fingers lightly down her back, kissing the top of her head. "Time to wake up, Channing." She sighed and nuzzled deeper against me. "C'mon gorgeous, we should get down the mountain before they send out a search party." And before the snow started falling heavily again.

That got her attention, her eyes fluttering open. "Hi."

"Hey." I kissed her sweet lips softly. "How are you feeling this morning?"

"Just gnarly," she murmured and I burst out laughing.

It only took us a few minutes to get dressed and gather all of the stuff I'd brought with us last night before I moved to open the door and release us and the magic of the night back into reality.

․․․

Channing

Son of a biscuit.

Last night I'd been flung off of a kicker that I didn't ever want to land.

Even though we'd been basically sleeping on the hard floor, I'd slept amazingly well, but I'd still woken with the familiar ache between my thighs. Only now it was worse because I knew what was possible. I hadn't lied when I said that my limited experience with sex hadn't been like this—it hadn't even been that enjoyable. I'd thought the kid, the snowboarder, Steve, was hot and he'd been the first boarder to show an interest in me, the rest unable to see me as anything other than one of the guys. We'd had sex twice, behind the rental shop because I didn't want my brother or our friends to know; the first time, I thought it was because it was my *first* time. The second time, I figured that it wasn't worth the trouble. So, I'd kept myself close to my brother and Emmett and eventually Steve got the picture that sex wasn't happening anymore.

Wyatt was not just a different story, but a whole different world. The rush, the thrill through my body was more than I could even describe. If I didn't believe that my body was made for boarding, I would swear that it was made for this—with him. And I wanted more when I woke up and I could feel that he did, too. But, instead, he insisted sweetly that we get dressed and head back down.

I dressed and waited patiently, coming up behind him as he reached for the doorknob and wrapping my arms around his waist, letting my hand drift down to where I could see his arousal pressing against the denim.

"Channing," he ground out, sucking in a breath. "We need to go. Your sister is probably freaking out."

I laughed—he clearly didn't know much about Ally. "I doubt it. I'm sure the longer that the both of us are gone, the more thrilled she will be." I pressed my palm harder against him. He turned and kissed me hard—and I thought I had won. Until my desire was greeted by a rush of cold air.

It was pretty chilly outside, the sky looking like it was about to let down another blanket of snow, but it did nothing to dampen the burning in my body.

"Are you ok?" I asked as he brushed the snow off of the seat and set the bags on the lift, fishing for the keys to go turn it on.

"Yeah."

I wasn't convinced. "Wyatt." He turned at the sound of his name and I put my hands on his shoulders and shoved him onto the seat, climbing on top of his lap. He groaned as I settled over his arousal. His eyes narrowed on me as his hands grabbed my waist, but he didn't push me off of him—*baby steps.*

"Why don't you want me this morning?" I was being totally brazen and I smiled because I didn't even care.

He slammed his hips up into mine. "Don't *ever* think that I don't want you, gorgeous. *This* has been the story of my life since the second you knocked over all of my boards."

Yeah, I was never going to live that down.

"Well, at least now you know how good I am at making wood stand up straight." I grinned coyly at him, finally putting a smile onto his face. "So, what's the problem?"

His hand slid down and squeezed into my ass. "Aren't you sore?" he rasped. "And don't lie to me. I wasn't easy on you last night, gorgeous, and fuck me, I should have been. I should have been tender and sweet and everything that I'd wanted to be when the time came—instead—"

"Instead," I interjected, "you took me like your life depended on it and I can't imagine why you would think I would have wanted it any other way."

He groaned. "I was too hard…"

"Well, you were that. I can't disagree with you there." I winked at him. "Seriously, Wyatt, I don't even know of a word to describe how perfect it was. You know me," my voice quieted now, my eyes watching as my hands traced down over his chest, "I like hard. I like fast. I like rough." I found his gaze again. "I'm a snowboarder, after all."

I rubbed myself against him, enjoying the catch in his breath and the way the chairlift began to gently rock us together.

"Alright, point taken." He pushed forward and kissed me and I sighed into the familiar haven. "Now that you've succeeded in eliminating my guilt," he kissed along my jawline to my ear and I held my breath in anticipation of what was coming next, "we should really head back down."

The air rushed out of me in furious disappointment. He clearly was still trying to be a gentleman about it all. Well, I wasn't having any of it.

I turned my head and kissed him again. He didn't push back when I deepened the embrace, my tongue demanding attention from his. Lifting my hips, I slid my hand down over the front of his pants, undoing the zipper before he could stop me.

"Channing…"

"Show me," I said, "show me that you want me." It was a dare. We lived in a world of dares—daring fate, gravity, mother nature—to stop us from getting what we wanted. And now, I was daring him to stop both of us from taking what we needed. "Here."

Alone on the mountain, we were its King and Queen. And the thought of him taking me on a chair lift that I'd ridden a thousand times soaked straight through my underwear.

"Stand and turn," his instructions were hard and demanding. I quickly complied. With my back to him, I felt one hand grasp the back edge of my pants and pull them down over my ass, exposing just enough flesh so that I wouldn't freeze in this process. His hand slipped around to my front, diving beneath my pants as I felt his teeth dig into the firm flesh of my ass. "Always so damn wet for me, gorgeous." His fingers slid over my folds and goosebumps covered my body. "Now, sit." His hand moved back onto my stomach and pulled me down onto his lap.

There was no warning aside from the brief touch of his fingers to assess my readiness as he guided me to sit, impaling me with his hard length. I gasped at the welcome invasion, my muscles were sore from last night, but it only made the fullness even more overwhelming.

Wyatt held me still for a moment, letting me adjust to him. Desire overwhelming me as I realized that we sat on the lift, fully clothed, except where we were joined. My hips begged to move.

"Ride me, Ryder."

I moaned and began to move up and down on his length, feeling the hot hardness of his cock slip in and out of me. His hand resumed its spot inside of my underwear, letting my movements allow my clit to rub against his fingers. Outside… inside… my climax assaulted me from every angle. I screamed into the silence, the delicious pressure finally bursting inside of me.

Just to confirm, it was as exquisite as it had been last night.

I heard his rushed grunts from behind me. He was thrusting up and into me now, the clenching of my core rocketing him over the edge. I felt his hips seize and the warm rush of his desire inside of me.

"You're going to be the death of me, Channing."

"Well, you are getting close to retirement," I mused teasingly. He laughed and gently pushed up on my hips, letting him slip out of me. Wyatt quickly pulled my yoga pants back up to make sure I wasn't cold before he tugged out a corner of a blanket to wipe himself and adjust his pants.

"Let's go, minx." He smacked my ass before going to turn the lift on.

CHAPTER
Twenty-One

Channing

"Ow!" I EXCLAIMED, FEELING THE HARD *THWACK* OF A PILLOW over my head.

"Channing!" Ally screeched, jumping onto my bed next to me.

I dove further underneath the covers. "What time is it?"

"Almost noon." She bounced obnoxiously next to me and I tried to hit her with my free hand. *Unsuccessfully.*

"Why are you doing this to me?"

"Because you were gone *all* last night—I know, because I waited up even after Zack left. And then you magically reappeared early this morning, only to pass out for another four hours in your bed." The excited sweetness in her voice was nauseating. "And then there's the fact that *your* Mr. Olsen had practically a breakfast buffet delivered to the house about an hour ago."

Damn gentleman.

"So, what happened? Spill!"

"Coffee…" I rasped, feeling her climb back over me. Only to have the covers yanked unceremoniously off of me. At least when Wyatt had dropped me off earlier, I'd had the wherewithal to change my clothes—and my underwear. "I hate you," I grumbled, pushing myself up.

"Only until you get your coffee and some food!" And then she flicked the lights on. "See you downstairs!" Ally grabbed the edge of the doorframe, pulling herself back for a second as I squinted at her. "By the way... about breakfast... I can't promise that I left a lot of the good stuff. Snooze you lose!" Her smile flashed as she disappeared from sight.

She wasn't going to leave me alone until I told her all about my night—and her giant grin when I appeared downstairs a few minutes later confirmed as much.

"So, what happened?" She repeated as I poured myself a giant cup of coffee. The snow had started again—a steady fall onto the inches we'd gained from the squall last night.

"We had a picnic." There was truly no better cure for anything than a good, strong, hot cup of coffee. I breathed in the energizing aroma, letting it bring me back to life.

"Yeah," she retorted. "I knew that much. Oh my God, Zack said it was hysterical the way Wyatt was in their kitchen cooking yesterday, getting everything ready."

Now, I was intrigued.

"Oh yeah? What else did the *other* Mr. Olsen say?"

"Nope. Sorry. Lips are zipped until you tell me what happened last night—*after the picnic.*" She raised her eyebrows.

I picked up a croissant and took a huge bite. "He took me up onto the mountain, for the picnic, where we ended up stranded because of the snowsquall." I shrugged—'stranded' might have been a stretch; even if we could have, neither of us would have left.

"And..." Ally grabbed half of a cinnamon roll. "Do I have to spell it out? *Fine.* Did you guys do *it?!* Did you sleep with him?"

I nodded, knowing that in another second, my blush was going to reveal the truth whether I liked it or not.

"AHH!!!" she screamed and began jumping.

I couldn't help but laugh. I mean, it was a big deal—a huge deal—to me... but her excitement came close.

"Why are you so freaking excited? You know I've had sex before..." I said it casually—like I had sex every other day—in an attempt to downplay the drama.

"Oh yeah? When? If it's been longer than five years it doesn't count." That was my cue to take another large bite of food in an attempt to avoid an answer. "Ok, seriously, Chan. I'm not judging you. Just talk to me…"

I felt stupid holding back from her. Maybe because talking about it—admitting to it—meant admitting to my feelings. Talking about it turned it into reality.

I wanted it to be a reality.

"Ok," I quickly responded, surprised by my thought, "let's go sit though."

We grabbed the coffee and the goods—aka the mass of breakfast food that Wyatt should have known was far too much for just us two girls.

"So, I'm sure you already know, but he cooked this incredible Italian dinner for us. I had no idea. I couldn't even believe when we pulled into the resort—I mean everything was closed because of the impending storm. I was so confused." I found myself smiling at the memory. "I didn't know about the dinner yet. Anyway, so he opens the trunk and hands me your snow boots—"

"I know! I was hoping they wouldn't be too tight!"

"No, they were fine." I took another sip of my black coffee. "So, we get geared up and then he starts walking towards the base of the trails and I'm thinking, 'where the hell are we going?' And then, the man pulls out a key for the freaking lift."

"WHAT!"

My eyes widened. "You didn't know that?"

"No! He just said he was taking you on a picnic at the mountain and that he needed my snow boots."

"Yeah, well 'at the mountain' meant 'up the mountain.'" I laughed, reaching for one of the glazed donuts. "So, he turns on the chair lift—mind you, I haven't been on that side of the mountain probably for a good year, so I have no idea what's at the top."

"Oh my *God*, this is so romantic."

"Do you want me to finish?" I scolded her. "So, we get to the top and we walk like a minute to the warming hut that's up there. It's open because… why wouldn't it be? If the lift is closed, how else would you get up there?" I took another bite, but continued to talk with my mouth full; *today, apparently, I was that kind of girl.* "We get inside, he turns the lamps on, and then proceeds to lay down a million blankets and his home-cooked feast. It was delicious."

"Yeah, I bet he was, too," came her sly response. "So how did it happen? Were you drunk?"

"No." I shook my head. "I mean, I had a glass of wine, but I wasn't drunk. We finished dinner and then he took me back outside to look at the stars; it was the most beautiful thing I've ever see, Al…" My gaze went hazy at the memory, remembering the infinite magical sparks above us.

"Well, I'm glad he didn't just take you to some five-star restaurant. I mean, that would definitely be romantic, but I don't think it would be you—and I'm glad he saw that, too."

I bit my lip as my smile tried to grow larger. "No, it wasn't a five-star restaurant—it was a five-million-star restaurant."

"Oh my God, you have it so bad." She began to laugh uncontrollably.

"Hey!" I sighed, lying into the back of the couch to try to stop myself from really over-indulging on the carbs.

"Alright, now let's get to the good stuff."

I rolled my eyes. "So, we came back inside and things got a little heated." No need to go into details about dessert. "And then he wanted to go."

"Wait, what?" The dumbfounded look on her face was pure comedy.

"He wanted to leave; he hadn't planned on staying the night—or having sex."

"Why? Is there… something wrong with him?"

"Oh my God, no. *No.* Definitely nothing wrong with him." My blush rose. "He… He insisted on leaving because he didn't want to or plan on having sex with me until after the Games."

"Why?"

"He didn't want me or Chance to think that he'd done it to throw Chance off in the competition." It was when Ally didn't response that I knew exactly what she was thinking. "I know…" I whispered, staring at the black pit inside my coffee cup.

"That you have to pull out of the Games?" She finished my sentence, transforming it into a query.

I nodded.

"Well that was convincing." I frowned and she put her hands up. "Alright, fine. I'll take your word that you are going to do it, but for posterity's sake, you need to let me say one thing," and she didn't give me a chance to do otherwise, "and that is that this guy is serious about you, Chan. Like *serious* with a capital—L." *What?* "Serious as in L-o-v-e. Sheesh. You need to withdraw from the competition and, not only that, but you need to tell him what you'd planned on doing; you need to tell him about Chance."

My mind spun through *that* conversation. For some reason, I'd come to the realization that I had to pull out of the Games, but I hadn't thought it all the way through to the fact that I needed to tell Wyatt about Chance. Ally was right though, there was no other way to explain why Chance wasn't here without more lies.

"I know; it's just hard." I put a hand up to stop her. "Not that I won't do it, but, I don't know, I guess I felt like I was finally going to be able to prove how good I was—not to anyone else, just to myself."

"I don't think anyone has ever doubted you."

I nodded; I didn't want to talk about this right now. I was still living off the high of last night and I wanted to keep that blissful bubble for as long as possible. "No, you're right." I smiled at her and continued, "Now, where was I? Oh, right. So, Wyatt wanted to leave and when he told me that he wanted there to be no doubt that I was more important than winning, I may have told him to prove it. Not to mention, by that point the snow squall had started so we were trapped."

"Oh, wow…"

"And then… yeah…" I ducked my head, moments flashing in front of my eyes.

"Don't just 'yeah' me! I want details! How was it? How many times? Did you…" Here, she chose to whistle instead of saying the word 'orgasm.'

"Hard to believe sometimes that you're my *little* sister." Maybe something was wrong with me, but I sure as hell didn't want the details of her and Zack together.

"Just once. Yes. And it was magical." I rattled, counting off on my fingers as I answered each of her questions.

"Must have been… if it was only just once."

"Ally!" I was tempted to throw the remains of my donut at her. "Yes, only once. At least last night…"

"*This morning?!*"

I smiled smugly. "On the chairlift." Her mouth literally fell open and for once, I enjoyed the deafening *silence* that came out of it.

"What the hell." Ally groaned as she fell back against the couch. "I don't get it. You're the one who's the freaking tomboy, you're the one who doesn't care about clothes or hair or make up or dates or boys—nothing except for snowboarding—and you're the one who ends up with Mr. Milk-Frother who is both impossibly hot and impossibly romantic. It's just not fair."

I started to laugh. "What do you mean? You and Zack are great together! I thought you really liked him!"

"I do!" She insisted, but her enthusiasm paled compared to how she'd asked about my night with Wyatt. "He's just not quite like that and I don't know. We're having a great time, don't get me wrong. I just don't know that it's going to last. I'm just not there yet."

"What do you mean?" It was my turn to pry, dear sister. "Does this have something to do with Emmett?"

Her head spun to me so fast I thought she was going to get whiplash. "Absolutely not. Why would you even say that?"

"Woah, no need to get an attitude. I just asked because there is obviously a problem between the two of you and I thought maybe you enjoyed being with Zack more because of how angry it makes Emmett."

Her arms crossed over her chest. "No. I don't care about Emmett and this has nothing to do with him. Maybe if he hadn't been the worst kind of asshole to me a few months ago, things would be different. But, I can't stand the man and I don't think I'll ever be able to."

"What happened a few months ago?" I was completely blown away. I hadn't heard of anything that had happened between them and she'd definitely never said a word.

"I don't—" Her refusal to answer the question was cut off by her cell ringing on the coffee table.

She picked it up like it was a lifeline. *"Hello?"*

"Hey, babe! What's up?

"Nothing, just talking with my sister."

"Oh yeah! That sounds like fun. Come over for six."

"Be careful driving. I'll see you then."

She hung up and turned to me. "Zack and Wyatt are coming over tonight for pizza and game night."

"We'll have to tell them that Chance is with Emmett." I don't know why that was the first thing that came to my mind and blurted out of my mouth, but it was. I saw Ally look at me disapprovingly because we'd just talked about *not* doing this anymore. "I know, I swear I'm going to tell him; I just don't think tonight is the night; I want to actually withdraw from the competition first."

"You better," she grumbled, standing up. "I'm going to take a shower."

And avoid answering my question about Emmett, I thought.

CHAPTER
Twenty-Two

Channing

"I HAVE A QUESTION." WYATT'S VOICE RUMBLED NEXT TO MY EAR. He'd stayed on the mountain to practice for the Games this morning after our training session, but not before he'd asked if we could grab dinner together before my shift at *Breakers* tonight. He'd followed me inside the equipment room when I went to put back all of the lesson gear, wrapping his arms around my waist as I tried to focus on standing the snowboards up neatly against the wall.

"And what is that?" I pretended not to notice how he bit my earlobe, the sensation turning my body on fire.

"I forgot to ask," he murmured, "but, why did Ally refer to me as 'Mr. Milk-Frother' the other week?"

I sucked in a breath. *Crap.* "N-no reason. She says crazy things—just look at how she was the other night when we were playing Apples-to-Apples." Granted, pizza and game night had also included alcohol, which meant that after about one drink, Ally had turned tipsy; it was a good thing she was cute—and that Zack was smitten. Needless to say, the game didn't end with any serious winner.

His hand snaked around to cup my sex through my black stretch pants that I had put on for work, his palm pressing against me.

I groaned, my hips returning the pressure.

This was how it had been all week. The heat, the tension, the pleasure. We weren't keeping it a secret, but we weren't advertising it either—which meant that our rendezvous were mostly hard and fast, hidden on the mountain or somewhere at the base. He refused to stay over while Ally was home.

I swore, it felt like I was trading in my spot in the X Games for a position in the Sex Games.

It was incredible—and not just because of the sex. It was the way Wyatt made me feel like I was the only goddamn star in the sky whenever he looked at me. The way my body felt like it had been made just for him when he touched me. And the way my heart beat into my brain just how hard I'd fallen for him every moment that I was with him.

Ok, but the sex was pretty phenomenal, too. Phenomenal and prolific.

"I don't believe you, gorgeous." He palmed me again, his index finger flicking over my entrance; I felt desire spill out of me.

"Not fair," I whispered breathlessly.

"Do you want me to play fair?"

I moaned, "No."

He flipped me around, my back now against the hard, smooth bottom of the snowboard that I'd just finished propping against the wall.

"Spill, Channing." His head bent and sucked my lower lip into his mouth.

I sighed. "Fine." I pushed my hips against his groin, my small act of defiance before I answered. "After we first met, when I told Ally about it—" I broke off, feeling his fingers along the waist of my pants. As soon as I stopped talking though, his fingers stopped too. "She asked if you were hot. S-so, I told her that y-you were so hot," I swallowed thickly, his fingers inching beneath my pants, "that s-she could stick your finger—" I groaned, his touch grazing over the top of my sex, "—in her s-stupid milk canister a-and use you to steam the m-milk for the espresso drinks."

He froze. And then I felt his body rumble against mine. Too bad there was still only just the slight touch of his fingers

"*Wyatt,*" I whimpered.

"Oh, don't you worry, gorgeous." He kissed along my jawline and I felt his hands begin to blessedly move, his thumbs hooking into my waistband and inching my pants down. "I'm going to froth you *so* good."

Son. Of. A. Biscuit.

I wanted to smack him. I wanted to yell at him for making fun of me. Hell, I wanted to just be able to groan at how *ridiculous* the whole 'milk-frother' comment had become. But I was just too damn intoxicated by the man to care how he was teasing me right now.

He pulled my pants midway down my thighs and dropped to his knees in front of me. *Looked like teasing time was over.*

My eyes found his—and his wicked grin. Then my legs were hoisted up onto his shoulders, his head fitting in the circle of my thighs that had been created with my only half-removed pants.

"I love seeing you lose control. Sexiest thing of my life," he rasped. The faintest hint of his breath moving over my slick center elicited a moan. I had no freaking clue. Burning… freezing… at this point, they both felt the same. "Mmm." His mouth kissed my inner thigh. "Let's see just how hot my finger can make you." As the words came out of his mouth, he pushed a finger all the way inside of me, curving it slightly into that incredible, emergency-explosion button that was inside.

My hips bucked at the sensation.

And then his tongue joined in. Sweeping from where his finger disappeared inside of me all the way up to my clit, savoring my desire. "Tasting pretty damn hot there, gorgeous."

And then his mouth covered me. Wyatt knew exactly how to send me right over the edge—and he'd only been perfecting it every day so far this week. The combination of his finger inside my core and his tongue on my clit was suffocating. It didn't take long—and neither of us wanted it to. And then, in the middle of our gear room—that was unlocked—with my back against a snowboard that some twelve-year-old had just been using, my legs clutched around his head, one hand buried in his hair, and the other grabbing blindly for one of the other secured snowboards next to me, I shattered against his mouth. My body arching against the source of my pleasure, the source that greedily lapped up every drop of my release.

He carefully disentangled us, righting my pants as my feet returned to the ground. I sighed, falling against his chest. The way his arms instinctively wrapped around me and held me to him made my heart pound.

"We should get you up to Breakers." I barely nodded. Honestly, I didn't want to go anywhere; I was right where I needed to be. "How do you feel?"

I pulled back slightly, looking up at him as his hands traced lazy circles on my back. "Thoroughly frothed."

If you can't beat 'em, join 'em. Or something like that.

We both laughed and, all of a sudden, the nickname grew on me. Still hugging him to me, I could feel how hard he was, but we both knew I didn't have time or I'd be late for work.

"I hate leaving you like this," I murmured as we walked out of the lesson building, hand in hand.

"I'll let you take care of me later." He winked.

"Yeah?" I turned with a devious smile. "Like when you stay over?"

"Channing, you know I—"

I turned in front of him, stopping him in his tracks. "I do know. Which is why I'm still inviting you over. Ally is staying over Tammy's tonight with Jessa; it's their monthly girl's night out—which is why I told her I wouldn't be able to make it since you and I had plans."

He eyed my skeptically. "What about your brother?"

I hated lying to him; each time it felt like I was adding another brick to a wall that I was solely responsible for building between us. "He's… uhh… going to stay at Nick's and help him with a project."

I crossed my fingers, hoping that was enough. "Alright."

I squealed, jumping and throwing my arms around his neck. It was ridiculous how the thought of sleeping with him in an actual bed—*in my bed*—could make me so ecstatically happy.

I also loved how he held me for just a split second longer than the embrace was supposed to last.

"C'mon, gorgeous. I need to feed you and get you to work," he said as he tapped my ass before pulling me against his side as we walked into the lodge.

He'd staked his claim to me and I was as happy as a snow bunny. Of course though, tonight of all nights, my eyes caught sight of Emmett and Nick sitting in the corner of the main dining room. Emmett's eyes immediately locked on me; Nick continued to talk for a few seconds until he realized that Emmett wasn't paying attention. As soon as he saw Wyatt and me, a smile broke on his face—*the knowing kind*—and he nodded to us.

Well, at least I hadn't lost both friends. I waved back at Nick.

Wyatt and I ordered our food—I, of course, choosing the *classic* chicken fingers and fries; my handsome date choosing a much healthier-looking chicken sandwich.

"You want to go sit with them?" he asked as we waited to pay.

I chewed on my lip. I did and I didn't. Mostly, I didn't know what was going to come out of Emmett's mouth and I didn't want to take the chance that it would ruin our night.

"C'mon, let's go sit with your friends." I sent up a silent prayer for fortitude.

Nick gave us a warm greeting—and in his own way, so did Emmett. And by that I mean he wasn't rude or obnoxious. He acknowledged us with a nod and a 'what's up?'

A quick glance told me that they were done eating which hopefully meant they wouldn't hang around too long.

"How's the triple coming, Lil?" Nick asked, taking one of my fries.

"Alright." I hadn't landed it yet, but Wyatt made sure that I didn't give up. His hoarsely caring and encouraging voice resounding in my mind, '*You have to get up every time you fall, sweetheart.*' His faith in me brought me to my knees.

"More than alright," my tempting teacher added on my behalf. "She'll have it by the end of next week." I swallowed painfully. If I did, that would be just in time for the competition that I was no longer going to be participating in.

As soon as I found a minute to let the committee know that 'Chance' was dropping out.

I swore I wasn't dragging my feet but I hardly got a minute to myself—up early to train, lunch with Wyatt, lessons, dinner with Wyatt, Breakers, and then bed. And any spare second in the day was wholly consumed with my gorgeous boyfriend.

Boyfriend.

I'd thought of him like that for days, but we hadn't explicitly said the words yet.

"Nice job, Lil." I raised my eyes in shock at Emmett's compliment; maybe his cooling off period had finally ended. "Chance would be proud."

Oh no.

"He is," I answered quickly, darting my eyes to Wyatt. "He's already seen me do it though, so he knew I was capable." *Pleasedon'tbecurious. Pleasedon'tbeconfused.* I stuck a fry in my mouth and then thanked God that Nick let up with a smirk, asking, "You guys are coming out tomorrow, right?"

Tomorrow…

"Your end of school celebration?" Wyatt jogged my memory; I'd completely forgotten about his invitation last week. *Crap.*

"Yup! Got one more final project that I have to finish tonight and then I'm home free for winter break!"

"Sounds like fun to me." I felt his hand on my lower back, tracing delicious circles again. "As long as my girlfriend can take a break from Breakers?" His gaze swung to me, knowing *exactly* what he'd said.

Of course. Of course he would make my eat my thoughts and would call me his girlfriend now. In front of my friends. In the exact moment I was trying to find an excuse for us not to go. And work would have been an excellent one.

"Can you get off of work, gorgeous?" Wyatt asked me quietly, but not quietly enough to prevent my friends from hearing and Emmett from snorting in disgust.

"Y-yeah. I should be able to." *I was in so much trouble.* "I'll ask tonight."

"Awesome! Big Louie's. Remind Ally." My sister's singing skills were infamous. I watched Emmett's face darken at the mention of her—and them.

I nodded just as Wyatt grabbed my hand underneath the table. "We should get going. I don't want you to be late."

"Yeah." We both stood, grabbing our empty trays. "Guess we'll see you guys tomorrow."

As soon as we were out of the dining room, he tugged my hand. "You don't seem like you want to go." I shouldn't have been surprised that he noticed.

"No—" I assured him. "—I do. I just forgot about it. There's just a lot going on in my mind." My mumbling quieted to nothing as we entered the building that Breakers was in.

"I see that. Care to share?" His thumb rubbed over the back of my hand.

"You called me your girlfriend." It wasn't that I didn't want to—or couldn't—tell him at least some of the things on my mind, but this was at the forefront, probably because of the way it tugged at my heart.

"I did." He smiled. "I thought that's what all this meant." Then his face turned serious. "Did you think I wanted something else from you? That this is just some fling for me?" The way he asked—and looked as he did it—told me that he would throttle anyone who suggested it—possibly including myself.

"N-no." I shook my head. I actually didn't think that. "No. I just… I was just surprised, that's all."

"Do you not want to be my girlfriend?"

I sucked in a breath, trying to hold in a smile as I answered, "I don't know—you snowboarders are all so cocky and demanding." The smile broke free. "I'm a pretty independent person, I don't know that I need—"

He growled and pushed me up against the side of the elevator as we climbed the eight floors to the bar.

"I haven't heard you complaining about my cock…iness all week, Miss Ryder." His mouth was hardly an inch from mine and I couldn't stop myself from trying to bite his lip. His knee wedged between my thighs. "So, tell me, Channing, what do you need, then?"

I tried to kiss him, but every time he pulled back. Finally, I groaned in defeat; my little tease backfiring. "You."

His lips landed hard on mine. "What else? What do you need me for?" He demanded.

"To be my boyfriend." The doors opened before he could kiss me again. My body sagged as he stepped back from me.

"Good," he rasped, leading me off of the elevator and wrapping his arms around me when he saw no one was around. "I'm warning you right now, gorgeous, this '*cocky and demanding snowboarder*' is going to be demanding a whole lot more than that. I hope you're up for the challenge."

I was always up for the challenge. *But, was my heart?*

"Go big or go home," I murmured, losing myself in his eyes. He kissed me tenderly before I walked into work, my internal timer beginning to count down the minutes until it was time to spend the rest of the night with my *boyfriend.*

Wyatt

I was so far gone and I didn't care who knew it.

I'd been ensnared by one feisty and fearless Ryder.

The way that her friends looked at me—especially Emmett—they thought this was just a game for me, just like the X Games next weekend; he thought she was just entertainment, maybe to throw off her brother or even not… I couldn't blame him for being protective, but I needed them—and her—to know just how serious I was about *us.*

I wasn't going to be obtuse about it; from the second I'd met her,

I knew that she hadn't just crashed into my snowboards, but that she'd crashed into my life—*into me*. From the second I'd kissed her, I knew that she was there to stay. And from the second I'd held her underneath the stars, I knew that I'd fallen in love with her. And *fuck* if I didn't want to tell her that over and over again, but there was still something standing between us. And that something felt a whole lot like her brother.

She continued to hold back from me—not physically—*God, not physically...* But I needed more and I wasn't going to give up until I not only won these damn Games, but until I won her heart. And I needed to figure out how to get her to trust me completely before I could share with her the plans that were almost solidified; every time I saw her, it burned on the tip of my tongue to tell her that I'd be staying in Hope's Creek after the competition was over—that I'd be staying to be with her. There was even more than that, but it wasn't finalized and wouldn't be until my parents got here this weekend with the paperwork. I didn't want to jinx anything about the fucking incredible future that I was building for myself—and hopefully, for us. I didn't know what was keeping her from me, but I didn't want to risk moving too fast on her and making it worse.

Tonight, she was going to get a little nudge. I was going to ask her to come to dinner with my parents and me on Saturday after they arrived. Not only was it what I'd wanted, but my mom was driving me crazy to meet the girl who'd changed my life.

I stood up off the wall that I'd been leaning against, quietly watching my gorgeous girl run her hand through her disheveled hair when she finished closing down the bar for the night. I saw the moment she looked around, wondering where I was; it was terrible of me to savor it—her worried expression, wondering why I wasn't there already—but I needed to savor it because it gave me hope that she wanted me like I wanted her.

"Ready?" Her head jerked towards my voice, a smile blooming over her face.

"And waiting," she tossed back at me.

"Sorry, I was just out in the hall." I held the door open for her to walk ahead of me.

"Doing what?"

I grinned. "Watching you." I bent and claimed a quick kiss, enjoying the soft blush that rose to her cheeks.

"Oh, yeah?" As soon as the doors shut she pressed up against me.

"How was work?" I didn't want to lose it now; I wanted to talk to her about dinner with my parents. *And then I wanted to finish what we'd started earlier in the equipment room.*

"Good. Pretty busy. I think more tourists are finally making their way out of the snow from earlier in the week." We both zipped our jackets as we walked outside into the cold. "What's on your mind? Why were you watching me?"

"Can't a man just want to enjoy the sight of his beautiful girlfriend?" I grabbed her hand, taking her fingers in mine, and pulling it up to my lips so I could kiss the soft skin on the back of her hand.

We broke apart to climb into her car. "That's the second time you've called me your girlfriend tonight," she said as she turned on the Jeep.

"Do you want me to stop?" I raised an eyebrow.

"No. I want you to say it again."

CHAPTER
Twenty-Three

Wyatt

My entire body hardened at her husky whisper. My jaw flexed as I looked over to her as she remained focused on the road, but barely.

We didn't say anything else for the remainder of the drive, our desire screaming through the silence.

I shut her front door, locking it behind me. When I turned, she stood frozen in the hallway, staring at me. The moment felt like forever and an instant—a beautifully brilliant contradiction. Just like the mountain. *Just like her.*

I stepped towards her just as she rushed towards me. And then just like the damn bird scene from the movie—*only better*—she jumped into my arms, wrapping her legs around my waist as my arms locked on her back, our lips coming home.

And then the scene quickly veered from that in the movie—*still, I couldn't complain*; the force with which she jumped into me knocked us both back against the door, my head knocking against the wood.

"Oh my God! Wyatt!" She exclaimed grasping my head as a groan escaped me. "Are you ok? I'm so sorry! I didn't mean to do it that hard."

I couldn't help the smile that broke out, laughter rising in spite of the momentary pain. "I'm fine." She still looked concerned so I kissed her again.

"Are you sure? Do you want me to rub it?" She whispered against me. "I know how hard of a head you have and all… but that was really loud."

"Oh, I'm the one with a hard head?" Mocked astonishment escaping me. She swatted the side of my shoulder even as she laughed. When her eyes found mine, I let her know just how sure I was. "I'm fine, gorgeous. Trust me, my head is not the ache that I'm worried about at the moment." I rocked my hips into hers, letting her feel another *very* hard part of me.

"Do you want me to rub it?" God, I loved it when she tried to be naughty—*and* when she bit that damn lip of hers. "Put me down and we can go upstairs and I'll take care of you."

"Oh, we're going to do those last two things, but there's a snowball's chance in hell that I'm putting you down right now." I kissed her again, my arms tightening as I began to walk us down the hall towards the stairwell. I carefully carried us up the stairs, trying not to lose myself in the hot honey of her mouth.

"Down the hall…" she moaned. I followed the directions to her bedroom, kicking open the door to see a room white as snow. The lights were dim as I carried her over to her bed, depositing us both on top of the white comforter.

"Finally, a real bed." My body cradled between her thighs. I felt better sinking against her knowing that she wasn't being pressed into the floor or a wall or the snow-covered ground. Her mouth parted as I kissed her chin.

"Were you planning something special for the occasion?" She laughed breathlessly as I kissed my way along my favorite trail—the one that led from her lips onto the soft skin of her neck.

"I was thinking—" I nipped her skin. "—of making slow, *sweet* love—" My tongue soothed where I'd marked her. "—to my *girlfriend*."

She rubbed her hips up against mine. "Say it again."

"*Girlfriend*." My breathing became ragged as she ground against my arousal again. "I'll say it a million times, Channing, but if you keep that up, you're going to ruin all my plans."

She sighed deeply as I pushed myself up, tugging my shirt over my head. Her blue eyes clouded over with desire as she stared at my chest. I'd always been grateful for my appearance, but when she looked at me like that, she made me feel like a fucking God.

My hands found the edge of her shirt, pulling it up and over her head before I moved to her pants and discarded them just as quickly.

A growl erupted from my chest. "How many damn matching sets of underwear do you have?" I stared down at the lace purple bra and matching thong that my girl had on, my erection butting against my pants.

"Do you really want to know?"

My lip twitched, seeing her nipples perk up against the lace. "For some reason, I think I'd prefer to be tortured finding out." I bent down, grabbing one of the peaks between my teeth and pulling it, along with the lace into my mouth, sucking her through the fabric.

Her chest pushed up against me, my hand kneading her other breast. This lacey enticement, luckily for me, closed in the front. My fingers quickly unclasped the bra, releasing her perfect breasts to me. One after another, I worshipped her sweetly soft flesh, drowning out the rest of her body and mine as they begged for more. All I knew was what was under my tongue, the supple bud firming as goosebumps spread over the surrounding skin; the way she tasted just as pure as snow.

"*Wyatt.*" My name brought me back, the throbbing of my cock hitting me like a freight train.

My hands grabbed ahold of her panties, sliding them down the toned muscles of her legs. I stood as I finished pulling the slip of fabric off of her, dropping it onto the pile of her clothes already on the floor.

God, she was almost as white as her sheets except for her lips and her nipples—small red beacons of what I'd already claimed. *Perfect. Pristine. Mine.*

Channing tipped her knees out and my eyes settled on the space between them. Even from here, I could see how drenched she was. Carefully undoing my fly, I pulled my jeans down over my aching flesh eagerly jutting out to point at exactly where it wanted to be. She moaned, her foot sliding slightly on the covers. I was driving us both crazy.

Stepping to the edge of the bed, I put my hands on her knees, letting one slide down her leg so my fingers could brush over her folds. My gaze returned to hers, heavy with need, as I moved back onto the mattress, the cloud-like softness bending under my weight. Her legs spread wider to accommodate me as I lowered myself slowly over her. I stopped, air hissing from my lips when the tip of my cock brushed her entrance.

I bent my head. "Slow and sweet, gorgeous," I whispered against her ear as my hips pressed forward, pushing me ever so slowly inside her tight heat.

Inch by inch, I let her muscles draw me further into her heaven. Her fingernails dug into my arms and I tipped my head down to watch my length disappear inside of her. It was then that I noticed her chest wasn't moving, that she'd been holding her breath as I filled her.

"*Breathe*, gorgeous," I ground out.

"*I can't.*"

Fuck. My teeth closed onto her collarbone, savoring the explosive stillness of being seated inside of her. And then my hips began to move—along with her chest as she exhaled.

Slow and sweet. I moved inside of her, our bodies finding the rhythm of the ride. I held it together as long as I could, but then she slid her leg up along my side, letting me sink even further inside of her.

"I want to give you slow and sweet." I forced my hips to comply with my words.

"Wyatt..." she moaned. The way her eyes looked at me, I knew what came out of her mouth next was going to shred my control. "I don't want a slow and sweet ride." She gasped as I pushed inside of her again. "I need you fast and furious."

I froze, pushing myself up slightly. Her leg bent easily as I inched it higher and locked it over my shoulder. "As you wish."

I slammed into her, claiming the deepest part inside of her. Channing lost it underneath me, her hips undulating uncontrollably, her body arching as her need destroyed her. Maybe we should have stuck to frozen grounds and equipment room walls; her bed shook violently underneath us. I felt her one hand gripping my shoulder and saw her other fist into the covers.

Covering her mouth with mine, I swallowed her moans. She bit my lip and my cock almost exploded. The waves of my climax began to grip me; I needed her release and I knew just how to get it. I tore my lips from hers, grabbing her nipple between my teeth, pulling before sucking her hard into my mouth.

She shattered and her orgasm claimed mine.

Channing shook so violently underneath me, my own release no less intense, that I couldn't hold onto her breast. My hips moved on their own, burying my cock inside the pulsing heat that milked me.

"*Holy shit,*" I exhaled, collapsing onto her chest. Our hearts pounded violently against one another, trying to slow their racing pace. I slid off to her side, but pulled her with me, unwilling to leave her warmth just yet.

Her big blue eyes looked up at me. "Who knew calling me your girlfriend would make such a difference?" Her lazy smile that flashed told me she was teasing.

Meanwhile, I wondered what would happen if I called her my wife; I bit my tongue and held that thought to myself. *It would happen, but not yet.*

"Oh, you think it was the girlfriend comment?"

"You have a better idea?" One eyebrow raised adorably.

"I might." My finger languidly traced down the side of her arm. "Now that I've finally had you in an actual bed, Miss Ryder, let's just say that you have been well and truly frothed." The words almost made it out before I burst out laughing.

My arms raised to cover my head as she grabbing the pillow from underneath her and proceeded to hit me with it. "How's." *Thwack.* "That." *Thwack.* "For." *Thwack.* "Frothing."

I groaned amidst my laughter as the movement caused me to finally slip out of her. The abuse stopped but the laughter didn't. Whether the delirium from the sex was a contributing factor, I couldn't be sure, but for minutes we just lay there laughing at ourselves—at each other. I couldn't remember any one of my gold medals having made me smile so big.

"I want you to come to dinner Saturday night," I said as soon as we calmed down.

She eyed me skeptically. "I have to see if I'm on the schedule to work. There's an event going on and I don't know if they need me or not."

"Well, tell them they can't have you." I cupped her cheek. "My parents are flying in Saturday morning and I want to take you to dinner so that you can meet them."

I watched in slow motion as she processed what I was asking, the look of anxious surprise spreading over her beautiful features.

"Dinner…" she mumbled. "W-with your parents…"

"They're flying in for the Games and not only do I want you to meet them, but my mother has been hounding me to meet you." I grinned, gently rubbing the pad of my thumb over her cheek.

"They know about me?" I laughed because she said it like she was my dirty little secret.

"Of course, they know about you, gorgeous. You *are* my girlfriend, after all."

"I have a feeling they knew about me before I was your girlfriend though," she grumbled underneath her breath.

"So, is that a yes?"

"I guess so." If she chewed any harder, she was liable to bite right through that lip of hers.

I pushed on her chin, forcing her teeth to let go of her flesh. "What's wrong?"

She looked away from me. "I-I've just never met the parents before."

I hated to see her self-conscious like this. "Channing, they are going to *love* you. Trust me." *Almost as much as I do*, I wanted to add.

"Hopefully." She tried to give me a reassuring smile, but I wasn't fooled. I could try to convince her now, but that wasn't how my girl worked; she needed to see things—do things—for herself to believe them. I had no worries though, the way my mom talked about a girl that she *hadn't* met yet had me thinking that Zack and I would soon be vying for second-best in her eyes.

Thud.

Our heads whipped towards the door.

"Did you hear that?" She barely breathed the words as we listened.

"Yeah." We'd both heard the loud thump that sounded like it was coming from somewhere in the house. We both lay perfectly still, barely breathing while we waited for confirmation.

I pushed myself up. There wasn't another loud noise, but a soft rustling that *definitely* sounded like it was coming from inside the house. "Stay here." I demanded tightly, quickly climbing over her and yanking on my clothes.

I carefully opened the door to her room, looking over my shoulder to see Channing sitting up in bed, watching me intently with wide-open blue eyes. With the door open, the shuffling and rustling became much more distinct. "Basement," I mouthed, turning and quietly headed for the stairs.

I moved quickly and efficiently down the stairwell. If there was an intruder, I had no idea what I was going to do when I caught him, but there was no way I was letting him get anywhere near Channing.

I located the basement door immediately when I saw light shining through the frame. *Someone was definitely down there.* I grabbed a knife out of the knife block, gripping it tightly in my hand as I reached for the doorknob. I slowly turned the knob, holding my breath until the door gave way. I pulled it towards me, letting more of the light spill out. The noises were definite now. Someone was pulling out drawers and moving paper around—at least that was my best guess. I put one foot on the top step, cursing as it squeaked slightly under my weight. The rustling immediately stopped. I imagined that the both of us—myself and whoever was down there—remained frozen, waiting to see who was going to make the next move.

All of a sudden, I heard something slam and then another loud thud, similar to the one that Channing and I had heard initially.

"*Fuck.*" I flew down the stairs, realizing what the thud was.

Nothing. Empty.

I was too late.

Whoever had been in what I assumed was Chance's bedroom was out the sliding door by the time I burst in.

I walked over and locked it. It was pitch black outside and the most I could see was a few trees; whoever had been here was long gone. Moving back, I glanced around the room. I'd never been down here before so I had no idea what the hell was missing or messed and what wasn't. For the most part though, I couldn't see much of anything that looked like it had been touched.

What the hell was going on?

I needed to tell Channing; I needed to let her know that she was safe.

"What the hell are you doing? I told you to stay upstairs." I couldn't help the edge in my voice. She didn't know it was safe yet and still she came down here when I explicitly told her not to.

She looked like she hadn't heard a word that I'd said; she looked like she'd seen a ghost.

"Channing." I tossed the knife onto the bed, walking over and pulling her into my arms. "What's going on?" I felt her shoulders begin to shake seconds before I heard her tears. "*Jesus*, sweetheart, what's wrong?" I crushed her tighter against me. "You're ok. We're ok," I tried to soothe her. "I don't know who it was, but they are gone now. Doesn't look like they took anything anyway." I kissed her head—her hair—gently rocking her as her sobs grew more violent.

I felt her hands curl into the front of my shirt, pulling it against her face to try to stop the torrent of tears that spilled from her eyes.

"You're starting to scare me, gorgeous. Please, tell me what's wrong. Tell me what I can do." The pain in my chest was unbearable, seeing her hurt like this.

I couldn't do anything else—couldn't say anything else. All I could do was hold her and so, I fucking held her like my life depended on it. I absorbed her shaking into my body, her tears into my shirt, her sobs into my chest. I took it all and hoped I was giving her whatever she needed in return.

Minutes later, she finally began to calm down, her shaking now only caused by her hiccups. My head turned down to hers as I felt her shift against me. I stared into her red-rimmed, broken blue eyes as she said, "I think it was my brother. I think it was Chance."

CHAPTER
Twenty-Four

Channing

I shouldn't have cried. I shouldn't have said anything. But I'd seen a ghost—or at least felt one. Only, he wasn't a ghost; he was my living, breathing brother. And he was gone before either of us had entered his room. There was no question in my mind that it was him; *he was my twin.* And he'd come home.

Except he'd tried to do it without anyone knowing.

Any hope that I'd felt was quickly doused and stomped completely out when it hit me that after all these months, after all the calls, all the texts, *every* attempt to reach out to him, he finally returns in the dead of night, trying to make it as though he had never been here. And that's the moment everything crashed around me—including the heart-stopping fear I'd felt coming down the stairs, wondering if Wyatt was ok, *wondering what I would do if something happened to him.*

How could Chance do this? Again…

The pain that had ripped through me the day I'd shown up at the hospital to pick him up after PT only to find out he was gone was there all over again, burning through my body like acid. All I could think was, *what had I done? Why didn't he want to see me?*

The harsh reality hit me that if Wyatt hadn't been staying over tonight, I—and Ally if she were home—would have been fast asleep and we never would have even known that he'd been here.

But Wyatt was here. And now he was surely wondering why

Chance had broken into his own house and why I'd lost my shit over it.

"Hey," he said softly. I felt his hands slide to my head, lifting it up to his. His light kisses sprinkled like snowflakes over my face. "What's going on? Why would you think it was your brother?"

I swallowed over the lump in my throat, framing my response cautiously. "Because only he and the guys have a key to get in here and the door wasn't busted."

"So then why are you crying, gorgeous?" His thumbs brushed the traces of wetness from my cheeks. "Forgive me for not understanding, but he's your brother. And this is his house, too."

"I-I know." *Think, Channing. And think simple.* "I was just so afraid that something was going to happen to you. T-that's why I came down here a-and then when I realized it was j-just Chance, all that unfounded fear and anxiety overwhelmed me."

"Fuck, sweetheart," his lips crushed mine, "you scared me for a second."

The shock of finding Chance was wearing off and the reality of losing Wyatt consumed me.

"I just realized that I don't know what I would do without you." The hushed confession didn't even sound like it came from me, instead, it echoed around us from a place so far down inside of my chest—a space that had been empty until Wyatt.

"Hey, hey, hey." He forced my gaze to his. "You don't ever have to worry about that." His fingers held my chin. "You don't ever have to worry about losing me. I will never leave you, Channing. Unless you ask."

"I would never ask."

The world stopped, only starting again when his lips touched mine. The next thing I knew, I was being laid in my bed. The warmth of his touch disappeared as he stood to remove his clothes and then he climbed in next to me.

"Don't go," I whispered groggily, feeling the alluring pull of sleep after the long, eventful day.

"Told you, gorgeous. I'll stay up with you all night, I'll hold you all night—whatever you need, I'll never leave." His lips against my forehead was the last thing I felt.

"You seriously expect me to wear this?" I held up the black dress that Ally had thrown at me. I'd asked her if she could give me something to wear to Big Louie's tonight because Lord knew I didn't have any bar-party clothes. *Aka I didn't have anything nearly as sexy as she did.* And since this was Wyatt's and my first night out, I wanted to look *hot*. I was also hoping some confidence in my attire would ground the nervous energy in my stomach.

This was our first date.

It wasn't really, but in public with my friends and *not* on the mountain, it was.

"Um, yeah?" Her blank stare daring me to argue. I hadn't told her about what happened last night.

This morning, Wyatt and I decided to take the next few days off from our morning training. It had been years since I'd woken up and not gone to the mountain—if I didn't count the days I'd been medically forbidden to. Instead, we woke up and went for coffee; it was so simple and so right.

Surprisingly, our conversation only briefly touched on the odd events of the middle of the night, but I assured my very protective *boyfriend* that I'd text both my brother and the guys today and ask if it had been either of them. The web I'd woven had become impossibly entangled; posing as Chance was one thing. Posing as Chance and falling for his biggest competition was another. If Chance had returned... the thought made me see that the plans I thought I'd built on solid stone were nothing more than a house of cards. I'd watched Wyatt drink his mocha, his eyes never leaving me, and for the first time, I'd felt like I was *enough*.

With Wyatt, I didn't have to try to be as good a rider as Chance, I didn't have to try to be one of the guys, I didn't have to try to be a girly girl. All I had to be was Channing Lily Ryder—*and that was enough.*

We walked out of the coffee shop and I promised myself that come hell or high-water, I was going to the registration office on Monday and pulling Chance from the Games. At which point, I would come clean to Wyatt about everything.

Pulling up in front of his and Zack's condo, I said, "I'll see you later, Mr. Olsen." Grinning, I looked into his eyes.

"That's Mr. Milk-Frother to you," he whispered just before his lips crashed hard onto mine. Then, he was gone—and I was left counting down the minutes until tonight.

I dropped him off at his place so that I could go pick up Ally and get ready for my afternoon lessons; I'd never been in the Aspen Grove's development before but holy shit were those condos and townhomes nice. Leaving the cul-de-sac of easily half-a-million dollar homes, I fought with myself over whether to tell Ally about what happened and ask her if she'd seen or talked to our brother.

In the morning light, what happened last night seemed silly. I told myself that there was no way I could be sure it was Chance. Whether that was the truth or it was that I didn't *want* it to be him, that I didn't *want* to believe that he'd actually come home and deliberately tried to avoid me. Instead, I told myself that he'd probably given Emmett or Nick the key to get into his room because they were like brothers. What I'd felt wasn't the eerie tug of my twin nearness but the anxious, tired, and sated sensations of a long, productive, and passionate day. And because I couldn't be sure, I'd thrown the e-brake on my Jeep and the notion that I should say something to my younger sibling.

When she got in the car, I was immediately bombarded with questions about my night with Wyatt—most of which I answered. There was no mention of the 'break-in' on my part and no mention of Chance on hers. I told myself that if she had seen him or he'd contacted her, she would have told me.

Ally turned to look at me, pausing her makeup application. "I mean, I *assumed* you wanted something sexy, otherwise you wouldn't have asked me."

"Well, yeah… but, you don't think this is too much? It's only Big Louie's." I chewed on my lip, looking down at the scrap of black cloth that was going to somehow transform into an entire dress.

"No, I don't. Plus, who cares? You want to look good for Wyatt; what does it matter if it's a little nicer than what you might normally wear there? It's for the best, honestly, because some of the things I see women walk in there with. *Good God*. It's like the Wild West out here when it comes to fashion sometimes."

She had a point.

"You're going to look hot in it, Chan." She winked at me. "He won't be able to keep his eyes—or his hands—off of you."

I held the dress up against me again, my head darting back up as Ally threw her brush onto her vanity. "Oh! Wait! I know what else you have to wear." She blew right past me, grabbing my arm as she went and pulling me back into my room. I watched her start to open and close all of my drawers.

"What are you looking for?"

"Stockings." She rifled through my sock drawer. I raised my hand to my face, something itching underneath my eye. "*Don't touch your face!*" Shit. I forgot I had makeup on again. This was probably the third time in the last thirty minutes.

"I don't have stockings." Did she not know me? *At all?*

A huge smile spread on her face. "Oh yes, you do." She slammed the drawer. "Yes, you do. When I made you dress up with me for Halloween, part of the costume you bought was fishnets. Where are they?"

I stared dumbly at her. We'd dressed up as sexy pirates, except the only thing I had in common with any kind of sailor was that I could swear like one; *thanks, Emmett*. She was right though, the costume had come with fishnet stockings.

"Well, where are they?" She tapped her foot. "I don't have all night. I'm already running behind after doing your makeup."

I turned. "I-I don't know." I tossed the dress onto my bed and thought for a second. "Maybe…" I opened my closet door, looking in the one corner on the floor, pulling out the box of random clothes—the ones you don't wear, but also don't get rid of. "Here."

I stood and opened the plastic bag, pulling out the stockings I had worn that night.

"Perfect." She smiled deviously. "Put those on with the dress. And then just wear casual black boots to help bring it down." She walked out of my room before I even had a chance to protest, leaving me standing there holding the damn hooker-tights in my hand like they were toxic.

"I don't know about this," I grumbled to myself, laying the stocking out next to the little black dress.

Closing the door, I stripped down and stared at the kicker in front of me. *A dress. Tights. At least there were no heels involved.*

You can do this, Channing.

Hands on my hips, I sucked in a deep breath. I had on a black lace bralette and matching lace cheeky's. The fabric on the dress was so tight that every floral detail on my ass was sure to show through.

And then I found myself smiling. I may not be a skilled seductress or anything even remotely close to it—but sometimes, I had good ideas. *And by good, I meant sexy.*

Wiggling out of my bottoms, I reached for the tights.

Wyatt wanted to tease me about my matching underwear, well, let's just see how playful he decides to be when he realizes that tonight, they won't be matching—they'll be missing.

Damn.

I'd thought the tights were cheesy when we bought them. I thought it when I'd first worn them. Heck, I'd thought it right up until I turned and looked at myself in the mirror, wearing *nothing* but the fishnets and my bra. The tasteless tights had transformed like Cinder-freaking-ella into a tantalizing temptation, obscuring and revealing just enough…

I shivered. I couldn't wait for Wyatt to see.

Then came the dress. I unhooked my bra, knowing there was no way I could wear anything under such a low-cut top. Picking up the black sheath, I shimmied it over my head, surprisingly remembering to keep it away from the makeup on my face lest Ally have a heart attack.

I turned and looked in the mirror.

The only way to tell the front from the back on this dress was because of where the tag was since both dropped into a dangerous V on both sides. I had no idea how Ally wore this with her boobs; it was only because I had none that there was no wardrobe malfunction when I turned or bent over. That was really the only detail on the dress. It clung to my body like my Under Armour, only this was making me hot for an entirely different reason. The dress was short, but so was I compared to my sister so thankfully, it wasn't too exposing—the top half was revealing enough.

Opening the other side of my closet, I dug through the mess of shoes on the floor that I never wore, searching for my pair of black ankle boots that did have a small, thick heel on them.

I slid them on, doing the buckles on the side.

"Smokin!" Ally stood in the doorway, grinning. "Oh! Wait!" She spun and ran back down the hall—in her heels, no less. I swear, running in heels sounded more dangerous to me than the triple cork. She returned a few seconds later holding her arm out with a leather jacket grasped in her hand. "This will be *perfect!*"

I stood and took the moto-looking piece from her, putting it on and turning back to the mirror.

My outfit walked the fine line of classy and sexy, a sophisticated rock chick with my fashionable dress and tights paired with the leather and buckles on the boots and Ally's jacket.

I glanced over at my stylist, willingly admitting to her skills at knowing just what would look good together. My baby sister looked good, too, in a small skirt, cut-off top, and thigh-high boots. But for the first time, her appearance didn't put a complete damper on my own.

I looked hot.

"Told ya." She winked at me.

"You did." I moved closer to the mirror to fix some wayward strands of my hair.

"Ok, I just have to put my setting spray on, fix my hair slightly, and then I'll be ready to go. We are meeting them there?" I nodded in answer to her question.

Wyatt had offered to pick us up, but that would have put the four of us in the same car at the end of the night and I knew Wyatt wouldn't be keen on staying with Ally in the house; I wished he would believe me when I said she slept like a freakin' rock.

My eyes kept going to my reflection in the mirror, obsessed with what I saw because I knew Wyatt would be, too.

"Ready!" Ally sang as her heels clamored down the staircase.

I grabbed the purse she lent me because I sure-as-shit didn't own one of those either, and followed her down.

"Wow! It's packed tonight!" Ally exclaimed as she walked through the door and I trailed closely behind her. Big Louie's was a happening place—especially when the Broncos were playing, which thankfully wasn't tonight. There was a small entryway room right through the door where the bouncer, Todd, checked our ID's; the second door that we'd just walked through put us directly in front of the huge pine bar that had at least forty beers on tap—many from local breweries. During the week, the place could be a little questionable, but on the weekend, it tended to draw a somewhat nicer crowd, especially with the Games coming up; not that that mattered to Nick, Emmett, or my brother—they loved this place.

The bar was in the center of the room with four widescreen TVs hanging above it; two had on college basketball and two were showing some coverage of Snowmass and the preparations for the upcoming events. It was probably the basketball game that was drawing the crowd, because all these people certainly weren't here for Nick.

Ally hooked a right, attempting to circle around the bar on that side to the back of the building where there were tons of high-tops and large windows that had snowy vistas of the mountain.

"Do you know where they are?"

"No," I practically yelled. I'd texted Nick after we parked, but I didn't get an answer. I knew he and Emmett were here though because I saw their trucks in the lot. I also noticed Zack's Range Rover parked out front too, so our guys were here, too. "Is there no karaoke tonight?" She stopped and asked as though if I said no, it would be a deal-breaker as to whether we would be staying or not.

I pushed my hands against her back. "Just keep moving before we both get run over."

We squeezed through the crush around to the back where the fewer number of TV's ensured fewer people. "There." I pointed over Ally's shoulder. Emmett's bright red halo glowed like a beacon in the crowd. As soon as I found our crew, my eyes immediately scanned for the one I was dying to see.

"There they are!" Zack exclaimed, hauling Ally against him for a kiss while Emmett stared bloody murder at them both. *Where was Wyatt?*

I walked up to Nick and gave him an awkward congratulatory hug for finishing his semester.

"Hey! Thanks for coming, Lil." His eyes glinted at me. "Or should I call you 'Pride?'"

He knew. I froze.

The world stopped.

How? What was he going to do?

"Lil." Emmett came over to us and restarted reality. "I see you've got that shit on your face again." The slight smile—and the fact that I'd grown up with him—told me he was teasing me. It appeared our delicate truce was continuing to progress—at least while he was preoccupied with being pissed at Ally and Zack.

"Well, you know how much I like to do things to annoy you." I shrugged with a laugh. His eyes quickly diverted back to my left—where Ally and Zack were talking and laughing amongst themselves.

"*Fuck*, I need to get something stronger," Emmett swore, downing whatever alcohol was in his cup.

"Have you seen Wyatt?"

"At the bar getting drinks for you and him," Nick responded. "It's a fucking disaster over there. I told him he should get two. Who knows how long it will take to make it back up there."

My eyes immediately went to the crowd waiting to be served. "Are a lot of your friends from school here?" I was still looking for Wyatt. Where was—*Found him.*

Hair done. Nice jacket. Button-down shirt. He was the only one here who looked like he could leave and go to a business meeting without having to change clothes.

"Some are. I think a bunch of them just parked." He pulled out his phone. "Walking in now."

I looked back over to Wyatt who finally looked like he was being served whatever it was that he had ordered.

"There they are!" Nick exclaimed, walking around me to the group of two… three… six… ten people—*mostly women*—that spilled into our corner of the room, leaving me effectively alone at the table; Ally and Zack didn't count because they were too engrossed with each other. I looked again for Wyatt, but he was gone.

No, he wasn't. Icy-hot shivers shot up my spine as my eyes found what I was looking for.

Mr. Milk-Frother was walking right towards me.

Narrowly avoiding the people in between us, his eyes were focused on the two drinks he was holding until he was just a few feet away from me.

I'd stopped him in his tracks.

CHAPTER
Twenty-Five

Channing

"Channing." The deep rasp of his voice made my insides crazy. He set the drinks down onto the table, his eyes never leaving mine. It was like the entire room disappeared as his hands found my waist underneath Ally's jacket, pulling me towards him. "*You're killing me,*" he growled just before his mouth claimed mine.

God, how was this man so good at everything he did?

If the X Games had a competition for best kisser, he would take gold in that, too. Hell, he'd take all the medals because there was no competition. I sighed into the kiss, knowing that we were probably worse than Ally and Zack right now the way we were blatantly making out by the table. *Did. Not. Care.*

He tugged me hard against him, jamming his tongue deep into my mouth before he pulled away. "What the hell are you wearing?" he rasped.

"A dress. Tights. Boots. Jacket," I answered casually, trying not to smile. *No big deal.* "Why? Don't you like it?"

His eyes left mine to look over his shoulder; I followed them only to realize it was a cover-up as he gripped my hips and ground his erection into me for a split second. "Does that answer your question?" Now, I smiled.

"What did you get us?" I turned towards the martini glasses he'd set on the table filled with murky white liquid and garnished with a cucumber.

"It's called an 'Effin' Good.'" Our mutually intrigued stares met. "I don't know. For some reason, I pegged you as a martini girl—somewhere between strong and sweet."

"I know what it is." *One of my favorite martinis.* "I've made it for customers at Breakers." I took a sip, letting the cool, refreshing cucumber flavor soak over my taste buds. *Somewhere between strong and sweet* was exactly what this drink was.

"Do you like it? I can get you something else." He picked up the other glass, watching me savor my first drink.

"It's one of my favorites." I licked my lips. Suddenly, I felt his finger tracing down along my sternum, stopping when it came to the lowest part of the V.

"Do that again and I'm throwing you over my shoulder and taking you out to the damn car to have my way with you." His low growl made me choke on the liquid that I'd already swallowed. I crossed my legs, watching as he took a long swig of his own drink.

At this moment, I realized how I hadn't quite thought through my seductive plan. These tights were not ideal at keeping my desire at bay.

I needed to sit.

Grabbing the nearest barstool, I pulled myself up onto it making sure my legs still remained crossed. Clearing my throat, "I'm surprised to see you drinking tonight, Mr. Olsen."

"What the fuck are you drinking, Olsen?" We both turned to see Emmett stroll over to our table. He eyed both of our drinks with interest as he set down his glass and pulled himself onto another stool.

"Emmett," Wyatt greeted him. "Effin' Good." Emmett's face belonged in the dictionary under 'what the fuck?'

"It's an Effin' Good," I replied, taking another delicious sip. "I've made them for you guys before." He nodded.

Ally's laugh radiated over to our table; she and Zack had joined Nick and some of his school friends. It looked like Zack had said something that had all of them laughing. *Except Emmett.* He took several long sips of the amber in his cup—Powers whiskey, *neat*, if I had to guess. "So, how's your *training* coming, Lil?"

"Good. My triple will be as good as yours by next week." That had him smirking.

"I'll be happy to prove you wrong there." He was responding to me, but I could tell that I wasn't the Ryder he was focused on. "Glad you'll be giving some of the other assholes a shot at the Open this year, Olsen."

My body tensed. Wyatt hadn't officially decided that he was retiring from competition yet; it had been suggested and apparently, Emmett decided to assume.

Only for Emmett, assuming didn't make him an ass; he *was* the 'ass' in 'assume.'

"Well, I figured it was only fair. Must suck to lose all the time." *Damn.* I bit my lip trying to restrain a smile. Touché, my dear boyfriend. Touché.

For the first time that night, Emmett cracked a smile—*ok,* maybe more like an exaggerated smirk, but close enough, Wyatt's inflammatory response creating some weird sort of respect for him in Emmett's eyes. "Well, pity combined with being almost as damn good as the best still attracts the ladies." My eyes followed his nod over to one of Nick's classmates—a busty brunette who looked like she'd been eyeing my friend up for quite a few minutes.

"And being the best landed me a Ryder." Wyatt put his arm around the back of my chair, draining the rest of his cocktail. He hadn't meant anything by the comment, but I saw the way Emmett's hand clenched around his glass and his jaw muscle spasmed.

"And how are you two *lovebirds* doing? Moving in yet? Meeting the parents?" His voice dripped with sarcasm.

"Yeah," Wyatt responded coolly, not taking his bait. "We're going to dinner with my parents tomorrow."

"Nice. A whole fuckin' family affair." His tone was scathing. Emmett never talked about his family—his mom really. No one ever went to his house. No one ever met his mom. The last time someone had brought her up… well, it ended with a trip to the hospital. Whatever happened in his family—to his family—made him cynical about everyone else's. He only really started coming to our house once my parents moved to Florida.

"Something like that." Wyatt turned his gaze to me, tiring of having to deal with Emmett's attitude; I didn't blame him. I wondered how I could stand him most of the time, but then there were days like the day that I fell, where he carried me to the doctor and never left my side. When he brought me home and made sure I had everything that I needed, that I was taken care of. When he made sure to check in on me in spite of his feud with my sister.

Those days reminded me that there was a good man buried beneath the bad boy. At this rate, though, that good man was going to be six-feet-under soon…

"Although, she's still left me wondering whether or not she's going to try to hide me from her parents when they get here." *Wait, what?* He was laughing, but I was completely confused. "I'm assuming they are coming to see your brother…"

Oh, no. No. No. No.

Sirens, flares, nausea, blurry vision. No, no, no.

"Well that would be a waste of a trip," Emmett interjected sarcastically.

"Why? The fact that he is competing in the Games is a huge accomplishment. I mean, I can't promise he's going to beat me, but he very well could from what I've heard."

I heard Emmett's glass slam down on the table. *Or maybe it was his jaw hitting the floor.* I didn't bother to look.

"I-I don't think they are going to make it up from Florida, actually. They don't like coming in the dead of winter like this; they'll probably just come up for the Open." I hoped my words came out as slowly and calmly as I'd forced myself to make them.

"Well, in February then. Unless you want to take a beach vacation with me." If all of my internal organs weren't in my throat, the wink he sent me would have had a much more devastating effect. "Oh, did you hear back from your brother about this morning?"

Oh, God. I hadn't thought it could get any worse. *Never* think that; it *always* can.

"Yeah, it was him. Nothing to worry about." I forced out a little laugh. "Do you want to get us another round?" I pictured Ally in my mind and the 'please me' smile that she had perfected and I prayed to God that mine remotely mimicked hers.

He did give me a strange look, but then it disappeared. "Sure." As he picked up the glasses, his lips swooped in for a quick kiss. "For the road."

I watched him walk away, feeling Emmett's black stare burrowing into my side. "Any chance you want to tell me *what the fuck* that was? Why does Olsen think Chance is competing? And why did you just tell him your brother was at your house last night?"

I gulped and slowly turned to him; this was not the plan. This was not how I wanted them to find out. Shit, at this point, I never wanted them to find out because I was going to withdraw.

"Lil." His voice was so hard I was surprised it didn't shatter the glass of the window next to us. "You have five seconds to tell me what the fuck is going on." I didn't need to ask, much less want to know what happened in five seconds.

I stared at the empty glass on the table, spinning it in my fingers. "Wyatt thinks Chance is competing because I registered him."

His black eyes burned like coal. "Why would you do that? Not only is he not fucking coming back, he couldn't fucking compete even if he wanted to. *You know that.*"

I did. I nodded and continued so quietly I was surprised that he could hear me over the hum of the crowd. "He wasn't going to be competing, Emmett. *I was.*"

Silence.

Awkward, frozen, debilitating… silence.

And then, just when I found myself willing to say anything to make it stop, he… *smiled?!*

Not a smirk this time. A smile that grew into a laugh. "Holy fucking shit." He shook his head in amused disbelief. "You… you're going to compete as Chance…"

"Not anymore. I'm pulling him—myself—out."

"Why?" His eyes went wide as he put the rest of the pieces together. "Oh, that's fucking rich, Lil. You signed up as your brother—and then you had the one person who could beat you, teach you how to win. That is so fucked up… hell, it sounds like something that I would come up with." Proud amusement radiated from every syllable, every pore of him. "And then you went and fucked him. I'm assuming, since you're giving up on the whole idea—it's because you fucked him."

"*Emmett…*" I growled.

"Holy *fucking* shit." He ran his hand over his mouth while I sat on the edge of my seat, waiting for the other shoe to drop. I was withdrawing; what else could he want me do? What else could he do? *Besides tell Wyatt.* All amusement wiped from his face. "Why did you tell him Chance was at your house last night?"

"Someone broke in."

"*WHAT?*" Protective rage flared, the volume of his voice drawing eyes from a few neighboring patrons.

My hands gestured for him to keep it down. "Not broke in. Someone came in to Chance's room through the back sliding door, but whoever it was didn't break in—they had a key. And the only people I know with keys are you, Nick, Chance, and me. I don't even think Ally has one."

"Did you ask Nick?"

I shook my head in the negative again. "I didn't have to. I know it was him; I know it was Chance."

"*Jesus.*" He stared into his empty glass as though he could will there to be more alcohol inside of it. "Why wouldn't he tell us… What the fuck…" Exactly my thoughts. "Does Ally know?" Now, his eyes looked tortured and I quickly shook my head.

I couldn't even respond and not because I was just as confused as he was, but because I was reliving the same emotions I had last night—the ones that could easily break me.

"Oh good, you're back, Olsen," the asshole mask was back in place and I froze, unsure what Emmett was planning with all of the incriminating information that I'd just dumped on him, "because I need another drink and to go introduce myself to that fine piece of ass standing over there." He stood. "Lil." He said my name, but what I heard was 'we'll talk later' and then he was gone.

"Can't say I really get that guy," Wyatt said, setting my drink in front of me. I managed a half-smile before reaching for the glass and taking two large sips of the liquid. "You ok?"

I nodded rapidly. "Yeah! He's just cranky about Ally. I-I don't know why."

Wyatt laughed. "I do." *What?* I stared at him. "He likes her Channing. You don't see that?"

Oh my God.

So many things made sense now—the anger, the fights, the rudeness, the *jealousy*. How did I not see it all before?

"I-I thought he was just being protective," I mumbled. Clearly my people perceptivion skills were abysmal.

"Maybe." He shrugged. "Maybe I'm wrong. I don't know him as well as you do." I took another sip.

"Olsen!" Nick exclaimed, coming around the table with a group of his friends. "I want to introduce you to some of my friends."

And just like that, our conversation was rapidly diverted from any potentially dangerous subject as Nick drew us into conversation with Matt, Sean, Laura… and two other girls whose names I didn't catch.

I rarely drank, so by the time I'd drained my second glass, I was feeling *really* good. My dazed attention drifted between the conversation and the way Wyatt's body moved closer to mine. At some point, I took off my jacket, relishing how Wyatt moved his arm possessively around my shoulders, his fingers tracing down my arm.

"We're going to have to go soon," he bent down and murmured in my ear.

"Why? I'm having so much fun!"

"Because I don't know how much longer I'll be able to keep my hands off of you."

My eyes widened. While certain sensations had dulled, the feel of my nipples puckering against the fabric of my dress was exquisitely excruciating. I shifted in my seat, the netting of my tights teasing over my sex. *Yeah, we might have to go soon.*

"Ready when you are." I licked my lips that had gone dry.

He pulled me up so fast that I lost my balance, tipping forward into his side.

"You need me to carry you?" His tone was teasing but his eyes were completely serious. He reached behind me for my jacket that I'd draped on the chair, holding it while I stuck my arms into the sleeves.

"Need or want?" I murmured. Before he could take me up on the thought, I stepped in front of him, to walk towards Nick.

"You guys leaving already?" I ignored his face that said he knew why.

"Yeah. I didn't get out on the mountain today, so I want to make sure I'm at least able to get some time in tomorrow morning." He nodded, completely understanding.

"Yeah, looks like some night riding to me." He smirked. "Enjoy."

I wasn't sure that I should talk to Emmett again tonight and when I saw him in the corner with the brunette he'd mentioned, his tongue about five-feet-deep into her throat, I decided against it.

Next, I looked for Ally. *Wow, there were a lot of people here.* Finally, I picked her out, but only because I found Zack who was half-a-head taller than most of the crowd. He was talking and laughing with another couple and for the first time, Ally wasn't looking at him enthralled or amused. In fact, she appeared completely detached from the conversation, her eyes burning a path straight through the room to where I'd just been looking—at Emmett and the girl. The look in her eyes broke my heart.

"Ally." Her head jerked to me; she hadn't even noticed our approach. "We're going to get going."

Her distress immediately vanished, replaced by the bubbly smile that fell easily onto her face. "Ok! Is Wyatt taking you home or…" Her brow furrowed.

"She's going to stay at my place," his deep voice rumbled from behind me. A pleasurable shiver ran down my spine.

"Oh, ok!" Her smile grew. "Zack can take me home." She glanced over at Zack but he was still in deep conversation with some other guy about what sounded like fantasy football.

"I'll talk to you tomorrow." I leaned in and hugged her, giving her an extra squeeze knowing that behind her smile, she was suffering.

"Ok! Love you."

"Love you." We didn't even bother to interrupt Zack. I would have, but Wyatt's warm hand on my back, underneath my jacket, was a steady force driving me towards the door.

I clutched my arms as soon as we got outside—it was frigid. And it probably would have felt much worse *without* the two drinks that I'd had.

"Keys, gorgeous." I blinked in confusion, then realizing that he meant to drive. *Good thinking. I was not in a place to be doing that.* I dug into Ally's small purse, fishing and finding the fob. My arm shaking, I handed it to him.

I heard the beep of the unlock as we approached the passenger side of the car. The next thing I knew, my back was against the cold metal of the door and my lips were against the hot drug of his mouth, his tongue lighting a fire inside of mine.

Good Lord, he tasted so effin' good.

I moaned into him and then his warmth was gone. "Just needed to hold me over," he rasped, reaching to open the door for me, helping my shaking body inside.

I blinked—he was starting the car. I blinked again—the snow-covered sign of 'Aspen Grove' flew by us. I blinked a third time and he opened the door into his condo.

"Oh, wow," I gasped, walking into the space. Dark hardwood, white and gray walls, cabin-chic furniture. I was barely able to take it in before I was hauled back against the hard wall of Wyatt and his mouth took mine again.

Not that we'd ever been restrained, but the alcohol flowing smoothly through our systems made everything hotter, heavier, and headier.

We were upstairs, my jacket lost somewhere along the way. The door to what I had to assume was Wyatt's room shut behind me, my back pressed against it as his mouth trailed down my neck. His hand found the zipper of my dress; I felt the cool metal sliding down along my spine.

"Wait," I whispered breathlessly, my hand on his chest. His breathing was labored, but he pulled back.

Finally able, I looked beyond him, taking in the room behind us. It was facing the mountain with windows that completely covered the far wall. On the right was a low dresser that had two columns of three drawers and a mirror on the wall above it. On the left was his bed, a plain dark gray comforter on top. The room didn't have any personal effects in it—which made sense since he didn't live here. *But I wasn't going to think about that now.*

"What's wrong?" His fingers rubbed impatiently on the skin of my back.

"Nothing." I smiled brilliantly at him, the alcohol giving me a seductive confidence that I normally didn't possess. "Go sit on the bed."

"Channing..." He growled.

"*Trust me.*" I pushed a little harder against his chest before he gave way; he didn't go without me though. His hand wrapped around my wrist, pulling me along behind him.

"Now what?" He bit out as he sat down on the edge of the mattress.

Freeing my wrist from his grasp, I bit my lip. "Now, you watch."

His eyebrows raised as I stepped back from him, the moonlight reflecting off the snow outside, illuminating me and the room with an ethereal bluish-white glow. Holding my dress to my chest, I bent and, as quickly as I could, undid the buckles of my shoes, kicking them off to the side. I stood, his gaze locked on me even while his feet slipped out of his loafers.

My arms reached behind my back to finish the task he'd begun, finding the zipper and tugging it all the way to the bottom.

His hands were gripped into the covers and he was bent forward as though he were about to spring off the bed and ravish me at any second.

"I swear, gorgeous," his hoarse voice floated over the silence, "if you are wearing another pair of matching underwear, I'm going to not only rip them off of you, but take them downstairs and burn them when I'm through with you."

I threw my head back and laughed. His eyes were on my throat, his lip twitching with the need to kiss it.

"No," I answered throatily. "They aren't matching." I grabbed the sleeves of the dress, lighting tugging them off of my shoulders and letting them fall. I didn't need to look down to know that the fabric of the dress had dropped just enough so that my hard, pink nipples peaked out from on top of it. The heat from his gaze was melting my body like snow. He looked ravenous—like a wolf that had finally found his prey, his body poised to strike.

My thumbs hooked underneath the edge of the dress. I bent over and tugged the fabric all the way down, careful to leave the tights in place. Rising slowly—*provocatively*—I gave him the sight that I'd planned. I stood before him with nothing but the fishnets, pulled high up onto my waist, my breasts exposed and my sex barely obscured by the tights. "Just missing," I finally whispered.

And his reaction was more than I'd imagined.

He swore and stood from the bed, ripping his jacket and whipping it off to the side of the room. Then his shirt—his poor shirt—was torn down the middle, buttons sprinkling onto the area rug on the floor. He didn't touch his pants, although the hard outline of his cock suggested that it might split them on its own.

He closed the distance between us, one hand cupping behind my head, tilting it up for his mouth to ravage mine. His other hand moving right between my thighs, his fingers threading right through the netting and into my core.

My body went crazy at his touch. Mouth. Hands. *Hot.* Tongue. Fingers. *Wet.* My mind a pool of desire unable to focus on anything but the pleasure that rolled through me.

His mouth bit and kissed along my jawline, the hand on my head tipping it to the side to give him better access. "Very clever, gorgeous," his hoarse whisper soaked through me. I moaned and my hands groped for his belt. His hips pulled back. "Not yet," he said painfully. "This will end far too quickly that way and I want to take *full* advantage of your little tease."

I sucked in a breath as I felt three fingers push inside of me. His smile spread against my cheek. "All's fair…"

And then he spun me to face the dresser and mirror—my face flushed, my lips swollen and red, parted as I tried to breathe through the suffocating pleasure, and Wyatt standing behind me looking like he'd been given the world on a golden platter.

His hands came around to cup my breasts, completely covering the small mounds. I watched as his mouth returned close to my ear, sucking on my earlobe as he kneaded my flesh, pleasure undulating through me in waves. "I love how sensitive your nipples are." I moaned as he pinched them both, my sex clenching, begging for release. "I wonder…" he rolled the tender peaks between his fingers, the sensation setting me on fire, "…if I can make you come just. Like. This."

I gasped. *I had no doubt that he could. No. Freaking. Doubt.* I arched into his hands. The delicious pressure twisted inside of me until I shattered. I shuddered against him, briefly registering his groan of pleasure before one hand was between my thighs, cupping my sex, allowing me to grind against his palm.

"*Fuck, I can't wait.*" He released me and I tipped forward, my hands catching me on the edge of the dresser. Through heavy lids, I saw him unfastening his belt, anticipation searing through me. The orgasm had been good—but nothing like when he was inside of me, losing his mind just like I was. *And that was the one I wanted.*

Jeans half-hanging off his hips, his hand reached around onto my stomach. "Not here," he rasped, turning me to the bed. "I want to be in you in my bed." I moaned, letting his steps behind me guide me over to the mattress. I didn't wait for instruction, I climbed onto the cloud-like structure. With his pants still half on, he reached for the waist of my fishnets. I lifted my legs, easing their removal.

Finally, his pants were gone. My sex clenched as he climbed onto the mattress, his head detouring onto my sex. My ankles hooked around his head as his mouth drew my body up to that peak again. I whimpered, another climax about to wreck me, and then his mouth was gone, his body coming up to cover mine.

"All I thought about tonight, gorgeous—how effin' good you taste."

"That's all?" I gasped, feeling the head of his erection tease my entrance.

"This too." And then he slammed inside of me.

I was deranged, left hanging on the precipice of pleasure and then filled entirely with Wyatt—not just my body, but my heart and soul, too.

Our bodies flew against each other, lacking all control.

I screamed as I came again, rocketing him over the edge with me. I felt him pulsing deep inside of me, marking that part of me that would only ever be his, and I lost it.

There are times on the mountain when you're practicing a trick that you *know* you aren't going to land. You realize when you are up in the middle of the air that sticking the landing isn't going to happen—that the fall is inevitable. Time slows in that moment, allowing you to enjoy the feeling of flying before you come crashing back down to Earth. That's how I felt right now: weightless, free-falling.

The difference? All my life, I'd been afraid of the fall; falling meant failure—until this moment. Like so many other words, Wyatt had flipped this word's meaning on its head. Tonight, falling didn't mean weakness; falling didn't mean losing.

Falling meant Wyatt; falling meant in love.

CHAPTER
Twenty-Six

Wyatt

I WOKE UP WITH THE WARM SOFTNESS OF MY GIRL PRESSED AGAINST me: one arm underneath her neck, the other over her waist, my hand cupping her breast, the light of the dawn streaming through the window in front of us.

This was how I needed to wake up every morning.

I didn't care what happened with my plans; I didn't care whether or not the venture capital donors I'd spoken to in Canada agreed to help fund the school that I was going to open—a school that didn't just give talented kids time to spend on the mountain on their own, but a school that taught them both on the mountain and off—a school inspired by the woman in my arms.

This morning I woke up with a clarity—a purpose—for the rest of my life. A purpose that wasn't a job or activity or thing—a purpose that was a person.

Loving Channing was my purpose and I wasn't going to let anything get in the way of that.

She moaned and snuggled back against me. I quickly bit into my cheek as her delicious ass brushed against my morning wood.

"Wyatt?" I kissed her neck.

"Good morning, sunshine." My thumb brushed lazily over her nipple. She half-turned back against me. "What time is it?"

"Time for the mountain." That opened her eyes. "Well, almost time."

I leaned over and kissed her, enjoying the way she immediately melted into me.

My hand trailed down over the soft skin of her stomach as my tongue teased hers.

"Last night…" she murmured against me.

"Was incredible." I finished for her as I raised her leg and placed it back on top of mine. My fingers slid up to her core, slipping down over her folds.

She moaned softly. "Don't we have to go?"

"Do you want me to stop?" I circled her clit, feeling more moisture seep from inside of her.

"No," she gasped. "Don't stop."

I smiled and kissed her again, slipping two fingers inside of her to prepare her before I pulled them out and replaced them with my cock. This morning's rhythm was nothing like the furious one of last night. This morning was slow and sweet.

I imbibed each of her moans as I slid in and out of her. My fingers stayed on her clit, pleasuring her from both the inside and out. I felt her leg tense against me, her breathing halt, her muscles squeezing against my erection; one more thrust and she came around me, my body tightening and then firing inside of her.

"Can you wake me every morning like this?" she whispered, her eyes still adorably shut as our bodies began to relax.

"I plan on it," I promised. Her sigh transformed into a smile. I drew in a breath, slipping myself out of her. "But now, it's time for the mountain."

I laughed as she snuggled deeper into the covers. Feeling for her ass, I gave it a light tap before throwing the covers off of me and sliding out of the bed.

"C'mon," I said over my shoulder, grabbing a new pair of briefs from one of the drawers. "You're going to land the triple today."

We'd been down the park once already. Every double that she'd pulled had been flawless and so I'd told her to go for the triple on the last one; she just missed the landing. I saw the hope diminish slightly in her eyes, but my girl was strong; I knew she wouldn't give up.

We made it back up to the top and she tried again. And again, she narrowly missed completing the last rotation and when she stood, I saw the anxiety and fear of defeat affecting not just her entire body, but her mind. So, I swung my board to a stop in front of her, my mitts grabbing the side of her helmet.

"Breathe, Channing," I said softly, my face inches from hers. Our helmets were pressed against one another. "I know you can do this."

"How?"

"Because I've watched you. You have everything that you need to nail this."

"What if I fall again?" Her question was tortured.

I could have told her that she'd get back up and try again. But that wasn't what she needed to hear—she already knew that. She wasn't asking about the fall, she was asking what I would think of her if she messed it up—if she failed again.

And so, I said the only thing that I could, the only thing that I'd been thinking all morning, the only thing that I'd been holding inside for days—weeks, even. I said the only thing that mattered.

"I will still love you, gorgeous, whether you land this or not." Her eyes widened in disbelief. "I'll be waiting for you on the other side."

I pushed off, leaving my sentiment hanging heavy in the air. She'd been surprised that I'd said the words, not that I felt them. After how things had been between us the past few weeks, it was unspoken between us that this was where our relationship was at—that this was how we felt about one another.

My hands flexed at my sides as I saw her start to move. She gained speed and then I lost sight for a second. Next thing I knew, I saw her fly up over the lip of the jump. And boy, she *flew*. I smiled, my hands coming together when she was still up in the air because I knew she'd done it; she'd executed perfectly, she was going to land it. Sure enough, a second later the distinct and definitive thud of the bottom of her board meeting the solid earth beneath it reverberated over the slope.

I bent down and unstrapped from my board, tossing my helmet and goggles next to it and ran over to my girl who was screaming her lungs out. She slowed as she approached me and I caught her underneath her arms, spinning her—board and all—around as we both laughed. Bringing her back down, I unsnapped her helmet, baring her face to mine, and kissed her hard.

"I'm so proud of you, gorgeous." She smiled against my lips, laughing. I tasted the saltiness of her happy tears.

"I… I love you." My heart stopped. "I love you, Wyatt Olsen. Thank you for believing in me."

"Always, Channing." I rained kisses over her face. "*Always.*" And then I kissed her again and again… until the whistles and hollers of the riders flying by us became too obnoxious to ignore.

"We should probably head down." I kissed her forehead, raising her helmet to put it back on her head. "You have lessons and I have to get to the airport to pick up my parents."

Channing

Best. Effing. Day. *Ever.*

I took another deep breath, trying to force myself to continue to believe it. I landed the triple because of Wyatt. But it was more than that. The trick was just a symbol of both everything that I'd worked towards and everything that I'd given up to get it; it was the impossible. And today, he showed me that the impossible was only possible with love—with letting someone inside a part of me that I'd convinced myself could remain empty forever.

I'd always had the skills, but the something—the part of me—that had been holding me back was my heart—afraid that I was going to let Chance down again, let Wyatt down, *let myself down.* And he saw that; he saw my fear and he'd conquered it with love.

I let out the millionth small squeal for the day, twirling in my room like the girliest-girl I knew—and I embraced her with every cell in my body; my heart so full I thought it might burst.

And then Ally knocked on my door. Tucking my towel around me, I let her in. "Hey. Good thing you're here, I will probably need to borrow something to wear tonight. You know, I'm surprised that you're not going... you don't look that ill." I gave her a skeptical eye. Zack had invited her to the family dinner, too, but she'd refused, saying that she wasn't feeling well after last night—but she looked fine to me. I almost turned to go back to getting dressed but stopped myself when I saw her face. "What's wrong?"

"Nothing..." She tried to smile. "Can I talk to you for a second?"

My brow furrowed. "Of course. What's going on?" I sat on my bed, patting the spot next to me. "Does this have to do with Emmett?"

She stopped in her tracks. "*No.*" Ally shook her head and then sat next to me. "No, it has to do with Wyatt."

"Oh." My hands gripped into the towel, dread coming over me. "What about him?"

"Have you talked to him about his plans after the Games?"

Oh. I breathed out. "No. I mean not yet. Why?"

"I... I don't know the details, but I wanted to tell you before you were in too deep." *Too late.* "Zack was talking the other night. H-he thinks that Wyatt is going to be opening a snowboarding school in Canada when the Games are over."

School. In Canada.

"Wyatt hasn't said anything to him, but he heard him on the phone with a Canadian company owned by a family friend of theirs talking about investing."

My head was swimming. I'd been on Cloud Nine... and now I was free-falling to ground zero. "He hasn't mentioned anything to you?"

"No." I cleared my throat, trying to disguise how my voice broke on the word and my heart broke on the reality.

"I mean, Zack could have totally misheard or misunderstood."

She laughed nervously; we both knew it was unlikely. "I just wanted to tell you. I just wanted you to talk to him before things got too serious."

Before? I stared up at the ceiling. My little sister might not put much weight into being with guys and dating them, but I did because I never did it. And apparently, when I did, I gave it my all.

"They haven't gotten too serious, have they?"

"No." I shook my head, laughing so lightly compared to the lead sinking in my stomach. "Of course not. I mean… they could. For sure they could." I stared blankly at the corner of the towel I was fingering before I raised my gaze to her concerned face. "Thanks for letting me know, Al. I'll definitely talk to him about it and see what's going on."

"Ok." She gnawed on her cheek before wrapping me in a hug. "I'm sorry, Chan. I'm sure it will be fine. I just don't want you to get hurt. And I don't want you to move to Canada."

I laughed because I couldn't cry. "I'm not moving to Canada, don't worry about that." Especially with Chance gone; I couldn't leave her. *Which meant that Wyatt would have to leave me.* I put my arm around her shoulder, hugging her to me. "I'll figure out what's going on. I'm sure Zack misheard." I wasn't sure if I was telling her or trying to reassure myself.

"Are you ok?" She whispered against my shoulder. I nodded against her head; I didn't trust myself to speak. "I didn't know if I should say anything."

"Yeah!" I exclaimed. "I'm completely fine. Now why don't you find me something pretty but *modest* to wear to dinner tonight?" I stood and she followed suit, heading back to her closet leaving me and my heartbreak in suffering solitude.

Why wouldn't he tell me that he was leaving? Why would he do and say all this stuff? Why would he tell me that he loved me if he was just going to leave?

I shook my head. It didn't make sense. Zack *had* to be wrong.

And that was what I repeated over and over again as I finished getting ready, as I walked out of the house, as I got in my car and drove over to his condo, and as I stood at his door with my heart in my throat wondering just how this night was going to play out.

"Hey, gorgeous." Wyatt immediately pulled me into his arms and up to his mouth for a kiss; the hours since he'd last kissed me felt like years. In the safety of his embrace, I prayed again that Zack was wrong. He pulled back, only then taking a good look at me, "You look beautiful."

His smile halted as the click of heels approached us. "Wyatt James Olsen, please stop hogging Miss Ryder all to yourself and introduce us!" Wyatt turned, revealing the woman who'd come up behind him—a woman whose face had the same chocolate eyes and the same smile as the man in front of me, although she could have been his sister, rather than his mother for how good she looked.

"Channing!" she exclaimed and hugged me like I'd been a part of their family for years. "It's so wonderful to finally meet you. I'm Wyatt's mom."

"It's nice to meet you, too, Mrs.—err Dr. Olsen," I fumbled. *Great. Nice one, Channing.*

"Oh, no. You have to call me Mary. Please." She pulled me further into the hallway and let Wyatt shut the door behind us, a pleased smile on his face.

"Mary," I said softly.

She wrapped her arm around my shoulder and we began to walk towards the condo's kitchen. "I want to know all about you—Wyatt hardly tells me anything. Oh—Dan," she broke off as we made it to the kitchen where a sharply-dressed middle-aged man sat. *Now, I knew where Wyatt got his fashion sense from.* "Meet Channing. Channing, this is my husband—Wyatt's dad—Dan."

"Hi, so nice to meet you." I began to stick my hand out, but he too stepped down from the counter stool to wrap me into a hug. Just like my parents, I thought, remembering the first time Emmett had some over and met my mom and dad; they'd both hugged him and he'd looked like a deer in headlights—like no one had ever done that before.

"Let's go sit on the couches and talk. We have some time before we have to leave for dinner, right, dear?" She looked to Wyatt who nodded. "Wonderful. Now, why don't you get us girls a glass of wine?"

She linked her arm through mine and we made our way over to the couches in the living room.

"How was your flight?" I asked, frantically searching for things to talk about with the mother of the man I'd fallen in love with.

"Oh, pretty good. Long—at least for me. I don't particularly like flying."

We sat. "How long was it?"

"A little over four hours." She laughed at herself. "So, I guess not really that long; I'm sure you and Wyatt wouldn't be phased by it and it makes visiting out here very easy."

What did she mean that we 'wouldn't be phased by it'? That it would make it easy for us to visit here?

Was he really expecting me to move to Canada? Without even asking me?

The man in my thoughts appeared in front of us, handing both his mother and me each a glass of white wine.

"Zack said he'll be here in ten. I think he was just checking on Ally. And then we'll get going."

I nodded.

"So, Channing, Wyatt tells me you are an excellent snowboarder?" I blushed and took a sip of the wine that was a little too dry for my taste.

"I don't know about excellent," I laughed.

"Don't let her be modest, mom!" Wyatt yelled from the kitchen. "She's one of the best I've seen."

I groaned and took another sip. "Well, I guess I can't argue with him, can I?"

She gave me a knowing smile. "Wyatt has always been the child determined to get his way—*to win*—some might say." She winked and I laughed, secretly wondering if his way was going to be to move me to Canada—away from my family, away from my friends. I gulped down the wine. "And somehow, it always manages to work out for the best. Especially with his new idea which he tells me was completely inspired by you."

My eyes widened in surprise, my mouth parting; I had no idea what she was talking about.

"Mom! Can I talk to you upstairs for a minute?" Wyatt interrupted again, his serious tone suggesting that Mary was about to tell me something that she wasn't supposed to. I looked at him over my shoulder as his mom stood up next to me.

"Of course." She gave me a smile as they both moved upstairs.

A minute later, just as Dan and I had started a conversation, the front door opened again and Zack walked through.

"Hey!" I watched as he walked over and gave his dad a hug. "So glad you guys are here." He turned to me. "Hey, Channing."

"Hey, how's Ally?" Dumb question since I'd seen her less than an hour ago.

"Ehh…" His face looked a little sad. "I think she'll pull through; we had a little too much fun last night, it looks like." He winked at me and I smiled, knowing the effects the alcohol had had on us as well. "Alright, where's mom and Wyatt?"

"Upstairs," Dan replied.

Zack looked at his watch. "Don't we need to get to the restaurant? Aren't our reservations in ten minutes?" I shrugged; I wasn't sure. Wyatt had just told me what time to be at the condo. "Alright, I'll go—"

"No!" I stopped him. "Let me go grab them. You stay and talk to your dad." The forcefulness of my tone was a tad too much but thankfully, it only caused him to pause before he nodded and started to talk to Dan about hockey.

I swallowed and made for the stairs. Guilt pooled in my stomach. I didn't want to eavesdrop, but I needed to know what was going on. I quietly climbed the carpeted staircase, hearing Mary and Wyatt's voices getting louder. As I neared the top, I slowed, trying to make out what they were saying.

"I'm sorry, Wyatt. I thought you told her already." Mary's soft voice floated down to me.

"I wanted to make sure everything was in order first but it looks like that's not going quite as I had planned." He sounded frustrated. "I guess I'm just going to have to leave sooner than I thought."

Leave? He's going to leave. Not us. Him.

"I did my best."

He sighed loud enough for me to hear. "I know, mom, and I appreciate it. I figured it was something that couldn't be done from so far, but I was hoping that I could at least get something definitive squared away before next weekend."

"I'm sure that it's going to work out regardless. They seemed very excited about the idea and can't wait to talk to you in person about it." His mom asked. All I heard was '*in person*' which meant in Canada. "Are you going to tell her?"

Silence.

"Of course. I was just trying not to put such a huge commitment on her shoulders this week with the Games coming and everything."

I think he continued talking, but the sound of my heart breaking drowned out the noise. I shook my head. *Dinner.* Just get through dinner, Channing.

The last three steps I made sure to be extra loud so that they could hear me coming, ending their conversation as I appeared on the landing.

"Zack is here." Hopefully, the smile I forced to my face was convincing.

"Oh, wonderful!" Mary exclaimed, pure joy lighting over her face as she put a hand on Wyatt's arm before walking past me and down the stairs.

I looked back to my boyfriend, my smile dimming slightly before I turned and followed her back down to the main floor. He'd looked like he wanted to say something—or maybe it was just my imagination. I heard him a few steps behind me as we joined the rest of his family.

Mary Olsen embraced her other son, my eyes straying back to

Wyatt who watched her intently—as though if he let her out of his sight, she was bound to let something slip that he didn't want me to know. *Like that because I'd told him I loved him, he expected me to move to another country with him.*

But nothing of the sort happened. Surprisingly, with another glass of wine, dinner went *really* well; if my heart hadn't been breaking, it would have been the perfect ending to the perfect day—meeting the parents of the man that I loved, talking with them, laughing with them, feeling like a part of their family.

I wanted it. I wanted it so badly.

But I couldn't leave Aspen. I couldn't leave Colorado—not even for Wyatt.

When we got back to the condo, I made my excuses for why I should head home, not in the least of which was to check on Ally which put Zack on my side.

"Everything ok, gorgeous?" Wyatt asked me quietly as he helped me put my jacket on.

"Yeah, just an eventful day." I smiled. "I told Emmett about the triple earlier so he wants me to ride with him tomorrow morning."

"Ok." He looked a little disappointed. "I should probably spend some time taking these two," he rolled his eyes over to his parents, "around before my afternoon practice. Meet for dinner?"

"I-I had to add a few hours to my shift because I took off last night and tonight, so I'll probably be eating while I work."

"Oh, ok."

I needed to get out of there. I needed to think. "I'll text you tomorrow." I moved around him to say my goodbyes to his parents, making promises to see them later this week that I wasn't sure I would be able to keep.

Wyatt came outside with me, walking me to my Jeep even though it was parked right out front of his condo.

"I'm sorry about earlier."

"What do you mean?"

"With my mom." He somehow knew that that was on my mind.

"She's been helping me with this project, but it's not going as smoothly as I hoped."

"I'm sorry."

He shook his head. "It's not your fault. Or hers. I just have to get on the phone with a few people and confirm the details on Monday and then I want to talk to you."

"About what?" My nervous laugh betrayed me.

"Us." He pulled me against him. "The future."

In Canada? I wanted to blurt out, but I held my tongue. The sad truth was that as much as I adamantly refused to move, there was a part of me that was already arguing how to make it work—that I needed to make it work for him because this kind of love doesn't happen all the time.

"But not tonight." He kissed my forehead and I released the breath that had been building inside of me. "Text me when you get home, gorgeous." I wanted to tear my gaze from his, knowing that he would see right into the broken pieces of my heart, but I couldn't pull away. As much as I wanted to distance myself from the hurt, all my body wanted was to draw closer to him.

His hand came up to cup my face and my eyes closed anticipating the kiss that I still craved. "I know something is bothering you, Channing. Just know that I'm here whenever you want to talk about it." And then he kissed my lips softly. "Just know that I love you."

I linked my arms around his neck and crushed my lips to his. His words tore tears from my eyes that I didn't want to cry. I didn't want to hurt. I wanted to kiss him and forget about everything that would stop me from being with him no matter the cost. He groaned and kissed me back just like I needed, his tongue wiping away all my worries. His body was a hard rock that I clung to amidst the storm.

Soon there was only us. Wyatt growled against my mouth. "You should go, gorgeous, if that's what you want. Otherwise, I'm about to throw you into your back seat and figure out the fastest way to get inside of you."

I shivered. The idea sounded so deliciously tempting. But I

needed to go home.

"Goodnight." I pressed my mouth to his one last time before I stepped back and opened my car door.

His eyes were glassy with desire as he watched me climb into the Jeep, shutting the door once I was settled.

I made it a half a mile outside of the condo development before I burst into tears.

CHAPTER
Twenty-Seven

Channing

For the first time, the mountain had no answers for me. It was there—solid and silent—beneath my feet. But no matter how many times I pounded into its snow-covered surface, it refused to respond.

The wind whipped snow across my face as Emmett swung to a stop in front of me. "You planning on riding this morning, Lil? Or just crying and feeling sorry for yourself?" *Dick.*

I glowered at him. Maybe it had been a mistake to ask him to ride. He was the only one I could count on. And he was as close to Chance as I had.

"You aren't going to win the Games by sitting there." I scowled even further. I was supposed to withdraw today. I'd planned on going after my lessons on my way to Breakers, but now I wasn't sure.

The mountain was all I had. Even though it didn't answer me, it also wouldn't leave me. It wouldn't force me to choose.

Losing Wyatt was going to take a piece of me that I didn't think was replaceable, but I could at least try to disguise that loss with a win. And now that I had landed the triple again, a part of me begged to stay in the competition and prove to myself that I could do it—and that I didn't need Wyatt.

"I was thinking of dropping out today," I said to no one in particular.

"Because of Olsen?" He scoffed. "Do whatever the hell you want. I think it's fucking hysterical you think you can get away with being Chance. I, personally, just want to see it."

"I was… but I don't know anymore."

He stomped his board. "Fuck, Lil. If you got something to say, then fucking say it. But I'll warn you right now, I'm not a fucking therapist."

"I think he's starting a business back in Canada and he wants me to move with him," I replied, my gaze moving from the snow in front of me to the surprise on Emmett's face. "I can't move."

"So then break up with him." I laughed and shook my head.

"I'm in love with him."

His hands smacked the side of his helmet. "Well, fuck."

"My sentiments exactly." I fell back into the snow.

"So then move. Your sister did. Your brother did." He paused. "Well I guess he technically didn't move, he just left."

"I-I don't know. I can't leave Ally or you guys. This is my home."

"Did he actually ask you to move?" I silently shook my head in the negative. "Christ. What is it with women? Then how do you fucking know that that's what he wants?" He shook his head, laughing harder. "You want my advice, my therapy session? Talk to him. And as much as I want you to stay in the Games incognito because I want to see Olsen get trashed by his girlfriend, I told you once before to stop living in your brother's shadow; this is literally the epitome of that. FYI, my rate is three-hundred bucks an hour—I'll bill you."

At least living in Chance's shadow was safe.

I rolled my eyes. "I will talk to him. But if that is the case, I want to be prepared for it; I want to be prepared with an answer. And I don't want him to find out that I lied to him about Chance. But, if he leaves and I-I don't do this… I will have lost so much more."

"And what if Chance is back?"

"Have you…" My eyes widened.

"No," he answered curtly.

After the other night, there had been nothing suspicious. I tried to call my brother again but it went straight to voicemail. I mean, there was a chance that he could have given someone else a key, but no, he was back.

"Why would he do this?" I wondered aloud. "Why would he come back and hide from us? His friends? His family?" I stared down the slope, feeling the cold air freeze the moisture brewing in my eyes. "Why bother coming back at all?"

"Because he's a dick." I glowered angrily at him for his callousness. "What? Don't give me that look, Lil. You know you've thought it, too. Yeah, we all feel bad for the fucker, but life sucks. Trust me, I know how it feels to be stuck with a hand that you never imagined you'd be dealt." He huffed. "I guess everyone deals with it in their own way, but if running is how you're going to do it, then *run*. Don't creep back here."

"Do you think he heard that 'he' was competing in the X Games?" I saw the coverage that had been on the other night at Big Louie's, but what was the likelihood that he'd seen it wherever he was… unless he was keeping tabs on the game. But that would be like torture knowing that he wasn't competing.

Emmett shrugged. "Maybe. But I would have come right to you and smacked you upside the head." I threw a snowball at him. "You know what I mean… Unless he doesn't realize that it's you that's doing it. Who knows? Who knows what he's thinking? And who cares? If he wants to be here, he'll be here."

I wished I did know. I used to.

"Well, then maybe I should stay in the competition and see if it draws him out."

I heard him curse underneath his breath. "I don't get you. Either of you women Ryder's for that matter. Then just do whatever you want. But right now, we're sitting in the middle of the park, so how about you just practice your triple because riding requires no thinking."

"What's going on between you and Ally?"

His face darkened dangerously. "We hate each other, Channing. Sorry. Not much I can do about it and I sure as shit don't need a friendly therapy session to figure it out." And with that, he spun and carved down the slope.

I pushed myself up and headed towards the next kicker.

Funny how when I met Wyatt, I was only worried about pulling my triple together. Now, I had the triple down… and it was everything else that was falling apart.

I threw myself into the rest of my day, trying to focus every ounce of mental energy on my ride, my lessons, my job. Wyatt and I texted back and forth throughout; he'd taken his parents around the town of Aspen earlier in the morning and had spent the afternoon preparing for the Games; the Slopestyle run was on Thursday, and qualifiers were on Wednesday. I responded to him as though his future after the competition wasn't threatening to tear us apart. I responded to him like everything was still perfect, each time hoping that it was, only to stop and remember that it all hung in the balance.

When I got home, I checked my phone once last time.

-Hope your night was good, gorgeous. Wish I was sleeping next to you again.

~Me too.

-I have a business call tomorrow morning now. I tried to move it later, but it was the only time.

~It's ok. I told Emmett I would ride with him this week since I've been MIA.

-Alright. Can I see you after work Tuesday?

I didn't respond right away. Burying deeper underneath the covers, I didn't know what to say. I didn't want to have the discussion. I was afraid of the discussion. I could move with him. I *wanted* to be with him. That was the part that scared me the most—not leaving, not what would happen to my friends or family, but the fact that I felt like I could do it so easily, without thinking twice, if it meant staying with him. I felt like I was betraying my sister with my feelings. And like Emmett said again earlier, dropping out of the Games, moving away, it would all be stepping—no, *leaping*—out of Chance's shadow, out of the path that we'd been following for our whole lives. For someone who was so comfortable with risking my life, when it came to doing it in this manner, I was petrified.

~*Yes, but I work late,* I texted back before I could think the better of it.

-*I'd wait all night to see you, gorgeous.*

It wasn't fair that even just texting me, he could make my pulse race and my thighs clench together. I waited another minute to see if he was going to say something else—*to see if he was going to say 'I love you'*—but nothing ever came.

I was a coward. It was as simple as that.

Turning off the Jeep, I stepped down into the crunch of icy snow covering our driveway. I left work early tonight, claiming that I wasn't feeling well and I only texted Wyatt about it on my way home.

I was a coward. But if I didn't talk to him, I didn't have to hear how his future after the Games was in Canada; I didn't have to make any hard choices. I told myself that the purgatory of ignorance was better than the finality of knowing.

I unlocked the door, walking into the kitchen and tossing my keys onto the counter.

"Oh, it's you." Ally's rush down the staircase slowed when she saw me. "Everything ok? I didn't think you'd be home from work this early."

"Yeah, I wasn't feeling well." Opening the fridge, I pulled out a can of La Croix, popping the top and taking a satisfying sip.

She made her way into the kitchen. "What's going on?"

I shrugged. "Nothing."

"Are we really going to do this?" She put her elbows on the counter, resting her chin in her hands.

"I'm just… at a loss. I haven't talked to Wyatt about what you told me. At first, I didn't really have a chance. But then he wanted to talk tonight and instead I chickened out and came home early from work."

"Why? Why wouldn't you want to know?"

"Because knowing makes it final, Al. Knowing means he's actually leaving with or without me. Knowing means that I can no longer pretend like everything is going to be ok."

"Well you can't avoid him forever."

I groaned. "I know. I just feel like everything is up in the air—Wyatt, our relationship, his future, my future, the Games…"

Her eyes narrowed. "I thought you withdrew from the competition?"

Crap. I ducked my head. "I… was going to and then you told me about Wyatt and… I couldn't."

"Channing, how could you?" The look on her face was the one that held me back time and again—the look that I'd let someone down.

"You don't understand, Al. Riding is who I am. Yes, there are other parts of me, but somehow, I can't seem to find them without Wyatt. I can't give up the only part of me that I know won't go anywhere, especially if he is leaving." I stared at the can, my fingers toying with the tab until it snapped off from the top. "I can't quit. I'd be letting myself down. I'd be letting Chance down. This was supposed to be for him." *I wasn't going to admit how that was part of the problem.*

"Channing!" My eyes flew to hers. She'd never yelled at me before; I'd only ever seen her this mad at Emmett. "Stop being a child."

"Excuse me?"

"You're being a child and you're running away. I may be your younger sister, but I know this because I've done it. Why do you think I moved back to this horribly cold place? You think that everything is up in the air because you like to think you can just live up in the clouds, on the mountain, away from your problems; you can't. It's time to come back down to Earth where we deal with our problems—our fears." I was in shock. Ally was fuming and at the same time looked like she could burst into tears. I was stunned speechless. "I know I said you can't move to Canada, but if that's what it takes for you to be with Wyatt—which I'm assuming is what you want—then that's what I want for you; I want you to be happy—and that doesn't mean you doing whatever you think will make me happy or protect me—or Chance for that matter, if he were here."

I couldn't believe what I was hearing.

"You need to stop running and talk to Wyatt. Fear can make us do stupid things—especially the fear of letting the ones we love down. It can make you move to Colorado even when you hate the cold. It can make you mess up a jump that you know you can land. And it can make you flee the hospital, with no note, no message, no explanation to any of your friends or family who care about you." The back of her hand rose quickly to brush a tear from her cheek. "We're all guilty of it, Channing, all of us. But I'm telling you right now that what I see between you and Wyatt is the real thing—it's doing the impossible trick, landing the impossible kicker, winning the impossible gold; it's everything worth fighting for. So, don't let me down, don't let Wyatt down, don't let yourself down—*don't give up.*"

"I…" I couldn't speak over the lump in my throat.

"And as for the Games," she continued unrelentingly, "I hate to break it to you, but winning a stupid competition isn't going to bring Chance back."

I tried to go to her, to hug her, but she put a hand up, the other wiping her cheek before she turned and fled back up the stairs into her room, the *slam-click* of the door indicating that this conversation had come to an end.

Wyatt

I stood at her door, hearing someone's footsteps as they approached. It was still dark outside, but I wasn't taking any chances. I knew that she was avoiding me. Ever since the night Channing met my parents, she'd become distant. And then last night when she'd disappeared from work, texting me to let me know that she was going home to go to bed because she wasn't feeling well… well, that was the last straw. The woman had my heart; I wasn't going to let her disappear with it without a fight.

"Wyatt." Her wide, blue eyes and parted mouth was the exact expression I'd wanted to see. I didn't tell her I was coming here this morning; I wasn't going to give her another chance to hide from me. "What are you doing here?"

"I came to talk to you, gorgeous." I held out my hand that had a travel mug and a little pastry bag in it. "Mocha and apple fritter. A peace offering."

She took them from me, standing back to let me inside. "Were we at war?"

I waited until she closed the door behind me before turning and trapping her against it. I wanted to kiss those damn lips of hers—lips I hadn't tasted in three days, lips that were barely an inch from mine, but I remained frozen, instead asking, "I don't know. Were we?"

I watched the subtle movement of her mouth as she swallowed. "I… don't think so."

"Good," I growled, my hands clenching at my sides to hold her, "because I'd really like to kiss you right now."

She licked her lips and I hoped that meant she felt the same because my mouth crushed hers. *I'd been right.* Her lips parted under the first touch of mine, begging my tongue entrance. Toying with hers, I savored every inch of her sweet warmth as my body vibrated with my desire to have her. But I needed to talk to her first and so, I settled for one *really* good kiss before I stepped back.

"I missed you," I rasped, watching her eyes refocus on me.

She bit her lip. "I missed you, too."

I moved back slightly allowing her to walk into the kitchen. I could see how she sipped the coffee I'd brought her like it would calm her. She was nervous that I was here and I was determined to find out why. Setting the bag down on the table, she turned to me, waiting for my next move.

"What happened, Channing?" I let her see the pain in my eyes. "Everything was perfect… beyond perfect. And then the other night you disappeared. You were there, but you were gone. Qualifiers start tomorrow and I'm not going into this with this wall between us. I'm not going into the Games without you by my side."

The sound of the pastry bag crinkling as she opened it was my answer.

"You can talk to me, gorgeous. You can trust me." *Woah.* Her head spun to me so fast I thought her neck might snap. Her eyes like blue ice, freezing my every thought.

"How can I trust you when you are keeping something from me?"

That's what this was about? I let out an exasperated laugh. "I told you I wanted it to be a surprise! I just hit a few road bumps, but I told you that you were going to love it."

"I'm not going to love Canada!" There were so many emotions written all over her body, I doubted if she knew how she was even feeling.

I laughed because I was at a complete loss. "What?" I ran a hand through my hair. "I mean, I think that's a little harsh if you've never been there." *Well, that was the wrong thing to say.* I took a step towards her. "Gorgeous, I don't care if you love Canada, I just care if you love me."

I raised a hand to her face, my thumb prepared to wipe the tear about to drop from her eye. And then she said the words that broke my heart. "I do love you, Wyatt, which is why I'll move there if that's where you'll be."

Shock. Confusion. Astonishment. The words weren't synonyms for how I was feeling—I felt every one of them separately. *What the fuck was my girl talking about?*

"Channing," I said quietly, "I'm not going to Canada. I wasn't going to ask you to move there." I saw the weight as it lifted from her shoulders.

"But… Ally said Zack…" Her brow crunched, trying to figure out how she'd made a mistake. "I heard you talking to your mom."

Tilting her chin back up, I made sure she was looking me in the eyes when I repeated. "I'm not going back to Canada, Channing. I'm not asking you to move away from here." I let out a deep breath before I gave her the *actual* news that I'd been waiting to share. "I'm moving here, gorgeous. I'm moving here to start a school. And yes, I want you to move somewhere, but that somewhere is just in with me—whether it's here or the condo or a new place. I'm moving here to be with you."

Finally, I forced myself to pause and let her respond, but she only just stared at me in disbelief. "I didn't want to tell you until I had the funding for the school squared away. And then, I didn't want to freak you out by asking you to move in a day after I asked you to meet my parents." She was frozen. I hoped she was at least breathing because she didn't move a muscle. "Please, say something, Channing."

Her arms came around my neck as she jumped against me, crushing her lips to mine. *Fuck, I hoped that meant she'd loved my secret.* My arms molded her against me as we devoured each other, the wall that had been forming between us melting in a second.

"I thought you were going to ask me to move to Canada," she finally whispered. "I wouldn't ask you to do that and leave your home, your friends." I kissed her again.

"But you'd ask it of yourself?" Her big blue eyes looked up to mine.

"Channing," I chuckled, "I haven't *lived* anywhere for a long time. Yeah, my parents and some of my friends are there but with competing and practicing, I'm hardly ever there. This is the most I've seen of my brother in probably a year." I pulled her against my chest. "Another reason I've been fighting against leaving the competition world. Where was I going to go? Back home to what? I haven't lived with my parents for fifteen years. I had nothing to do. No where to go. Until I met you, Channing."

Her body quaked with the shaky breath she inhaled. "I feel like such an idiot."

"Don't—" I cupped her cheek. "Don't ever think that. I should have said something earlier. I didn't know Zack overheard and misinterpreted. I only talked to my mom about it, but I should have said something to you."

"It's ok," she mumbled.

"No, it's not. I was afraid. I was afraid I was going to ask too much, too soon of us—*of you*. I was afraid of losing you." My lips touched her forehead.

"We all know how unfamiliar you are with that sensation." My laugh shook my whole body. Only my girl would tease me about losing right now.

When my smile faded, I asked the question that hung in the air. "Well, did I? Did I lose you?"

"I would have moved to Canada had you asked, Wyatt," she answered me incredulously and then I remembered that she *had* said that. "I think that's as far from losing me as you're going to get."

"*Thank fuck.*" I didn't realize until she said the words just how afraid I'd been that I would never hear them. I kissed her again—ravenous with relief that my girl was *mine*. I was only a few seconds into her sweetness when I realized that I needed more. "I want you so fucking badly, Channing."

"So, take me." She ground her hips against my arousal.

"Ally…?" Even as I asked my hand snaked down over her ass, fingers delving underneath her to where her entrance was. Through her sweats, I could feel the heat radiating from her core.

"Upstairs. Sleeping." I swore. "She won't hear." And then her hand grabbed my throbbing cock and I lost the fight.

"Turn around," I bit out. My hands guided her around, her palms slapping onto the granite countertop as my hands snaked around her—one up her shirt finding her nipple hard and begging, the other down her pants to her sex that was hot and soaking.

My finger tuned her body better than any board I owned. Within minutes, she was shuddering against me, her body about to break. Releasing the flesh of her breast, I freed my erection.

She bent over farther, giving me the perfect view of her pink slit, wet and ready as I pulled her pants down just far enough. I grabbed her hips to anchor myself and steady her, putting my head at her entrance and then ramming into her. She exploded on contact—my cock hitting that sweet spot all the way inside of her. Her orgasm broke around me, muscles clenching as I pushed inside of her. My thumbs dug into the sweet flesh of her ass, watching as my erection pulled out, coated with her desire, only to disappear back inside her haven. Two more thrusts was all it took, the waves of her climax too strong to resist, before I came.

My tongue bled from where I bit it, trying to silence my shout, as we collapsed over the countertop.

"Sorry," I groaned, kissing her shoulder, waiting a few more blissful seconds inside of her heat as my cock pulsed, releasing every last drop of my desire.

"Don't—" she gasped as I slid out of her, righting her pants, "—apologize."

I grabbed a tissue and quickly wiped myself, checking the stairs every few seconds to make sure Ally wasn't about to walk in on us. "That wasn't what I was planning when I came here."

"Oh, no?" she asked coyly, resting an elbow on the counter. "And what were you planning?"

I pulled her against me. "I was planning on making sure that my *girlfriend* knew that I'm looking for something much more permanent than just 'girlfriend.'"

The happy moan that escaped her made my whole fucking body vibrate with how much I loved her. "Mmm… well, mission accomplished, Mr. Olsen."

"Good." My teeth grabbed her lower lip and tugged. We stood there for several minutes just holding each other. The details would come later. Right now, this was all we needed. "Alright, Miss Ryder, go finish getting ready and we can ride over to the mountain together."

She pulled out of my embrace with a brilliant smile on. "I like the sound of that."

"Me too, gorgeous. Me too."

CHAPTER
Twenty-Eight

Channing

I COULD HAVE SCREAMED. OR CRIED. OR JUMPED AROUND LIKE A lunatic when Wyatt told me that he was moving *here*. However, I think I preferred the quick and dirty kitchen sex to celebrate.

I'd been an idiot for not talking to him the past few days and now I felt like my heart could explode with happiness. *He was moving here. For me.*

To be with me.

I didn't care where we lived or any of those details. I wouldn't have to leave my family, my friends, or my mountain. And, most importantly, I wouldn't have to leave him. *How did I get so lucky?*

Immediately, the cool breeze of guilt brushed over me. I was lucky because Chance fell—because his dream had been taken from him—and left us. If he hadn't left, I would have never gone to registration, I would have never crashed into Wyatt's boards, I would have never met *him*. The guilt that all of my happiness had stemmed from the one thing that had destroyed my brother's life and taken him from us was very, very real. But, so was my love for Wyatt.

Chance couldn't stay away forever. And I couldn't keep blaming myself for it either.

Grabbing my jacket, I shoved my feet into my boots and headed out the door; Wyatt was already in the car, warming it up and waiting for me. I barely shut the door before I asked the next thing that consumed my mind.

"So, you're opening a school?" Obviously, the fact that he was moving here and *not* asking me to move to Canada had taken precedence. But now, I wanted to know everything about his plans.

He laughed, throwing the Range Rover in reverse and backing up to turn down the driveway.

"Yup," he grinned, "and completely inspired by you."

"Me?!" *What was he talking about?*

"You told me I was a good teacher. Well, not just you… but you were the first." He shrugged. "After that and hearing about the type of school that you and your brother and your friends went to, it got me thinking. I thought it was great the way that your classes and time was flexible so that you could spend more time on the mountain, but I want to be able to offer more than that. I want to be able to offer not just freedom to go to the mountain, but instruction there as well. I want there to be a professional training component to the curriculum."

"That's… that's amazing." My mind was already racing with the possibilities—with all of the things that Chance and I could have accomplished had our time on the mountain been somewhat more structured, instead of relying on lessons from the resort or private lessons from another rider.

"You think so?"

"Seriously? I think that's an incredible idea. If I had had that kind of opportunity, especially to be taught by someone as skilled as you are, well, the triple would be the least of my problems." I grinned excitedly at him.

"Good." He paused and I knew there was more coming. "Because I want you to teach there too." My head whipped to him and I stared. "If you want, of course. I'm not going to force you. But, I've seen the way that you are with the kids; I may make a good instructor, but you aren't too bad yourself there, missy."

"You… you want me to help you?" I clarified. *God, I was turning into a damn watering pot this morning.* I reached for the tissue box that was on the floor as Wyatt turned into the resort.

"Gorgeous, I want you to be a part of my life in any and every way possible. So, if you want to, then yes, I want nothing more than for you to be a part of this with me because, without you, I'd still be a lost asshole, flying down a mountain, up into the air, and hoping that when I landed there would be a future for me waiting at the bottom instead of just a medal."

I couldn't help but chuckle. "You know you love the medals."

"Not as much as I love you." He winked at me and I almost lost my shit *again*.

"So why were you on the phone with people from Canada?"

He parked, grabbed his gear from the back and continued to reveal more of the story as we walked towards the training room to grab my equipment. "I know some people in Montreal who are both friends of the family and who have also sponsored me in a bunch of competitions in the past. I wanted to reach out to them for venture capital. Not that I can't fund the entire thing but I guess I wanted to know that people with a business mindset thought it was a worthwhile investment as well."

"Oh…" Everything was starting to click into place.

"I had a few phone calls with them. I also spent a few mornings going to some of the schools in the area. At first I thought about just working at one, but none of them seemed interested in adapting their curriculum to add a sports training component. Anyway… everything was going really well after the calls. The one guy, Vaughn, his wife works with my mom. I emailed my mom a business plan, proposed funding needs, etc. and had her take it over so that she could gauge his reaction first-hand. But, I guess stuff with work happened and then he wanted to talk to me personally—which was fine, but it just took longer than I was hoping for. You know, I even had a feeling that Zack was listening to me on the phone the one day, but he had headphones on and was watching some show on his laptop, so I figured he wasn't paying attention; I'm going to have to have a small chat with my little brother."

I shook my head as we sat on the lift. "Don't yell at him. It wasn't his fault. I should've said something as soon as Ally mentioned it, but I was afraid. First, I thought you were just going to leave and then it spiraled into you wanting me to move with you…" It really did seem crazy how it spun out of control in my mind.

His mitt grabbed mine. "Told you, gorgeous, I'm not leaving you."

The bar went up on the chair and we slid down off of the lift. Stopping at the beginning of the park, we both strapped in.

"Let me guess," he said, "you're a pro at the triple now and you no longer need me."

"Well, I *may* be an expert at it now," I grinned, "but, I think I'll still keep you around."

He laughed and began to carve down the slope. I stayed for a second longer—taking in the view, taking in my life.

I wasn't just on top of the mountain—*I was on top of the world.*

It was only when we parted ways after lunch that I remembered the elephant in the room. *The Games.* Crazy to think about how an international sporting competition that began the next day had slipped my mind, but what can I say? Love can make the rest of the world disappear around you.

The argument in my mind was nothing new, but qualifiers were tomorrow; the reality was that I couldn't back out now. And that meant that I had to pray that Wyatt wouldn't be running his pass close to mine—that he wouldn't recognize me. I wasn't even worried about winning; Wyatt was far too good for that. Plus, I actually wanted him to win.

My anxiety about the upcoming two days plagued me through my lessons. I'd taken off from Breakers in preparation for getting a good night's sleep for the competition; I told Wyatt that they didn't need me and that's why we could actually spend some time together tonight.

He was waiting for me outside the equipment room when my lessons were over and I wondered if the warm electricity that spread through my body would always be there when I saw him; I had a feeling that it would.

"Do you mind if we get Thai?" he asked on the way back to my house. I shook my head; that was fine with me. "For some reason, I always crave Thai right before a competition."

"Ahh, so now you're giving away your competition secrets!" I exclaimed. "The secret to winning—Thai food!"

We laughed and continued talking like we'd known each other for years instead of just a few short weeks, stopping in town to pick up dinner and then heading back to the house.

"What is Zack going to do?" I don't know what made me think about it, but I realized that Ally could be in the same position that I was in. Zack was only here because Wyatt was competing. What happened afterward?

I glanced over and saw his mouth firm into a thin line. *Uh oh. That doesn't look good.* "I'm not sure. I haven't told him about the school. I'd really like him to come teach skiing there. Well, maybe not teach," he laughed, "but coordinate the skiing program maybe."

"You don't think that he will?"

He sighed as he turned the Range Rover into the driveway. "Honestly, I have no idea. I don't think Zack is at the point where he really wants to settle down; he likes traveling, competing, 'living life.'"

"Oh." That didn't sound good for my sister.

"Maybe Ally will have changed that." Wyatt knew what I'd been thinking.

Holding the take-out bag, I shut the door behind me. "As much as I like to think of her as my baby sister, she's a lot wiser and stronger than I give her credit for. I'm sure whatever happens, she'll find a way to make the best of it."

"If I could make him stay, I would." He held the door open for me and I walked into the hall.

"I know."

At that point, our conversation transitioned back to our own future and the school—all Wyatt's ideas for where it should be, who should be hired, how many students we should have in a class.

I remembered when I'd first met him, the barrenness that had come over his face when people mentioned his retirement or asked him what his plans were—even when he told me about working with some of his sponsors. Nothing had inspired him. Nothing had excited him. The thing that was so poignant to me, though, was the fact that the X Games began tomorrow—his *last* Games—and nothing could have been further from his mind.

He'd come to Aspen clinging to this competition like it was his last chance at living and doing something meaningful. Now, he'd found something so much more—something that he wanted me to be a part of with him.

The front door opened just as we were finishing up.

"Hey, Ally." Wyatt greeted my sister, being able to see her first from where he was sitting in the kitchen.

"Oh, hey, Wyatt," Ally said, walking into the kitchen. "Didn't expect to see either of you here this early."

"I… had off tonight because of the event, so we just grabbed some take-out." I risked a glance at her.

"Gotcha. Well, I won't interrupt."

"Do you want some Thai?" Wyatt asked her, walking over to my side and putting his arm around my waist. "I'm actually going to get going in a few." He kissed the top of my head as I turned my face up to his. *Why was he going?*

"Actually, that sounds amazing." She reached across the counter for the rest of my Pad Thai.

"You're leaving?" I asked him quietly.

He chuckled and leaned closer to my ear. "Gorgeous, I need to get some sleep tonight for the competition." I felt the hand that had been on my waist drift down over my ass. "And if I stay here much longer, I won't be able to leave. And I *definitely* won't be getting any sleep."

I groaned softly; *he did have a good point.*

"Ok," I pouted. "I'll walk you out."

"Bye, Ally."

"See ya, Wyatt!" she returned, her mouth full of noodles.

When we made it to the front door, I didn't even get to the doorknob before he had me up against the wood, his mouth claiming mine. We kissed for several long—*but not long enough*—minutes.

"I'll see you tomorrow," I said breathlessly.

"And every day after," he growled, kissing me hard again before reaching around and opening the door.

It was frigid outside, but I held the door open, watching him get in the car and drive down the driveway. Only when he was out of sight did I finally shut it—and realize how frozen my nose was.

"I take it you had the conversation and it went really well." Ally didn't even preface her statement as I walked back into the kitchen.

"What gave it away?" I asked wryly.

"Well, your not-so-silent whispers—TMI, by the way. Your fifteen-minute good-bye at the door before I even heard the door open—unless being over thirty means it takes him that long to make it to the front door. And the way you look like Rudolph the Red-nosed Reindeer from standing looking out the open door."

"Oh, only that?" I returned cheekily.

"Well…?"

"He's not going back to Canada, Al." I couldn't stop smiling. "He's moving here. And opening up a school for kids with talent to learn from him—from us." She raised her eyebrows. "He wants me to help him."

"That's awesome, Chan!" She wrapped her arms around my neck and I felt her sigh with relief into me; she would have been crushed if I'd left.

"I know! I'm so happy!" I laughed against her as she continued to hug me. Part of me debated whether or not to mention anything about Zack, but after everything that had just happened between Wyatt and me, I didn't want to start another round of skepticism and miscommunication.

"Why do you have off tonight?" Her tone fell but she didn't let go.

"I requested off when I first registered as Chance." I knew what was coming next.

"Are you still competing?"

"I… I thought Wyatt was leaving. So, I never got that far. And now, it's too late. I'm afraid it will look suspicious." Shit. She began to pull back. "The last thing I want is for someone to realize that Chance isn't here and his name to be dragged through the mud after his career is already over."

"But you signed him up no problem?" Ally's arms crossed over her chest. This was going downhill.

"Because Wyatt was there and vouched for me!" I ran a hand frustratedly through my hair. "I-I don't know what to do, Ally. Every option seems wrong. If I pull out, there will be questions—and not just from the Games committee, but from Wyatt. And if I stay in… there's no chance I'll win against Wyatt. There's a chance he could realize it's me. But also, that he might not."

"You just don't want to give it up, do you?" She asked sorrowfully, shaking her head. "Do what you want, Channing. Clearly, you are going to anyway. I just hope that one day you realize that you have nothing to prove to any of us—not me, not Chance, and definitely not Wyatt; we all love you. I hope you finally figure out what it is you're trying to prove to yourself."

"Ally…" I didn't even know what to say, but she saved me from having to figure it out.

"Don't worry about it, Chan. It's your life. Do what you want. I'm going to bed." And with that desolate statement she turned and went upstairs. The *slam-click* of her door was becoming a familiar punctuation mark in the story of my life.

CHAPTER
Twenty-Nine

Channing

WHATEVER I'D BEEN EXPECTING, IT HADN'T BEEN THIS. THERE were people *everywhere*. It was the X Games and I should have known, but the sheer mass of snowboarders, skiers, and spectators was nothing to balk at.

I led the way towards Cup of Joe. Ally was walking behind me; we'd rode over in complete silence. She didn't bother to suppress her disappointment or hide it from her eyes when she saw me head down to the basement—to Chance's room—with a bag to pack his stuff into.

"Ready?" I'd asked, attempting a smile only to feel her draw farther away from me. Grabbing her purse, she just walked out the front door towards the car.

I'll take that as a yes.

I woke up to a text from Wyatt saying that he and Zack would meet us at Cup of Joe this morning before the events of the day got underway. I wondered if we were even going to fit inside the coffee shop with the number of people around.

I pulled the door open and sure enough, there was a crush of customers inside. "Looks like you have your work cut out for you today, Al."

She ignored me and walked through the door only to run straight into Emmett as he turned from the bar, holding a mug of coffee in his hands.

"Well if it isn't Little Miss sunshine." He grinned and I winced. Ally was *not* in the mood this morning, which meant Emmett was about to have his ass handed to him.

"Get out of my way, asshole."

"Woahhh," his hands went up, "did Prince Charming leave your panties in a bunch this morning?"

Oh no. "Emmett, just leave her alone," I finally interjected, glaring at him, trying to force him to move out of our way. Except he didn't look at me, his eyes remained on Ally, waiting for *her response.*

"Did you bring a change of clothes?" Sweetness dripped from her words and I knew a scene was about to me made.

"Why? You plan on taking them off?" He laughed. *And then she did, too.* "WHAT THE—" An impressive display of expletives echoed through the coffeehouse as Ally tipped his coffee mug over, spilling the steaming contents down the front of his shirt. "What the hell is wrong with you!"

"Oh, my gosh! Did I do that?" her tone dripping with mock innocence. "I am *so* sorry."

I moved to step around them when Emmett grabbed my arm, his eyes burning with rage. "What the fuck is wrong with your sister?" he yelled.

"I told you to leave her alone!" I huffed and pulled my arm from his grasp, noticing Ally smiling sweetly at him as though she hadn't just doused him in hot coffee.

I saw Wyatt watching the exchange from the corner and I was about to turn and make my way to him when I saw Emmett step closer towards my sister. I paused, watching as he leaned in and whispered something in her ear—something that wiped the smile right off of her face and painted her cheeks red. He dipped his finger into what was probably only a few drops of coffee left in his mug and traced it down her cheek.

I had to give Ally credit, she didn't flinch away from him; instead she stared him down, wiping her cheek with her sleeve, as though she would destroy him if it was the last thing she ever did. In that moment, I realized that what Wyatt had suggested had much more truth to it than I'd given it credit for.

"Who needs to watch today's events when your sister can put on a show like that?" Wyatt teased as I walked up to him and the coffee that he had waiting for me.

Wrapping my arms around his neck, I raised up on my tip-toes, claiming the kiss that had been coming.

"I can't wait for the next two days to be over," he rasped against me.

"Why?" I pulled my head back. "It's your last Games! You should enjoy it!"

The warm breath of his laugh brushed over my cheek. "I'd rather be enjoying you. Every night. *Every way.*"

I shivered deliciously. "Promises, Mr. Olsen?"

"You bet, Miss Ryder." He kissed me quickly and then we searched for a seat to drink our coffee.

By the time we found a table, Emmett was gone, Ally had her apron on and was behind the counter, and Zack had arrived at some point and was chatting with her.

"Guess the show is over," I mused wryly.

Wyatt laughed. "Looks like it's up to the rest of us to keep the masses entertained." *If they only knew.*

"Are there always this many people?" He nodded affirmatively. "Crazy…" I drained the last of my coffee. "What time is your run?"

I already knew when it was because I was holding a copy of the schedule in my pocket—a schedule that listed my own time on there, too. Thankfully, Wyatt was running at the end of the heat and I was just after the middle; so, there were probably about six or so riders separating us. This meant he would still be in queue when I finished, giving me time to change and watch his pass.

"Looks like I'm closing today." He smiled.

"You would think that you would go first since you won last year."

"I'll go first tomorrow." *Oh, that made sense.* We both stood, needing to go get ready.

"Alright, I have to go get ready for Big Air, gorgeous." He bent down and kissed me. "You gonna watch me?"

"Oh, I'm going to do more than watch you," I answered with my best—yet, still somewhat lacking—seductive voice.

He laughed, his hands coming to my waist as his fingers teased the top of my ass. "Let's go."

I gave Ally a smile and a wave as we walked out; I don't think she saw either of them.

Wyatt and I walked to the main lodge, hand-in-hand; my other hand hanging guiltily at my side, feeling like I was going to stab him in the back in just a few short hours.

He wasn't going to know.

I walked with him as far as the blockades would allow, knowing the pass with Chance's name on it in my duffel bag would let me by.

"You ready?" I teased him. He looked so completely calm and confident—like this was every day for him; it was just the X Games, no pressure or anything.

He laughed. "I've been ready for a long time. I'm just glad that you're here for my last go at this. The perfect close to an incredible ride."

"And a perfect beginning," I murmured. We both smiled at each other like one of the scenes from my chick-flicks—the ones where men usually grunt and groan at how sappy they are.

He crushed me against his snow clothes—*too many layers, way too many.*

"Where are you parents?"

I felt his head turn side-to-side. "They're somewhere around here. I know Zack was going to sit with them. Probably your sister, too. You want me to call them?"

I shook my head. "No, I have a better spot to watch you from."

"On the mountain?" I nodded with a devious smile. There was no way I was going to watch his run on the stupid jumbo-tron.

"Alright, gorgeous. I'll find you when I'm done with my run?"

When his lips left mine, I hesitated, "I... I have to help Chance with all his stuff, so I'll just see you once Slopestyle is over?"

I could see he was surprised to hear me mention my brother's name since I hadn't been practicing or helping him at all these past weeks. But, because he loved me, he believed my lie. And because I loved him, I hated myself for it.

"Sounds good, gorgeous." He kissed me again, deeply this time. "Just taking some of that for good luck."

"I don't think you need luck there, Mr. Wyatt-Always-Wins-Olsen."

"You're right, I just need you." And with that, his hand smacked my ass and he was gone, jogging out onto the slope towards the entrance to the lift.

The one benefit of being a local in this moment was that I knew exactly where I could get the best vantage point of his qualifier. He ran last in this heat, since he won the gold in it last year, too. I pushed through the standing crowd, avoiding the giant cameras everywhere trying to get photos of the riders as they began to congregate on the mountain.

Most people were sitting on the right side of the slope, watching the big-screen projectors that would be showing the run. Instead, I took to the other side of the trail where there was a double lift still taking visitors half-way up the mountain. I got a few strange looks as I got on the lift with no gear, but when I got off, instead of going to the left where the other open trails were, I went to the right, cutting through the wooded area that would take me down along the side of the Snowmass pipe. From there, I could watch from right at the end of the massive jump and not down several hundred feet where the rest of the spectators were.

And there I waited for the other riders to complete their pass. Pulling out my sheet, I counted down from the twelve that were on the schedule until it was finally time for Wyatt's run.

My heart beat out of my chest; the funny thing was that I was sure that he wasn't nervous at all. But I wanted this for him. I wanted him to go out on top. And then, I saw him drop from the top of the slope, gaining speed before he approached the single huge kicker that comprised the Big Air competition. Unlike Slopestyle, where there were three jumps at the end of the run, Big Air gave you only one shot—your highest shot—at nailing the most insane trick you could accomplish.

I watched him carve, controlled and confident, through the snow, my mouth parting in awe.

Some people are touched by a photo or a piece of art; some are enraptured by a piece of music or a song; for others, a dance or performance captivates in a way that nothing has before. Well, that was me right now, watching my boyfriend perform arguably the most difficult jump ever attempted up to this point in time: the Quad Cork.

The strength, skill, and precision of every muscle in his body to coordinate its movements, to gain the right speed and angle off of the snow, to flip and rotate in perfect synchronicity—it was a work of art. *He was a work of art—one that it seemed impossible to put into words.*

In slow motion, I watched him spin, opening up through the air. It was only seconds that he was up there, but the way he floated felt like it could have been minutes. The thought of him falling never even crossed my mind. No, this was a man who had been practicing this for a long time—a man who had taught me the same lesson: don't practice until you get it right, practice until you can't get it wrong. *Wyatt could not get this wrong.* He performed the maneuver as easily as an inhale of breath; the solid sound of his board hitting the landing a firm exhale. *And the crowd went wild.*

"Sometimes, Wyatt Olsen's riding is simply indescribable…" I heard the announcer boom over the speakers.

He didn't have to attempt the quad for qualifiers; he could have easily made it in with a triple. I saw his head jerk towards my direction as he flew by; he saw me. That was why he did it. The damn man wanted to impress me even though he knew he didn't have to. And tomorrow, I knew he was going to get out on this slope and do the exact same thing and win. No one else who'd gone would ever attempt the quad; their only hope would be if Wyatt bailed on the landing tomorrow.

Which I could tell them right now wasn't possible.

I checked my watch. *Shit.* They were going to call the Slopestyle riders soon now that Big Air was done. I jogged down the rest of the trail, sticking to the back of the crowd so I could move quickly—and so there was less of a chance that I would run into Wyatt, his family, or my friends. I wove in and out of the bodies—some that were leaving the stands, some heading to them for the next event—when suddenly, I felt a chill down my spine. It wasn't the chill that I got when Wyatt was around—no, that one was warm and intoxicating. This one was cold and calculating and it stopped me in my tracks. I glanced around for a few seconds, trying to find a face that I recognized, but I came up empty. And then the chill was gone.

It's your nerves, Channing. Stop freaking out and just get this over with.

With that slight delay, it took me longer than I would have liked to get over to the training building. I was unlocking the door to the equipment room when I heard the announcer come over the loudspeaker.

"Ladies and gentlemen. We're going to begin the Slopestyle event in a few minutes. If all participating riders could make their way over to the lift, we will begin shortly."

I ducked inside, making sure the door was shut and secure behind me. Grabbing my duffel bag out from underneath the bench I started to strip. Under Armour, black snowpants, black jacket—all baggy, all-concealing. I dumped the miscellaneous gear—gloves, hat, etc.—onto the bench, reaching into the bottom of the bag for my rider tag and RFID card that they scanned to let you onto the lift.

Chance Ryder.

I swallowed over the lump in my throat, cinching the strap around my arm before I could think any further about it. I turned back to the bench. *My last defenses.* I pulled on the black helmet that was adorned with the same local sponsor stickers that Chance had on his. *Everyone loves when twins wear the same things.* Last came the mirrored goggles—the only spot of color on my outfit.

Unzipping the board bag, I pulled out Chance's board, trying not to think about anything right now other than doing solid on my pass.

I took a deep breath, hand on the doorknob. *Go big or go home.*

Wyatt

I was on cloud-fucking-nine after finishing my Big Air pass. Everything had gone perfectly, not that I had expected anything different, especially because I knew my girl was in the crowd watching me, cheering me on, and most likely critiquing me—one of the things I loved about her. I could be the best—I *was* the best—and she would still push me to be better.

I looked for her in the crowd but didn't spot that blue gaze. Usually, I waited near the end of the slope with all the other riders to watch the rest of the heat, but I wanted to be with her; I figured she'd be down here somewhere watching her brother.

I apologized as I pushed through the crowd, my snowgear making it even harder for me to move through the crowd with any appreciable speed. I didn't see anyone that I knew, not even Zack and my parents or—

"Emmett!" I yelled, cupping my hands around my mouth. His fire buzz-cut was impossible to miss. Black eyes whipped to mine. He, surprisingly, stopped and waited for me. "Have you seen Channing?"

He smiled; I didn't like that smile. "No, I haven't." His thumb came up and brushed over his nose. "I'm sure you'll be able to find her easier once the qualifier is done."

"Yeah, but I wanted to watch with her; I'm assuming she's down here watching her brother…"

His face broke into a smile again briefly as he cleared his throat. *Something was going on and this fucker knew what it was and wasn't planning on telling me.*

"Emmett, what's going on?" I let a dangerous tone enter my

voice—one that rarely came out, but was easily accessible for the woman who held my heart.

He shushed me. The motherfucker shushed me as the announcer came on, giving Chance's name.

"Emm—"

"Watch," he bit out. "If you watch you'll find her."

What the fuck was that supposed to mean? My mouth thinned in frustration as I looked around one last time; I didn't see her anywhere. Guess I was going to meet up with her after the run was over after all. Turning my gaze to the giant TV screen, I watched my girl's twin brother at the top of the slope, all in black, about to drop.

I'd never seen him this close before—I wasn't a big fan of watching the competition. But now that I was, the similarities between him and Channing were insane. Their board stance, their posture… on the mountain, they were identical.

And that's when it hit me.

Slow at first, a gentle tugging of my mind back to a dark place where anything was possible—*anything like this.*

It couldn't be.

The rider—or Ryder—began to move down the course. The grind and rails told me nothing. The body moving with a smoothness that I'd observed for weeks now.

They are twins, Olsen. They've been training together since practically birth; of course, they are going to move the same.

My heart beat faster and much harder than it had all day. I watched as the camera panned as the rider approached the first jump.

Switch backside 1260.

Perfect execution. Nothing to tell me whether or not this rider was Chance or…

Switch double Underflip 900.

My eyes narrowed. I saw something as the rider came out of the jump, something that I recognized, but couldn't remember; something that told me the pit in my stomach wasn't unfounded.

Bile rose inside my throat as anger and hurt crashed in my

stomach. The rider approached the last jump.

Frontside 1080 double cork.

What in the living fuck had I just seen?

My heart stopped. The doubles were what we'd spent hours on and fuck me if that flawless feat didn't look exactly like Channing.

I would have bet my life that it was her on the board at that moment, carving triumphantly toward the end of the trail. But that wasn't what convinced me. Yes, I knew her body and the way it moved on the mountain… and on me. But what solidified it had nothing to do with the jump or the double or her technique. What told me it was her was something so small that no one would have ever thought twice about it. *No one but me.* Because I *saw* her—*all* of her—down to every last worry or breath that passed through her body. And down to every. Last. Tick.

Including the one that I had teased her about the first time we were out on the park; the adorable little habit she had of wiping her glove off on her pants as soon as she stood from the landing.

It was adorable and it was her undoing.

I burned with rage as I turned towards Emmett who it seemed had been looking at me, smirking the entire duration of my revelation.

"Did you fucking know?"

"Of course I fucking knew," he answered casually. Honestly, there was nothing else to say to him. I didn't really give a shit if he knew; I wanted to know why *I* didn't know and there was only one person who could—and would—answer that. I turned to walk away when his voice gave me pause. "Those Ryder women really know how to fuck you bigtime, don't they?"

For a split second, I felt bad for the asshole. Trapped and tortured by his feelings for Ally that he would probably rather die than admit to. I, on the other hand, had no problem admitting how I felt about Channing and how much I needed her.

And yet, somehow, it seemed like we were both equally as screwed.

CHAPTER Thirty

Channing

I BREATHED A HUGE SIGH OF RELIEF AS SOON AS THE BOTTOM OF MY board smacked confidently against the landing of the last jump. And as soon as the breath was out of my lips, I immediately began to scan for Wyatt in the crowd. He wasn't at the bottom with all of the riders; that was when the first hint of dread came over me.

No, Channing. It's for the best that he's not there.

Unless he was looking for me.

My board hadn't even come to a stop before I was unstrapping from it, lifting it from the ground. I dove to the side of the crowd as my eyes scanned for the quickest way back to the equipment room to change.

Had I left the door unlocked?

I pushed inside the dim room, rushing to my bag, and propping my board against the wall as the door shut. I turned around to go and lock it and I realized that I wasn't alone.

Wyatt.

He was leaning against the wall opposite the door, arms crossed over his chest. He still had his snowpants on, but his jacket was missing, his cold gear stretched tight over the hard muscles of his chest—muscles my fingers itched to touch. But his face, his expression, it stopped my heart. If it were Ally, I would have seen disappointment; if it were Chance, I would have seen anger. In Wyatt, I expected both.

Instead, I saw pure, unadulterated betrayal.

"That was an excellent run there, gorgeous." His stare burned right through to my soul. "Or should I say, *Chance*?"

"Wyatt…" I exhaled his name because that's what he was to me. *Oxygen.*

"That's me, Channing. That's who I've always been. But, I'm wondering just exactly *who* are you?" He stalked towards me. "And what could I have possibly meant to you for you to do this?"

"Please…" I begged. "You don't understand." I shook my head. I was frozen—like when I'd bombed the triple last year at the Open; I was frozen in failure.

"Don't I? Because it seems pretty straight-forward to me." He stopped inches in front of me, glancing over at the board against the wall. "You registered in the *men's* Slopestyle competition under your brother's name, which—" he broke off with a laugh, "—ironically, probably wouldn't have happened if it hadn't been for me."

I tried to say something, but he cut me off, continuing, "And then, I began flirting with you and you realized what an *opportunity* you had—not just to get me to help you, but to distract me from winning the last Games of my career." He swore, rubbing his hand over his mouth. "And you know what the most fucking fantastic part about all of this is? *It's all my fault.*"

My head began to do that thing where it shakes back and forth because you want to deny so badly what the other person is saying, but you either can't find the words or they won't let you speak them. So, instead, it shakes 'no' over and over again, beating into your brain that you deserve this; that I deserved what he was saying. Tears streamed down my face like blood from the open wound of my heart being ripped from my chest.

"*I* was the one who got 'Chance' registered. *I* was the one who pursued you. *I* was the one who offered to help you with your triple. What a fucking joke that must have been; I bet Emmett got a good fucking laugh about how the asshole you were trying to beat just offered to help you do it. *I* was the one who gave in and fucked you. *I only have myself to blame."*

"No!" I finally yelled, my hands quickly wiping over my face. "No… I didn't… It's not your fault." *Goddammit. Nothing was coming out like it should.* "I registered Chance because he is gone." It probably wasn't the best thing to start with, but it got his attention. "Chance was injured and y-you were right, it was t-to the point where he couldn't compete again. And then, o-one day, I showed up to the hospital and he. Was. Gone. Do you know what that's like? Do you know what it feels like to have the one person who was literally a part of you from before you were born ripped from your life *by choice?*"

I sucked in a breath, my hurt and anger holding the sobs at bay. "Some days, I think it would have been easier if he had died because then I wouldn't have to wake up knowing that he left me with no note, no explanation, no goodbye, *on purpose*. And I know that's a horrible thing to think, but hell if I can help it. I want to sympathize, I want to empathize, but how can I do that with him gone? Without knowing what he feels or thinks? And for everyone else's sake, I've been holding that anger and hurt in for months and finally, I realized that I couldn't expect him to come back. But, I could still try to achieve our dream. Yes, Chance was injured, but I wasn't. So, I registered under his name."

My arms crossed over my chest, my hands gripping into the side of my jacket, not in anger, but in an attempt to literally try to hold myself together.

"I didn't… plan on running into you—or your boards; I didn't even know who you were at that point. I didn't *plan* on you following me. I didn't *plan* on wanting you. When I was with you, I forgot about the competition. You weren't just helping me learn the stupid fucking triple; you were helping move past something so much deeper than that. I didn't realize it at first and when I did, I knew just how hard I'd fallen for you. I didn't plan on you, Wyatt; I didn't plan on falling in love with you."

"Then why are we here?" he ground out.

The tears began to fall again. "I was going to pull out—pull Chance out—after the night on the mountain but then Ally told me what Zack said; I thought you were going to leave and I felt like everything I had gained was ripped right back out from under me and the only thing left was the competition."

"I told you I wasn't going to leave you."

"I was too scared to believe you." I confessed softly. "I wanted it so badly to be true. But all I could think was how Chance left... my brother... my twin. He was never supposed to do that either. And when you and I finally talked, it was too late; I couldn't drop out without it looking suspicious. Chance may never compete again, but I couldn't ruin the name he'd made for himself."

"Or risk your future in the sport?" he asked harshly.

"I don't—" I choked, unable to get the rest of the words out. *I didn't care about my future in the sport, but why would he believe that now?*

"Why didn't you just tell me, then?" His exasperation was evident. "Why didn't you just tell me what you had planned? What did you think I was going to do—report you? Turn you in? The woman I love?"

My eyes shot to his. '*Love*' not loved.

"I-I just thought that I would do it and forget about it; that you wouldn't have to know. I didn't want you to think..." I wiped away more tears. "Everything that you are thinking right now. Everything that I would be thinking right now if I were you."

"And if you were me, Channing, what would you do now? What would you do knowing that the woman you'd give up everything for doesn't believe in your love for her?" He laughed harshly. "No—even worse than that, what would you do knowing that your woman doesn't even believe in herself? In her own worth?"

"I-I don't know," I replied, my voice wavering. He sighed heavily and turned towards the door. "Where are you going?"

"I don't know." He threw his hands out in frustration. "I have no fucking idea. You asked if I could imagine how it felt when your brother left? When someone who was a part of you left you and ripped away everything that you knew? How about when someone you love, who was going to the biggest part of your future didn't leave you, but was never there to begin with? Does that count? Because they both sound a whole lot like someone who you thought loved you enough to trust you with their pain decided to leave you hanging up in the air."

"Wyatt—" The door shutting behind him was his response. And I didn't—*couldn't*—blame him.

The sound was like the wind being knocked out of me. As soon as he was gone, the first pain of impact registered followed by the immediate assessment of my body's damage; only after those first few seconds did I realize that the one thing I needed to survive had been robbed from me.

And I'd been the one to steal my own happiness away.

I didn't stay. I ripped off my snowclothes—the stupid loose-fitting garments had never been so difficult to get off; then again, I didn't bother to turn on the lights or try to stop the tears from falling from my eyes. I changed in a watery darkness and then fled.

I didn't check to see if I had qualified, chances were that I did, but in spite of what Wyatt thought—*I didn't care about the Games anymore.*

The drive back to my house had never seemed so long. In my distress, I forgot to put on the emergency brake in the Jeep until I was halfway out the door and the car started to roll back. *Get it together, Channing.* I yanked the stupid thing into park; the next thing I knew I was opening the front door, my sobs distorting my reality.

The front door slamming behind me echoed through the empty space.

Empty—just like me.

Again, I blinked and I was in the kitchen, my footsteps through the hallway nonexistent in my mind. I didn't remember what I came in there for. Water? A tissue? A frozen heart?

"Lil." I halted. *First, I wasn't registering my movements and now, I was hearing things.* I would have laughed in self-pity if I wasn't already sobbing so hard. I needed to lie down, that would help. I needed to calm down and then figure out how to fix this.

"Lil." I wasn't imagining it. The sound—my name—was real; someone had said it, someone was here. *Someone who never should have left.*

I stopped breathing all together as I turned slowly towards the living room. My eyes registering the body that was sitting in the armchair next to the couch; I stared in shock at the eyes, the face, the voice that I'd known from before birth. I stared at myself—I stared at my twin. *I stared at Chance.*

Chance

My sister was the mirror of my disaster.

Channing looked like how I felt inside; she looked how I did months ago. Now, I was just better at hiding it.

Fuck. Why did I even come back here?

My jaw tightened. I wouldn't say that I'd been happy in LA, but it had been easier to forget about here in a place that was the complete opposite of the one that I'd called home.

Her mouth fell open, the word 'what' barely escaping from it in shock. The only sound in the room was her uncontrollable hiccups from the abrupt stop of her sobs. I pushed myself up off the chair where I'd been lounging, wondering which sibling I would encounter first.

Channing continued to stare at me like I was a goddamn ghost. And I might as well have been for what my life consisted of anymore. Without being able to ride, I had nothing, I was nothing, and I just wished I could have been invisible.

I stopped a few inches from her, so many—too many—emotions fighting inside of me, but they weren't important right now. What was important was my beautiful sister, standing in front of me, shattered in a way I'd *never* seen her before.

She breathed my name again, finally realizing that I was there and that I was *real*.

And then she crumbled against me.

My arms locked around her as sobs wracked her body, her tears drenching my shirt within minutes. I held her, my hand coming up to rub the back of her head as she cried. A new wave of guilt washed over me for leaving her.

But I hadn't had a choice.

I don't know how long we stood there, but I would have held her for as long as she needed. Channing had always carried too much weight on her shoulders; I'd hoped that by leaving, I wouldn't have added to it. Instead, I'd come back to find her broken anyway.

Finally, her cries began to subside, not because the pain had but because all of her strength had been sapped. I felt her pain, through the bond that we shared; I felt every excruciating crack of her heart crumbling inside of her.

"W-why are you here?" Her voice as wet as my shirt. "W-why d-did you c-come back?" I felt her grip around me loosen as she pulled back to look at me.

I exhaled deeply, knowing the answers to those questions went far deeper. "C'mon, Lil. Why don't we sit? You look like you're about to collapse." I put my arm around her shaking shoulders and led her towards the couch. Once she was seated, I walked up to the entertainment center, opening the top cabinet, and pulled out my stash of Powers whiskey.

She watched in exhausted silence as I grabbed two cups and filled them generously with the liquid. "Drink." She needed to calm down.

I took a sip, hoping it would incite her to take one as well. Instead, she stared at the liquid in the glass. "Ally called me," I began, watching as her eyes immediately rose to mine. "She called and told me what you were doing—competing in my name."

"I'm sorry..." she whispered as her face turned red.

I laughed harshly, taking another sip. "Don't be. I don't give a shit about that." I leveled my eyes on her. "I do, however, care about you."

"So, you only came back to stop me?" she whispered.

"Something like that." I watched the amber liquid shift in my glass as I held it. "I thought I could just show up and withdraw my registration, which is why I came to the house that night looking for my letter and license..." I trailed off knowing the next part was going to hurt her. "But I didn't find it in time."

"So you just wanted to stop me, but without actually seeing or talking to me?"

I was a fucking asshole.

"Lil—"

"No! Why, Chance? Why come back? What did I do to you?" I could see her tears threatening to overtake her again. "*Why are you running from me?*"

I didn't answer, opting to respond with a question of my own. "Why did you enter under my name?"

"Because I wasn't invited."

My eyes narrowed. "Don't be smart."

Her gaze fell to her glass and she finally took a long sip. "I-I don't know. At first, I thought it was because you deserved it; you deserved to compete... even if you couldn't. Then... stuff happened and I realized that maybe I had done it for myself—not because I realistically thought I could win or anything. I thought if I placed it would make up for the Open last year; I thought if I placed I would finally be as good as you; I thought that I should—that I had to—because it was our dream for... as long as I can remember. And I guess, maybe I also thought if I did, you might see and you might come home—that you might forgive me for letting you down."

"Fuck, Lil." I speared my hand through my hair; it was a weird feeling—to have hair to run a hand through—since I'd always kept my hair as short as Emmett's. "Why the fuck do you think you let me down?"

"I don't know. Because I didn't place at the Open. Because you got hurt. Because I didn't do enough to help you... to keep you here."

I groaned, wiping my hands down the length of my face. *This was exactly what I didn't want to have happen.*

"Channing." I took control of the conversation using her full name. "First, you didn't let me down. *At all.*"

"Then why did you leave?"

There were a lot of answers to that—many that I was still unwilling to acknowledge—but there was one that I could give her; and it was the one she needed to hear. "You are right. One of the reasons I left was because of you—*but,—*" I emphasized, seeing her eyes go wide, "—not because you did something wrong, but because I didn't want to hold you back."

"I don't understand." Her expression echoed her sentiments.

"Lil, when I was in the hospital I realized two things. One was what had happened before I got there and the other was what was going to happen when I left." I refilled my glass; *I was going to need it.* "For a long time, maybe forever, it's always been you and me, learning, riding, competing. And I wouldn't have traded that for the world, but somewhere buried under our need to push each other has been a sibling rivalry. Not malicious, but no less real. And when I fell, I realized just how much of our lives it had consumed. Now, me, I had no choice; I couldn't continue even if I wanted. But you, I saw you and I saw you still stuck in a cycle that neither of us knew how to break."

Fuck, I hoped I was making sense. The way she looked at me made me feel like I was speaking Greek to her.

"The mountain is a part of you—a part of me—and that's not wrong, but it's also not everything and when I was injured, I realized that it had become everything—especially to you. I realized why I'd been so excited for you to land the triple, only to tell you not to do it in competition. Because you were pushing yourself farther and faster than was safe; I just thank fucking God you weren't injured worse when you fell. Do you understand what I'm saying?" I asked, frustrated with myself. "Being as good as me, being the best, *not* letting me down—it's consumed you. And I don't judge you because it consumed me, too. So, part of me left because I wanted to break your cycle. If I stayed, you would have tried to continue to best me. I never thought though," I paused to chuckle, "that if I left you would try to *be* me."

It was moments like this when I felt like there wasn't enough whiskey in the world to ease the pain inside of me. *Emmett would agree.*

"I know what you try to carry—all the jobs, the responsibility, keeping the house together, keeping us assholes in line. How do you think you would have felt going to the mountain every morning to ride with our friends knowing that I couldn't? Competing knowing that I never will again?" *Fucking fuck. Saying it hurt so much fucking more than thinking it had.*

"Guilty."

"Exactly." I downed another mouthful of fire. "And my injury was in no way your fault, but you would have blamed yourself anyway. It would have been just one *more* thing for you to feel like you'd disappointed me. The mountain… snowboarding… it isn't everything, Channing. I had to learn that the hard way; I don't want you to have to."

I still hadn't learned it. But she didn't need to know that.

The sadness in her eyes was as deep as the ocean. "I know, Chance," she whispered. "I figured it out, but I was too late. I found something that meant so much more than the mountain, but, like every other time it seems, I didn't have enough faith in someone who loves me to believe it." She bit her lip and I knew she was trying not to cry again. "I should have believed you when you told me that I wasn't ready to compete with the triple… just like I should have believed Wyatt when he told me that he loved me and that he'd never leave me."

Wait, what? Hold the fucking phone. "Wyatt… Olsen?"

She nodded again. "It's… a long story."

"Yeah," I scoffed. *And I was sure that I didn't fucking want to hear half of it.* "So that's what Frost was being so fucking shady about."

"Nick?" Her brows furrowed.

I nodded. "I've been staying with him. And don't—" I gave her a hard stare, "—give him shit for it."

"I'm sorry," she said quietly, "if you're upset about Wyatt."

"I'm not upset, just protective. How do you know he wasn't using you to get to me? Or you, posing as me?" I didn't want her to be fooled. I may have left, but I would protect her at all costs.

"Because I was the one who had to convince him to be in a... relationship." I tried not to read into the slight pause. "He insisted on waiting until after the Games because he didn't want me... or you... to think that."

"I see." There is was again, the completely shattered look on her face.

"What happened?"

"Everything. Nothing." Her self-deprecating laugh killed me. "He told me he loved me and that he wouldn't leave me. And at the first test, I readily believed that at worst, he was moving back to Canada after the Games, and at best, that he was going to ask me to move with him. Turns out he was moving here... for me. But, I didn't trust him, so I never pulled out from the Games."

"So, you didn't tell him you were competing as me?"

She shook her head. "I also had him help me relearn the triple. So now, not only does it look like I was trying to mess with his head just to win, but I also asked him to teach me how to do it."

"Oh, shit."

She laughed and her head fell back against the back of the couch. "Exactly."

"So how are you going to fix it?" Her head snapped back up and she looked at me like I'd just asked her how she was going fly to the moon.

"I don't even know if there is a fixing it."

"Seriously, Lil?" It was time for some tough love.

"Yes, Chance!" she yelled. "I hurt him, I betrayed him. I didn't use him, but he thinks that I did."

"Woah, woah, woah." I held up my hands. "I don't need to, nor do I want to know all of the details here, but there is only one thing that I need to know: do you love him?"

Her head cocked to the side, looking at me with a face that said, 'does a bear shit in the woods?'

"Yes." She let out a small laugh. "Yes, I do. I love him."

"Did you give up snowboarding the first time that you fell? How about the millionth time? Did you give up the first time you lost a competition? Or the time you bailed at the Open? How about the first time you got hurt? Or the tenth?" Now, I just took a swig from the bottle. "No. The answer is always and emphatically 'no.' We don't give up when we fall, Lil; we get back up. We don't ever give up on something or someone that we love."

Unless life forces us to—but that was my fucked-up story, not hers. What I told her was the truth—it just wasn't a universal truth.

A smack on the back of her head would have been just as effective and much less painful, in my opinion, but I did this for her.

"So, what are you going to do about it?" I asked again. "How are you going to fix it?"

She gnawed on her lip, staring at the black screen of the TV that wasn't on. She sat there for minutes on end and I could see scenarios, plans, ideas flitting through her mind like snowflakes flying on the breeze. But I waited. I waited because I owed her this. I didn't regret leaving; part of me regretted coming back. But none of me regretted helping my sister pursue a love that was her own.

Finally, her head turned and her blue eyes met mine.

Finally, she responded. Her tone that of dazed revelation, she said simply, "I'm going to fall for him."

CHAPTER
Thirty-One

Wyatt

WHAT THE FUCK. I PUSHED MINDLESSLY THROUGH THE CROWD, heading for the parking lot.

What was she thinking? What had I done?

"Wyatt! Where have you been?" Zack ran up behind me and clapped his arm around my shoulder. "Mom and dad have been looking for you!"

I kept walking towards the Range Rover. "I'm heading back to the condo."

"Wait, what? Don't you want to celebrate? You ran fucking amazing out there, bro! You're totally going to take both events tomorrow." Zack laughed with excitement. We'd come a long way since our destructively competitive days. "What the hell is wrong?"

"I'm a fucking asshole, that's what's wrong." *How could I have used her hurt against her? Yeah, she didn't tell me what happened with Chance and yeah, I was confronting her about it but she still told me, regardless of how we got there. She told me about her pain and I threw it back at her because of mine.*

Zack stopped—but I didn't, so he jogged to catch back up with me. "What are you talking about?"

"You mean you don't know?" When I looked at him, I saw Ally trailing a few steps behind us. "Ask your girl back there; I'm sure she does." Zack glanced over at her.

"Oh, no. Did she tell you?" Her soft voice drifted up to me.

My jaw tightened. "She didn't have to. I've spent hours out on the slopes with her; I know the way her body moves on the snow, over the jumps. No amount of snow gear is going to hide that from *me*."

Zack's head jerked back and forth several times. "Wait… are you saying… Holy *fucking* shit. That was Channing out there?" He continued to look between us. "She signed up and is competing as her *brother*?" He at least had the decency to remain shocked; anything else might have tempted me to punch him if for no other reason than as an outlet for my frustration. "How? How do you even do that? What happened to Chance?"

I laughed harshly. "Chance was never here. He was never competing; it was always her."

"Zack," Ally caught up to us, "can I talk to Wyatt for a minute?"

I groaned. I just wanted to get out of here and figure my shit out—and *not* have to deal with any Ryders.

Zack looked between the two of us. "Ahh… sure. Guess I'll just go let mom know that you're heading back to rest for tomorrow." And then to Ally, he said, "Text me, babe."

"Ally, I'm not trying to be a dick, but I'm not in the mood." I hit the button to open the trunk of the SUV, waiting impatiently to be able to pack my gear inside and get out of here.

"I'm… sure." Her arms hugged herself nervously.

Fuck. "Alright, what do you want to ask me?" I just wanted to get this over with. I slid my board into the back, before looking to her for her response.

"The only important question. Do you love her like you said you did?" Damn, those blue eyes of hers only made me think of Channing.

"Yes." There was no hesitation, no doubt, no anger. Only 'yes.'

"Ok, then that's all I need to know." I shut the trunk, watching as she turned to walk away.

"That's it?" I was floored. I was expecting a whole conversation.

She glanced back to me. "I only needed to know how you felt; you're the one who has to figure out what to do about it." And with that, she walked away, pulling her phone out of her pocket, probably to text my brother.

I hit the radio button to turn the music off as soon as the car started; I needed silence. Pulling through the lot, I saw Ally at the edge of the cars. I almost stopped because she looked irate and was yelling at someone, but as I moved forward, I saw that it was Emmett whom she was yelling at.

Channing had lied to me. She'd used me. She'd kept herself from me.

It all sucked and it fucking pissed me off, but that wasn't what hurt.

What hurt was that she'd done it all because she was too afraid to trust that I loved her—that I would support her and wouldn't leave her.

And what had I done?

At this first instance, this first test, I made her feel like shit for it and left; *I proved her right.*

I could tell myself a thousand times that I was in the right, that I had no reason to feel guilty about how I felt or what I'd said, but that would be a thousand more lies to add onto her one.

I didn't give a fuck that she was competing as her brother; I wouldn't have given a fuck even if she won as him. I finally found something that mattered more to me than the damn competitions and that was the only thing I was fighting to win—*her.*

Wanting something quick and easy, I stopped and picked up a sub on my way home, knowing there was no food at the condo.

Ally had asked the only important question with the most important answer: I loved her.

I loved her.

It blew through every part of my body as I turned the car off and walked into the condo.

I saw how truly afraid she was that I was going to leave her, which meant that the only way to prove to her that I loved her was to show her now that I wasn't. No matter how angry and hurt I was, I wasn't going to leave her or give up on her.

I took my sandwich up to my room, groaning as I peeled out of my coldgear.

I remembered one time when Zack and I were young, and my mom made spaghetti and meatballs one Sunday. I'm sure that we'd had it before, but I didn't remember any time before that day; that Sunday, it tasted like it had come from heaven. We'd laughed, talked, played some games, and both cleaned our plates. Then, the following Saturday, we'd run up to her and asked, "we're going to have spaghetti and meatballs again tomorrow, right?" The expectation had been built. It wasn't just the food—it was family time, the conversation, the happiness, the delight—every event and emotion had coalesced into what seemed like a simple meal. One meal, one night, was all it took as we stood there unwilling to take no for an answer. From that day forward, until I started traveling so much for practice and competitions, we ate spaghetti and meatballs every Sunday because the expectation was there.

I sat down on the edge of my bed, glancing around the room, and felt that same sense of expectation for love, happiness, and peace. All it had taken was one woman and that first night for me to know that I needed her *every. Single. Night.* It wasn't just my desire for her—it was everything that she made me feel, everything that she inspired inside of me. I wasn't willing to compromise and I hoped that, even after what I'd said, that she wasn't either.

I was almost done eating in when there was a soft knock on the door. "Yeah?" I yelled, figuring it was probably Zack.

"Can I come in?" My mother's voice asked.

"Yeah." I crumbled up the wrapper as she entered. "Thought you were Zack."

She waved her hand at me. "No, I think he is taking Ally out to dinner."

"Sorry, for jetting out of there right away," I mumbled. "And for bailing on dinner; we can go tomorrow though once this is all over."

"Oh, don't worry about it. It was silly to suggest it. You should do whatever you feel that you need to." I walked over towards her, tossing my garbage in the trash. "You did great today though, honey."

"Thanks, mom." I turned and pulled her in for a hug, grateful for her support.

She clasped her hands in front of her, her 'concerned-mom' face appearing. "Wyatt, are you ok?"

I nodded. "Yeah," pausing before I admitted, "I will be. I just messed up. With Channing." I exhaled deeply. "She made a mistake and I said some things that I shouldn't have; she needed me to pull her closer, instead I pulled back."

I looked over at her, surprised to see her watching me with wide eyes and a small smile.

"What?" I asked. I'm sure as a mother it's fun to see your kids tortured sometimes, but I wasn't sure this was really one of those times. "I didn't think you were the type to enjoy my suffering. Zack? Definitely. You? Not so much."

She shook her head. "Oh, sweetheart, I'm not," she sighed. "I'm really not." And then the smile was back. "I just... when I asked if you were ok, I meant about the competition. Tomorrow is your last day in this phase of your life—a part that you've been holding on to for some time now. Some might say you were in denial that it would ever come to an end..." Now she was teasing me.

"And?"

"You don't see?" She stepped closer to me. "You've been holding onto the past for so long and now, the only thing on your mind is your future—*with* Channing. It's silly, but as your mom, I just felt like you've been stuck—you were stuck after last year, you were stuck when you came here. And then you met her. And now, the thought that tomorrow is your last day as a competitive snowboarder—that after tomorrow you will be *retiring*—hasn't even crossed your mind." Her smile grew bigger. "I'm sure whatever happened between you two, you'll figure it out. You've always been so empathetic, Wyatt, always so good at reading people's feelings and knowing just what to do about them; I don't need to tell you that or give you advice. I just wanted to make sure you see just how far you've come and that I will always support you wherever you decide to go from here."

She was right. I hadn't even thought about this weekend as the end of my career. I couldn't even remember the last time it had crossed my mind. Before Channing, ironically 'B.C.,' it was all I could think about. Dreading either retirement or having to explain once again why I was continuing to pursue competing instead of going out on top. In this moment, I was excited for tomorrow because it was no longer an end, but a beginning.

"Thanks, mom." I hugged her again, letting her faith in me and the change in my perception sink in.

I was going to fix this because I gave myself no other option. But I wasn't going to fix it tonight. If she needed to compete tomorrow for herself—to help deal with her brother being gone—I wasn't going to fuck with that.

But she better believe that as soon as her feet left that board tomorrow, I would be in front of her and on my knees, asking her to still be mine.

CHAPTER
Thirty-Two

Channing

WHEN YOU'RE A MOUNTAIN PERSON, YOU UNDERSTAND THE brilliance and beauty in contradiction. The way the land and snow can be your greatest teacher. How something can be both grounding yet elevating, intoxicating yet soothing, wild yet serene, demanding yet patient.

I stood at the top of the slope, waiting for the rider ahead of me, McManus, to finish his run before it was my turn.

My brother and my sister were both at the bottom cheering me on; I'd come downstairs this morning to see them in a tearful embrace, Ally just realizing that Chance was back. I guess that even though her voicemail had been the reason he returned, he hadn't seen her.

I assumed Wyatt was down there, too. He'd already won Big Air with the quad cork and his Slopestyle run had been no less flawless. I woke up to a text from him this morning—a simple: *'I need to talk to you afterwards. I love you.'* I knew he would be there watching, that he would be there for me in spite of what I'd done.

And we would talk, but there was something that I needed to do first—something for him, but also for myself. So, I left the message without responding, jetting out of the house early to hang with Emmett and Nick until my run. I didn't want to see Wyatt or talk to him before because I didn't want to lose my nerve—and I also didn't have the right words to be able to tell him what he needed to be *shown*.

I needed him to see that I did trust him and that he was so much more important to me than any of this—the Games, winning, even snowboarding. He was everything.

In this moment, like the mountain, I was a contradiction as well. I was broken yet whole. I was imperfect yet perfect. And I was going to win even when I lost.

The announcer droned on like white noise through my helmet and I knew he was announcing me—*announcing Chance*. I moved up to the top of the trail, tightening the straps on my bindings one more time, snapping my helmet on, and tugging my neck-warmer up over my face.

I'd talked to Chance—told him what I was going to do—to make sure that he was ok with it since it was technically *him* competing after all. Like I figured, he hadn't cared.

The buzzer sounded and I knew it was time.

Dropping onto the slope, I kept it simple over the rails, gearing up for the big part of my run. The first kicker approached and I pulled another perfect double just like yesterday. Now, it was time for the real show. The second jump came in slow motion and everything that Wyatt had taught me resounded in my mind and my muscles. It was nothing like the last time I'd attempted this in competition. My nerves were calm because they weren't listening to me; they were listening to Wyatt—moving according to his instruction as I took off, twisting and flipping through the air. *One. Two. Three rotations.*

Smack! My board landed confidently on the snow and I heard the crowd cheering below.

'*Backside triple cork 1440!*' The announcer roared over the speakers.

I approached the third jump.

I crouched down, gaining speed and flying off into the air,

And I did nothing.

I savored the weightlessness, the nothingness of being completely still. I knew the judges and the crowd were probably watching in complete shock as I attempted no trick on the last kicker of the run—ensuring a huge loss in points. But that wasn't enough. I came back down to earth and as my board touched the snow, I gracefully let my balance slip towards the heel-edge of my board, tipping me back until my butt landed on the cold snow. I let myself fall further onto my back, spinning and sliding down the rest of the slope.

All the while, I was laughing. I was laughing so hard, tears were streaming down my face and I couldn't hear the announcer even if I wanted to. My face hurt from my smile being so large.

If they had cameras on me, the crowd probably thought I was insane; I'd just completely tanked my run and I was laughing and crying like I'd taken the win.

The funny part was, I was laughing and crying *because I had*.

Today, losing became the most important thing. In order to win, I needed to lose.

And I had. I'd lost the competition, but I'd won myself. I'd broken the cycle. I'd won out over my fear of being a failure. And most of all, I'd won Wyatt.

Finally coming to a stop, I began to push myself up only to be swarmed by the paramedics, thinking that I must have injured myself from the way that I'd fallen and then stayed down.

It certainly wasn't comfortable, but I was fine.

"Don't move! Don't move your head." The one paramedic instructed me. "You could have a concussion."

I opened my mouth to tell them that I was fine, but before I could get the words out Wyatt was there.

"Move!" He yelled, pushing the smaller EMT out of the way; he protested but the look Wyatt gave him sent him into silence. "Channing, are you ok?"

He unhooked my helmet, his warm hands tugging down my neck-warmer. "Tell me you're ok, gorgeous."

"Yes, I'm fine. I fell on purpose, Wyatt; I'm fine." I hadn't thought that the EMT's would come. Maybe my fall had been a little *too* dramatic. "I'm sorry. I'm fine."

"I've got her," he said curtly to the two men in red who were watching intently. He unstrapped my boots from my board.

"I'll take that." Chance's voice resounded behind Wyatt, who turned and was probably shocked to see that my missing twin had returned. Chance grabbed my board with a small nod of what looked like approval and then walked off into the crowd.

By now, the cameras had moved off to the next rider, which meant that when I sat up and pulled off my helmet and goggles, only those in the immediate vicinity were greeted with the female who'd just competed in the Men's Slopestyle competition.

"Let's get you out of here." Wyatt hoisted me into his arms and carted me off to the side of the slope. I let out a slight squeal, burying my face into his chest as we disappeared through the crowd over to the neighboring slope that was closed after the skiing event held their earlier.

He gently set me down on my feet. My heart skipped a beat when he didn't let go of me.

"I'm sorry, Wyatt. I'm sorry for not telling you. I'm sorry for not believing you," I blurted out, my apology spilling from me like water from a faucet. "I hung onto this competition like it was all I had, when it ceased to mean much to me weeks ago. I hung onto it because I was afraid to let go; I was afraid of falling for you." My hands gripped into his jacket, pulling me even closer to him. "You were right yesterday; I didn't trust you to love me and not leave me. More than that, I didn't trust that there was more to me than this competition and then when I realized that there was—that there was you—I fought it, afraid you would disappear like Chance did."

"Fuck, Channing, no." His hands came up to the sides of my face. "I was an idiot yesterday. God, you were afraid that I would leave and that's exactly what I fucking did." My heart wanted to explode with how much I loved the man who insisted on punishing himself for me. "I was angry and hurt, but I shouldn't have said what I did; I didn't think that you were more concerned about this than you were about me. I was just… an ass."

"You are not an ass." I laughed through the happy tears that had begun to fall.

At least he cracked a smile when he began to disagree with me. "No, I was. I was and I plan on making it up to you every single day from now on." His thumb brushed a tear off my cheek. "I plan on showing you every day just how fucking stuck with me you are."

A watery laugh erupted from my lips again. "I love you."

"I love you, too, gorgeous," he growled and his lips crushed mine.

I melted against him—against his love, his warmth, his safety, and into our future. His tongue claimed every inch of my mouth and I drew him in, wanting more of him. When we finally broke for a breath, I was jealous of the air that passed through his lips, that was how consumed I was by this man.

"You've shredded me, gorgeous. Absolutely fucking shredded..." he whispered against my lips and I smiled back.

"You're not so bad yourself, Mr. Milk-Frother," I teased, earning me another one of his thigh-clenching growls.

"Careful, Channing. You use that too much and soon, you're going to be stuck as *Mrs.* Milk-Frother."

I sucked in a breath, my pulse racing. Had he... Was he... "Soon?" I squeaked out.

"Told you I wasn't leaving you, gorgeous. *Soon.*"

I sighed into him, murmuring, "Well then, soon isn't soon enough."

I didn't even get the groan this time before he kissed me again, his arms locking my body flush against his. I pushed myself further into his delicious kiss, feeling even through all the layers of snow gear, how hard he was. *And knowing, underneath all my layers, how wet I was.*

"We should get going," he rasped against my lips. *Yes, home. To a bed. To each other.* "My family and your sister... and brother... are probably looking for us."

Crap. I'd forgotten about Chance and that I'd forgotten to explain how Chance had returned. For now, at least.

His arms relaxed around me. "I have one more question, gorgeous." His brow furrowed and I assumed he was going to ask about my brother—and why he had come back. "What were you thinking out there?" he asked hoarsely, nodding towards the slope we'd exited minutes ago.

Guilt rushed through me again. I hadn't expected that they would think I was injured and send the EMTs over; I thought I'd executed my fall as pretty overtly purposeful. "I'm sorry." I shook my head. "I didn't mean to worry you—or anyone. I didn't even think that they would send the first aid crew out. I thought it was obvious that I did it on purpose."

He shook his head. "Not that. I knew that you fell on purpose—it *was* obvious." He chuckled.

Oh. Now it was my turn to look confused. "I don't understand."

"*Why* you fell on purpose is less obvious, gorgeous, and *that's* what I want to know." His tortured stare met mine. "You worked so hard and you were killing it out there; I wanted you to place, Channing. I was rooting for you knowing that you wanted this so badly even in spite of what happened between us, and yet you tanked your last two jumps. Why? Why did you fall, gorgeous?"

I blinked up at him, finally finding the words so that he would understand—echoing the story he'd told me weeks ago at the top of the mountain. "Because, Wyatt," I whispered, "some people are worth falling for."

***

By the time we walked off of the slope, most of the crowd had dissipated with the events done for the day. I pulled out my phone and texted Ally.

"Looks like everyone is back at our house," I read, "celebrating your win… without you." We both laughed. As much as I wanted to celebrate in private with him, this was a big day not just for us, but for his whole family and he deserved to enjoy it with everyone.

As we walked through the resort, the TVs blared with the news that Wyatt Olsen had taken the gold *yet again* in both Big Air and Slopestyle. Everyone was speculating on retirement, but he hadn't confirmed because he'd been with me.

"I'm going to tell everyone tonight." He opened the passenger side door of the Range Rover for me; it looked like Chance had taken not just my board, but also my car back to the house.

"The news?"

"No, I'll do that tomorrow. Tonight I just want to be for us." My lip caught between my teeth as I smiled.

"Have you told Zack that you are moving here?"

He shook his head. "Not yet. Guess there are a few things I need to share with everyone tonight." We held hands as he drove towards my house. "So your brother came back?"

Oh, right. I nodded. "He showed up at the house last night—just in time, you could say. I guess Ally called him and told him what I was doing; she was pretty upset when I told her that I thought it would be too risky to leave the competition."

"What did he say?" Wyatt asked quietly.

"All the right things—for me… for us… that is." I sighed. Chance had changed—and not just physically; he'd changed the moment that he'd been injured. The brother that I'd grown up with wasn't the same person that he'd been a few months ago and truth be told, I didn't know if things between us would still be the same. "After his injury, he said he saw the cycle that I was in and he thought that if he stayed, it would be one that I would never make it out of."

"That's not the only reason."

"I know. But it's the only one he was willing to give…" I looked out the window, sadness seeping through me.

Wyatt squeezed my hand. "Everybody deals with things in their own way, gorgeous. I'm sure he'll tell you when he's ready."

I hoped so, I thought as we turned into the drive. The house was lit up and alive—for the first time in months—and it felt really good to be home.

"Channing! Wyatt!" Ally's shriek was all the announcement that we needed as we walked into the house. Inquisitive eyes peered at us from the kitchen.

Our hands were still locked tight as we joined the whole group—Ally, Zack, Wyatt's parents, Nick, Emmett, Tammy, and Chance.

"Congratulations, sweetheart!" Mary Olsen embraced her son and it was the only legitimate reason I would accept for him letting go of my hand.

At the same time, Ally skipped up to me, wrapping her arms around my neck.

"Are you ok?! I was so worried," she gushed into my ear. "Chance told me right away that you'd fallen on purpose, but I was still scared."

I laughed. "Yes, it was on purpose and yes, I'm fine." I pulled back. "I can't believe you called Chance." My eyes narrowed even though I wasn't really that mad.

Which was a good thing since she replied unapologetically, "Well, you weren't thinking. And you were so happy, Chan. That night before I told you Wyatt might be leaving, that was the happiest I'd ever seen you; I didn't want you to lose that because you thought you had no choice."

"Thank you," I whispered and she nodded, turning to grab her beer as we both tried to blink back tears.

"If I could have everyone's attention." Wyatt's voice boomed across the lull of the conversation. "I just want to thank you all for coming to be with me… to be with us tonight. I'm sure you've heard on the news, but I wanted to tell all of you first. I've decided that this was my last competition." His eyes flicked to me and I warmed all over with excitement.

"Yes, I am *finally* retiring," he joked and a soft laugh spread through the rest of us as we continued to listen. "I am retiring because I've decided to start a winter sports school. Here." I immediately looked to Zack, seeing the surprise register on his face, and not miss the way Emmett's face darkened at the revelation. "I don't want this to just be any private school, but one where we also focus on cultivating the students' skills on the mountain." He turned to face me and my face began to redden before he even spoke my name. "My gorgeous girlfriend, Channing, has already agreed to help me in my venture and now that the news is out, I know some of you will be hearing from me in the near future. But, I wanted to tell you now and thank you for all of your support up to now and into the future that I am *very* excited about."

I wiped away a stray tear as the group clapped and cheered. Wyatt pulled me against him and gave me a quick, hard kiss.

"Last," he continued and I wondered what more he could have to say, "I thank you for all of your congratulations, but I would like to redirect them to the amazing woman standing next to me right now."

Oh boy. My face was on fire.

"Ladies and gentlemen, may I present Channing Ryder—the first woman to ever successfully land a backside triple cork in competition." Now the hoots and hollers were obnoxious—especially from Emmett and Chance. "Zack." he nodded to his brother, who stepped forward and handed him something. *He couldn't be proposing. He just joked about it earlier—there was no way.* Still, my racing heart came to a screeching stop. He turned to me.

"Channing, you have worked relentlessly and uncompromisingly over the past few weeks to nail that jump. You have been my inspiration for so many things, but not the least of which has been your dedication to bettering yourself." I wiped tears that kept falling from my eyes, my hand pulling my sleeve over my knuckles and then up in front of my mouth. "Your run yesterday was flawless and your run today would have been, too, had that been what you wanted. You are one of the most talented snowboarders I've ever met and even if you had finished your pass today, *you* would not have been the one to get credit for it. Which is why…" he trailed off as he pulled the arm he had around me away, glancing down to whatever was in his hand, slowly unwrapping the cloth covering it.

Oh my God.

"I would like to present you with the gold medal for today's Slopestyle competition. Not because I love you—even though I do." I was full on crying right now I could barely see the damn thing he was holding. "Not because today you fell for me—even though you did." With that everyone laughed, including me even though it was more like a watery gurgle. "But because you are good enough—you are talented enough—and you fucking deserve it."

I couldn't speak, tears clogged my throat, as he lifted the medal up and placed it over my head. My shoulders shook so hard I was surprised that the thing wasn't bouncing against my chest.

Everyone was cheering, but all I knew was that Wyatt pulled me against him, my arms winding around his neck as he kissed me.

I'd never been so happy.

Wyatt

I loved making her cry like this—the kind of cry that was from an overload of happiness. I held her as she shook against me—whether it was from the tears or the happy laughter, I wasn't sure. After a minute or two, everyone else went back to their conversations, which was when my girl finally raised her head from my chest; I had a feeling she'd been trying to avoid the attention.

"Don't," I said in anticipation of her telling me that I didn't have to do what I'd just done. I wanted nothing more than to take her upstairs and show her exactly how amazing I thought she was, but it was probably time for us to mingle with the rest of the crowd.

"I don't know how to thank you," she said softly.

I quickly touched my lips to hers, "You don't have to, but I'm willing to let you try any way that you want a little later." I grinned at her, enjoying how her eyes immediately clouded with desire. "Now go see your friends."

She nodded, her hands rising to the heavy gold medal around her neck, finally looking down at it.

"I think that's a little too big for your neck, Lil!" Emmett yelled from across the island where he was standing with Chance and Nick—all three of them looking at Channing like a sister. I watched her roll her eyes at him and begin to move their way.

"Well, it's a good thing you didn't win it then, Emmett, because I don't think the strap is long enough to fit over your big head," Ally chimed in with her sweet sassiness.

A collective "Ooo" resounded from around the room and Channing glanced back to me; I think she now saw what I did. Only before, Emmett would have shot back at her. Tonight, he just smiled and laughed as though he was completely unaffected. I was surprised. *Ally* looked even more so. But the most important response came from Chance, who'd been gone the past several months, who'd missed everything else that we'd seen between Emmett and Ally, and so, who now looked on as if there was nothing more to see.

I wondered how long that was going to last.

Not long—if I were a betting man.

"I'm so proud of you, Wyatt," my dad said as he hugged me, bringing my attention back to my parents and Zack who'd come over to talk about the school.

Everyone hung out in the kitchen for some time, chatting, laughing, enjoying the company. Aside from Ally and Emmett who purposely avoided each other, Channing and my worlds meshed into one.

Eventually, the group dwindled. First, Zack left to take my parents back to the condo. With Zack leaving, Ally had decided to go home and stay with Tammy for the night. The move was partially to get away from Emmett, but also so that Channing and I could have the house to ourselves.

The only wild card was Chance. I caught him looking over at me a few times as Channing was talking to them, but it was only once my parents were gone that he approached me. Emmett and Nick's eyes followed him over, prepared to back him up for the protective-brother speech that I knew I was about to get.

"Olsen." He stuck out his hand and I grabbed it firmly.

"Ryder." I nodded. "Funny to think how this is how we would meet; I figured it would have been on the slopes."

"Yeah, well, life likes to throw fucking curve balls, doesn't it?" His smile was tight.

"You could say that."

"I won't lie to you, Olsen." *And here it was.* "I can't say I'm too fucking pleased about the whole idea of you and my sister, but thank you."

What? Thank you? "Ahh…for what?"

"For being there for her, taking care of her… everything." He downed the rest of the beer from the bottle in his hand. "I wouldn't be happy seeing anyone with her, but if it had to be someone, I guess she could have done worse."

I laughed briefly—that was as close to a compliment and acceptance as I was going to get. "I may be the competition, but look on the bright side—at least I'm not a skier."

Now *that* had him laughing; when in doubt, rely on the mutual, comedic distaste for our winter sport counterparts.

"Funny." He nodded to me, his expression darkening again. "But, I'm not your competition; I'm nobody's fucking competition anymore."

I heard in his voice the same worthlessness that I'd felt thinking about retirement, fueled by the thought of what purpose I could possibly serve if I wasn't competing.

"Well, I'm going to need instructors in a few months," I offered casually. I wanted to ask Channing about it first, but the moment was here and knowing where he was coming from, I had to say something.

"Yeah…" He glanced down and then up and out the window; *clearly, this would have to be a topic for another time.* Then came the words that I'd been expecting. "Anyway. Just wanted to say that if you hurt her, Olsen, I know seven different spots on this mountain where the snow never melts."

"I'd die for her." I held his gaze—his eyes just like Channing's, except his were haunted.

"Good." He turned back to his sister and friends who were now all watching us intently. "Channing, I'm going to stay with Nick."

"Oh, for the night?"

"For indefinitely," was his hard response. "Let's go."

The three of them strolled from the kitchen like their crew being reunited meant that hell was about to freeze over. They all shook my hand as they brushed by me and I felt bad for whoever was at their destination; those three were wild and looking for trouble.

CHAPTER
Thirty-Three

Channing

"**You ok?**" Wyatt walked towards me slowly, concern written on his face.

I'd been in a slight shock when Chance said that he wasn't going to be staying here—in his own home—for the 'indefinite future.' This was a new Chance and I didn't know much, if anything, about him right now; I hoped that our friends would find a way through to him even if I couldn't.

"Yeah." I sighed as he wrapped his arm around me.

"He'll come around." He kissed the top of my head gently.

"What did he say to you?"

He laughed. "The usual—that he knows several spots on the mountain where he could bury my body and they would never find it if I hurt you."

I laughed and shook my head—now *that* sounded like my brother and it gave me hope that he was still in there somewhere.

"In the meantime, I won't complain that we have the house to ourselves right now because all I've thought about for the past hour is taking you upstairs and taking off all these layers."

I moaned, wrapping my arms around him and giving into the need to stare dreamily into his eyes. "So, what are you waiting for?"

The growl was my answer—the growl that told my body I was going to like what was coming. I squealed, finding myself hoisted up over his shoulder as he carried me, giggling, around the island and upstairs to my room.

Barely inside the threshold and I was right-side up again with his mouth on mine. Hard and hungry, just like I liked it. My hands dug for the edges of his shirt, tearing it up and over his head; I managed to undo his belt buckle before he pulled back.

"Your turn."

I carefully lifted the medal from my neck, still holding it in my hand as he pulled my Under Armour shirt off, revealing my red-lace bralette underneath. He reached for the clasp, deciding against it for the moment in favor of removing my pants.

"Tell me they are fucking matching again," he rasped. I bit my lip hard, knowing the answer—and what his reaction was going to be. Desire seeped from me as I heard the string of provocative expletives leave his mouth seeing the matching red thong.

"You should... probably... get used to this," I said breathlessly, my voice catching as his finger reached out to trace around my nipple through the fabric, slipping down onto the front of my panties. My fists clenched as he nudged the lace to the side and dipped his finger inside of me.

"I'll never get used to this," was his hoarse response; drunk on desire, a second finger thrust inside of me and my legs shook. "I do, however, plan on *frothing* you in each and every one of these torture devices." His eyes twinkled with heady humor.

I grinned, the heavy metal weight in my hand sparking an idea. "Sounds like a *really* good plan," I began, my free hand pulling his out of me so that I could take a step back, "but not tonight."

His eyebrows raised as my free hand reached around and unhooked my bra. I let it fall to the ground, watching his mouth part, hungry for my naked breasts.

"I don't think," I hooked my thumbs on the edge of the thong, "that I properly congratulated you on today..." I teased the fabric down over my legs, standing back up completely naked in front of him.

He was losing control—and I loved every second of it. His eyes were impossibly dark as he began to undo the waist of his pants, his erection forcing the material wide at just the slightest amount of give. "And how are you going to do that, gorgeous?" He pushed his pants down, my own mouth going dry at the sight of his *excessively* evident arousal.

I smiled brilliantly, lifting my hands again, feeling the familiar fabric come to rest on the back of my neck. The medal slid down to rest just between my breasts and my body broke out in goosebumps—but not from its coldness.

"By letting you take the gold."

Need rolled through me in wave after relentless wave as Wyatt consumed my body—his mouth on my mouth, his hands on my breasts... his hands and mouth on my core.

My body flew so many times before he finally pushed inside of me, enjoying every clench of my sex around him. And when he was fully seated, he grabbed the gold medal and pulled it up and off of my neck, tossing it onto the floor.

Because it meant nothing to either of us anymore—we had everything we needed.

My orgasm sucked me in and then burst through my body just like my love for him had—with an intensity that I could no sooner describe than I could contain. And he followed me into the fury.

Much later, after much more *frothing*, I lay with my head against his chest, our heartrates still not quite back down to normal. My mind ran back through the events of the day. *I wouldn't have changed a thing.*

"Do you think anyone realized that I wasn't Chance?" I wondered aloud.

"I think your secret is safe, gorgeous." He chuckled, tipping my chin up and kissing me lightly. "So, does this mean I can tell everyone that you fell for me?" he teased against my lips.

"You're so cocky sometimes." I laughed, tilting my head back. "I'll agree to it, but only if you answer me one thing."

"Anything." His thumb brushed against the skin of my neck, stroking warmth throughout my body.

"When did you fall in love with me?" The question was breathless, waiting for his answer to fill up my lungs with life.

He smiled—that devastatingly brilliant smile that still managed to stop my heart—and said, "Somewhere between the snow and stars."

Emmett

I sucked in a huge breath of the frigid night air; I needed it to freeze me from the inside out because I was burning. I was burning with rage and burning with desire.

Wyatt Olsen was staying in town. *Congratu-fucking-lations, Lil.* What that meant to me was that his douchebag of a brother would most likely be staying too. And if he was staying, he'd be staying with Ally.

Just because she wasn't mine didn't mean that anyone-fucking-else was allowed to touch her. *Especially a goddamn skier.*

Especially him with all his compliments and touching and caring consideration. Fuck him.

We were like fire and ice, she and I, and the burn I was feeling right now told me that the fire was winning. The past few months had been torture. Without Chance here, I'd felt responsible for the two of them—his two sisters. I was already responsible for one human and yet he'd saddled me with two more. Thankfully, Lil knew how to take care of herself. Ally, on the other hand, was a goddamn daisy and a disaster all rolled into one; she was warmth and sunshine, kindness and caring—everything I wasn't and everything I didn't deserve to have. She was also young. *Christ*, I was almost ten years older than she was; I told myself that a million times—that it didn't matter that she was twenty, *that she was legal*; she was Chance's kid sister.

And I hated her for it.

I hated her for rubbing it in my face—her youthful, carefree nature;

the way life hadn't fucked her like it had fucked me. I hated her for rubbing that douchebag in my face. I hated her for tempting me with the thought that she could be mine for the taking. Little Miss Sunshine and her perfect life; *I so badly wanted to shatter it and keep all the brightly broken pieces for myself.*

I was pissed that Pride left, but it wasn't my call; I was more pissed that it had put me in closer proximity with the one person I couldn't have—the one person I shouldn't have—and the one person who certainly didn't want me.

I needed Chance back because I didn't know how much longer I could take the torture. I needed the SnowmassHoles back because I needed the mindless distraction of riding—both mountains and women—to let me forget about my piece of shit life that hid inside a sparkly cage for just a few hours.

Mostly, I needed Chance back because without him, I'd allowed myself to forget the most important piece of this puzzle: that Ally was his sister. It didn't matter who I was; it mattered who she was. Even SnowmassHoles have a code—and that code included not fucking your best friend's sister.

"Thank fuck you're back." I growled as we approached Frost's truck. I couldn't tell him how much, but I could tell him that.

He better be staying because I wasn't sure that there was anything left standing between me and showing that little girl just how far down I could drag her—and just how delicious it could be.

Nick

Quiet, unassuming, distracted, and generally considered the nicest out of the three of us. I was the worst kind of asshole; I was the kind that masqueraded as decency. I hid it so well that sometimes I could even fool myself into thinking that I wasn't *who* I was.

I was the wolf in sheep's clothing.

I was the one with a smile on my face and the knife hidden behind my back.

Not for them, of course. But for anyone else who tried to get too close. I had goals and I had rules. There was no compromising.

They thought I was a stoner and easily distracted. The truth was I just didn't give a shit about anything except one tiny, living, breathing thing that was being held hostage from me. But no one knew that because I was better at hiding things than the rest of them.

I saw things that they assumed I missed. I saw the dick who'd harassed Channing that night at the bar; I saw and I watched to see what would happen. At some point, I would have nudged King and let him play the hero, but Wyatt had shown up first. I also saw the way King looked at Ally—the way he was dying to fuck her. I thought it was fucking hysterical.

And Pride? I saw that he didn't want to be here almost as much as we wanted him back. I saw the martyr he was making of himself, but who was I to judge? I needed the SnowmassHoles back so that I could go back to hiding in the background, letting Pride and King take the spotlight so I could focus on getting back the one thing that belonged to me—the one thing that was a part of me; I needed to be back in the darkness that was my home, where I could let out every ugly thing that allowed me to keep my pleasant persona intact.

I wasn't pissed that Chance had left. I wasn't pissed that he was back. I wasn't pissed about Wyatt or Channing. And I wasn't pissed when Chance turned to me as we approached my truck and held his hand out expectantly, waiting for me to give him the keys. I didn't care that Emmett immediately made for the passenger seat, leaving me to the back. I didn't care about any of it. I had an incredibly long fuse—so long, most assumed it was never-ending. There was an end, an end with a very big bomb was just itching to be ignited.

All I cared about was that we were going somewhere where the darkness could relieve that itch for the time being.

Chance

"This lying low has been bullshit," King muttered, walking around the car to the passenger seat. There was no question when I held my hand out for the keys to drive, leaving Nick to drop his keys in my hand and open the back door.

I didn't want to be back. I never wanted to come back, but for my sister I would do anything. Including returning to the place that held nothing but painful reminders of everything that I had lost.

At least if I hung with these two, they wouldn't ask me why I left, what had happened, or why I was back. They wouldn't ask questions because that's not what we did; we didn't ask questions.

King and Frost were desperate to keep us together—to keep me back here. We were the Three SnowmassHoles of Aspen. Together, we took what we wanted; apart, we were just three more rowdy snowboarders too full of themselves to matter. Channing had kept us at bay—more or less—and I'd always been slightly more inclined to her side of reason, but I had a feeling that she was going to have a different male figure on her mind than any of us assholes and the shenanigans that we got ourselves into.

I saw where they were coming from; I saw what they saw—only it wasn't the truth anymore. It wasn't the truth because I was fucked. But maybe that was a good thing because I was no longer inclined towards reason. There was no meaning to my life which meant the only thing left for me to do was enjoy the fuck out of it. *Go big or go home.* Except my version of 'go big' wasn't going to be fit for any fucking Disney movie.

I wasn't a snowboarder anymore. Definitely not a competitive one, probably not even an amateur one. When I'd picked up Channi— *my* board—earlier, it'd been like a fucking brand on my hand; it had been the first time I'd touched a board since the accident and all it did was taunt me—like handing a recovering alcoholic, three months sober, a glass with vodka in it. The board teased me, whispering my name straight into my soul, tempting me to ride her again. *Not fucking happening.*

I sat almost as quiet as Nick, turning on the truck and heading away from the house; it wasn't home anymore. And because I was almost as quiet, I realized just how far I'd fallen. It's always the quiet ones that are the most dangerous. I may not know all his secrets, but I wasn't fooled into thinking that he didn't have any.

"You weren't serious that we were going to Frost's, were you?" Emmett broke the silence again. And I shook my head. "Good. I need a hard drink or a good smoke."

"Both."

"And a hard fuck," he finished, Frost murmuring his agreement.

I floored it out of the driveway, heading towards Big Louie's. I'd shown up at the mountain today, but there were too many tourists for any locals to have noticed. At Louie's though, everyone would see that I'd returned. And everyone was going to see that this Chance Ryder was *not* the one they knew—I was not the one who'd left almost four months ago. I was no longer a Wonder Twin. I was no longer the mountain hero. I was, however, still an asshole—for better or for fucking worse.

Aspen better look the fuck out—the SnowmassHoles were back.

The End.

THANK YOU FOR READING!

I hope you enjoyed Channing and Wyatt's story! I would love to hear what you think, if you want to head over to Amazon to leave a review! **Reviews play such a big part in not just how I get feedback on my work, but on how other readers make their decision on whether or not to check out my writing. It would mean the world to me if you would share your thoughts!**

You can also contact me directly at: author@drrebeccasharp.com

Xx, Rebecca

Want to stay updated?

To be emailed with pre-order announcements, chapter samples, and release date info, sign up for my mailing list here:
www.drrebeccasharp.com

For details about projects I'm working on, cover reveals, excerpts, and more—follow me on Facebook and Instagram!

www.facebook.com/drrebeccasharp
www.instagram.com/drrebeccasharp

For exclusive previews, new project details, giveaways, and all-around discussion, check out my reader's group—Sexy, Sharp Readers—here: www.facebook.com/groups/1539118689482683

Acknowledgements

This book means a lot to me. Ok, ok, they all do. But this one is special to me because it hits so close to home. I'm not good at sports. None of them except snowboarding. Snowboarding has been my passion ever since the first year I could join ski club. From that point forward, winter became synonymous with the mountain. I'd rather be cold than hot, on the snow rather than on the sand. I am no expert that is for sure, but I do love this sport. I hope this book—aside from the love story—gives you a sense of just how much the mountain means to me.

M.W.—Thanks for agreeing to take snowboarding lessons with me the first year we did ski club—over 15 years ago. (We won't be too specific haha.) Here's to all the mountain dew and lodge food and hot chocolate (but only from the lower lodge!) that we lived on during the season. Remember the time we snowboarded with bunny ears on? #snowbunnies. What else? The bra tree? Hidden flasks? Risking our lives to make it to the mountain for the fresh snow. Oh, and here's to the time we got caught on Cliffhanger (a double black) that was a sheet of ice and you broke my tailbone. I still love you.

N.B.—This goes out to you for that one night. Ski Club. High school. The night it was so FRIGID that our lift tickets (back when they were stickers) wouldn't even stick to the little metal holder because it was so cold. The night that my nose was so cold that I couldn't even suck in air through it without my nostrils collapsing. The night that I successfully landed my first frontside grab and you dubbed me 'the Queen' of the mountain… loudly… for everyone on the park (probably on the whole mountain) to hear. Thank you.

A.R.—Thanks for letting me teach you how to snowboard and showing me that it can be completely normal for someone to be on the park doing rails and jumps on their third day on the mountain. #sonotnormal

To my husband—thank you for letting me suck you in to this world so eagerly. Thank you for not being too mad when I leave you on the beginner trails with our friends so that I can make my way to the top of the mountain and try to get some windburn coming back down. Thank you for not yelling at me when I tell you that I can't feel my feet anymore because they are so cold but *'please just let me do one more run?'*

Ok. Almost done.

Lastly, I want to thank the mountain. Thank you for teaching me *hard* lessons. Thank you for grounding me. And thank you for teaching me how to fly.

Thank you, my lovely readers, for taking a chance on me! I hope you enjoy the ride!

Xx, Rebecca

Other Works by
DR. REBECCA SHARP

STANDALONES
reputation

WINTER GAMES SERIES
Up in the Air (Book 1)
On the Edge (Book 2)
Enjoy the Ride (Book 3)
Nick & Tammy (Book 4)—Coming Early 2019

THE GENTLEMEN'S GUILD SERIES
The Artist's Touch (Book 1)
The Sculptor's Seduction (Book 2)
The Painter's Passion (Book 3)

THE PASSION & PERSEVERANCE TRILOGY
(A Pride and Prejudice Retelling)
Complete Series Available Now
First Impressions (Book 1)
Second Chances (Book 2)
Third Time is the Charm (Book 3)

ANTHOLOGIES
The Kocke Chronicles (Kocke CEO)
No Limits (A Taboo Anthology) (Hypothetically)—Early 2019

Made in the USA
Middletown, DE
06 December 2018